GYNECOCRACY.

A narrative

Of

THE ADVENTURES AND PSYCHOLOGICAL EXPERIENCES

Of

JULIAN ROBINSON

(afterwards Viscount Ladywood)

UNDER PETTICOAT-RULE,

written by himself

VOLUMES FIRST, SECOND, THIRD

BIRCHGROVE PRESS
MMXI

http://www.birchgrovepress.com

ISBN:
978-0-9870956-5-7

Gynecocracy was first published clandestinely in 1893, most probably by Leonard Smithers and the booksellers Robson & Kerslake. Authorship is attributed to an English lawyer, Stanislas Matthew de Rhodès (1857-1932), who is also credited with writing *The Yellow Room* (1891) and *The Petticoat Dominant* (1898). Stylistic and thematic differences between these three books suggest that they may not have been written by the same author. Indeed, it is worth noting that *Gynecocracy*, which is the most sophisticated of the three, has also been attributed to the English psychologist, Henry Havelock Ellis (1859-1939).

Gynecocracy is significant for the novelty of its focus on the punishment of a young man through enforced cross-dressing: it represents the first extended treatment of this practice, which was discussed in Victorian popular media, in literary erotica. Earlier references to it (in erotica) are brief and fragmentary. See, for example, *Madame Birchini's Dance*: 'I whipt upon [my maid's] back last night / A French Duke, and two English Earls: / the first of which, with frock and sash, / I drest just like a full-grown Miss; / Then gave him many a vig'rous lash, / For giving footman John a kiss! / I taught this fancied Miss a dance— / I made him caper to the ceiling'. (Hotten, 1872: 29)

The Yellow Room, *The Petticoat Dominant*, and *Madame Birchini's Dance* are available from Birchgrove Press.

GYNECOCRACY.

VOLUME THE FIRST

CONTENTS OF VOLUME I

'Petticoat influence' is a great reproach,
    Which even those who obey would fain be thought
To fly from, as from hungry pikes a roach;
    But since beneath it upon earth we are brought,
By various joltings of life's hackney coach,
    I for one venerate a petticoat —
A garment of a mystical sublimity,
No matter whether russet, silk, or dimity.

Much I respect, and much I have adored,
    In my young days, that chaste and goodly veil,
Which holds a treasure, like a miser's hoard,
    And more attracts by all it doth conceal —
A golden scabbard on a Damasque sword,
    A loving letter with a mystic seal,
A cure for grief — for what can ever rankle
Before a petticoat and peeping ankle?
                            — *Don Juan*

Avant Propos

Wholesome meats to a vitiated stomach differ little or nothing from unwholesome; and best books to a naughty mind are not inapplicable to occasions of evil. Bad meats will scarce breed good nourishment in the healthiest concoction; but herein the difference is of bad books, that they, to a discreet and judicious reader, serve in many respects to discover, to confute, to forewarn, and to illustrate . . . . Good and Evil, we know in the field of this world, grow up together almost inseparably; and the knowledge of good is so involved and interwoven with the knowledge of evil, and in so many cunning resemblances hardly to be discerned, that those confused seeds which were imposed upon Psyche as an incessant labour to cull out and sort asunder, were not more intermixed. It was from out the rind of one apple tasted, that the knowledge of good and evil, as two twins cleaving together, leaped forth into the world. And perhaps this is the doom which Adam fell into of knowing good and evil — that is to say, of knowing Good by Evil. As, therefore, the state of man now is, what wisdom can there be to choose — what continence to forbear without the knowledge of evil? He that can apprehend and consider Vice, with all her baits and seeming pleasures, and yet abstain, and yet distinguish, and yet prefer that which is truly better, he is the true warfaring Christian. I cannot praise a fugitive and cloistered virtue, unexercised and unbreathed, that never sallies out and sees her adversary, but slinks out of the race when that immortal garland is to be run for, not without dust and heat. Assuredly we bring not innocence into the world, we bring impurity much rather; that which purifies us is

trial, and trial is by what is contrary. That virtue therefore which is but a youngling in the contemplation of evil and knows not the utmost that vice promises to her followers, and rejects it, is but a blank virtue, not a pure; her whiteness is but an excremental whiteness: which was the reason why our sage and serious poet Spenser (whom I dare to be known to think a better teacher than Scotus or Aquinas) describing true temperance under the person of Guion, brings him in with his Palmer through the Cave of Mammon and the bower of earthly bliss, that he might see and know, and yet abstain. Since, therefore, the knowledge and survey of vice is in this world so necessary to the constituting of human truth, how can we more safely and with less danger scout into the regions of sin and falsity, than by reading all manner of tractates and hearing all manner of reason? . . . *Liberty of the Press*
JOHN MILTON.

Chapter I

Introductory

By this time I am thirty years of age, and well aware of it.

Home-staying youths, some poet or wiseacre has said, have ever homely wit. Whether I have a homely wit or indeed any wit, I do not know. I have never endeavoured to form an opinion, deeming the question not to be one into which I could hope to enquire impartially; in fact, not one for my personal judgment But though I have been a home-staying youth, I have had experiences; experiences of the world, that is to say, of woman, whom I regard as a complete epitome of the world — and if anyone, home-stayer or otherwise, has had experience of *her* in all her moods and whims, and has passed through all the psychological and physical gymnastics by which her varying caprices and lusts can conduct his soul, his passions, and his senses, and still preserves a homely wit, he must be an arrant duffer!

For *Woman* is a complete education.

By my own experience, I have reason to respect the petticoat and *chemise*, the drawers and long stockings, the high-heeled boots and tight corsets — and what they contain — and to believe that good may accrue to a young man by being disciplined by a smart girl. This may be thought a very peculiar view.

To give one instance, a young man of my acquaintance was sent at nine years of age to a fashionable preparatory school for Eton, and was expelled eighteen months afterwards. It was considered futile to send him to another school. Three tutors successively resigned on the ground that he was altogether incorrigible. At a loss what to do, his guardians enquired in all directions, and answered innumerable advertisements of persons professing to devote themselves to the reformation of backward and refractory boys, until, at last, it was suggested by a friend of the family, who had had some German anthropological experiences, that the lad should be taken in hand by a lady. The idea was astounding! A great, rough, strong boy of fifteen who had defied the discipline of private schools and tutors, and of specialists who devoted themselves to such characters, would never yield to a lady. The friend, a person of position and reputation, pledged herself that he would be completely broken in; she had known similar cases in which the plan she advocated had proved successful beyond all possible expectations. After protracted discussion, her suggestions were adopted. A *pension* was quickly found, The Grafin von — stipulated that the lad should be left absolutely under her control for two years, and at the end of that period he turned out a model of docility and obedience, courtesy, and chivalry, and with remarkable intellectual development and self-possession. His friends acknowledged with wonder and gratitude the marvellous transformation which the pretty demure German Countess had wrought. Naturally, they were curious to ascertain by what magic she had worked this miracle. I do not know whether they succeeded in learning; probably not, as they were English; but having been through the same kind of discipline myself, I possessed the key. When we met, we accordingly compared notes, and he confessed that the magic was wholly feminine. She had impressed him with the subtle and subduing influence of sex, under which he was perpetually kept. She, as I guessed, employed not tutors but maids, who, notwithstanding his age, treated him in all respects as a child. She used female clothing — first a girl's, then a young lady's — and made the use of masculine habiliments, or even the desire for them, an offence of the deepest dye. She subjugated his rude male propensities to her softening womanly influence, to which he was compelled to do perpetual homage. She punished rebellion in the most ignominious manner, with the birch; and the same sharp instructor was used to brighten his wits, teach him his lessons, and enforce her precepts. I remember he made a particular complaint of the fact that, to his shame and disgrace, he was usually punished before girls. This he felt acutely. He described his feelings to me upon the first occasion of his shocking exposure to a bevy of laughing girls. He was held down across an ottoman by a couple of buxom country lasses. The mere narrative made my blood boil and electrified me. He detailed his efforts to repress all expression of his sufferings, in which they revelled and gloried; how he writhed; how, by degrees, his fortitude vanished through stress of pain, whilst consciousness of the youth and sex of his beholders maddened him; how, ultimately, as the cutting strokes administered by the white round arm of a woman continued to fall with cruel regularity, he was obliged to abandon himself absolutely and helplessly. He could no longer withstand the sense of abject humiliation, the necessity for yielding unreservedly to his fair mistress. He spoke of the subjugation and the galling nature of the conviction that they had, despite himself, thoroughly mastered him. But, he added, he could have held out against a man; what sapped his strength was not so much the torture of the punishment as the sorcery of gender. It was the triumph of the petticoat. He could at last have grovelled on the ground before these fair but relentless conquerors, and have begged their permission to breathe.

Enough, however, of his experiences. In the following chapters I purpose narrating my own adventures of like kind.

Chapter II

Downlands Hall, Suffolk

I was what women are fond of describing as a "nice youth": ruddy complexioned, fair, tall, well-made, and rather over fourteen years of age, when it was decided to send me to school.

This resolution was come to, because one fine afternoon, being on the stairs behind our pretty nursery maid, a lively and brisk piece of feminine flesh, as she was carrying the tea tray up to the nursery, in the exuberance and precocity of my animal spirits, I seized the advantage of her hands being engaged in holding the tray, and lifting her petticoats behind up to her waist, I indulged in a long look at her stalwart legs, thighs, and plump bottom. Then, my eager hands slipped through and touched something hairy between her warm legs. Whether she would have objected to this part of the performance, I do not feel sure. I believe she would have reserved the matter for private scolding and settlement at a convenient moment, but, as soon as she felt my hand, it had an altogether unexpected effect, for, blushing crimson, she incontinently dropped the tea tray, and, as the milk ran one way and the scalding tea and boiling water went drip, drip another, and the cups and saucers rolled down the flight and broke themselves quite leisurely, she exclaimed, looking a picture of loveliness in her confusion: "Oh! Master Julian! Oh, you wicked, wicked boy!"

In the midst of the clatter and exclamation, out came the head nurse. She found the girl as red as a peony, and myself looking utterly foolish. She took in the situation at a glance. No supper, but bed, and a severe application of an old slipper were my portion that night. A report was made to headquarters, and to school I was sent, and remained there for nearly two years.

I left school, because it did not agree with my health. Delicately brought up, and accustomed to luxuries at variance with the rigour of scholastic discipline, school was found unsuitable for me. So I came home again.

My parents were a great deal too much occupied with fashionable society and parliamentary affairs to look after me. My father expected to become before long a member of the government, under which he then held a subordinate office. His expectations were fulfilled, and he was subsequently rewarded with a seat in the

Upper House and an Earl's coronet. I was delighted to become a Lord; but, in the meantime, a large old house which had belonged to my father's brother, who had died leaving three daughters, was my destination. It was a fine old place near Stowmarket in Suffolk, with a thousand acres of woodland and pasturage. My cousins Maud, Beatrice, and Agnes, charming girls, were being educated there by a sweet young French governess, to whose care, in consideration of an extra fifty pounds a year salary, I was also consigned.

Mademoiselle de Chambonnard was tall, svelte, possessed a beautiful little figure, with masses of black hair, large black eyes, and pallid complexion; and dressed and comported herself like a young Queen. Her air of *espieglerie* and mischief, and her womanliness bewitched me. But there was about her a resolution and determination, indicated by her firmly compressed mouth and beautifully shaped lips, which rather terrified me, and with reason. Her eyes laughed; her mouth never relaxed.

My cousins were equally charming, and seemed to have imbued much of Mademoiselle's frolicsomeness and playfulness. They were all dressed in the height of fashion. Maud was just twenty, Beatrice eighteen, and Agnes sixteen. I fell in love with Beatrice at once. She was the *bete noire*, and I suppose we intuitively felt we were kindred spirits. I at once observed their dainty feet and shoes, their faultless deportment, their pretty short frocks, and enough of their underclothing to perceive its exquisite character. Agnes was the coldest and the favourite; Beatrice, always in scrapes, the warmest hearted and most beautiful; and Maud the provokingly faultless one. I cannot describe my sensations, when deposited by my father's man after a drive of nearly twenty miles, amongst these young ladies, with the full knowledge that my fate was in their hands. Mademoiselle received me, and observed that she had heard of some of my doings, adding that they would all find it odd to have "a male thing" amongst them, but that she hoped I should be a good boy and very obedient. She then rang for the maid, ordered her to show me my room, and told me to join her and my cousins at the schoolroom.

Mary conducted me to the bedroom, and looked after me much more than I liked, and in a peculiar manner which I could not make out, and felt disposed to resent. She poured out the water, tempered it to the heat she considered right, helped me off with my jacket, waistcoat, and collar, asked me for my keys, told me to wash myself, and, I verily believe, had I not been quite a stranger she would not have left the room at all, which I should have found decidedly inconvenient. Then it was her good pleasure to tie my necklace for me, and when I explained that I was quite capable of doing it myself, she exclaimed: "Oh, are you, my pretty young gentleman? Perhaps you will find before long that you are not allowed to do as many things for yourself here as you like."

On our way to the schoolroom, we met a tall, handsome young woman, who was evidently standing there purposely to see me. She had lovely dark eyes and an oval face. She was Miss Elise, Mademoiselle's maid. I entered the schoolroom a little ruffled and out of temper, which Mademoiselle was quick to discern. She introduced me to my cousins, and I greeted them formally with that dignity on which I prided myself and thought becoming in a young man. But Mademoiselle, at once, made me supremely ridiculous in my own and everybody else's eyes by insisting on my asking each of them for a kiss. That put me to great confusion, for the kisses were not readily given, and I was compelled to go on begging until, with much reluctance and great condescension on their part, I got them. Mademoiselle then rated me for being ill-mannered, and peremptorily ordered me to kiss her own hand, which she extended for the purpose. I did so with an ill grace, earnestly wishing myself anywhere but where I was, and sat down sullenly enough, in a frame of mind which provoked the immediate remark from Mademoiselle.

"Come, Master Julian, behave yourself, or I shall send for Elise to put you to bed!"

The suppressed giggle which this provoked increased my ill temper, but I resolved to pass it over and show self-control and command over my temper, trusting that my nonchalance and imperturbability would make her duly sensible of the manly manner in which I treated her indecorous freedom, and that it would convey a just rebuke of what she would evidently see I regarded as her bad taste, and I expected she would then be properly abashed accordingly.

Her maid put me to bed! The idea!

But unfortunately, Mademoiselle was not in the least abashed. On the contrary, she acted towards me with unseemly levity, and positively betrayed a disposition to treat the matter with inconsiderable impatience and anger, and although she then took no further notice of my demeanour, I felt that she intended to make a note of it, and an uncomfortable foreboding again stole over me.

The evening passed without further incident. Amidst the warmth and brightness of the room, and the pleasant chatter of the girls, my stiffness wore off; but I was destined to make an ass of myself. The pretty girlish forms, the graceful contours of which were admirably revealed and suggested by their dresses, gave me a delicious sense of voluptuous ease. I therefore became graciously condescending, although a curious twinkle in Mademoiselle's eyes ought to have awakened me to the ridiculous figure I was cutting. My foolish serenity was, however, undisturbed until the next day, when I had a rude awakening. I had no suspicion at the time that she was only fooling me in the most finished manner.

Her conversation was easy and engaging. She drew me on to talk quite confidentially, to tell her of my likes and dislikes, and reveal my real self to her to an extent, which quite startled me when I reflected upon it afterwards in bed, with the uncomfortable doubt as to whether she was really my friend or only trotting me out and secretly quizzing me the whole time.

She reclined in a low chair with a fan with which she coquettishly played in her lovely dimpled hand — one foot on the steel bar of the fender, her *seduisante* attitude revealing a good deal of her slender limbs and open-work stockings, and affording occasional glimpses of exquisite lace and white under-raiment. Of course, it was my *role* not to appear to notice anything, and I played it to perfection, being insouciant to a degree that must have astonished and discomfited her. However, in my own mind, I thought her extremely nice, and felt I should become really fond of her.

Alas! Before long I had reason to think of that low chair in quite another manner.

Maud, as the governess and myself chatted, pored over some book, seemingly resolved not to interest herself in the least in our conversation. She had, apparently, quickly come to some conclusion. I felt, though, that her carelessness was strongly tinctured with contempt for me.

Between Beatrice and myself there had already been established, from the first, a tacit intelligence and friendliness. The dear girl was evidently much disconcerted and greatly concerned for me.

About Agnes' mouth there played a cold but amused smile. She said nothing and gave no sign.

I found they led a delightful life, taking high tea at half-past five, dinner at half-past eight, bed at half-past eleven, breakfast between nine and ten, and luncheon at two.

I enjoyed my dinner that evening hugely. The exquisite *toilettes* and low dresses surprised and delighted my susceptible nature. Every one was merry and free, and lessons were not mentioned.

That night I soon fell asleep; and so ended the day of my arrival at Downlands Hall.

Chapter III

Mademoiselle Hortense de Chambonnard

The next morning I woke up miserable. Since my father's servant who had brought me here had departed, I had not seen a single male about the place. My sensation of utter loneliness at the full realization of this fact, which was vividly borne in upon me on awaking, made me completely wretched. What would become of me amidst a pack of women and girls, with no companion in an uncongenial feminine atmosphere against which I instinctively revolted?

I anticipated that I should be shorn of my manhood and made effeminate and good-for-nothing, that my strength and virility would be suppressed. I worked myself into a passion of rage and resentment against my parents for putting me to such a position, and resolved to write at once and expostulate in strong terms. I did not understand then that this was the very discipline they considered desirable. I arose with rebellion surging in my breast, and with a determination to give battle at the earliest opportunity and to assert myself.

All my surroundings felt strange and unnatural to the last degree as I indignantly dressed myself; and when Elise came to show me the way to the breakfast room, the climax was reached, and I told her roughly that I could find my way there myself. She looked angry, but merely said she was to show me the way and she whispered something to Mademoiselle when we got there.

Mademoiselle and the girls were dressed in charmingly simple dresses, and looked so fresh and beautiful that, for the time, I completely forgot my isolation and resolutions. An opportunity for battle soon arose. There were two letters for me, and Mademoiselle actually took them and opened and read them before my eyes, and would not let me look at them, or even tell me from whom they came. She merely remarked that they did not need any reply, and that I was neither to write nor receive any letters without her express permission. I protested, remonstrated, and expostulated; but it was useless. The girls looked on amused, but never uttered a word. I could, in my fury, have burst into tears and torn the letters from her. Mademoiselle remained quite collected and exasperatingly calm, gazing at me with a peculiar light in her eyes. I think she was revelling in my helpless raving and storming. She severely observed that I certainly did not know how to behave, and that she would give me a lesson afterwards in the schoolroom (at which I noticed the girls looked at each other very significantly), and bade me sit down, eat my breakfast, and hold my tongue, or that she would send me out of the room. I saw there was nothing else for it, so, very crestfallen, I at last sat down.

The hour for assembling in the schoolroom was half-past ten, so Mademoiselle told me when I had finished and she added I might go.

"Let me have my letters," I cried passionately. "I will have them," I added, walking up to the head of the table where she sat with them open in her right hand.

"No," she answered very calmly, "you shall not have them. Leave the room."

A little after half-past ten, I sullenly made my way to the schoolroom. Mademoiselle had not arrived, but the girls were there.

"Oh, Julian!" said Beatrice, looking up from the Dante she was conning over. "You will catch it! How ever could you be so rude and violent?"

"Catch it!" I rejoined. "What do you mean? I have a perfect right to my own letters; and I call her conduct dishonourable."

"You won't talk like that in an hour or two, my boy," remarked Maud from her easel in the window.

"A little smart feminine discipline will certainly make a great change," chimed in Agnes, who was arranging some flowers.

"Nonsense," said I, wildly. "That she can't do!"

"Do!" they ejaculated in chorus. "What can't she do?"

"I suppose," added Maud, "he has never heard of a riding whip. Mademoiselle has a horridly cruel little whip. Ay! How it bites!" and she laughed.

"Or of the *regime* of the stay-lace, or of fifty other ways young ladies have for breaking in refractory boys," went on Agnes. "Never mind," in a tone of mock consolation, which maddened me, "he will soon be initiated."

"She whip me! At my age, and before you, girls! You must be mad to think she would dare to do such a thing. You are only laughing at me. I should fight. I am much stronger than she is."

"You will like petticoats, however," said Maud. "You will find you have to submit to them. And she is sure to punish you in front of us. You will not have many clothes left to conceal your hidden charms: and if you turn out to have as nice a figure in reality as you seem to have now, I shall get Mademoiselle to let you pose for me as a model for an Apollo."

"Julian," said Beatrice, "take my advice and submit quietly, dear boy. Your resistance will only make things worse."

"I believe you're gone on him already, Bee," laughed Agnes. "Mind, you'll have to go shares!" At which they all laughed.

I was horrified and disgusted. Could such things be? My first impulse was to fly, to rush to my own room, lock myself in, get together a few necessaries, and escape. But, at that moment, Mademoiselle entered, very determined-looking. She spoke a few words to each of the girls about their work, and then sat down in her low chair, very elegantly and gracefully.

"Now, Master Julian," she said, "you have to realize that I am your governess and that you are my absolute slave. Don't interrupt! From you I shall expect and shall exact the most implicit obedience and the most abject submission. You will tremble hereafter at the mere rustle of a petticoat; by it you are to be governed. If you are sufficiently foolish to continue your insubordination and the ridiculous temper you displayed this morning, it will be the worse for you."

"Mademoiselle," I broke in, "I do not understand you; my father sent me here because I am too delicate for school."

"And too unruly for home. Too indecent!" (at which I blushed). "Too inquisitive! Too anxious to know what young ladies have under their petticoats." (I was dumbfounded, and furtively glanced at the girls who were eagerly listening.) "Yes! I know all about it. The petticoat will have its revenge now, and you will be under it in more senses than one for some time. Kneel down there at my feet." (I hesitated, especially seeing the girls highly amused.) "Kneel down at once," she repeated, settling herself in her chair, and assuming a more erect attitude, "and put your hands behind you."

This was not very bad after all, and I felt so abashed and ashamed, and had so little to say for myself, that I complied somehow. Then Mademoiselle rang a hand bell.

"Elise," she said, "strap this boy's elbows behind his back as tightly as you can."

Elise grasped me firmly by the upper part of the arm. I was

surprised to feel her strength. The little resistance I made was soon overcome. I cannot describe the mixture of sensations I experienced with her standing over me, my head level with her waist, and at her pulling me about roughly as she delighted in executing Mademoiselle's order. I noticed what Zola describes as "a powerful feminine perfume" — the *odor de femina*.

At last two straps were buckled tightly round my arms, just above the elbows. In each strap was a small metal ring. Elise passed a white cord three or four times through these rings, and then proceeded to pull them as closely together as possible. Oh, how she hurt! I thought she would have broken my arms. I cried out, I resisted as much as I could, but the improvised pulley was too much for me. I writhed in my endeavours to get free, but she stood over me and kept me down.

"Tighter," said Mademoiselle.

And at last, when my elbows nearly touched each other, Elise fastened the cords and stood up, looking very pretty with the flush upon her smiling comely face caused by her exertions.

"Now, Elise, make him kneel quite close to my knees. Put that belt round his waist, and fasten his ankles to it at the back, so that he cannot get up. Now, Master Julian," she went on when this had been done, "you are in a fit state for punishment and you shall have it. You were rude to me about those letters." Smack, smack, in my face, one on each cheek: one with the left, the other with the right hand. How those soft, lovely, dimpled hands stung! How my cheeks tingled! How I struggled in absolute helplessness to get free! "You object to a governess, to feminine domination, to petticoat-rule" — giving me two smacks at each enumeration. "I think I shall convert you. You see" — smack, smack — "you must endure it."

I would not have believed two dainty little hands could have caused such pain. Kneeling at Mademoiselle's pretty feet, in close proximity to her, and seeing her graceful figure each time she raised her arms to inflict me punishment, was I own, at first, some assuagement of my pain. But at last the smacking she gave my cheeks made my head swim and I became so silly and bewildered that I was almost unconscious by the time she put the backs of her hands alternately to my lips and made me kiss them and thank her.

"Oh, please undo my arms and let me get up." I longed to move about and to put my hands up to my face; but she refused.

Instead, she enquired of Elise whether I had not been rude to her.

"Yes, Mademoiselle, very rude. Master Julian spoke to me most rudely when I went to his bedroom to show him the way to the breakfast room."

"Very well, Elise. Out of school hours Master Julian is to be under you tomorrow and the two following days, and by that time I trust you will have made him respect you. And now, Julian, you shall be deprived of your trousers. Take a long leave of them. When you will see them again, I do not know; they teach you all sorts of resistance and naughtiness and make you assume airs of ridiculous superiority which you do not possess. We must make a girl of you. Elise, make him stand up and take them off."

"Oh, Mademoiselle! Oh, please do not before you and the girls. Oh, don't —"

Elise, however, speedily unfastened the straps which kept me kneeling, but kept my elbows still confined, and busied herself in unfastening my buttons. Maid like, she tore open all the front first, to my intense shame, and then fumbled round my waist with both hands at once, kneeling before me. I cannot describe what I felt at being close to a girl in this condition with her hands busy about me, the front of my principal garment opened and violated, and my person almost coming into actual contact with her swelling bosom as she proceeded with uncompromising promptitude and rapidity to unfasten my trousers, my governess and the three girls looking on with amusement. I myself felt like a fowl about to be roasted and was nearly stupefied with shame.

Presently the braces were unfastened and Elise at once pushed my trousers and drawers down to my heels, not hesitating to move her hands freely about my person, even putting her arm between my legs to effect her purpose. In the midst of my abasement, I noticed an incipient sensation of what I felt when I had lifted the nursery maid's garments. Truly the tables were turned on me, for now, before women and girls, my own legs, from the end of my shirt to my ankles, were bared and displayed, naked. Elise next, with little ceremony and much disconcerting violence, pulled off my shoes and socks; then tore off the drawers and trousers, rolled them up, and deposited them on a chair.

My cheeks burned and I felt horridly defenceless.

"Now, Julian, how do you feel? To enforce your subjection to the petticoat, the emblem of the female sex, and to show your domination by it, you shall stand in the corner with one over your head until half-past twelve, when lessons are over. Elise, fetch one of my red flannel petticoats out of the soiled linen basket in my room." Elise soon returned with the garment required. "Tie it together at the top — so! Now throw it over his head. There, now he is under the petticoat! Put him in the corner; and at half-past twelve, Julian, she will come and take you to my bedroom, where I shall birch your bottom for you as smartly as ever a boy's bottom was birched."

I winced at her threat and at her talking so freely of my bottom. There was not much to hide it from sight and they must have caught glimpses of it as Elise hustled me sharply into the corner. What could I do, my arms fixed immovably, my head wrapped up in a red petticoat of Mademoiselle's, and myself overcome by the pungent odour I was then quite unacquainted with, but with which I subsequently became only too familiar? I was also terrified to think of the birching in store for me.

Lessons went on just as if I had not been there. Beatrice made some blunders with her Dante and (would that I could have seen!) had to lie across an ottoman, have her petticoats turned up, and receive a dozen cuts with Mademoiselle's little whip, and then be deprived of her drawers for the day. I heard her muffled sobs and imagined the scene, the smallest peep of which my pinioned arms and the petticoat covering my head prevented my obtaining. I trembled at the sound of the punishment and already began to repent and make resolutions of obedience. Obedience, alas! I did not know then that the infliction of punishment, whether deserved or not, was an integral part of my handsome governess' discipline and system, and that I should be whipped merely for being a boy! A great deal of courage had left me with my trousers, and, smothered as I was, I longed for some covering for my bare legs. I wondered what on earth would happen to me during the three days I was to be under Elise.

At last, half-past twelve arrived. The girls went off and so also did Mademoiselle. In a few minutes Elise came for me. She whipped off the petticoat, and taking hold of my ears from behind, roughly and angrily hustled me off in front of her, giving me every now and then a dreadful thump behind, first with one knee, then with the other.

"Get along, Master Julian, you bold young rascal. What! You complain of my being rough to you — I will be as rough to you as your tongue was to me. Wait till tomorrow, and the next day, and the next, when I shall have you in my power! You will have some reason to complain of my hurting you then!"

In this ignominious manner, out of breath, my ears feeling as if they were being torn out, my arms aching as though they would break, and my head in a whirl with the slapping I had had, I was bundled into Mademoiselle's bedroom to have my bottom birched by her.

Chapter IV

The Birch

A sort of mesmeric influence seemed to have crept into me from that intensely feminine garment which had been in such close contact with Mademoiselle's own person and then so long over my head and face as I stood disgraced in the corner. It seemed to have sapped my strength and all my powers of resistance, to have undermined my self-respect, to have rendered me contemptible in my own eyes; in short, to have completely emasculated me. I had felt my virility ebbing away during the hours I had stood with the red thing enveloping my shoulders, touching my eyes and nose and mouth, conscious all the while that it was a woman's petticoat which had been worn, and that a thing so essentially feminine had, willy-nilly, been forced upon me. I had gradually, step by step, to give in to the flood of feminine associations which rushed upon me, and yield by degrees to the power of woman. I was keenly aware that nothing could save me, that all opposition was useless and hopeless, and I was slowly drifting towards the knowledge that I must sooner or later abandon myself absolutely to it. I stood before Mademoiselle, cowed and humiliated, not so much at the prospect of the beating as at the sense of my own helplessness in her hands, because she was feminine and could therefore do with me what she liked. Whatever it was, I knew I had no power left to resist, and trembled at the inevitable acknowledgment of this fact to myself. She seemed the embodiment of triumphant womanhood as I was hustled into her presence, shaken and pulled about by another woman, to be whipped by her.

As I stood before Mademoiselle, my hands still tied, my ears red and tingling from Elise's rough usage, panting and out of breath, my back sore from the rude thumps of Elise's knees, my courage gave way and my eyes filled with tears, which the poignant sense of my abasement caused to overflow. I could only hold my head and yield in silent resignation and despair.

Let not the reader, however, imagine that I was subdued at once. No, there was many a reaction. A constant revolt of all my manhood which required many severe lessons to quell and conquer finally. But I must confess that as time went on, my disgust lessened, these revolts were divided by longer intervals, and at last I became a wretched petticoat-slave.

Mademoiselle looked on haughtily. Her form dilated and expanded with the sense, so agreeable to a woman, of power over something male. She looked like a magnificent bird of prey, a regal and feminine eagle, about to swoop upon her victim. She stood erect, her head thrown back, consciously displaying her well-developed bust and elegant figure; her air of determination and pretty wilfulness much enhancing her charms. There was something arch about her manner as she quizzed me upon my first introduction into a lady's bedroom. She asked me, as she significantly handled a light, long, and elastic birch, how I liked the prospect of my first assignation. She remarked that I had been introduced in all due form by her maid to whom she proceeded to give a guinea out of my pocket money (which Mademoiselle had charge of) in recognition of her services. Mademoiselle produced a sovereign and a shilling and gave them to Elise before my eyes, to my intense and ill-concealed annoyance, which increased her merriment, and Elise thanked me with mock politeness and gratitude.

Mademoiselle promised me by way of consolation, that the maid should be sent out and that consequently I should have the advantage of an entirely private *tête-à-tête* with her, and enquired whether I was not rejoiced at my good fortune? I do not know what it was, but something or other in these words, or what they suggested, quite changed my mood, and I let my eyes rest on her affectionately and admiringly, and said that I indeed appreciated the favour; a remark which brought me a sound slap in the face. Again disconcerted, I determined that nothing should allow me to be made a further fool of, and resolved not to utter another word.

The room was a large one and very handsomely furnished. The extremely pretty bed stood under a heavy silk canopy across the angle of the room farthest from the fireplace, the canopy suspended from the ceiling and the carved oak bedstead standing clear of the walls. There were several quaint, cosy-looking chairs about, and bowls of spring flowers. Mademoiselle stood between me and the light, tall and graceful in her severely simple black *mousseline de laine* dress, displaying her womanly figure to the fullest advantage. As I contemplated her in my wretched condition I felt yet more abjectly humiliated. A novel sensation of awkwardness again replaced my habitual self-possession, an inveterate stupidity my ordinary sprightliness and vivacity. There I stood, a great boy, trussed like a fowl, with nothing to conceal my bare legs but a shirt, which did not reach to my knees.

Mademoiselle ordered Elise to place a long carved bench of black oak, about a foot wide, in the middle of the room, and to put upon it a feather bolster which Elise, by means of tapes, tied to the bench. I was then compelled to stand across one end while Elise strapped my ankles close together underneath and then left the room. Mademoiselle went to the door, shut and locked it, and then turned full upon me. I could not but note as I trembled how her whole form glowed with smiling and triumphant satisfaction. She walked deliberately up to me, lifted my shirt up behind, and, to my intense shame, intently contemplated my back for some seconds; then, still holding up this undergarment and standing a little way off, she took up the birch and gave me some stinging lashes with it. I had never felt anything like it before. I had no idea that it would hurt one-tenth as much as it did, and was compelled to cry out.

Mademoiselle then, to my horror, unbuttoned my waistcoat and lifted my shirt with both hands high up in front. I could not move. I was speechless, as she stood facing me and examining my most secret possessions over which and along the front of my things she several times passed her dimpled hand. Then she let the shirt fall, untied my elbows, and taking up a lady's jewelled riding whip, she remarked that I should be flogged naked. Standing at my left side she ordered me to take off my jacket and waistcoat. I hesitated and fumbled. Looking round she gave me a touch of the whip on my bare legs. If the birch smarted, that vicious little thing bit like fury. I yelled and clapped my hands to my legs, but only to get them lashed also. She went on until, in desperation, I tore off my jacket and waistcoat.

"Now your shirt! Quick!"

Up went the whip, her eyes sparkling savagely. This time, without an instant's hesitation, and without thinking about it, I whipped off my shirt more quickly than ever I had done before. And there I was, perfectly naked before her, red and overwhelmed with shame and smarting with pain. She leisurely regarded me, evidently intending not to spare me a single pang. She moved her hand along my back and shoulders, remarking that she thought the whip would mark my skin easily, and, by way of experiment, she gave me several more smart cuts with it on various parts of my body, each stroke causing me intense anguish. I cried out, and implored her to desist; but she merely gloated the more over my torture.

"Now," she at length said, "your bottom must be put in a proper position for me to punish."

"Oh, Mademoiselle, forgive me! Oh, I am sorry for my disobedience and folly! Do forgive me!..."

"I never forgive! Lie down on your face."

I saw there was nothing for it but compliance; so, with a sigh like a gasp of despair, I obeyed her. She placed her hand on the back of my head and pressed it into the bolster. The wide bench separated my thighs, pressing my most sensitive parts cruelly. She fixed a strap round my neck and passed it under the bench, placed another round the seat and my waist, and lastly fastened my hands together underneath the bench. My posture and the soft bolster (which soon became pleasantly warm) gave me a certain voluptuous feeling soon, however, to be dispelled by my sufferings.

"Now we shall see whether a girl can properly punish a boy's bottom!!" How she dwelt on the shameful word! "Whether a youth is or is not to be subject to feminine discipline and rule and to his governess." And, putting her hand from behind between my legs, she caught hold of what I was ashamed she should know I possessed, and pulled it about until I confessed to myself that I was her slave body and soul. Then, for the first time, was revealed to me the secret source whence woman's power springs. A keen sense of the difference of sex was communicated to me through her taper fingers. Her skirts caused me an electric shock each time they touched me. The feminine characteristics of her form, as she stood over me, became indelibly stamped upon my being, and acquired for her and for the rest of her sex an absolute dominion from that moment over me. A look or the rustle of petticoat is enough for me now. At either I tremble.

This sway was established and emphasized by the cruel punishment of the most secret portions of my body which I then underwent at her hands. Regularly and deliberately was the birching given; the methodical administration of which I could not interrupt. I protested and swore; but I had to learn how cruelly women can punish — how relentlessly they slake their vengeance — what a lust they have to satisfy, when they have a male at their mercy, to deal unmitigated torture out to him. How they exercise that dominion over him which is so real, although often unacknowledged. Men are not subject to these motives and never punish so cruelly as women.

Only once was my torture stayed. Mademoiselle had flogged me from my right side and from my left. My sobs had given place to screams and yells; but Mademoiselle said she should insist on my taking punishment quietly, at which threat I gave a delirious laugh. She calmly opened a drawer, and took out a plum-shaped piece of wood with a leather loop at its thickest end, through which loop she slipped one of her scented handkerchiefs. Then she forced the plug into my mouth, and tied the ends of the handkerchief tightly behind my neck. I was nearly choked, and effectually gagged. Perfectly indifferent to my sufferings, she resumed the punishment, merely remarking that I should have ten minutes more of it for making the gagging necessary.

When the ten minutes had expired there came an interval when the strokes, which had fallen with the even regularity and swing of a pendulum, the swing of which I had ascertained to the fraction of a second, ceased. I hoped it was over. I could not express the hope in words, so I groaned. Mademoiselle had been whipping me across both ways. She now came to the top of the bench at my right, daintily lifted her skirts, and put her right leg across me. Then, almost sitting upon my neck and smothering me with her petticoats, the back of which fell to the floor over my head, she proceeded to flog me lengthwise. She was looking down my back, and I knew that behind me the wardrobe mirror reflected my open thighs. Although the strap had been loosened I could scarcely move my head; when I tried to do so, however, she pressed me more closely. I can give no idea of what I felt at my novel posture underneath a young woman. She now struck lengthwise, more slowly but more viciously; the strokes cut like hot iron, and, as the pliant ends of the birch hit what lay between my thighs, I felt I was being murdered. The anguish was maddening, and if I recollected what she could see by lifting her eyes to the glass, it was with utter recklessness to the exposure.

"There, Master Julian, that's enough for the first time. I think I have whipped you pretty severely. You will not care to set me at defiance again," she complacently remarked, throwing herself into a great saddle-back easy chair, apparently somewhat exhausted.

I lay utterly prostrate, powerless to speak even had I not been gagged; all my strength was gone, and I smarted as though I had been seared with red hot wires. Presently she unstrapped and ungagged me, I could scarcely move. I was in a cataleptic or comatose state and only semi-conscious.

She resumed her seat, and bade me kneel at her feet. I obeyed mechanically. Had she bade me walk into a fire, I think I should have done so. I was thoroughly exhausted, my head sank upon her lap, and my tears flowed softly, but I soon began to feel better. She then bade me kiss her hands and the remains of the rod, and thank her humbly, but sincerely, for whipping me. Whatever she ordered I at once obeyed, deprived altogether of my own volition. She made me stoop down and kiss her feet and legs; for one delicious moment she held my head in soft imprisonment between her thighs. Beside myself from the effect of the pain, I am astonished still at the recollection of how my feelings towards Mademoiselle then underwent a most unreasonable but complete alteration. I loved her as violently as I had detested her before. I fell hopelessly in love with my cruel governess. I loved her because of her cruelty and became suddenly enthralled by a strong and anxious desire to press and fondle her. I worshipped the very ground on which she walked. Why was this?

Chapter V

Metamorphosis and Luncheon

Mademoiselle reclined for some minutes in her chair, whilst I knelt between her knees with bowed head, drinking in, as it were, the luscious radiance which I had suddenly discovered encompassed her. She did not speak; she allowed the influence of her being and spirit to silently overcome me.

At last she rose, and pouring some wine into a large bohemian glass, she bade me drink; then, pointing to some clothes Elise had left behind her, told me to put them on.

I suppose the red grape juice made me defiant, for, on perceiving them to be a girl's dress, I protested. Mademoiselle simply said she was sure I should obey her. Strange to say, that was enough, and I complied, only remarking that for her sake I wished to be a boy. She smiled and promised that I should tell her all about it after luncheon in her *boudoir*. With her help I then put on a *chemise*, long stockings, drawers, petticoats, a corset which did not fit, and I was buttoned up in a bodice. How strangely embarrassed I felt. But these feelings were swallowed up by a sense of disgrace when I found that outside all, I had to wear a pair of Mademoiselle's own laced drawers, the waistband being tied round my neck, and my arms thrust through the legs as though they were sleeves. These were fastened with garters at the wrists. In that guise I was to appear before the girls at luncheon in token of my subjugation and defeat, and of the rout and discomfit of my virility. Petticoats were difficult enough to put up with; this addition of a pair of drawers completed my abasement. However, the novelty and discomfort of the attire served somewhat to divert my attention from the intense humiliation I suffered, as did also the effort necessary to walk at all decently; for what with the high heels of the girls' boots, which buttoned high up my legs and which felt like mountains under them — and what with the agitation of my nerves and my soreness from the severe whipping I had received at Mademoiselle's hands — walking was no easy matter. I blushed like a girl as I felt the feminine garments against my legs and saw the drawers about my arms. The delicate, minute, ladylike handkerchief, all laced and of no practical use whatever which I had to hold in my hand, made me feel really girlish; and when ushered into the luncheon room and introduced to my cousins as — "Miss Julia, instead of that very naughty boy Master Julian, who has been sent home" — I began positively to wonder whether I was not actually a girl. They made great fun of me in a quiet and exasperating way, saying the sleeves reminded them of a bishop under his wife's thumb, and Agnes slyly suggested a cushion when she noticed that it hurt me as I sat down.

When I looked at Beatrice's girlish figure, I felt I was a boy dressed up, and feared she would despise me forever. She, however, said nothing; but when I handed her a plate and upset her wine glass in so doing, Mademoiselle bade her smack my face. She did so with a severity that startled me. Whatever her real feelings towards me were, it was evident I need look for no mitigation of my punishment from her.

"You clumsy hussy," exclaimed Mademoiselle, flushing angrily, when the leg of that damned linen thing upset Beatrice's glass, sending the red wine all over the tablecloth, on to her pretty frock, and I stood dumbfounded by her.

"Beatrice, smack her face. Stand still, Miss, and keep your hands down!"

And Beatrice, with a half-vexed and half-amused air, who was rubbing out with her napkin the wine which had stained her gown, gently put the napkin down, and calmly stretching out her right arm to free her hand from its cuff and sleeve, she smilingly opened her pretty plump hands and looking full into my eyes gave my left cheek a stinging slap delivered straight from the shoulder.

Before I had time to recover she repeated the process on my other cheek.

"Resume your place, Miss Julia," Mademoiselle directed in calm tones, "and remember, if you are so clumsy again, she shall slap you elsewhere."

At this remark, Beatrice slowly lifted her eyes to mine, a little mocking smile playing about her mouth, and, by her expression, she plainly enquired how I liked the prospect, which prospect I can safely say I did not relish.

Quite cowed by my own awkwardness and its prompt punishment I sat down in disgrace and confusion, my cheeks tingling terribly. I should not at all have desired to be exposed to the tender mercies of Maud or Agnes, who seemed to be very contentedly awaiting an opportunity, and of the arrival of which, sooner or later, they evidently had no manner of doubt. And I am sorry to say that they were quite right as it happened in the sequel.

But Beatrice was the one who silently, as far as circumstances would allow, took me into her own irresponsible charge and whipped me whenever she thought I deserved it, or she had a mind to do so, at her own sweet pleasure. At odd times she gave me private instructions and lessons on various details as to how she wished me to behave and how to conform to the discipline I was subjected to. Of its relaxation she would not hear a word.

Thus it was that I soon found I had more governesses than one. Mademoiselle ruled by a mixture of sex and force — force which her sex made irresistible; but I could evade and escape her to some extent. Beatrice ruled by love, and her pains were sweet though sharp. My relations with her were too tender and too intimate to make it possible for me even to wish to elude her. From her I could not keep a secret, and from the very first she took it for granted that her wishes would be my law, and I tacitly assented. I had still a great deal to learn and have much to describe before reaching that period of my life to which what I have just written relates.

Chapter VI

A Lesson in Psychology

This afternoon, which I well and vividly remember, was full of novel and startling revelations and experiences for me. I had no real knowledge whatever, nor did I recognise the character of my passions and instincts. Although now wide awake, they were then totally blind, and perplexed me with doubts and curiosity as to their significance.

Of a subtle and indefinable influence I was very conscious, but its source was still a mystery to me, and its sway a puzzle. The company of a young woman affected me very differently from the companionship of men; why, I knew not. I supposed Mademoiselle's hand had excited me only because she had touched and played with an organ of which for some reason I felt ashamed, especially in connection with a woman. Why the drawers and petticoats kept me in a perpetual and delicious tremor of excitement, and made that organ grow inconveniently and painfully large and distil in an altogether unusual manner a pellucid essence, I did not know either.

To think of all this in connection with the propagation of our race never once struck me. How the human race propagated seemed to me like one of those dry matters to be found at the commencement of geographies with the explanation of the seasons, the revolution of the earth round the sun, &c.

The pretty *boudoir* was trimmed and pranked with rose-coloured silk and exquisite water colours, until it looked a perfect feminine thing. Its statuettes were feminine. A bust of Omphale; a replica of Hercules in the Borghese Casino, in her clothes; an Aurora conquering a reluctant Cephalous, who was on one knee, his arms bent back in her hands, and his shoulders entangled in and imprisoned by pretty legs.

The high priestess of this charming sanctuary, sunlit, rosy-coloured, perfumed, and delicious, was Mademoiselle. Never had I seen her so alluring! She had promised to let me tell her "all about it" in her *boudoir* after luncheon and was keeping her word. She had given directions that we were not to be disturbed. She told me with winning softness that I had her now all to myself. My faults were all ignored or forgotten. Luncheon had revived her. Her spirits had lost that archness which had so disconcerted me, and she had become affectionate and gentle; yet I did not feel towards her as if she were my sister. There were cravings which unconsciously affected me but the magic secret had not yet been imparted and I was content to admire as I reclined upon the luxurious divan. Her masses of black hair had become loosened, and its thick rolls contrasted with her white skin in a marvellous manner. Her ruby lips and white teeth, her pink ears, and lovely head so admirably poised upon an adorable bust, dazzled me with their beauty. Her body was thrown back in her big *dormeuse*, her ankles and even higher being exposed to my view. She had been pretending to read, and was sipping black coffee, and petted me with cake and red Burgundy, rich as nectar.

When suddenly I called to mind how she had treated me, and what she had seen, my cheeks burned more than they did from Beatrice's slapping, and I noticed that the thought produced a strange medley of sensations on the organ violated by that beautiful hand and those taper fingers. I thought that some of my remarks brought a tinge of colour to her cheeks, but it may have been only the reflection of the rose-tender light of the apartment. She spoke in soft melodious tones, and although only twenty-three years of age, she appeared a complete woman of the world and entirely free from girlish ignorance.

"Now, Julian — for you wish to be a boy for me, and I will not now call you Julia, you have many things to tell me and here you have me in an amiable mood, all to yourself. What is it you have to confess? Begin."

"Oh, Mademoiselle, I do not know. Many, many things; but how to describe them is beyond me. I thought — I should be so wretched here, with only girls, and now —"

"You think you will change your mind. Do not be in too great a hurry to do that."

"You seemed as though it would be impossible to be friends with you, and — and you punished me so severely; but the strange thing about it is that it has made me like you — made me quite fond of you. I want to be close to you, to be always with you. I want —"

"What do you want?"

"Oh! May I say it? I want to love you."

"Do you, indeed? Well, you have a mark of my favour in the garment you have about your neck. I do not think any cavalier could bear a more distinguished or intimate mark of a lady's favour than her drawers; but, as I believe they are usually carried on the helmet or shield, I will, if you like, muffle up your head in them."

"Oh, no, Mademoiselle; because then I could not see you!"

"But, if it were not for that, do you really think you would like it?"

"Yes."

"You would be over head and ears in love then," she rejoined, laughing, "and I fear I should be compelled to punish you again. But, come, how would you like to love me?"

"I should like to be close to you — oh, so close — to feel you as close to me — to hold your hands, to look into your eyes, to kiss you, to expire for you."

"If you think of kissing my lips, some day, years hence, if you are very good and very obedient in the meanwhile, and have a moustache — well, perhaps then, if you remember, you may ask again."

"But how could I wear a girl's clothes with a moustache?"

"I do not think it is good for a youth without a moustache to kiss a lady's mouth. It is only after long and devoted service, after winning his way upwards in her favour by slow degrees, that such a delight could be permitted."

"But may I," I asked eagerly, half-rising, "kiss your feet? I have done so once. Let me begin at the beginning. Let me do it again, and perhaps I may get a little higher, because — because —"

"Because what?"

"When you were whipping me you — you stood over me, and perhaps — might — kiss your —"

"Kiss what?"

"Your leg," said I with bated breath. I was intoxicated with the recollection of the contact of the warm soft flesh and the satin skin.

"And would you really like to kiss my legs again?" enquired Mademoiselle archly, moving them ravishingly. "Well, we shall see. I have something here I want to read, when we have done talking; and then perhaps I may let you put your lips to my ankle. But you must first tell me about your experiences of a petticoat — you were very inquisitive about them. What could have induced you to lift up that girl's petticoats? What did you expect to see underneath them? Your affection for petticoats made me put you in them, Julian. That is what your curiosity has brought you to."

"Oh, I lifted them out of sheer mischief. What is it that girls hide so carefully underneath them? I only saw a pair of fat legs."

"I dare say you will know before you are much older. Mischief! *Mon Dieu*! Did you not feel naughty?"

"I felt carried away by some passion or other. Is that feeling naughty? It is rather a nice feeling."

"Did you feel the same under my petticoats?"

"A little."

"And whilst Elise was marching you off to be birched by me?"

"Yes."

"And whilst I was punishing you?"

"Yes."

"Especially, I suppose, when I lifted up your shirt?"

"Yes."

"Now, cannot you guess why?"

"No. Have girls the same thing under their petticoats as I have under my shirt? Is that why they wear them?"

"Have you never seen a girl naked?"

"No."

"Look at those statues. Look at that Venus; look at Aurora. Have they got the thing you complain of?"

"No; but I always thought that was because they were only statues."

"And you don't know what that thing is capable of, and why women have not got one?"

"No."

"I must really give you a psychological lesson, Julian, and put you in possession of knowledge which a great boy like you should have. At present you are unfit for life and for the world, and much of the discipline you are having would be thrown away if I did not instruct you."

So Mademoiselle got up, and radiant with amusement, she reclined on the great ottoman at my side, with her left arm across me. She settled herself comfortably, and then turning her head and looking over her shoulder into my eyes, she questioned me archly as to whether her being so close to me did not make me feel naughty? I was almost suffocated by the violence of my feelings, nor did she wait for any reply, but rapidly slipping her right hand under my petticoats and moving it along the front and inside of my things, she caused me inexpressible emotion. She then caught hold of the thing in front of me.

"It is here you feel naughty, you bold boy. Another time I should whip you for this." These words made me worse.

"Yes! Yes!" I gasped in hushed tones.

"How it has grown!" she exclaimed, as she held it tightly in her hand.

Leaning close to me, she mingled a little pain with my pleasure by drawing the foreskin up and down several times, each time further back. I wriggled and said she hurt me.

"It is very tight," she remarked, and then finally grasping it and the testicles together in her hand, she squeezed and opened her hand frequently, sending a convulsive thrill each time through my body, so that several times I nearly threw her off me and jumped up. But she held me tight in that delicious thraldom and persistently continued her movement.

"Oh! Oh! Mademoiselle. Oh! Miss de Chambonnard! Oh, how nice! Oh, how I love you! How I adore you! I — I — worship" (squeeze, squeeze) "you! Oh, let me go! Oh, don't! Oh, how nice your hand" (squeeze) "is there! Oh, how I love you!" clasping her slender waist round from the back with my disengaged arm.

"Oh, take your hand away! Something awful — something dreadful will happen. I am sure it will, and I cannot prevent it. Oh! Oh!" For all answer, squeeze, squeeze, squeeze, uninterruptedly and determinedly continued.

When she worked me almost into a frenzy, and my movements, jerks, and exclamations showed me to be *in extremis*, still holding me and pressing me more tightly, she again turned her head to look into my eyes. I noticed her own eyes were swimming. She squeezed me and crushed me more energetically, not uttering a syllable, but pressing against me with her whole form.

At last a convulsive shudder shook my frame from head to foot, and finally centred and concentrated itself in what she had hold of. Completely beyond myself and without my control, it went into a violent spasm of throbs, causing me such a sensation of delight and satisfaction as I had never dreamt of in my wildest moments, spouting out something time after time into her dainty hand, which was now still, and only quiescently grasping me.

"Oh," I gasped as I lay exhausted, and she arose, "*if only I could do that to you!*"

"Where should you put it, Master Julian?" she asked, laughing.

That, I confess, puzzled me.

As I lay recovering, my eyes rivetted on Mademoiselle, I understood why women have such power over men, why men will go through so much for them, and how truly they may be named "mistress." It is because they have it in their power to do that with his body, which can convulse him with inexpressible and delirious joy. I began to feel the subtle pleasure of being wrapt in a woman's garments, which seemed hallowed from their resemblance to those which enveloped Mademoiselle herself, as she stood a little distance off, wiping her dainty hand with a handkerchief, and putting on a pretty and amused air of delicate disgust.

I had been introduced to Love, and made acquainted with one of the secrets of its influence and power. Love was no longer an abstraction, but the sweetest and most desirable reality. Venus had, however, so far only uncovered her face. I felt the want of some complement of my ecstasy, of some participation in it. The veil had fallen to the Goddess's shoulders, not yet to her feet!

Mademoiselle again ensconced herself in her easy chair, and taking up her book, turned over its leaves somewhat at random. Her breasts rose and fell more quickly than before; and upon her cheeks there was just the slightest possible flush — such a flush of pink as a delicate white rose sometimes has. And in her dark eyes shone a glorious and laughing light, which she allowed to radiate upon me, reminding me of the laughter-loving Venus, and revealing the significance of that Homeric epithet.

Chapter VII

A Mouth with a Moustache

I felt convinced that there was some way as yet undisclosed — some means by which I could comprehensively and entirely love and be loved.

I had already become sensible of the rapture of possessing in some degree the secret of the concealed springs which, duly worked upon, rose in fountains of overwhelming volume and transported one in floods of delight.

I felt that at last I had begun to live instinctively, that there was something to live for. It could be no mere hallucination that the future had still some mystery to disclose, and some more perfect tuition to offer. A dim vision of the happiness to be enjoyed by the human creature when it perfects itself by the discovery and coalescence of its sexual affinity was thus unfolded, and, on the other hand, I easily perceived the misery it must endure from unsatisfied yearnings.

There was evidently more in the education I was receiving and in the discipline to which I had been given up than was apparent on its surface or than I had supposed.

Mademoiselle had indeed thoroughly given me a psychological lesson. I had taken it to be a joke. I had not dreamt it was possible for that little hand to teach me so much.

At last my fair instructress looked up, and speaking as though she were putting some restraint upon herself, said significantly: "Well, Julian, I think we have talked long enough, and I am now going to read."

"Oh, Mademoiselle," I said, "won't you give me more?"

"You silly boy," she rejoined, laughing, and now really rosy, "you do not even know what I am going to permit you. Come here."

She was seated in a low and long-seated armchair, and placing her knees against its left elbow, she directed me to seat myself on the floor, with my legs underneath the chair, and with my face close to the front of the seat.

I found this no easy matter, and went to work rather clumsily, receiving one or two playful but sharp slaps, "for not carrying out a lady's wishes with more alacrity." When at last I had succeeded, she unfastened and took off the drawers from my arms and also the body of the dress I was wearing, leaving my arms, neck, and shoulders bare. I was much incommodated by the corset, which was really a very ill-fitting one, and felt exceedingly awkward in my unfamiliar attire, and indeed hurt myself with the busks of the longwaisted thing as I assumed the required posture. My long legs, uncovered by the petticoats, which in my efforts to seat myself as bidden had worked themselves quite up to my knees, were disposed in a very ungraceful and clumsy heap beneath the chair. I sincerely trusted Mademoiselle, martinet and stickler for elegance as I knew her to be, would not notice this, dreading the consequences if she did. Perhaps, however, she considered the irksomeness and the discomfort of the badly arranged drapery beneficial. For although she must have noticed the bundle and my immodestly uncovered legs, yet when she had got me close enough, she gave me no further directions. By a dexterous movement and half-turn, accomplished before I had time to guess what she meant, she whisked her petticoats over my head and lodged her right leg across my left shoulder. The result was that I found my head again between her soft and warm thighs, each voluptuously pressing one of my cheeks. Her legs were enveloped in exquisitely fine linen undergarments; and there was wafted to me a fresher and stronger prevalence of that strange intoxicating perfume which I had noticed about the red flannel petticoat. My natural impulse was to retreat, an effort promptly prevented by a tight grip of Mademoiselle; stooping over she lifted up her skirts and looking at me with a strange fierce light in her eyes but with a rosy smile upon her face, said: "Now, Julian, if in the course of your incursions underneath my petticoats you should encounter a mouth with a moustache you may kiss it; and, in fact, when I press my heel against your back — like this — you are to kiss it — you understand — and to continue doing so as long as I press you."

She then again dropped her voluminous garments over me and threw herself well back in the chair. My head, already well above her knees, came to the open part of her drawers where I felt her satin-like skin and soft warm flesh, this time naked, against my cheeks. To my astonishment, my nose, mouth, and chin were tickled by some hairs. This must be the moustache thought I, and before I had time to determine what to do, Mademoiselle gave a wriggle and holding me close with her legs, rubbed something very hairy and moist all over my face, my eyes, my nose, and my mouth in a very lingering manner. In the midst of the hair I found what seemed like a mouth set lengthwise instead of across, and felt a little protuberance near its top, which was pressed forcibly against my own lips and which appeared to be excessively sensitive. At the same moment I felt her heel pressed against my shoulders and I gave it a kiss. It was instantly pushed into my lips and my mouth was forced wide open; unable to kiss it, I tickled it with my tongue.

Mademoiselle's movements as I did so became more and more vigorous, her hold of me grew tighter and tighter, and she pressed me still more closely. Feeling her foot heavily against my shoulders I continued to play with what I concluded was her raw flesh, to bite it gently with my teeth, and to lick it with my tongue, especially that little protuberance, as I soon discovered the transports which that gave her. To my wonder the aperture still grew larger and larger until I seemed actually to lose my face in it. It had wet me and appeared to cover me all over in it. I felt as if I was some distance inside her body and I grew furious with a strange excitement which increased with her own. Mademoiselle's throbs became more and more convulsive, indeed as violent as mine had been on the ottoman.

At last, centring herself upon my mouth, there came a series of violent spasmodic throbs lasting for some seconds then becoming gradually slower and slower, whilst there was jerked into my mouth a warm sticky fluid tasting something like the white of an egg only a little bitter. I could hear Mademoiselle's exclamations although her garments partly smothered the sound. At last her efforts ceased, her grasp relaxed, and she seemed to repose as she let my head rest against one of her knees.

What an experience! There was no longer any need to describe to me how a man differed from a woman. How delightful that she should be so formed and possess an organ so receptive, so responsive, so capable of appreciating and returning the passions of my own, which, whether it was intended or not for the purpose, I longed to place inside hers. How exquisite would be the pleasure if our movements could take place simultaneously, and whilst I was inside her. I was overjoyed at the intimate knowledge of a woman to which I had been so agreeably introduced and wondered whether everyone had equal good fortune, feeling convinced that they could not otherwise obtain anything like a perfect acquaintance with her. I was overjoyed, too, that that woman in my case was Mademoiselle.

I burned to express my feelings in words, to implore her to permit me to carry out my idea of inserting in her the engine of mine which she had manipulated. I conceived the idea to be original and I thought its communication would be welcomed by her as an inspiration of genius.

Not knowing what to do with the liquid with which my mouth was filled and needing some fresh air and a relief from the constraint of my position, I endeavoured to rise; but Mademoiselle instantly clasped my head tightly between her knees and prevented me. A horse's strength is in his loins, a lion's in his jaws, an elephant's in his trunk and weight, an ox's in his neck, and a woman's is evidently in her thighs. I again tried to free myself only to receive a tighter and more prolonged and suffocating squeeze followed by a smart blow on my back from her heel, which almost knocked the wind out of me. A little chagrined and disappointed, I thought it wisest to give in, and resolved to await events, passing my time in contemplation of my delicious situation under a young lady's petticoats. To enhance my sense of it I recalled her lovely features and figure to my mind, picturing her to myself seated there. And then I remembered that I was in full possession of the secret of her most private charms. I gently rubbed my head against her, up and down the insides of her thighs. She relaxed her hold and her lascivious motions told me how this pleased her.

I revelled in the contact of her undergarments and in the warm atmosphere and pungent scent of the locality. I gloried in the discovery of what petticoats actually did conceal and I swallowed the liquid in my mouth with a voluptuous thrill.

Mademoiselle was evidently reading, and I had opportunity for moralizing. I began to wonder whether there was anything wicked in all this — whether it was impure? Was it adultery, fornication, or lasciviousness to be beneath a maid's legs, kissing them and gratifying her and myself by dalliance with my lips and tongue with her "mouth with a moustache," simply because that mouth was between her legs and usually hidden? The concealment was conventional as dress, founded on the decorum and decencies of life. Was it wicked to kiss the mouth of an Eastern woman because, when walking abroad, it was covered by a Sash-mak? Brushing aside the conventionalities in the shape of skirts and drawers gave a poignant relish to the embrace that seemed perfectly legitimate. So I hugged Mademoiselle closer and kissed her legs again.

In a few minutes any further disposition on my part for reflection and analysis was cut short by a firm but gentle pressure of her dainty leg and little heel on my back. Again I glued my mouth to what seemed the compendium, the embodiment, the full divine revelation of Mademoiselle herself in her most intimate soul, and, on this occasion, with fewer scruples and with more avidity, with greater knowledge and keener skill. I bit the tender succulent lips, I inserted my tongue further and tickled the little protuberance more persistently, absorbing the yielding flesh more greedily. Mademoiselle's motions were in proportion more violent, her transport, her loss of self-control completer. All our efforts were directed to bring about a repetition of that convulsive and spasmodic agitation of her being which seemed to delight her and affected me. It took much longer this time and required more effort; her legs were thrown wider apart and she exerted herself (and I also) more vigorously. At last it came! The spasm took place more slowly and endured longer. She lay back with a sigh or gasp of relief and satisfaction, and I was becoming a little weary; no ethical questions this time presenting themselves for analysis and solution. The novelty of the situation was wearing off. Besides I felt the need of a repetition of the operation upon myself and was anxious to communicate my idea to her. However, I was not allowed to rise.

Mademoiselle read on. She moved and adjusted herself, giving me pleasure by the fresh and unavoidable contact of her flesh, each time she did so. But it seemed as though I were never to be released, and it appeared an interminable time before I again felt the signal on my back, and, on this occasion by the exercise of a little compulsion, was forced a third time to repeat the delicious process.

A few minutes later Mademoiselle threw down her book, lifted her leg off my shoulder, and told me to get up.

What a delicious flutter she was in! And how proud I felt at having been permitted to become so intimately acquainted with the secrets of her being!

"You may get up now, Julian, you dear boy, and we will have some tea. I want it, I can tell you."

I got up and stretched myself. I glanced at the Sevres clock, leisurely ticking away the hours as though it controlled Time with its fat and lazy motion.

For two hours had I been under Mademoiselle's petticoats in close communion with her!

Chapter VIII

How Babies are made — What an Idea!

"Well, Julian," said Mademoiselle Hortense, looking at me with eyes full of kindness. "Well, Julian!"

How can I express the coyness, the solicitude, the tenderness with which these two words were uttered? They meant so much after all I had been permitted to learn. I was encouraged to believe that nothing could now be denied to me.

"Oh, Mademoiselle! Oh, Mademoiselle, how I love you! How I thank you!"

"Do you really? Well, you have been very good and you discharged your duty admirably. And now that you know what ladies have under their petticoats, as well as what they can do to you, are you satisfied?"

"Ah, Mademoiselle, alas, no! A bright idea has struck me which I implore you to consent to. I am sure if you would only try it, it would be Paradise."

"You greedy youth! What more can you want?"

"I want — I want you to let me put — put what I — have got — into what you have, where my tongue was; and — perhaps what happened to you and what happened to me on the sofa might occur at once, at one and the same time. And *that* — that *would be* ecstasy. Oh, Mademoiselle, do let me!"

"No, Julian, I cannot. The idea is not new; it is as old as the world. That idea brought you and me and every one into existence. It is, I admit, the sole remnant of the joys of Paradise which Adam and Eve left us; but I cannot allow you now — not for years — not under other than entirely altered circumstances. You must be content with what you can have; had I not been fond of you I should not have given you so much. However much I should like it, I cannot give you that. It might result in — in a baby."

"In a *baby*?" I shouted in utter surprise. "Do you mean to say that is how babies are made?"

"Yes," she answered, "it is."

For some minutes utter silence fell upon me whilst I considered the rapture it must be to make a baby and to reproduce in a little pink and white crying thing, endowed with life and form, all the exquisite and inexpressible emotions and sensations with which one has been inspired and affected by the woman, to whom they have been communicated in that perfect mode, when beyond one's self and carried away by one's sense of all her charms, of all her loveliness — communicated at the instant of the culmination of passion with all its force.

"Oh, Mademoiselle," I exclaimed, in rapture, "what can be greater happiness, what can be holier, what can be more exquisite than — than —?"

"Than the consummation of love," she suggested, chillingly.

"Love," I exclaimed, "is not immoral."

"Exactly," said Mademoiselle. "But, my dear Julian, you cannot go about begetting babies on every girl who takes your fancy."

How these words desecrated what I held holier than religion.

"Certainly not. I have these feelings, these longings for you alone. It is but to one woman that a man ought so to reveal himself. I should live for you alone and devote myself to you only."

Mademoiselle smiled amusedly. But there was a little incredulity, or perhaps a tincture of contempt, mingled with this smile, which was certainly cynical.

"You must learn the lessons of the world you live in and solve the problems they suggest as you can. I have given you a necessary part of your education and I see you have already derived much benefit from it. In France ladies afford many favours and many harmless privileges, but they draw the line at what you ask for. I shall tease you as much as I like, and when I like, and make you please me frequently; perhaps for the remainder I shall put you into another lady's hands — Lady Ridlington's for example. She is very fond of breaking in amorous youths. But you must be content with what I have allowed you, Julian, as far as I am concerned, and the discipline will be wholesome."

"Oh, Mademoiselle, how cruel!"

"Not so cruel as I should be if I laid you across my knee, turned your petticoats over your head, and smacked your bottom, which must still be sore from your birching, for daring to propose such a thing to me; and yet, if you continue refractory, I shall certainly do so! You must learn self-control — it is the foundation of good breeding. Come! I am going to ring for tea. Put on your bodice, Miss. What is all this," looking reproachfully at me, "on your *chemise*?"

What Mademoiselle had said and her entrancing manner of

saying it, only made me feel worse. The notion of being laid across that lap of hers in the position she had suggested could have no other effect; but the necessity of replying to her question, which I felt to be an awkward one, diverted my attention from the pleasant idea.

"Oh, Mademoiselle, I — I — I swallowed in the first time, and the second, but the third —"

"You spat it out! And yet you have the impudence to profess you love me," retorted Mademoiselle indignantly. "Very well, you shall swallow something not half as nice in my dressing room after tea, for punishment!"

I changed colour, but dared not reply.

Elise then entered with the tea things, and looked at me very curiously. As she went out, looking straight at me, she ominously observed: "Tomorrow, and the next day, and the day after that!"

Mademoiselle laughed.

"If it were only!" I ejaculated, much disturbed.

"That is the whole point of it. It will not be I," was all she replied.

Mademoiselle's appetite astonished me, and I thought she gratified it most immorally. She devoured crumpets and muffins, and plum-cake, and *bonbons*, and cups of delicious fragrant tea. She made me sit near her and follow her example. Her manner towards me was most winning and affectionate, with a strong spice of tantalising coquetry. She even indulged in some little endearments of a peculiarly alluring character. For instance as she sat talking to me she rested her elbow on my lap quite casually, but would not notice the emotions it excited, or the movements and looks it evoked.

Chapter IX

The Golden Elixir of Mademoiselle's Dressing Room

Tea over, Mademoiselle glanced at the clock. As I arose I shook down my petticoats with contempt and some indignation of a keener mind than I had yet felt. Mademoiselle complacently noticed the action but did not attempt to give me any consolation.

"It is just an hour and a half to dinner and you will now come with me to my dressing room, Julia."

What a strange thrill the name Julia gave me! She led me rather crestfallen to her dressing room, warm, cosy, and bright. She bade me take off her shoes and stockings, and, having permitted me to kiss her feet, I put them into dainty fur-lined slippers. Then she took off her dress, and I saw her admirable bust and glorious arms, but she would not allow me to kiss them although I prayed her to let me do so. Instead I had, in my turn, to divest myself of every single article of clothing and to lie flat on my back in a long, narrow, shallow bath, in which she fastened me by means of a strap over my breast which prevented my rising. The bath was slightly tilted up at the foot.

She then took off a slipper and struck what I was so anxious to put into her seven or eight times, hurting me greatly, observing that it deserved punishment and no further kind treatment.

Her altered mood caused me great astonishment, but, as I have remarked, the gymnastics through which a woman's caprices can put one's soul are a principal portion of education received by any one subjected to her sway.

When she had amused herself in this manner, she said she would teach me not to spit out the choicest possible marks of a lady's feelings!

I felt very much frightened. Ignorance of my fate increased my fears.

She repeated that as I had not swallowed what I had wooed from her in response to my own efforts, I should now have to swallow something less nice which she would be glad to get rid of.

This terrified me much more. The idea struck me in an instant what it was possible she might mean. No; she could not mean — she would not dare — she would not so treat me! I should have started up but for the restraining strap. As it was, I did start as much as it would allow me, for the terrible idea gave me a strong shock.

I was not reassured by what took place next.

She stood across me in the bath ravishing me with a sight of her pretty figure overhead, her legs bared to her frilled drawers; and coquettishly lifting up her petticoats with both hands to her middle, she carefully drew the drawers well apart, disclosing to my full view what I had been kissing that afternoon, with entrancing glimpses of lovely pink flesh.

Great Heavens! There can be no doubt what she intends to do to me! I shall die of disgust!

"Mademoiselle," I cried, "don't! Don't. I will swallow what you like; but don't do that."

She looked at me with an amused and satisfied smile.

"Why should I not? It would serve you right!"

"I dare say!" I exclaimed. "But I am very sorry. I beg your pardon!"

"And did you really think I would?" she exclaimed with a merry laugh and blush. "What a fright I have given you! Well, not this time," she continued, * adding, with an uplifted finger and a sparkle in her eyes: "But beware, in future. On this occasion I shall commute your sentence to half a tumbler full of *Eau Amere de Pesth*, commonly called "Aesculap." You must have some punishment; and it will serve my purpose better than the tumblers of water which the Empress Catherine compelled her refractory courtiers to swallow as penance. In the meantime though, I must really give you a *douche*, you saucy boy." And, lifting a large can of tepid water, she drenched me with it. I sputtered and blew, but the torrent poured on. The stream fell full and impetuously upon my lips, my nostrils, my eyes, and my whole face — blinding and suffocating me — running into my mouth and down my throat, almost choking me, to Mademoiselle's delight. Would the can never be empty? Would she not tilt it up and be done with it? Over my chest, over what she had been playing with, over my legs, the now attenuated stream trickled, my hair gradually getting soaked through and through, and I drowned in the water; the bath being small and tilted at its end submerging me to my ears and chin.

---

* The late Lord — was actually placed in this jeopardy by a German mistress in Fulham who was not so merciful as Mademoiselle.

At last the stream ended, and she then gave me the drops that had run past the mouth of the can. I turned my head away only to become more drenched and to get my mouth fuller. There were five inches of the fluid about my head; it came quite up to my lips and if I moved got between them and went, perforce, down my throat.

"There!" said Mademoiselle, exultingly, having at length exhausted the reservoir. "Now, Master Julian, just contemplate what that water *might have been!* Just think what you might have been lying in — what you might have been made to swallow. Take care. Another time I may not let you off. Think of all this; and then I do not believe you will play me that trick again."

I was disposed to agree entirely with her, but dared not venture upon a word, not feeling particularly thirsty at the moment. On a subsequent occasion I ran an even narrower risk of the same punishment.

This time the half-tumbler of Aesculap, bitter and a little nauseous, which she made me drink, willy-nilly, effectually confirmed my good resolution. I felt angry, in fact, furious at this drenching. It was so ignominious; but I confess that the fear that she would carry out her threat, together with the idea that the water about me might have been of a different kind, and if I offended again, would be, gave me a strange delight.

With a laugh at my discomfiture and at my look (I felt my eyes gleaming), Mademoiselle left the room. Returning in two or three minutes, she calmly sat down before a large glass to do her hair at great leisure. The least she could have done would have been to release me; but that, she showed not the slightest intention of doing as yet. I had to lie in that deluge quite half an hour, while she bade me reflect what a pickle it might have been, and unconcernedly let down and combed her magnificent hair.

When, at last, I was released, I felt well soused. Certainly the milk of Venus was pleasanter to swallow than that nasty water, yet they both might have come from the same place, and from Mademoiselle. I think, on the whole, that I really loved her the more for the fright I had originally experienced: a strange overpowering longing to devour her; to be intimately united with and yet subject to her; to nourish myself with her being; a craving which I endeavoured to slake with kisses; and which was subsequently much more effectually gratified by my absorption of her raw clinging flesh, expressing in a humid language of its own the fleeting vanishing emotions of her soul.

It was hard that she should use a force originating in myself only as an engine for my own training, for the subjugation and taming of my virile ferocity; thus compelling me myself to provide a weapon for my own chastisement.

At last she snipped the stout threads of the strap-buckle which held me, with a pair of long scissors to avoid wetting her dainty fingers and bade me get up. How I longed to throw the whole contents of the bath over her, hair and all! However, all this time the water was running down me, drip, drip, drip, like the water from a rat rescued from drowning, into my eyes, over my lips, over my shoulders, down my back, down my breast, and along my arms. Mademoiselle gazed at me with amusement. I was too wild to speak and yet dared not do anything. She might otherwise have made me drink it. She was quite capable of doing so. Horrible notion, horrible peril! I dared not give the slightest sign which I thought could possibly provoke her displeasure. To my relief she gave me a towel, but I was not yet out of danger for she would not allow me to rush away as I desired. There was that Aesculap. Bitter stuff!

Chapter X

"Now Dress Me!"

No; I had now to discharge an office which, being about Mademoiselle's person, was, I grant, extremely agreeable. The remarkable manner in which she racked and harrowed my feelings — now doing that which provoked my bitterest dislike and disgust, then what attracted and excited my warmest feelings towards her — reduced me to a state of great trepidation and nervousness, effectually depriving me of self-control. When, quailing beneath her gaze, I had hastily dried myself as much as she thought necessary, she slipped off her dressing gown, and said peremptorily: "Now dress me!"

Her evening stockings had to be put on ceremoniously and carefully, the ends of the suspenders dexterously caught and attached to them; her low shoes found, and because I could not immediately discover where they were, I received several cuts of her stinging little riding whip to sharpen my wits and quicken my movements. Then her corset had to be changed — the evening one laced to her satisfaction. The fastening, adjusting, and lacing of a lady's tight corset is a difficult and ticklish process, and her gown had to be put on and hooked. She then complained that one of her stockings was wrinkled in her shoe, which I had to remove and smooth the delicate fabric.

No sooner had I replaced her shoe than she sprang up, and I suddenly and quite unexpectedly became conscious of the weight of her pretty little foot by the receipt of a sound kick in the rear. I called out and clapped my hands to the part. Mademoiselle continued the exercise, dancing about the room after me with surprising agility and astonishing spirits, kicking me as she did so, first with one little foot and then with the other, always aiming at my back. It was a novel edition of the skirt dance, which I did not at all appreciate, though, doubtless, Mademoiselle looked charming and her laughter and exclamations of delight put a merry aspect, from her point of view, upon the performance. Her pointed shoes hurt confoundedly, and the sweetness of the vision did not allay the pain. I was soon black and blue.

Mademoiselle laughed until I thought she would have had a fit. I, on my part, felt much more disposed to cry more from the ridiculous figure I was made to cut than from anything else. My love laughed at, and I was myself kicked naked about her dressing room by my adored one.

At length, fatigued, she summoned Elise to finish her hair and complete her *toilette*, and to lock me up for the time being, amongst her skirts and petticoats in the wardrobe.

When I was released in about another half hour, Mademoiselle had left the apartment, and not without some apprehension, I found myself left to the tender mercies of her maid. She roughly jerked me out of the cupboard by the arm, administering with the other hand, as she did so, a succession of sound, stinging slaps on various parts of my body, and expressing much curiosity as to what I had done to get myself made water upon by a young lady, and especially as to how I liked it. I indignantly denied it. "None of your Les to me, you nasty dirty boy. I know very well what she did. I ought not to touch you with the tongs. I know where that water came from; don't tell me! Come off to the bathroom at once. Quick! We have no time to fool about!" peremptorily ordered Elise. A hot bath and a big sponge were very welcome. It was curious being washed by a maid. And when she soaped the flannel and washed me like a baby between the legs, I squirmed and blushed and felt utterly foolish. The skin of my bottom was quite sore from the birching and kicking. Elise heeded this very little, in fact not at all, and rapidly dried me with warm rough towels; then taking me to my room, as rapidly dressed me. Silken vest, *chemise en coeur* (I had a plump breast and well-rounded arms), drawers, a corset which fitted much better than the first, stockings and the rest; in short, a young lady's evening *toilette*. Even my hair was done up like a girl's with a broad ribbon round my head after the Grecian mode; it was not long enough for any other style.

I must not omit one particular article which she added to my attire, and which gave me peculiar inconvenience as the evening wore on. At the end of my long-waisted corset in front, about four inches apart, were two hooks. As soon as she had tightly and severely laced that horrid instrument of torture, she proceeded to adjust a square piece of linen, to two corners of which were attached two tape loops. These she slipped over the hooks; and through the loops she inserted a folded napkin, and drawing it between my legs, tied its ends together, after putting one through a broad steel eye, which was sewn into my corset at the back. It was pulled quite tight, and the effect, of course, was to drag down the square piece of linen in front, and envelope in it what I had there, so that that thing was kept straight down, and also, the napkin being mercilessly tight, well between my legs. It was a most uncomfortable affair and incommoded me dreadfully.

But my protestations were altogether unheeded as a matter of course. Elise remarked that some contrivance was imperative, to prevent any indications on the surface of my petticoats which would belie my sex; and that if I had the privilege of being dressed and looking like a girl, I must put up with some punishment for being in reality a boy!

The friction of the napkin against the tender skin and sensitive nerves between my legs gave me my only consolation. It caused a pleasant titillation, and kept me in a perpetual condition of delicious naughtiness, the usual expression of which, however — erection in front — was quite, and designedly, out of the question.

At last I was dressed. It was a painful business. To give me a colour before I descended to the drawing room, Elise, who was really a beautiful damsel, frivolously inserted her right hand and arm under my skirts from behind, and severely rubbed and pinched my bottom, not forgetting to give the prisoner in front an energetic reminder or two, slipping her hand through from behind for that purpose. This proceeding did, indeed, bring the roses to my cheeks.

Chapter XI

Lord Alfred Ridlington

I was positively astonished and dismayed to find five or six men, in faultless evening costume, in the drawing room downstairs. I had no idea that there would be any strangers — men above all — to witness what I had to go through! Fortunately, my great confusion was interpreted as sweet and pretty bashfulness and ingenuousness. By degrees, I rather entered into the spirit of the joke, especially as Mademoiselle took an early opportunity of whispering into my ear that she would expose me and flay me alive unless I behaved myself. She then introduced one of the men as Lord Alfred Ridlington and myself as Miss Julia Robinson. He appeared to be good-naturedly amused at my fluttered demeanour and at once tried to set me at my ease. He succeeded to a very considerable extent, but there was something in his eyes which to my mind suggested that he was in the secret; an idea which kept bringing a succession of hot blushes to my cheeks and neck. The other men regarded me with ill-concealed looks of respectful and profound admiration. They were, it was plain, jealous of Lord Alfred Ridlington's good fortune and without any idea of the truth; but I could not rid myself of the notion that he had some inkling of it. The restraint of the bandage speedily became a subject of thankfulness; without it, some indication of what I began to feel would inevitably have made its appearance and have entirely destroyed the illusion.

Lord Alfred Ridlington took me down to dinner, and, of course, sat beside me. He took a proper solicitude in my welfare, exercising a watchful care over me such as I conceived to be the duty of a cavalier towards the maiden whom he had been deputed to look after. And I, for my part, comported myself as much after the fashion of a young lady as I possibly could. I was careful not to encourage him too much, and gave myself all a girl's airs and graces, her pretty fastidiousness, her little wilful ways and arch caprices. Maud, Agnes, and Beatrice were all too fully occupied with their own cavaliers to notice me much, or I doubt whether my assurance would have proved equal to the occasion.

Lord Alfred Ridlington himself aided me materially by the perpetual flow of small talk which he kept up unceasingly for my entertainment. It admirably served to cover any little confusion arising at odd moments when I felt slightly at a loss. I was hungry, in fact very hungry, but the wretched corset was so desperately tight that I was compelled to eat like a real young lady and dared not drink much.

I filled up the time by wondering where I had heard Lord Alfred Ridlington's name, which seemed familiar to me, and, at length, recollected it had been mentioned to me by Mademoiselle herself during my discussion with her in her *boudoir* that afternoon. She had threatened to hand me over to Lady Alfred Ridlington, whom she said was particularly fond of breaking in amorous youths. This, I thought, must be that lady's husband, and I immediately cast at him a glance expressing so much interest that he noticed it. Ignorant of its true motive he seemed much gratified by the look, and we thereupon became greater friends than ever. He was a very good-looking young man, fair, plump, with a beautiful mouth, teeth, ears, and hands, and rejoicing in an enormous expanse of snowy white shirt front, fastened with three brilliant diamond studs. I observed how white and unusually well-formed his neck was, and a certain softness, even effeminacy, about him and his air suggested the question as to whether he had ever been subjected to the same discipline that I was going through. I sadly reflected how bitterly disappointed he would certainly be if he ever discovered that I was a boy.

Chapter XII

The Conservatory

After dinner there was a carpet dance. One or two of the other men were at first my partners. How odd I felt, and how feminine! But I naturally enjoyed most those waltzes which I had with Lord Alfred. He waltzed capitally. After several turns, however, he suggested a stroll and a rest; and although I was sure Mademoiselle would notice our absence and was by no means so sure how she would take it, we soon found ourselves in a cosy and sequestered nook of the conservatory, where, seated close to me, he began to make hot love. His advances were delicate and insinuating. Aggression would at once have put me in arms. When he hoped he was not altogether disagreeable to me, what could I say? I could not be rude. But my unprotected position, the knowledge that I could not respond, which grew upon me with increasing intensity, filled me before long with a feeling approaching dismay, and I positively longed for a chaperon.

I had never been in such a fix before. I liked being made love to; but when he discovered that I was a fraud! Confound Mademoiselle and all her ways!

What on earth to do — whether to confess what I was, say I could not help it, and rely on his honour not to tell — I did not know.

The idea of running away occurred; but what a fool I should look, and, besides, it very soon became impossible and I was obliged to abandon all thought of it; for he put his arm round my waist and held my thighs pressed closely to him. How a girl would have enjoyed it! But me! I could only behave as I conceived a maiden would have done.

To add to my confusion, and to hasten the catastrophe, his other hand, in some inexplicable way, got up one of my legs underneath my petticoats. Then I felt there was no hope left! The murder would soon be out, and he would indignantly expose me to Mademoiselle, and she! But between my real and imaginary sensations I was in such a state of tremor and excitement that I could only rest gasping against him, be the consequences what they might.

After several minutes of the most deliciously exciting but yet most embarrassing dalliance with my legs and undergarments, and after many whispered soft nothings in my ear, he slipped his hand right up to my waist and got a firm hold of what was fastened there between my limbs!

Now, thought I, surely all is over! And I prepared myself for the outburst I conceived imminent, and to meet the consequences as best I could. But to my intense relief and no small astonishment, he proceeded to play with his fingers and hand, until I was almost beside myself. The softness and warmth of his form surprised me much. I wondered whether I should treat a girl so. Certainly not, I concluded, if I discovered her to be a boy. However, he evidently thought otherwise, for he continued torturing me in this nice fashion for some time, and appeared to take an unaccountable pleasure in it. At length, he went further; he set me, or, to speak more correctly, an important part of me, free by slipping the loops of the bandage over the hooks in front, and then leaning quite over me, he took hold of me afresh, this time more vigorously and more comprehensively. The same crisis soon occurred (but under a completely different set of emotions) as had happened on the sofa with Mademoiselle, and, strange to say, his enjoyment of it seemed to equal, if not to surpass hers. It puzzled me how it could give him pleasure, and I felt no longer a girl. There was no mistake about it, his eyes swam, his lips were glued to mine, and he seemed to be carried away by a strong corresponding passion. *Was he a man?*

After a few minutes spent in imbibing as slowly as possible the deliciousness of the sensations we had evoked, he readjusted the linen bandage, gave me a final kiss, helped me to rearrange my disordered garments, and to smooth my ruffled hair, and then he proposed that we should rejoin the company in the drawing room. Although my cheeks were on fire, even if there were no other telltale signs, we were obliged to do so, for I felt sure that our absence would have been remarked. But returning did not accord with my wishes. I longed to tear open his shirt, his trousers, to investigate for myself, to solve the tormenting question without delay. Could he be a woman? He must know now that I was not one. What could he be? He gave me no chance, however, to ascertain. He availed himself of my dread that Mademoiselle would notice our being away, and said that my looks would confirm her worst suspicions, so we hurried off at once, and I was very glad to join energetically in the waltz we found just started when we got there. It would be some explanation of my flustered condition. Did all young ladies, I wondered, who left the ballroom or sat a dance out on the stairs meet with an experience like mine?

But I was doomed to disappointment. Mademoiselle had not failed to notice our absence, and proceeded in the presence of the entire company, to my horror, to rate Lord Alfred soundly for having carried off one of her charges, and upon his improper behaviour, paying scant attention to his excuses. Then, turning to me, she informed me I was to go off at once to my bedroom, there to be well smacked with a slipper, and put to bed by her maid for my forward behaviour. Whether this was to Lord Alfred's delight or chagrin I cannot tell, but it was to my own inexpressible confusion, and I was on the point of tears. I stood dumbfounded and foolish before everyone. I did not want any more whipping (I was still sore from what I had had), nor did I wish to lose the evening's enjoyment. But they started off for the next dance, and poorly I had to march off.

Chapter XIII

The Maid and the Slipper

I knew by the stern glance which Mademoiselle threw at me across her partner's shoulder, as he led her gracefully away into the swimming mazes of the dance, that there was no hope whatever of mercy. There never was as far as I could see! Was it not enough to torture me with the birch, to mortify my manhood with the imposition of feminine dictation to such an extent as almost to crush it? Was it necessary to cause the cup to overflow by the addition of gratuitous wrong? It really had not been my fault. My indignation knew no bounds. However, there was no help for it, and if Mademoiselle caught me there, when the waltz brought her round to that part of the room again, I knew my fate would be worse, so I slunk off in a very sullen mood to my bedroom.

I certainly heartily agreed with Mademoiselle about Lord Alfred's deserts. But then, why was she so unjust?

It was all horrid affectation on her part in order to be the more cruel to me!

It was certainly all his fault — entirely his fault, from beginning to end — he had been amusing himself with me, and now I had to suffer! He did not seem to care in the least and made a joke of it.

What horrid, selfish, despicable creatures *men* are! I should never have expected it of *him*!

In my bedroom I was quickly joined by Elise, to whom Maud had communicated Mademoiselle's orders without loss of time. She came with indecent promptitude and haste in order to execute them. I am sure she was only too happy to have the opportunity!

How can I relate what happened? The reader can easily guess all!

Elise pretended to be in a very severe and magisterial, quasi-judicial mood; treated me just like a big naughty girl, and was conscientiously deaf to all the expostulations and explanations which appealing to her sense of fairness, I rapidly and breathlessly gave her. I did not want — I felt I could not bear — any more punishment. My only chance to escape lay in persuading her to let me off. I might as well have tried to persuade a hungry dog out of its bone. She came into the room with a large old slipper in one hand, smacking her other hand with it to give me a foretaste of my fate.

She took off my dress and drawers as callously as though she were a machine, alas — a slapping machine — and then sitting down on the couch, she laid me across her lap, getting me well under her left arm. She turned my petticoats up to my waist and smacked my bare bottom with the old slipper till I roared for mercy and struggled frantically. I was between her legs, her right leg confining mine, and she must have enjoyed my struggles and what they shew her. They were certainly useless for any other purpose, as I could not get free. I thought my cries and the sound of the blows must be audible in the drawing room. Smack, smack, smack! Yah! Yell!

When she had quite tired herself out, which was not until I had been smacked black and blue, she let me get up. I walked wildly about the room, with my hands clapped to my back to ease the pain, which was very bad. But even this consolation was soon to be denied me, and it was an unfortunate gesture, for it suggested further torment to her. She flourished the slipper and threatened me with a second edition, if I did not hold my noise, as she elegantly expressed it. And then suddenly noticing how I was endeavouring to alleviate my pain, she declared that she felt certain my hands had been in mischief also, and that she would make them smart too.

She compelled me to hold them out one after the other, and gave each of them two dozen sharp stinging blows with the same slipper with all her force, a most exasperating quiet smile playing on her face. I longed to knock her down. My arms tingled up to my very shoulders, and I was mad with pain, when she had done. As she had anticipated, I had no longer any desire to place my hands at my back. I danced about the room, clasping them together, and to her amusement tried everything I could think of to stop their throbbing without much success. However, she contented herself with this, and did not again attack my bottom, for which I was most thankful. She announced that she had the satisfaction of giving me a thorough and well-deserved punishment, and that there was nothing which could have given her greater gratification; and putting the slipper down, she then proceeded to completely undress me. When this was done she slipped over my head a long, laced, embroidered, feminine nightdress of Mademoiselle's, which made me feel very immodest. Possessed by this feeling I looked tenderly at the smart winsome maid, and pressed the back of one of her hands to my lips. Surprised for a moment, she said she was pleased to find I could take my punishment properly and be grateful for it.

As reward, she pushed me backwards across the bed, and standing close to it, between my legs, leant down right over me with her arms twined round my back and her bosom on mine, and kissed my lips five or six times, lifting her head and looking affectionately into my eyes between the kisses. The contact of her warm rosy lips was very agreeable indeed, and I enjoyed the long lingering wet kisses extremely. The close proximity and weight of her person gave me intense delight and had a most soothing effect on me. She made no bones about deliberately pressing herself against me, showing that she did not hesitate to recognise, and to let me know she recognised the fact of her intimate closeness and of her lying between my legs, keeping them even inconveniently wide apart. The lower part of my body was quite helplessly exposed to whatever crushing she chose to bestow on it with the corresponding portion of her own. And that was no small amount; the pressure was designedly heavier and more constant there. She wriggled and ground herself against me, especially when in the act of kissing me, exactly as I must have done against her as she was whipping me in her lap.

The notion of the three days to be spent "under her" was suggested by my position, and now recalled itself to my mind, devoid of most of its terrors. Indeed, the prospect seemed rather pleasant; but I was reckoning without recollection of the weight of her arm, although I had just experienced it, and was also ignorant of the exquisite cruelty in which she revelled, and of the many ingenious devices she possessed for exercising it.

If that bandage had only been removed, I should certainly have enjoyed "my reward" much more. It was very much in the way; besides which, it enabled her, when she clasped me closely, to press me yet further down, in exactly the contrary direction to the natural one. This caused me positive pain. I have not the slightest doubt she knew it; but to such an adept in the art of mingling pleasure and pain, the fact could only be an additional source of gratification.

It is true she had taken off the corset to which the bandage was attached, and I had had hopes that I was going to be freed from it. No such luck. She replaced it, fastening it even more severely than before, by means of a band round my waist underneath my nightdress.

After some quarter of an hour had been spent in this tantalising fondling, Elise made me stand up, and producing a broad leather belt with three or four small straps to fasten it, she buckled it very tightly round my waist outside the only garment I had on. At each side of this girth, just over the hip, two narrow straps were sewn. I could not conceive what these were for. They curled outwards in a menacing mode, and I felt sure portended nothing good. My suspicions were soon confirmed. They were to confine my wrists. In a very matter-of-fact style Elise took hold of each of my wrists and buckled them tightly one to each side by means of these straps.

"There," she remarked complacently, "your hands must be kept out of further mischief, and I don't see how they can get into it now. And you may thank your stars that I do not slip a strap through your elbows and draw them together at your back. I will do so next time. Get into bed!"

In my helpless state, deprived of the use of my arms, I accomplished this feat with difficulty. My hands were so rigidly fixed that I felt as if in a vice. The only use to which I could put my arms was to flap them against my sides, and that did no one any good and was ridiculous into the bargain.

Added to this, there was the restraint of the other bandage under my nightgown, so that altogether I really did not feel my own self. The sensation was quite novel, and I did not know what to make of it. I had much to put up with, for if I had made any sign Elise would surely have punished me smartly. I could have made good use of my hands. I wished for one thing to rub my bruises; besides, I hated being confined. Mademoiselle had not ordered it. I wanted to have free use of my hands. In my own bed surely I might have loosened that unnatural bandage, surely I might sleep as I pleased. Yet here they were, fixed so absolutely that I might just as well have been without hands at all. It was most unfair and unjust.

This phase of mind, these germs of rebellion in the land which the inflexible strictness of my fetters prevented from germinating and fructifying, were soon obliterated by the advent of a very formidable necessity bearing the endorsement of nature herself, one which was not in any sense of a sentimental character, and which I felt, as I turned restlessly on my back, would admit of no compromise. It forced itself on me relentlessly and with momentarily increasing vigour. The sheets were clean, so was my nightdress, and besides there was the bandage, before and behind. More whipping, more torture, more shame, more disgrace, more contumely, more ignominy, I knew well would be my portion if there was the least stain or the least moisture. And yet what could I do? I writhed and I trembled. The sphincter muscle was strong, but so were the opposing forces. I had not eaten, neither had I drunk much, but I wished I had eaten and drunk less, I wished I had not eaten or drunk at all. Of course there had been champagne between the dances, and there must have been some artistically designed decoction of onions in the soup or in the *entrees*, or in some dish or other to give such subtle power to this pressing demand. Elise had thrown the bed clothes over me and left me in the dark. But what would be the advantage of getting up? I could grope with my feet for the necessary article, but what use would it be when found? My hands were not at my service, and, in addition, I was tied up! In that condition, with the door of a closet gaping in front of me and its welcome promise of relief before my eyes, I should have been no better off. Nor had I even the benefit of the voluptuous sensation that this had been intended by my female persecutors.

Chapter XIV

Beatrice

At least an hour and a half of this excruciating torture and fear!

Then there was a gleam of light outside my door, which shone through its chinks, and I hailed it with the un-calculating hope of despair.

Whoever carried the light did not pass the door. She came in. It was Beatrice! What a mercy! Her curiosity had brought her and her flat candlestick in on her way to her own room. Elise had told her she might safely count on half an hour with me, as Mademoiselle had only just gone to her apartments with Lord Alfred Ridlington. With *Lord Alfred Ridlington!* I had heard him say she might do what she chose with him, but I never dreamt he would be taken *au pied de la lettre*. Was she chastising him? I heard no sounds; yet the room was not so distant. What was she doing? Incarnating his love, his babies? Horrid thought.

"Oh, Beatrice!" I cried.

Beatrice looked very beautiful! She was flushed with dancing, her cheeks were aglow, her eyes sparkled, her bosom heaved, her form was dilated with pleasure, and vivacity shew in her every movement, mischief in her every glance.

"Oh, Beatrice!"

"Well, Julian," she laughed, putting down her candle and giving her skirts a whisk, "a nice day you have had; you must be quite tender."

"Beatrice," I repeated, "for goodness sake, for the sake of all you hold dear, if you love me, at any price —"

"Good gracious, Julian! Whatever is the matter?" she asked with maddening equanimity, calmly sitting down near me. "I know you have been smacked and sent to bed. I have heard all about it from Maud. I know you spent the afternoon with Mademoiselle in her *boudoir*, and I have come to hear all about it from you. I know you were birched in the morning — a fine day you have had — your first too, but whatever can be the matter with you now?"

"Oh, Beatrice, you know you and I were friends from the first," I began, frantically.

"I know you spoilt my gown, you clumsy boy, at luncheon," she rejoined, determined to preserve her *sangfroid*.

"Yes, but I have paid for that."

"And I am glad to see you have not forgotten it! Shall I give you my own idea of the punishment it deserved? Slaps, indeed! One dainty soft one on each cheek! A nice punishment. Look here!" lifting her delicate leg and taking off and brandishing a slipper menacingly at me. "Look here!" giving me more than a glimpse of the paradise under her petticoats, as she lifted and retained her foot across the other knee. "Look and tremble. You have settled scores with Mademoiselle and Elise; now you have me to reckon with."

"Oh, Beatrice, do not jest, do not make sport of me. It is unkind; it is much too serious. It is a matter of health."

"I have heard of people dying for love. What is the matter with you — shall I kiss you? Will that do?"

"Yes! Yes! But first — first —"

"First what?" she enquired, astonished.

"First, unfasten me!"

"Anything more in a small way? Unfasten you? A fine time I should have then. No; certainly not."

"Oh, I promise, I promise, I swear I will not touch you. I promise to let you do me up again. On my honour I do. Unfasten me just for a minute. There's a closet near, I know." Beatrice went into a fit of laughter, stopped, and laughed again; took out her handkerchief to wipe her eyes — laughed till she cried, and then laughed again.

"Poor boy," she said at length; "I understand *now*."

"Will you?" I gasped.

"On one condition," she replied.

"Any condition — *any* — name it!"

"Don't be in such haste. On condition that you give yourself to me body and soul for five years. Give yourself to me to be my absolute slave. So do all I tell you and nothing that I forbid you, whatever the consequences, Mademoiselle, your father, your mother, Maud, Agnes, and perhaps, most important of all, yourself, to the contrary notwithstanding. If you will promise this on your honour, perhaps —"

"Elise," I suggested.

"Oh, you are not so hard up as I thought; however, Elise and I are fast allies."

I felt like Jacob selling his birthright, but I glanced at her and thought I might have a worse fate, and the exigencies of the case did not leave room for much hesitation. She was a lovely girl. What a bust and pretty head, what bewitching hair, what grace, what a splendid form, what a splendid little foot and ankle to have on one's neck! But five years was a serious matter. "Whatever do you intend to do with me, Beatrice?"

"Never mind; I won't discuss the question. Yes or no."

"You want me to leap in the dark," I said, reproachfully.

"Do as you like. You see me, and where you are leaping to," she said with a smile of entrancing archness.

"Very well. I will. You will undo me directly?"

"Consider, Julian."

"I have considered. Yes, for five years, I promise."

"Absolutely?"

"Absolutely."

"On your honour?"

"On my honour."

"Very well. There is a kiss," stooping over me, "to ratify and seal the bargain. You are mine now," she added, standing over me, "to do what I please with, and you must do nothing without my leave — you understand," and she looked lovingly into my eyes, "and whatever it may cost you if I refuse."

Then, with a sweep of her arm, she threw the bed clothes off me, unbuckled the belt, pulled up the nightdress without any ado, and unfastened the bandage. She did not stop to look. She gave me new life with my freedom.

"Run along, Julian. I give you five minutes! No more!"

On my return, I felt much better, and was able to contemplate my position, and the price I had been obliged to pay for a freedom to which the natural rights of humanity entitled me. I felt a little injured. This contract with Beatrice was indeed immoral, and I dreaded to think what Mademoiselle would have to say to it. But then I looked at Beatrice. What do girls care for immorality? What indeed! Nothing; unless it serves their purpose to care or to seem to care.

Beatrice's first order, when I returned and the door had been shut, was to tell me to take off my nightdress. She blushed as she bade me do so.

Now Mademoiselle was all very well, and Elise too. They were hardened sinners. But Beatrice, a mere girl, younger than myself. What harm I might do her! How degrading, too, to me.

I hesitated, and she reminded me of my oath.

"What about your honour, Julian?"

I still hesitated.

"Must I summon Elise to help me to enforce my rights?"

I looked at her.

"Yes, *my rights*," she repeated, stamping her little foot.

"Beatrice!"

"Take off that nightdress directly."

"How can you wrong me by talking about Elise?"

"Very well then, do what I tell you," she said laughing. I did not laugh, needless to say. I wanted to have another kiss, to get into bed as I was, and to wish her "good night." I was tired, and with reason.

No prospect of that, as I soon found. We looked at each other for a few minutes. She was inexorable. And before that girl, in her ball dress, which shew all her bosom, with her bare arms and smiling countenance, the personification of grace, beauty, and girlhood, I had to divest myself of my sole garment, and stand stark naked. She gazed at me from head to foot, whilst I covered my face with my hands. A woman, I suppose, would have adopted the attitude of the Venus de Medici.

"A fine girl *you* are, Julian, with a big thing in front of you," she said presently, blushing all over.

She then passed her hands over my shoulders and my body, along and between my legs, made me walk up and down the room, lift my legs, stand with them apart, bend over and touch my toes with my fingers, whilst she contemplated me from behind, sit down, kneel down, and go on all fours, and kiss her feet.

"How you have been punished!" she said. "Your — bottom — is black and blue. Tell me, you have had your bottom punished?"

"Indeed I have, Beatrice, severely."

"You must say it; come."

"Say what?"

"Say you have had your bottom punished — those very words; and ask me, your dear Beatrice, to pity you."

"I have had my — bottom punished, my dear Beatrice" (what a thrill these senseless words caused me and her also).

"Please, pity me."

"Lie across that chair then, with your head on the carpet and your feet on the ground."

I adopted the degrading posture, and she stood near me, speaking consoling words and rubbing the afflicted part with her soft hand. She did more than rub it.

"How naughty you have made me feel. I was bad enough when I came in. I must see, what consolation you can give me. Lie across the bed on your back, with your head over the edge."

I did so. I felt like a dog turned upside down. But what could I do with this uncompromising damsel? She stood over me, purring deliciously, and handling me, looking into my eyes, which were fixed somewhat reproachfully on her.

"Do you like that?" she asked.

Reply was unnecessary, and I was a little indignant.

"Now you must please me," she went on.

I knew what was coming. I had not spent the afternoon for nothing. I felt that I was beginning to understand women and their little ways. They were all alike. Precisely the same words, too.

She lifted up her skirts and threw them over my breast, put my head between her legs, and held it there, and rubbed herself against my mouth. I knew what to do, and did it. She was much smaller there than Mademoiselle, and there was a wall inside, beyond which I could not get. Her throbs were also more pronounced. She moved herself, she rubbed and pressed me more severely, and used her hands more freely. Added to which, she applied her tongue to me, and sucked what she was playing with in her mouth, stooping over me for the purpose.

She stopped once or twice, and slightly withdrawing herself, and lifting her soft, warm, garments, looked at me, and asked whether what she was doing gave me pleasure, and whether I liked my task.

I replied, "Immensely," and so I did.

She recommenced; the crisis arrived! Remembering my lesson about a lady's choicest favours, I did not hesitate to swallow, and, indeed, swallowed willingly what she shot into my mouth. She was not content until she had made me come also in her mouth. I did not like the idea of doing it and tried to prevent myself, but her hands and tongue were too much for me.

A moment after, Elise entered, and found me in the position I have described, prone on my back on the bed, enveloped from my breast upwards in Beatrice's skirts, which lay across me; my head out of sight under her petticoats, between her taper legs, and my face still closely pressed against her body.

"Pretty goings on," exclaimed Elise, nonchalantly. "I am sorry to interrupt your amusement, Miss Beatrice, but the half hour is up, and you must not remain longer. One minute, though. I must help him to recover. Put his legs across your shoulders, Miss; yes, and lift them up — one over each. Now clasp your arms round them and hold them firmly. Now, Master Julian —"

Smack, smack, smack, smack, smack, went Elise with her open hand and all her strength on my defenceless and sore bottom. I was quite powerless, effectually deprived of the use of my legs which Beatrice clasped just below the knees. My feet reached just a little way beyond her neck, and I was unable to spring up, as her own legs tightly encased my head. My posture not only admirably exposed me, but also drew the skin quite tight. I wriggled and struggled, for the slaps were stinging ones, but Beatrice easily held me. Her position gave her such a purchase. I ground my face into her. It was my only consolation.

"There," said Elise at length, "now he will be fit for Mademoiselle."

Beatrice then let me go. She was on fire, and well she might be.

"Good boy! she said. "You have done me so much good. I feel quite revived."

"Has Mademoiselle done with Lord Alfred Ridlington?" she asked Elise a moment later, with a curious little emphasis on the "Lord."

"Yes," Elise replied. "Sent him off scarcely able to sit down in his carriage."

"Good gracious," I thought as I lay on the bed quite naked and equally careless of what these two young women who had so intimately acquainted themselves with all my secret anatomy thought or said, "so he has been punished after all, and he must be a man then! Well, I am glad he did not escape scot-free."

"Now, Julian," said Beatrice to me as Elise began fooling with my legs and pulling them about, "I have one thing to say to you. I heard Maud announce that she wished to have you as a model for an Apollo. Now mind! *That* I forbid, positively!"

"Don't you think I am fit for it?" I asked mischievously.

"Never mind my reasons; remember I forbid it. Good night, dear," kissing me.

"And, Elise, let him wear a pair of my drawers tomorrow, instead of Mademoiselle's," she added.

"Yes, Miss, certainly; that is" (aside) "if he wears any at all. Good night, Miss."

"Good night," and Beatrice went.

Chapter XV

The Preparatory Ordeal

It was some alleviation of my circumstances to know that I had a confederate in Beatrice, and (to some extent) in Elise also. So far as their own designs upon me required, I knew they would support me in withstanding Mademoiselle, Maud, and Agnes. And that thus a sort of defensive alliance had been established which would occasionally yield me a certain amount of protection. But at what a cost the alliance would be upheld! Of course all the friction would be upon me. I should always be the victim and probably should have to endure pains and penalties from both sides. Except for the sentimental consolation arising from being in league with Beatrice, and from the pleasure I took in doing her bequests, I felt it would be better for me to have but one mistress. It would be impossible for me to please all. Already I saw trouble ahead concerning the Apollo. Maud would insist. So would Beatrice. Mademoiselle would side with Maud. Beatrice would not dare to side openly with me. I should then have to obey Beatrice and disobey Maud and Mademoiselle. There would be a battle royal, the whole brunt of which I should have to bear. It was extremely probable that in the clash of contending forces they would tear me to pieces.

Possibly also, Beatrice was only carrying out instructions of Mademoiselle, with whom, for all I knew, she might have some secret understanding. It might be some deep and insidious design of Mademoiselle to make my discipline and trials more severe. It might be her game to secretly instigate rebellion for the delight of wreaking vengeance upon me; to put me in a position in which, whatever my conduct was, I should be unable to avoid incurring her anger, and be tortured also by the necessity of silence and the sense of wrong. I felt instinctively what exquisite enjoyment and pleasure she would take in such a state of affairs, and how natural such an idea would be to so artful and intriguing a young lady. So far as she was concerned, it was extremely likely. But ultimately I felt sure that Beatrice was incapable of such perfidy, and so felt more secure.

"Now, Sir," said Elise peremptorily, but serenely, "get up — put on that nightdress this instant, and — come with me!"

I was obliged to obey her, and she re-attired me in my white nightdress and led me to Mademoiselle's bedroom.

I found Mademoiselle seated in a cosy chair near her dressing table, attired in a ravishing peignoir which was negligently unfastened. Her magnificent hair was let down, falling about her shoulders. She looked sleepy, and was in the act of yawning as I entered. A vicious-looking riding-whip lay on the top of one of the pedestals, which flanked the glass. Not far from her stood a stool covered with blue satin.

She glanced at me as I entered in my white raiment, which was so long that I had to hold it up in front to avoid stepping on it, but did not speak to me. She addressed Elise.

"I am far too tired and sleepy to do anything more tonight, Elise, and shall not be able to put him through the trial and lesson he ought properly to receive before being permitted to sleep with me in my bed. I dare say, however, he is also too tired to be really dangerous. Just try him, however. Strip him," she added, yawning again.

She evidently did not mean to mince matters or to allow any fooling, and was in a very businesslike frame of mind. Her eyes, however, gleamed when she saw me the next moment absolutely naked before her, and she looked at me contentedly and approvingly.

"He is a nice boy," she said. Elise waited a few seconds, also regarding me; but in that respectful manner, which the presence of her mistress necessitated.

"Go on, Elise," presently ordered Mademoiselle.

"Lie across that stool on your face," said Elise to me severely.

Suppressing a sigh, perhaps a groan, I obeyed. I wondered what fresh torture I was to undergo. Surely not more whipping.

Elise put one hand very heavily on the small of my back, pressing all the wind out of me, and rubbed and pinched my bottom and the backs of my thighs very violently with the other hand, which she also rapidly inserted between my legs, and as rapidly withdrew, until, at last, she found she was working me up into a state of extreme excitement; then she said:

"This is to teach you how to contain yourself. Mind, whatever I do, and I shall do more, you must restrain yourself. If there is the slightest mark on the cushion, you will have three dozen cuts — like this," and she gave me a frightful cut across the legs with the whip, at which I yelled; "and instead of being allowed to sleep with

Mademoiselle, you will be tied up naked with your hands above your head to the post of her bed, and you will stay there all night."

She waited a minute or two, and then she asked in a hard voice: "You understand?"

"Yes," I answered.

"And promise?"

"Yes; if I possibly can."

"*If* you can! You *must*. There's another reminder."

"Yah! I do promise. I will, indeed."

Bracing myself up, I resolved, whatever she did, not to allow anything to happen. The resolution was rash, but I set my teeth. Three dozen like that! It was only a question of muscular restraint. And to be tied up all night. Anything would be better than that, tired as I was. So I set my teeth firmly. I was in for it. The whip was awful, cruel beyond expression.

Elise immediately stood across me. I sighed and trembled, but fixed my thoughts on the pattern of the carpet, not allowing them to wander upon her. She soon recalled them. She inserted her left hand underneath me and caught hold of me, putting her right hand behind me. She worked the right one over all the lumbar muscles, both vigorously and relentlessly, for quite five minutes. I resolved not to give way. I refused to let an idea of what she was doing cross my mind, and remained absolutely passive. When she found this the case, she tried all the harder, and began to suggest thoughts about being under a maid's legs (pressing me with them), and her having what she had in her hands, about my nakedness, about Mademoiselle. Everything she could think of to excite my feelings, but I hardened myself and turned myself to stone. I would not be overcome. I reflected on the pain of the whip, and on what I should gain by victory. I resolved to be a stone, and succeeded. Elise tired herself uselessly. It hurt me dreadfully, and the strain occasioned by my determination to contain myself, and hers to overcome and defeat me, made me sore and aching. At last she stood from over me.

"Let me look," she exclaimed.

I also gave a glance. Surely there could be no mark to defeat all my efforts.

"I declare there is nothing!"

I looked at her triumphantly.

She made another minute examination. The blue satin would at once have shown the slightest stain.

"Ah! Ah! Elise," said Mademoiselle, to Elise's chagrin.

"Now on your back," said the discomfited Elise, who would have had the whipping of me, and did not like to be done out of it.

So I laid down on my back.

"Put your legs as wide apart as they will go."

Then she briskly stood over me, so arranging her petticoats on this occasion, that I was right under her bottom, with nothing between it and my face, but here and there her drawers, and these she rubbed away, until she felt her naked flesh against me. This was much harder to bear. She caught me in front with both hands, rolled the testicles, slipped her hands down and endeavoured to excite each nerve in turn. She evidently knew all about it. As I could not now hear anything she said, she could not excite my imagination and so find a traitor within the citadel by her words. But this advantage was counterbalanced and more, by my actual contact with her flesh, and with her mouth with a moustache, which was in a state of great excitement, very wet, and constantly rubbing and pressing against my mouth and all over my face. No words could have so completely conveyed the idea as the actual reality did. I was overwhelmed by that sense of the female sex which exacts immediate sexual acknowledgment from anything in the least degree worthy of being named masculine. An exaction made more irresistible by the use of her hands, and by the knowledge of what she and Mademoiselle could see. To all this I shut my mind. I had no carpet to contemplate. I closed my eyes, and I refused to remember where I was. I simply passively endured. I shut my teeth and lips firmly, notwithstanding her reiterated attempts upon them. My will stood me in good stead. I conquered. But instead of loving, I hated Elise. I hated Mademoiselle. I loathed women. And when she got off me it was all I could do to prevent myself from saying so.

"You stubborn boy," indignantly said Elise, who had really tried her hardest; "I will give it you tomorrow."

Mademoiselle laughed, and, bidding me kneel at her feet, told me I must exercise as great control throughout the night under a worse penalty. Meanwhile Elise continued to dart angry glances at me.

"I will conquer him yet," angrily said Elise, "even if I have to have him myself!"

"Well, not tonight at any rate," said Mademoiselle, amused.

"Get into my bed and warm it for me, Julian. I dislike a cold bed above all things. I will come in a moment when Elise has undressed me."

So I jumped into bed. How delicious, soft, and delightful it was to stretch oneself out and await Mademoiselle's coming.

What ecstasy!

No sooner, however, had I put my head upon the pillow, than Elise flew at me.

"You monster! You wretch! How dare you put your head on Mademoiselle's pillow? Get down into the bed at once" (striking my head several blows with her open hand), "right down! My goodness, what can you be thinking of?"

Chapter XVI

Mademoiselle's Bed

The pretty bed was a single one. To lie as Elise tyrannically and unreasonably directed, I had to curl myself up very uncomfortably. She threw the clothes over me, and I lay like a hot water bottle. My head was on my arm, my knees well up to my chin. Presently I heard the door closed, and felt some one take hold of the sheets and blankets and turn them down, but not far enough to uncover me. Then some one got into bed and two white little feet came down close to me. I put my arms out and clasped them. Mademoiselle arranged her pillow and settled herself snugly. She allowed me to get under her nightdress. I kissed her legs all over, and twined my arms under her dress, round her exquisite form. She opened her thighs and caught my head between them from behind. She lay on her left side — her left leg became my pillow. She moved herself deliciously against me, until we had both arranged ourselves quite comfortably, she moving just as freely as if I had not been there, and without the slightest embarrassment. Then saying "Good night, Julian!" she fell asleep, and I also.

When next I awoke some time elapsed before I could make out where I was. I was stifled and in want of air. The contact of her warm soft flesh reminded me. When I found that my movements did not awaken her, their only effect being to make her turn over, the idea suggested itself in a dreamy way to me that now I might attempt to carry out my wishes. I slipped my hands underneath her garment, right up to her breasts and put them round her. I had to move to do this.

How delicious her form was — how lovely her bosom, as it rose and fell evenly! I must have half awakened her, for she very soon pushed my head forcibly down to her waist and put her right leg over me, clasping me tightly with the fleshy portion of the backs of her legs against my face. Presently she gave a wriggle, and my face was pressed against her bottom and kept there, her legs and knees at my back pushing me up against her. Sleep again overcame me and I did not awake until the morning. I was dreaming that I was in a press or cupboard which was too small, and that some one was hammering me into it, when I awoke to find Elise had turned the clothes down and was belabouring me with a slipper, whilst

Mademoiselle was quietly smiling at me.

"We thought we should never have succeeded in awakening you, Julian, and as Elise declared smacking you hurt her hand, I sent her for your old acquaintance of last night. How have you slept?" she asked as soon as she saw my eyes were fairly open.

I sat up and rubbed them, yawned, and stretched myself.

Elise had brought delicious chocolate and hot cakes and butter. I had no corset on now and felt famished.

Mademoiselle looked so lovely, rosy, and fresh in the morning light. She must have had a bath before she had succeeded in arousing me.

What a delicious perfume exhaled itself from her! How charming she appeared in her loosened *robe de nuit* — the voluptuous richness of her figure plainly appearing, and her wealth of hair admirably crowning her coquettish little head. I was not yet sufficiently awake to speak, so, as she reclined on the bed, I clasped first her bosom and then her legs tightly to my breast and face, by way of answer.

"Elise, come back in an hour! Julian," she continued, "you are a good boy and I do not see why I should deny myself and you. No; not so fast! You will see what I mean presently. But I can see how longingly you look at that chocolate. Sit beside me here, draw the table across the bed — it will swing round — and let us have breakfast together. Then you shall *confer fleurettes*, eh? All work and no play makes Jack a dull boy, doesn't it?"

Chapter XVII

The Morning

I settled myself comfortably and closely to Mademoiselle in the place she had so graciously indicated, covering myself up to the waist with bedclothes, for, whether the reader remembers it or not, I had nothing on but was quite naked, exactly as I had been packed into bed the night before.

Elise had drawn the blinds and curtains and left the window open. The fresh fragrant air of the May morning entered, reviving and exhilarating me. The sun was shining brightly and the birds were singing gaily outside, as they hopped about on the dew-laden lawns. There was a gentle and sweet breeze which wafted in the scent of the flowers and made low melody with the boughs of the ornamented trees; and I was seated by her own desire close to a young woman who each moment disclosed fresh beauties and charms. I was in her bed — petted, fed, and caressed by her. What a multitude of little endearments she showered upon me! She placed her dainty fingers against my lips and let me drink from her cup. She let me try to cover myself with the masses of her wealth of hair, and rested her head lovingly against my shoulder. Presently to crown all, having pushed away the table, she slipped her hand underneath the sheets, and playfully taking hold of that portion of me which Elise had so tortured, asked me with a bewitching look for my experiences of the night and whether I felt at all naughty. Her air was most engaging and fascinating and her manner full of encouragement. I responded at once and described to her how I had enjoyed my slumbers, and she asked what I had dreamt about.

"Of you, Mademoiselle, and, oh, I do feel so naughty."

"No need to tell me so, Julian, I can feel it," pinching me meaningly. "And, do you know, so do I, a little." Who that was human could have helped it, in that luxury and that paradise, a perfect garden of delight, the golden day so young, the rich scent of the May wafted in by the lazily moving air, the voluptuous couch, the freedom from care? A feeling produced by such causes could not be naughty. If only the lovely being at my side had been my wife! As she had taught me that then only could she allow me what I instinctively felt was necessary to existence and could alone crown my felicity!

"What are you thinking of, Julian!"

"I was wishing you were my wife — how happy married people must be."

"Your wife — you naughty boy, I know what you mean. I shall put you down there and punish your naughty mouth, unless you take care!"

"Oh, do, Mademoiselle! Oh, do."

"Or do what I did to you on the couch?" she suggested, half reclining upon me.

"Yes, yes."

"Or would you like to lie in my lap better?"

"Oh! Mademoiselle, yes, yes."

"Which?"

"The last."

"Push that table a little further away. Let me arrange the pillow — now," opening her arms, "lie *between* my legs, you goose; down on my breast, so. No, *no*; you must *not* remove my nightdress; whatever are you dreaming of?"

"Oh Mademoiselle, only once, only for a moment, just once."

"Do you mean to say you could restrain yourself now as you did last night, and with me?" said Mademoiselle, half in doubt. "No, I see you can't. Come," putting her arms round me, "lie down outside as I told you, and don't tantalise me."

But I saw I had some faint advantage, some chance now if ever, and was not going to throw it away without an attempt at obtaining what I wanted. So I hugged her close and excited her without adopting the position she indicated, leaving in her full view what I knew she must be aware would give her the enjoyment she desired, for had she not confessed that she was naughty, and said that I was tantalising her?

I coaxed her to let me put it against her, only just once; just to put it in a very little way, promising on my honour to do no more. I saw what a struggle she had to refuse, and wondered what on earth the motive could be, which was strong and powerful enough to make her hesitate. She did not reply. She drew me to her waist, leaving only just enough to cover the entrance, twined her legs round mine, and clasped her arms round my back. Then looking lovingly into my eyes, she hugged me closely, moving up and down, and exciting corresponding movements in me.

I felt the transport of my exquisite fetters, of my proximity to her.

Her bare legs touched mine and held them; she was under me, the front of her nightdress was open, and my breast touched her bosom. Her breath entered my mouth and nostrils, her lips were against mine. She felt and judged the growth of my emotions and passions and her reciprocation of them, which I, on my side, was fully cognizant of, fanned them. Our transports acted and reacted upon each other. When I at last thought I was really about to expire in rapture, the spasm overtook me, and I sank on to her yielding form, a welcome and cherished burden. She allowed me to repose for some minutes in close communion with her. I had peeped into heaven. Would that I could have entered it! Would that she had consented to the incarnation of all she had affected me with and had caused me to express, by the throbs repeatedly ceasing and recommencing of that organ constituted for their communication. This expression she had refused to receive as a woman should receive it, an expression which should have resulted in a child born of her — what a child, what a love it would have been! Instead it had been wasted on her nightdress. What a crime! It was a grievous loss, a waste, a cheating of nature, for no moment can return, no opportunity once passed be seized again; never again might there be such a morning; or, if there were, it would be the second, not the first. It was the loss of the reproduction of myself upon my love, for she was entirely my love then, which deeply afflicted me; afflicted me much more than did the privation I knew I had suffered of the sensual happiness of which I had indeed had a partial enjoyment.

"Julian, how sad you look — how uncomplimentary."

"Oh, Mademoiselle, I would rather not do it at all than have to do it otherwise than in the proper way. If it is only a form you require me to go through, let me go through it. Let me marry you. That is not, cannot be the act of a priest, it must be the act of those who love. Who could be more married than we really are?"

"Oh, you ridiculous boy! Marriage, what foolery. I certainly shall not permit any such *betise* with me. Do you take me for a fool?"

"Then, Mademoiselle, it is a mere form, so let us be married without it."

"Indeed I certainly shall not so degrade myself. You should be grateful for what I allow you and not make me such a return. Come, I am not half satisfied. Come, you must be rested now."

"No, Mademoiselle," I said, "I do indeed love you. I do indeed wish to respond, I do not mean to be uncomplimentary or disagreeable, but I won't unless I may do it properly."

"Hoity-toity! What masterful airs! You will and you won't! Has not your discipline of yesterday taught you better? So I am to love you all in all or not at all, eh?"

"It is such waste!"

"Waste?"

"Yes; all the ideas with which you inspire me, all my conceptions of the loveliest forms suggested by your own beauty, all worked up into the most perfect expression, to be absolutely wasted on your nightdress. What can your nightdress do with it? It cannot incarnate the creature of my soul! You wish me to acquiesce in this — in your being cheated of conceiving, in my being cheated of — of — of conception by you!"

"Julian, on the subject of incarnation and conception you are mad — stark staring mad. It is a perfect mania with you. I expressly wish to avoid incarnation and conception. You selfish animal," she burst out. "In plain language you want me to have a baby!"

"Of course I do," I answered imperturbably, "of course I do; it is my right. You have given me the right; you have created, fostered, and inspired the idea; you have made me perform my part, and received it in the front of this," scornfully exclaimed I, holding up the front of her garment wet with my spermatozoa. "Of course I do," I indignantly continued. "Imagine, with my devotion to you and your kindness and goodness to me, which develop that devotion to its fullest extent — imagine Hortense, my own, what a love, what..."

"Julian, Julian," she cried, grief in her voice, "stop! It would be illegitimate."

"Illegitimate," I retorted. "What does that matter? To whom, except to hypocrites, is that of importance? Label it what you please, it would be our — our — child. Oh, my love!"

"Julian! Oh, my own, it breaks my heart. Some day, not today — not today — I cannot, I will not."

"Mademoiselle!"

"No, no, no! Come here. Lie down."

"I will not."

"You must; you *shall!*" and stretching out her arm to the table, she rang the hand bell, holding me very tightly all the time with her other arm across my back.

Elise entered almost before she ceased ringing. "Get a birch," said Mademoiselle. Then she added to me: "You must do what I tell you; you must not suggest such ideas; you must gratify me, obey me; you must, waste or no waste, please me, whether I incarnate and reproduce you or not."

What a thrill the words "reproduce you," from her mouth, caused me!

"Lady Alfred Ridlington will, if you like, lend herself to your whim." Cruel addition!

"I do not want to be incarnated by Lady Alfred Ridlington. You are cruel to me, Mademoiselle."

"Kinder than you think," she answered, getting me into position, clasping her arms round me, and again twining her legs about mine, which she stretched apart. "Now, Julian."

"No."

Elise had returned.

"Elise, birch him until you see he gives me good proof of his sex."

I was wild with rage. What profanation, what desecration!

Elise performed her task. I was birched, flogged into obedience, once, twice.

"Waste," exclaimed Mademoiselle, laughing and satisfied.

"Julian," she said, "I am sorry you should have clouded a day with so bright a morning, and made yourself so sad. Get those ridiculous notions out of your head, like a good boy. He will die of love, Elise. Dear boy, no one has ever shown me such true devotion. Some day, Julian, some day!"

"Today, Mademoiselle, can never return! If some day, it would not be the same."

"How absurd you are! As if that made any real difference. It is purely fantastical of you. But, anyhow, it cannot be today, that's certain. So there. Come," she added cheerily, seeing my countenance fall yet more, "come, you are a true knight and I will kiss you. I really will! Had you told me an hour ago that I would do so, I should have jeered at you! Go, Elise, and get my toilette ready. There, Julian, I will kiss you with a real kiss of love, such as your love inspires. I do love you, my dear Julian. I do indeed, and wish I could give you your desire. I cannot however. Marriage is a diabolical invention for persons circumstanced as we are; the embodiment of everything anti-aphrodisiac. Even married people find it so. If we were married, should we be spooning like this, *par example?* But we live in the world. And what could become of the brat? What would become of me?"

I was compelled to acquiesce. The divine fury had all been whipped out of me by that time. I enjoyed the kisses; sweet delicious long ones they were and they helped to heal the wound. But it was one that had truly added indelible sadness and years to my life.

I could not dispossess myself of the idea that a beautiful being had been summoned by my spirit and the co-operation of Mademoiselle's which had worked upon mine, she being at that period my feminine complement and completion. And that, having been thus summoned, it had been obliged to go weeping away, wronged and defrauded of its expectations, unable to linger, unable ever to return here, back into the nothingness out of which it had been evolved only to be disappointed and cheated; never to be clothed in the red earth which had been promised it, never to live.

I felt as though I had potentially lost a child * and my spirit was grieved.

---

* Emasculation was prohibited among the Jews. According to Josephus, it killed beforehand children who might otherwise have been begotten. The reason is intelligible but illogical.

Chapter XVIII

Under Elise — First Experiences

It will be remembered that Mademoiselle, before there had been established between her and myself any of that sweet and intimate knowledge which had since so worked upon and so changed my disposition, had as a punishment for my rudeness to Elise condemned me to servitude under that lively young woman for three days. Whether Mademoiselle regretted it now, I do not know. She had never shown me such true tenderness or manifested such feeling towards me as on that morning; her kisses still burned upon my lips, and I could recall the sweet pressure of her recent embrace. Notwithstanding this, she did not revoke the sentence. Almost as soon as I had had my last kiss, Elise returned. She carried me off naked to her room, away from the dear presence of my Hortense — my Mademoiselle. The three days under her had commenced, and, upon that morning, resistance was futile, expostulation I abstained from, under the sway of an indescribable medley of feelings.

The three days under her had commenced, and, upon their threshold, I saw a whip fastened to Elise's waist belt, a long thong, such as with a snap on the handle is occasionally used as a leading string for dogs. My curiosity as to what was to happen at once received a rude shock, and I dared not anticipate. She led me to her room.

To its ceiling there was attached a hook. She buckled two leather straps, broad and lined with thick felt, round my wrists. In each strap was a ring, through which she passed a cord. I had to mount a pair of steps which stood directly under the hook in the ceiling of this rather low room. She swung the cord over this hook.

I demurred about mounting the steps, being fearful of her object. She whipped me until I obeyed. Then, leaving the cord fixed over the hook and to each of my wrists, I had to raise my hands over my head, and to descend the steps until the end was tight. She then dragged the ladder away, and I swung by my wrists in mid-air, some three feet from the ground.

My cries of anguish, bitter as they were, remained unheeded. She put a leather belt, a foot or more in width, round my waist, and buckled it excessively tight, and then fastened two straps round my ankles of a similar kind to those round my wrists. To their rings she attached two cords, which were slipped through two staples fixed in the floor underneath me three or four feet apart. She then drew the ends of the cords together and knotted them. To this loop she tied a third cord, and putting it through another staple which formed a triangle with the two first mentioned, she caught the cord but a very short distance from the floor. Then, with all the purchase given by the expansion of the muscles of her knees and back, contracted by her having stooped down to take hold of the rope, she strained it as tightly as her force enabled her, and fixed it with a plug of wood which fitted the staple and allowed the cord to slide only one way.

My legs were dragged apart and my body pulled down in a way which racked me excruciatingly and felt like tearing my arms from their sockets. My weight only was enough to rack me cruelly, depending as I was from my wrists. The distension of my legs, and the constant downward pull, added fearfully to my torture. I implored Elise to loosen me. I assured her that my own weight occasioned me punishment sufficient. She took no heed whatever of my talk, not even bidding me hold my tongue.

My male organ was forced into undue prominence and isolated from the usual support and covering of my thighs by their separation. It was about on a level with Elise's face, and to my surprise it grew large.

When I was fixed, Elise addressed me: "I shall counteract," she said, looking at me viciously, her eyes full of a ferocious light, "the effect of Mademoiselle's treatment of you, and restore some manly vigour to this wretched thing" (thumping, twisting, and pulling what I have spoken of). "I shall elongate your figure and compress it too — that belt will give you a nice waist, you beast — and now," grasping her dog whip, "I shall give you something to think about."

I trembled. I had already felt that terrible whip, for it had taken a great deal of its persuasion to get me into that position. She stood a little distance off, eyeing me — and resting her left arm on her hip she swung the whip to its full length, and gave me a dozen whistling lashes with it. At each lash I emitted a piercing yell, plainly causing Elise to rejoice. She smiled at my torture as she slowly and deliberately continued the wanton cruelty, lifting her arm each time sufficiently to make the whip unfold itself to its full length.

Before she had finished I had become delirious. Mad with

anguish, I bit my tongue, my lips; I yelled and shrieked. Could Mademoiselle know what I was enduring? Could she permit it? I felt it would be useless to appeal to her, and dared not mention her name out of fear of further exasperating her. Besides, Mademoiselle was, I knew, inexorable. I began to feel — as long as I could feel anything but pain — deep resentment, hatred of her for her infidelity, treachery, and callousness, tormenting me, as she seemed to be doing, in every possible way by kindness as well as by cruelty. How could she give me up to this fiend? At last I could think no more. The room whirled round me; whether I yelled or screamed I did not know.

The cessation of the punishment was like Heaven. Spent and exhausted, almost fainting, I was left still hanging in a weak dreamy state, Elise having desisted to go and dress Mademoiselle. I do not know whether I fainted or slept, but I remember the strange fact that the following lines rang in my head with a vividness that frightened me. I remember too that this terrifying exaltation of my memory and other mental faculties filled me with an unspeakable dread that ere long I should find myself, in consequence of what I was undergoing, a jabbering idiot. In my anguish indeed, I almost hoped so. I felt it would serve Mademoiselle and her brutal maid but right.

> Lo! the Queen of pleasing pains,
> Linking Loves in mutual chains,
> Wreathes the myrtle bowers between
> Cottages of living green;
> And commands her virgins gay
> Through the mazy groves to stray.
>
> Full three nights in joyous vein
> Might you see the choral train,
> Hand in hand promiscuous rove
> Through thy love-devoted grove;
> Crowned with rosy breathing flowers
> Under myrtle-woven bowers.

These verses of John Dryden hammered in my head until they nearly drove me frantic. I can scarcely repeat them even now without a feeling of sickness.

My experiences under Elise were of a far more cruel description, as will already have been gathered, than anything I had yet endured, although the birching Mademoiselle had given me had caused me exquisite suffering.

A minute description of all I underwent is out of the question, but Elise's cruelty affected my animal nature only. She could not temper her inflictions with the same sweet mercies as Mademoiselle, notwithstanding that, as the sequel will show, she went further in the attempt than Mademoiselle, but ineffectually. Mercy and kindness from Elise were matters of indifference to me so far as my passions or emotions were concerned. She was undoubtedly a charming woman; her figure was very good, and I remember how she impressed herself on me with her full round bosom as she stood in her simple dark grey dress the moment before she commenced lashing me. But she was coarser and more brutal. She did not possess the ravishing spirituality of Mademoiselle. As a woman she affected me merely from an animal point of view.

In the intellectual appreciation and intelligence of her mistress I had found, even while undergoing her severest punishments, solace and consolation. Mademoiselle directed herself more to working upon the mind and the spirit and used other measures judiciously and discreetly only as they served this purpose.

Elise was purely, ingeniously, and most wantonly cruel for the sake of cruelty itself, in which she appeared to take a fiendish pleasure. I do not believe Mademoiselle would ever have strapped me up in that manner. It was essentially a maid's notion. To elongate my figure indeed!

There was no coquetry, no attempt, no suggesting of dalliance or flirtation about Elise's method. No love; it was absolutely material. She directed herself entirely to the body, not to excite sensations, but with no apparent object beyond her own gratification. In consequence, I could not even feel the satisfaction arising from obedience to a mistress. Nothing appeared to ameliorate or sweeten my fate. I had no hope, except for the termination of these three days. I was absolutely in her hands, at her mercy completely, to wreak what vengeance upon me she pleased. Why had Mademoiselle handed me over to this abomination of desolation? I saw afterwards that she had an object she herself could never have accomplished or which her endeavours to accomplish would have hindered and spoilt the effect of her other influence over me. It was a wise and economical division of labour. The lesson had to be learnt and none was so gifted for inculcating it as Elise. The animal needed taming by brute force without the aid of spiritual agencies, and of that force Elise was the priestess.

It is quite plain that the incidents of my three days purgatory cannot be set out *seriatim*. If the history of thirty-six hours has occupied so much time and space, and even *that* has not been dealt with in every detail, how much space would an equally diffuse narrative of the events of seventy-two hours require? I should never have done. Moreover, I have to relate not only the story of those three days, but of subsequent years. I should be interminable!

If any one burns for more nimble details, let him obtain a verbal account from some victim who, like myself, was forced to the sacrifice as a sheep to the slaughter. There are verily and indeed many such; the case is not rare in England nor in Scotland, less rare in Ireland, and still less rare in Germany and Austria. And it is by no means new. It is mythological and classical; it was known at Pompeii, and practised also at Rome. Such matters are in this country veiled in the closest secrecy. Many a haughty dame, respectable and so to speak irreproachable, could vouch for the truth of the assertion; the walls and closets of many a palace could, if endowed with speech, tell the same tale. In olden days this mystery was not thought necessary. But the world was pagan then. This cult, this luxury, exists only amongst the most highly educated, the most intellectual and most refined; amongst the classes vulgarly described as the "Upper Ten Thousand." The middle classes and their children are ignorant of this discipline and excess of voluptuousness.

It was on a Friday morning in the beginning of May when Elise first "tackled me," as she called it. Friday, Saturday, and Sunday, and the nights of those days! How they are stamped and burnt in my recollection! What a martyrdom I underwent!

Elise was tall and handsome, her face the most perfectly oval that I have ever seen, her teeth were white, and her lips full and cherry-coloured; her nose was a little fat, her hair dark brown, her eyebrows were heavy, her limbs admirably moulded, but her figure, notwithstanding her height, gave one the impression of being rather thick set, owing perhaps to her neck being a little short. Her hands were strong, her shoulders broad, and her muscular strength perfectly astonishing. She was always dressed with severe simplicity and was thoroughly a lady's maid in her ways, possessing vigour instead of delicacy, and just appreciably bearing a rankness of person perceptible to the nostrils, which seems inseparable from vigorous growth and life; or, at any rate, inseparable from them in a servant. This added to my punishment, for being constantly brought into the closest possible contact with her, effectually destroyed all romance and sensual gratification which I might have had.

Her bust, however, was a magnificent one, her fully developed breasts were soft, full, large, round, and white! Whatever relief or pleasure I did manage to obtain was from these warm, sensitive, substantial cushions.

Her age was seven and twenty. She had been in the service of some Princesses in France before she had come to Mademoiselle, and her experience of life, of human nature and of physical nature was limitless. The Princesses must assuredly have gone the pace, and have been as dissolute, as sensual, as indifferent to the sufferings of others as the coldest, haughtiest, and most wanton Roman ladies of the Augustan age, some of whom, indeed, they claimed to number in their ancestry.

I began to come to myself.

My physical sufferings were intense. The pain at the sockets of my arms, at my wrists, and under my shoulders was fearful. My weight and the feet forced my hands into the manacles from which I hung suspended and I got a fearful cramp in them. The belt pinched me terribly, impeding my breathing.

The accumulation of my sufferings and the sense of helplessness soon made me hysterical. I durst not cry out again, even if I had sufficient power left in me to do so. I sobbed convulsively, tears running down my face. A violent pain gradually asserted itself up the back of my head, resulting in a sense of deadly sickness; a clammy cold sweat broke out all over me; I nearly suffocated.

In a dreamy, hazy way I was conscious that there was the bed where Elise had slept, there the wash-hand-stand at which she washed and where the slops still remained. The sunlight entered at the window — a door leading into another room stood ajar.

All other ideas were obliterated. Mademoiselle, Beatrice, and the girls appeared to be the phantom creatures of another universe, the events of the morning but glimpses of a delusive visionary existence. How long I hung there, I knew not. At length the door opened. It seemed far off and did not concern me. I did not care to notice who entered. What did it matter whether it was Elise or anyone else? I felt no interest in anything. Presently I felt a hand upon that part of my frame which conclusively denied my girlhood. Mad and exasperating tomfoolery that pretence was! So essentially a woman's notion!

I opened my eyes.

"Gracious lawks!" the creature exclaimed. "I thought you were asleep, Master Julian. He! He! I beg pardon; Miss Julia, I mean. A fine miss, truly. He! He!"

I looked at her; surely I had seen her before. It was Mary.

I groaned.

"Don't — don't touch me," I gasped.

"Likely — likely indeed; we, poor maids are not to have feelings — not touch you indeed! I'll touch you," rubbing me violently, "my fine young gentleman. Miss Elise is to have all the pleasure, is she? Not if I know it. What a fine bottom," pinching it. "My lawks! If it wasn't that Miss Elise," putting her hand through my legs, "might come in at any moment, I'd take you down and make you do your duty like a man. Yes, I would. I'd have him. I'd make him rear his head inside me, just as he's doing now. It ought to be cut off, it ought. What business have you with it, Miss?" giving it a series of vicious pulls. "Come, I'll jerk it off for you. My gracious, it really does one good to see a self-opinioned young rascal strung up stark naked. My! I'd make him work."

Then standing a yard or two away in front of me, she rapidly lifted her skirts, displaying her stalwart, well-shaped legs. She was a comely damsel enough, very coarse. She gathered up the garments so as to expose to full view a hairy region, and an enormous affair in the centre. It horrified me. Much larger, much fiercer than that of Mademoiselle or Beatrice. What a monster, what an engine! Capable of sucking the very life out of one. I trembled.

"Come, how do you like it? It would make you work. Pity I can't get you between my legs. Ay!" dropping her skirts.

"You don't speak; none of your airs. I'll cure you of those," and standing at my side, she smacked my bottom with her hard, red hand. "I'll warm you; ask my pardon at once, or" — smack, smack — "I'll make you kiss it the first chance I get, although that's a nasty, dirty trick. There, you've quite warmed my hand."

I could only groan.

"Beg my pardon, or I will make Miss Elise punish you. Wait till she'll tie you again. Now that I've seen your thing I'll have you on the bed under me in a trice."

"Oh, Mary."

"Mary, indeed! Beg my pardon. Nice to be under your governess' maid, isn't it? She'll lend you to me and Susan tonight, she will. Susan is my bed-fellow. Who's Susan? Why, the scullery maid. We'll have you between us — promise!"

The idea of being prostituted by these animals filled me with a sickly terror. All my beautiful dreams dashed to pieces.

And yet what was the difference between their lust and Mademoiselle's love, which I had so ardently desired? Elise came presently, looking vicious.

Mary got the steps and put them by me. Elise, without a word, gave me a few gratuitous lashes with her whip, unfastened my legs, made me mount the steps, unhook my hands, and descend.

I tottered and almost fell. Elise threatened to make Mary lie back on the bed with her dress up, and to rub my face well into her disgusting parts, much to that wrench's supreme delectation. She was covered with blushes, when Elise had finished speaking, and looked most repulsively love sick. Elise undid my swollen hands, and marched me into the next room where I found breakfast. Here she ordered me to lie down on the floor at her feet, confess the outrage I had put upon her the evening before, clasp her knees, and humbly and abjectly ask her pardon for the insult.

I lay down and she kicked me. It was repugnant to my very soul to confess that what I had done, or rather refused to do, was an outrage. It had been the price I had paid for my night with Mademoiselle.

"You insulted me, you wretch!"

"Indeed, indeed, Elise!"

"How dare you call me Elise?" (kick, kick). "Lie there. Don't dare to get up, you beast! Say Miss Elise!"

"Oh, Miss Elise, I had to —"

"Yes, you dog, although I favoured you so — under my petticoats, my word! — and in my hands; an ugly old bitch would have affected you more."

"Mademoiselle?"

"What is that to me — you set *me* at defiance. Mademoiselle gloried in the insult to me" (more kicks). "You wretch, you," and she became quite red with vexation. "It was an outrage. Confess."

I acknowledged it, although a great part of my life went with the acknowledgment. I clasped her knees and servilely begged her pardon — implored it, prayed it. She smiled with satisfaction at the depths of humiliation to which she reduced me.

Taking me by the ear she led me into her bedroom and placed me across her bed, flat on my back, as Beatrice had done, my head again between her thighs as on the previous night. Then she worked me into a state of tremendous excitement, having previously, under threats of the severest penalties, made me promise on her account to "go off," as she called it. When I had grown enormously large she held me tightly with her legs and hurt me there fearfully. I thought she was tearing that sensitive part of me open. What she really did was to push the tight foreskin back, and she left it so. I danced about the room in anguish for this was the first time this had ever been done.

In that state I was bathed, then dressed as a girl with a tight corset of Beatrice's. Before she dressed me she replaced the skin with some difficulty. I was in such a state of nervous trepidation as to be scarcely able to eat.

When lesson time arrived she took me to the schoolroom and just outside the door she slyly slipped her hand under my skirts, got hold of that thing, and with a vicious vigorous tug, at which I nearly fainted, dragged back the skin and left it so. Then, opening the door, she pushed me in.

Mademoiselle and the girls were there. They immediately noticed my condition and laughed. Mademoiselle made me sit down. I could not sit still, but wriggled and fidgeted, and could not keep my hands quiet.

At last, Mademoiselle, tired of correcting me, gave me two bad marks and made Maud tie my hands behind and smack my face. I could not get the thing right. I was so bewildered I could not attend to lessons. My fidgeting continued until Maud was directed to hold me down across the ottoman and Agnes to birch me.

Still I was not cured.

Mademoiselle then enquired what was wrong. I could not tell her.

More birching till I could tell her. When I did so, she laughed delightedly and I had to lift up my skirts in front and stand whilst she gave leave to anyone who choose to take compassion on me to put me right.

No one moved. Could it have been expected of girls?

I had to go and ask each one in turn.

Maud gave me a blow for the insult.

Beatrice tickled my raw thing with her quill.

Agnes said she would not touch the horrid nasty affair.

Mademoiselle ultimately took pity on me.

That shameful part of me was, of course, prominently exposed to Mademoiselle and her smiling pupils.

I suppose the mad craving which I have heard exists in some men for being whipped by ladies is due to the possession in which it puts those ladies of the private structure of their bodies. It is an anticipation of the delight, resulting from a woman's conquest and control of their animal natures, gained by her in the act of copulation. But it always seemed to me to be founded upon a morbid appreciation of shame, and a morbid delectation in it.

Punishment by and before men would, of course, be a totally different matter.

The mystery of this fleeting evanescent feeling which I could not catch and analyse worried me.

When Mademoiselle spoke to me of being in that condition in the presence of ladies I had the hardihood to remark naively that it was natural I should be in that condition before them!

A peal of laughter greeted this observation.

Chapter XIX

Under Elise — Animals!

At half-past twelve, when lessons were concluded, Elise again made her appearance to claim me as her prisoner and I resigned myself to the inevitable with a sigh and accompanied her with a cowed, hang-dog, crushed, and humiliated feeling in which, in the presence of her petticoats and peeping ankles, I positively, to my surprise, found myself taking a queer sort of delight. It was of the same nature as that sensation caused me when I lay face uppermost between her bare legs, closely pressed to her body, exciting and forced to devour her living raw flesh. How oddly things strike one! I wondered whether this craving and gratification of mine were akin to those which the Israelites experienced in the desert, and which they satisfied with quails.

Logically or illogically, rightly or wrongly, I reflected that they had had the quails. And so I was confirmed in my determination to get any animal satisfaction I could out of Elise. That was not much.

Mademoiselle must have set bounds to it. Elise, Mary, and Susan, all threatened to make me do with them what I had implored Mademoiselle to allow me to do with her, but they never carried out their threat. Elise took me to the workroom. There was a wickerwork-stand there which was used for hanging dresses on while making or finishing them. It resembled half the divine female form, from the waist to the ground. Elise silently grasped me round the waist and inserted her hand under my skirts from behind. I trembled and gasped. I knew what was coming. She pressed her hand against my bottom, pushed it through my legs, caught hold of that affair of mine in front, and violently drew the skin down. I jumped, but could not escape from her grasp.

My petticoats rubbing against my more than nakedness hurt me severely. I changed colour, became pale, and then, a deep flush spread itself over my face. As soon as she had let me go I bent over in anguish, not daring to set myself right.

"Oh, Miss Elise, how severe you are." I did not forget the "Miss" this time.

"Oh," she said triumphantly, "strip yourself, Miss. I will have the maids in to see you like that when I have caged you."

I at once proceeded to undress, cured long ago by her whip, of all idea of hesitating. She then tied my hands behind me with a tape.

"You were elongated this morning, you shall be packed together again now," she continued, unfastening her whip from her waistband where it hung by a spring catch. "Get under that dress stand. At once!"

"Yah! Yah!" as she lashed me. "I will. Stop!"

I huddled myself under the accursed thing as best I could, crouching down, sitting on my haunches. I had obeyed instantly; the lashes were wanton and gratuitous. She padlocked the stand in two places to the floor. I felt like a caged beast. There was that thing of mine in front of me grown to an enormous size, strangulated, and swollen by the stricture of the skin, hurting me horribly as it wagged its raw head under the influence of excitement I could not prevent, and my hands all the time absolutely behind my back.

I felt as monstrous as Priapus, and was literally dismayed at the prospect of being exhibited like that to the gaze, the curiosity, and the ridicule of a number of maidservants, for I did not doubt for an instant that she would execute her threat. I knew the show she intended to make of me would afford her infinite amusement.

In the meantime she inserted the whip between the wicker bars of my prison and diverted herself hugely by poking and tickling me with it. The contact of the whip was most painful against that raw thing, tender and sensitive as it was. Then, raising her skirts, she pressed herself against the bars and made me kiss "Miss Elise" through them again and again. To my horror, she then summoned Mary and Susan; the last I had not seen before.

Mary repeated the poking process after which she minutely examined me.

Susan came next. She was a ruddy, comely, country lass, but filthy. She went to work in the knowingly cunning fashion that characterizes rural ignorance. About the kissing talk she was very shamefaced. Elise, however, insisted.

"Come, Susan, no nonsense: you will find how nice it is — up with your skirts."

"Oh, Miss Elise, I'd much rather not. Indeed" — with a deep blush — "a young gentleman to kiss me *there!* I never heard of such a thing, I couldn't do it, I couldn't."

However, Mary on one side, and Elise on the other, caught hold of the reluctant girl, and, despite her struggles, they displayed her coarse, common, and dirty underclothing, and got it way up above her waist. Elise put in her hand behind my head, and gave my face a good rub in it. Susan was nearly suffocated by her emotions, and gasped something about a lesson to teach her young man. When they let her go, she rushed off.

"Where's the fool gone to?" asked Elise. "Call her back, Mary."

She came back of her own accord with a pail full of stinking water from the scullery, which, before the others knew what she was going to do, she lifted up and poured over me.

"There," she exclaimed, "you filthy beast to ask to kiss young ladies so!"

What a slander! What a wrong!

The two maids rolled about holding their sides, roaring and shrieking with laughter until the tears ran down their faces, and ejaculating: "Well done, Susan!"

"Well I never!"

"Serve him right, Susan!"

My spluttering and blowing vastly increased their merriment; the water was cold and gave me quite a shock, and then noticing Susan's air of indignation, they laughed the more.

When they had done laughing Elise amused them by pulling me about and rubbing and pressing me through the bars of the wicker cage. Afterwards she uncaged me and made me lie across her lap while she spanked me before them. She then combed and brushed very roughly the downy hair about my middle, and finally tied a blue ribbon about Mons. Priapus, announcing that I should remain like that all the afternoon.

Then my hands were again bound behind my back and I was packed into the cage, over which a skirt was thrown, and left to digest in wet gloom and in a cramped and miserable position the treatment which had been forced upon me.

It was soon time to dress me again as a girl in spite of Mons. Priapus's contradiction, for school hours recommenced at half-past three. It was a beautiful afternoon, although the day had been oppressive, and to me particularly exhausting. I was done up — felt it and looked it — mentally and bodily. Mademoiselle observed my state with some compassion. She took me to her room and made me lie on her bed. She undid the blue ribbon and put me right, gave me some of her famous burgundy and cake, petted me, sat by me, and ultimately kissed me. The relaxion of the excessive tension brought on a flood of tears — a fit of weeping. Mademoiselle loosened my dress, removed my corset, and soothed me; and as I fell asleep threw a dressing gown over me and told me I was under her protection.

Would that I could have lived for her and have been hers alone! I remembered Beatrice but had not energy enough to settle the suggested difficulty.

That night Elise put me to bed quite naked with her and made me spend a portion of the night under the sheets in close contact with her secret anatomy. I have said she was beautiful; I felt as though I was becoming as well acquainted with women's private parts as with their faces. While my head was between her legs, Elise sucked Monsieur Priapus, bit him, and pulled him unceremoniously about. All this time she kept my hands tied behind me.

In the early morning, while she was still in her *robe de nuit*, I was ordered to lie in her lap. After which she turned on her face, and in token of subjection, I had to kiss her bottom. The sight of it excited me very much, and when directed to lie upon it, placing Mons. Priapus between its cheeks, I obeyed. I marvelled at Elise's buck-jumping and prancing, but I found out she had got what is called a *dildoe* underneath her in front, and had inserted it where she did not venture to insert me. This drove her into frantic eroticism. I was to be congratulated that the idea of inserting it into me did not suggest itself to her.

I helped Elise to dress; though she was kind she used frequent threats of the whip and birch, and ordered me about very peremptorily. I had had such doses of both that the threats were quite needless. Whatever she bade me do I instantly set about. She was more *exigeante* than Mademoiselle. Her stockings needed the greatest care — their ribs had to be placed with mathematical precision; the stockings themselves drawn to exactly the right tension, and the suspenders adjusted to the correct length. Before I put on her drawers I kissed her shapely legs above the knees having gallantly begged permission first. "Miss Julia," said Elise, "you are such a good boy" (hermaphrodite already, thought I) "that, if you like, you shall some day give me a portion of that which you long to give Mademoiselle."

I must add by way of epilogue to this portion of my experiences that it was not pleasant to kiss and lick a bottom, although a maid's. It gave one a shocking sort of thrill such as the ancients may have known when sailing through the Symplagades. They dreaded that the giant rocks might close and crush them. I did not feel sure what a bottom might not do. I had had a fright in the bath. Mademoiselle had not made me kiss hers. If she had, I should have had no fear. With Elise it was different. I wronged her by my fears, however. The contact of her flesh was very sweet and she did nothing indelicate. Would, Lady Alfred Ridlington, I could say the same of you! But I am anticipating.

After breakfast I was hung up again. I urged all I could think of, imagine, or invent. I begged, I prayed Elise; I grovelled on the ground and besought her to let me off this terrible maddening punishment.

She only answered with her dog whip.

In the afternoon, I was made to sew in the workroom — the task was only an excuse for tormenting me. At frequent intervals I was laid across the sofa and, my clothes turned up, a handkerchief stuffed into my mouth, and I was lashed for clumsiness and for not performing the impossibilities I was ordered to accomplish.

Chapter XX

Under Elise — Lent to Maud

I was driven to distraction, my eyes were full of tears, my hands trembling. I could not sew; and Elise had jumped up to practise some newly invented torture upon me when steps sounded outside. This awakened a faint hope of rescue, to be extinguished almost as soon as alive, for who would interfere to protect me? Who could it be, on that day, at that time? For it was Saturday, a half-holiday.

Maud came into the room, and to my great surprise, calmly begged Elise to lend me to her, telling her that she wanted to birch me, to pull me about, to have me at her mercy, and to make me obey her during the afternoon. Elise at first was obdurate, said she feared Mademoiselle, and dared not take the risk, as she would lose her place. At last, however, she sold me. Maud offered her three pounds. Elise would not hear of it. "Four!" — Nonsense, she would take nothing; it was not a question of money. — "Five!"

"Well, really, Miss Maud, you are too importunate; but five pounds are not to be gained every day, and — and — Mademoiselle is out and she need not know anything about it — and if you give them me now —"

Whereupon Maud took out her purse and told down five golden sovereigns, which Elise greedily snatched up.

"Now listen to me," she said, addressing me, and smacking my face and head till my ears sang, "one word of this to Mademoiselle and I shall hang you up for three hours tomorrow. That will be Sunday and there will be nothing to prevent me doing so. Three hours whether you die of it or not."

Maud had already got me by the ear.

"There he is, Miss Maud. He is yours till teatime, anyhow. Take him."

"Come along," said Maud, giving my ear an unpleasant jerk.

Maud was the eldest of the three sisters and was the very proper and faultless one. I believe she would have expired of spleen, had she been convicted of a fault, so implacable did she regard herself, and so thoroughly was she convinced of the fact that whatever she did must necessarily be right. She was cold, hard, proud, and formal; she spoke in measured phrases, never on any occasion betraying the slightest agitation; thoroughly wrapped in herself and her own perfections, her selfishness was astonishing.

As soon as we were outside the workroom door she let go my ear and stared coldly at me from head to foot.

"You look like a girl," she said in a disappointed tone. "I wonder whether after all you are really one. Follow me to my room anyhow." And she led the way to the back stairs, which, holding her skirts up daintily in front, she slowly ascended. As she did so immediately before me I could not help seeing what a nice girl she was. Her skin was white, her hair a delicious brown, wavy, and thick. Her form was elegant and with a girlish promise of development about it that was exciting; all her movements characterised by a graceful ease that gave her swing a decided charm.

She had two rooms on the third floor opening into each other and overlooking an Italian garden. One was furnished as a bedroom and the other as a studio. It was in elegant and artistic disorder with all an artist's litter about. Maud's forte was painting, drawing, and modelling in clay.

She took me through into her bedroom and locked both the outer doors; each room having a door opening upon the landing.

The bedroom was girlish in its simplicity. Maud's own precocious corporeal development was no doubt attributable to her habit, originally compulsory, afterwards persisted in from pleasure, of tight lacing; her mental precocity or pruriency was attributable both to Mademoiselle and to nature. I noticed several clever pictures in her bedroom; all studies of the nude.

Turning to me she said: "I want an Adonis or an Apollo. Strip and let me see whether you can fill the part. Besides, I want to — to — to analyse you. I need knowledge of anatomy for executing the drawings I love. Besides which I love the study of male anatomy for itself. I shall therefore study you. So far as I am concerned you shall always remain masculine. I admire virility. If I punished you it would be for effeminacy. How disgraceful to allow yourself to be treated as you are. How degrading! Mean creature that you must be. But while Agnes was flogging you yesterday, I saw enough of your legs and back to make me wish to see more. Undress!"

She then sat down at her ease in a low armchair, calmly waiting to have her order carried out.

I leant against the bed, half sitting upon it. I had naturally expected by this time to have become hardened and indifferent to the ordeal of being divested of all my garments by a girl and compelled to expose my nakedness to her. But, to my surprise and consternation, I found I experienced quite as much trouble and confusion upon each repetition as upon the first occasion. Shame did not wear off. The idea of undressing before this elegant girl, alone with her in her own room, caused me the greatest perturbation and confusion.

Steadfastly gazing at me she noticed my hesitation and reluctance. A queer light came into her eyes, and she moved her body in her low chair in a certain manner which I recognized and knew to portend mischief. She was resting her cheek on her hand, and her skirts, never too long, had worked halfway up to her knees. Her ankles were delicate and pretty. When she saw me looking at them, with a becoming consciousness, she tried to shake the garments down.

I wondered how much she knew.

I commenced a calculation of how far she would go. What it would be worth my while to do.

She was evidently in a flutter herself, and without that self-possession and repose so characteristic of Mademoiselle.

She was nervous plainly and sensible of the want of that impelling magic or mesmeric power which compelled obedience to Mademoiselle's orders however shocking and outrageous they might be.

So, feeling my advantage I began to sulk.

"Julian," she said, "do as I desire. I shall whip you if you don't." I twinged, and considered whether she could. "Undress yourself directly. Come, I have no time to lose; besides, I will not pay five pounds for nothing! Undress, I want to see you."

I still hesitated and only looked at her mutely.

"You are wasting all the time," she said, angrily. "If you do not undress at once I declare I shall call Elise and make her bind you, and will lash you without mercy myself. Come!" she said, half rising. "Must I, or will you do what I wish?"

Now the appearance of Elise on the scene would have spoilt all. I much preferred a quiet *tête-à-tête* with my cousin uninterrupted by Elise and her brutalities. But Maud made a great mistake in invoking another power instead of relying upon her own. I said so.

"I might do for you, Maud, what force and Elise could not make me do." I hazarded a gentle emphasis on the pronoun.

"Very well, then, be a good boy, and please me. I do not like force; I think its employment inelegant. I wish to conquer by my — by my — what Mademoiselle would call — charms," she said, with a most winning air of pretty embarrassment, coyly looking down as if frightened by her own temerity and uncertain of the response.

She had touched my weak point. "Indeed," I instantly answered, with a look freely expressing the admiration I felt, "they are sufficient." And my frank tone conveyed the sincerity of my conviction. The effect was magical.

"You *nice* boy," she said, rushing at me with girlish abandon and kissing me.

And then, with her hand upon my shoulder she said, looking into my eyes: "Undress! I wish you to do so. Now, we shall both enjoy it. I will help you."

Affairs had taken a very pleasant turn. It had become a task of love to obey her and the sacrifices involved were sweet and thrilling. We were both in a flutter of pleasant excitement as I yielded to her wishes. She threw the feminine garments one by one from me with disdain. My blushes were materially increased by the loss of my petticoats and the exposure of my bare arms and neck, while my nether limbs were covered by dainty shoes, long stockings, and wide heavily frilled drawers. She laughed gaily at the picture I presented and asked me how I appreciated the ignominy of being condemned to wear a lady's things.

Then followed two or three thrilling moments, while her fingers were busy with the strings about my waist, her arms often round it as she fumbled with the fastening of my drawers. Her taking them off, caused us both an infinity of delightful confusion. I felt the air against my bare legs and made a vain attempt to catch the mischievous pair of hands that were so ruthlessly invading my privacy with the undisguised intention of entirely depriving me of it.

She slipped down on the floor in front of me to pull off my stocking. Again a thrill and a gasp, as she petulantly pulled away the *chemise* and finally pushed her hands under it to get at the end of the stocking which was halfway up my thigh. I felt her soft cool hands on my bare leg and for an instant they went up higher than necessary. The next instant the stocking was jerked off without compunction and one long limb became as naked as my arms. She paused to look at it with approval and satisfaction before she attacked the other leg. With a pretty pout and an amused air she forcibly took hold of the other leg and its stocking and rapidly drew off the delicate silk thing. I felt worse than naked. Without a word she loosened and unfastened my corset and there was but the chemise left.

"Now," she cried, "I shall punish your ridiculous attempt at concealment," and, not waiting to take the *chemise* off, she slipped her left arm round my back and with her disengaged hand lifted it right up to my breasts and gazed at me intently with a very rosy face. I was forced to acquiesce although blushing from head to foot and hanging my head. Resting her shoulder against me to prevent the garment falling down again, she touched me. I could resist no longer. I threw my arms round her and kissed her cheeks and neck. She gave me some coy slaps, and, turning her head, placed one burning kiss full on my mouth.

We lost ourselves for some seconds in the sweetness of the embrace.

"Now," she said at length, "we must take this off, too." And gathering the chemise up with both hands she slipped it off my arms over my head.

There I stood before her absolutely and entirely naked without the slightest possibility of the least concealment and she gazed at me steadfastly from head to foot. I felt embarrassed and awkward. I did not know what to do. Partial concealment, I felt, would but emphasize the rest of my nudity. She passed her hands over my legs and thighs and between them, and played with that male thing in a most tantalising fashion, observing that she was glad to make the acquaintance of so handsome a gentleman.

"How it grows when I play with it!" she said quizzically; adding, "He looks much nicer now than when I saw him last in the schoolroom."

She next made me lie back on the bed and knelt between my legs. Her heavily drooping lids, her swimming eyes, her quickly heaving bosom, and her voluptuous movements, gave a promising and encouraging account of her own condition. I suggested that I should undress her and then we could have a reciprocal lesson in practical anatomy. She laughed, but not heeding my suggestion, wanted to know as she handled it, whether this bag contained babies, and how many.

"Oh, Maud," I said, electrified, "lie down on the bed and it shall tell you."

I remembered the conversation with Mademoiselle and the knowledge I had derived from it. Maud was not Mademoiselle, neither was she Beatrice, but in the height of my transport this was a mere detail which did not affect me, and indeed of which I never thought.

She stood up over me occasionally stroking me and passing her hands over and along my arms and shoulders which she said were admirable. By a dexterous movement I slipped my hand under her petticoats while she was thus interested in studying me. She started, grew fiery red, made a pretence of resistance, which was, even to my inexperienced eyes, plainly unreal — instinctive not intentional.

It is at this juncture that a man loses if he is fainthearted. But I was far too much excited to be fainthearted. I insisted. I touched her. A complete change came over her instantly and it seemed to me miraculously.

"Oh, Julian, Julian," she ejaculated, "you mustn't. What will Mademoiselle say? Oh, you mustn't!" After a few moment's pause: "How would it tell me?"

"It would tell you there," I said, placing my finger on the spot.

"There! Oh — oh — should you put it there?" she asked, awaiting the answer with evident anxiety.

"Yes, there!" I answered. I had got hold of her completely; her legs were well separated, and she moved lasciviously backwards and forwards, rubbing herself against my hand. As I repeated the words I pressed my middle finger well into the lips of that feminine mouth with a moustache to which Mademoiselle had first introduced me.

"Oh — oh — oh, Julian! What would it do?"

"It would throb — throb — throb," I replied, poking her with my finger each time I said the word and gazing laughingly at her, "and make his way right — into — you!"

"Would it — it — this long thing?" (holding it). "Just fancy! And these — this too inside me!" (with a delicious blush and exquisite confusion; and as she moved lasciviously, I felt my hand being moistened). "Oh how dreadful — but how nice it would be — but wouldn't it be awfully naughty? Have you," as a thought struck her, "ever done it to anyone, to any girl? I mean, are you sure it is right — the right way I mean?" with a look of arch simplicity, covering her head and endeavouring to conceal her rosy face against my breast as she knelt over me.

I could not but smile; I felt triumphant. There was a friend within the citadel who would hand the fortress over to me. So, for all answer, I moved my hand again. It was a most potent and convincing argument. After some inarticulate sounds, and one or two passionate movements, she cried, as I followed up my advantage and pressed the matter home:—

"You must — you must — you must! How shall I lie?"

Now I was a novice, but I guessed.

"Lie down on your back on the bed, Maud, dear," and I withdrew my hand and made room for her.

"So?" enquired the charming girl as in pretty disorder she abandoned herself helpless and absolutely to the divine impulse of nature and cast herself down — her legs wide apart, her petticoats up to her knees.

I gazed enraptured at her lovely uncovered limbs in their stockings and lace drawers, at her heaving bosom, at her beautiful features.

"Get between them, you naughty boy, directly. Lie down upon me this instant," extending herself to clasp me. "How dare you stay looking at me like that! Come, you naughty boy, at once — you naughty naked boy!" grasping me and drawing me on to her. Before I had time to throw myself into the Elysium beneath me she had twined her arms and legs about me and clasped me in a close and rigid embrace.

The voluptuousness of the position was most intoxicating.

My naked thighs pressed against hers underneath her skirts, ruthlessly encroaching upon the sanctuary of the feminine divinity. My breast oppressed her palpitating bosom, her throbbing form lay vanquished and confined beneath mine. No maidenly coyness, no ladylike reserve could avail her to the smallest extent now. Her face was a sweet and close prisoner which I could kiss at pleasure. I myself was a close captive between her legs, two warm round soft cushions, two wilful and unrelenting jailers grasping me with arch feminine severity.

There was a delicious scent of summer flowers emanating from her, and her violent and unembarrassed movements as she adjusted herself to her satisfaction, thrilled my sense of touch. She settled herself without the slightest hesitation or awkwardness and with a bewitchingly careless disregard of me, retaining her tight grasp of my body all the while. Her magnetic power gradually stole over me and possessed me. Her touch thrilled me through and through.

"There," she ejaculated in a transport, speaking with the clear distinctness of one who knows her own mind exactly and is determined to fulfil it at all hazards, "pull my petticoats out of the way — come up closer — now, Julian — so," wriggle, wriggle, "now put it in there — at once — directly in, as you said, or — or — or — I shall squeeze you to death!"

All my fatigue, all the exhaustion caused by the discipline I had undergone vanished as if by magic. I was carried away by the realisation of my fondest dreams before me and the intensity of the physical happiness of my situation. I knew instinctively that I was on the brink of tasting the fullest earthly bliss and of draining the cup. It could not be dashed from my lips now.

It was not with the person with whom I desired it, I confess. But love is wayward and capricious, seldom giving exactly what one wishes. One must often content oneself with the good the Gods provide without insisting upon choosing for oneself. And I was so excited and Maud so lovely that this never struck me, and I do not think I should have regarded it for one moment if it had as I lay quivering in her arms.

"Oh, Julian," gasped the lovely girl as I obeyed her orders and sank into her embrace.

We blundered considerably, but perhaps this was fortunate, stimulating our ardours the more and working us up into a yet higher pitch of excitement with its continually recurrent thrills of exquisite sensation.

At last to my astonishment and alarm she cried that I was hurting her and the tone of her inarticulate expressions of pleasure changed. Her eyes were suffused with tears. I began to have misgivings as to whether I was right after all. She was courageous, however, and insisted. There appeared to be some obstacle. She complained of being sore, that I was tearing her. She bit me as my mouth sought hers to silence her protests with kisses. She asked me to draw back for a moment and even tried to push me away. But my transport was such that, even had I wished, I could not have complied. Carried away by my feelings I only pressed onwards the more. I felt the climax had come and I forcibly overcame her resistance.

In a paroxysm of passion I threw myself upon her with fresh

vigour and forced myself well into her despite her opposition. I felt mad, furious, like an animal which has tasted blood. The obstacle soon vanished; I burst through it; and not heeding her screams, I thrust forward inside her, holding her with my arms about her neck as in a vice, pressing her down against the bed so that she could not retreat. Throb — throb — throb, I sank onto her breast and she seemed to faint in a delirium of joy, her pain gone with the sound of her screams.

At that instant she was stamped upon my mind with such strange and astonishing vividness that I still recall it with awe and wonder.

At the moment of consummation when her response and my convulsion satisfied the hunger I had not until then known how to allay, there was a perfect picture of her impressed upon my sensorium. And as our flesh mingled it was as though I fed upon her beauty and tasted the loveliness of her ankles, her thighs, her bosom, her features, her whole form — drank it in, absorbed it, lived upon it.

This then is love I reflected, as we reposed in ecstasy in each other's arms and I gazed upon her as she lay with her head resting on my shoulder and a leg still thrown across me as if to signify that she had not yet done with me.

Would it be a boy or a girl?

Would it resemble its mother? Her swimming eyes were closed, her cherry-coloured lips open, her fragrant breath fanned my cheek. Maud, who had brought me upstairs to study anatomy objectively, with a view to moulding inanimate figures, had had a subjective lesson of the most thorough nature which would doubtless result in a perfect and living study in clay.

The Apollo Belvedere or Venus! Which would it be? Could Beatrice have intended more than her words conveyed when she had issued her prohibition?

A tap at the door. Maud, who was in a light slumber, half-awaking moved and giving me a cooing caress, again slept.

Another knock; this time louder. The sun was sinking towards the west, already faintly gilding the attendant clouds with his evening greeting.

A third knock, and a voice in alarmed, hushed tones called:

"Miss Maud! Miss Maud!"

I recognised the voice. It was that of my tormentor, Elise. How I hated her. Would Maud be able to save me?

"Maud," I said gently, putting my hand on her shoulder.

"There is Elise. Let me send her away."

"Who — what — eh?" murmured Maud, startled. "Elise — oh, Julian!" and overcome with love, she gave me a hug.

"Miss Maud! Miss Maud!" again cried Elise. "Whatever are you about? Make haste and let me in at once. Mademoiselle has just returned."

"Goodness gracious!" exclaimed Maud, startled and thoroughly awake now, and thoroughly frightened also. "Whatever shall I do, Julian?" she asked, starting up. And then she shouted:

"All right, Elise; in one moment," adding to me: "Jump up, Julian; jump up and let me put myself straight."

I had knelt up.

"Great heavens!" I exclaimed, terrified and in horror. "Look there, Maud."

Could I have been right after all? Her *chemise* and the coverlet of the bed were drenched with blood. Whatever should we do? Maud turned white, but her presence of mind did not desert her.

"Let Elise in at once; it is the only thing we can do. She will know."

I trembled, but flew to the door and unlocked it. Elise rushed in, angry at having been kept waiting, and in a wild state of apprehension lest Mademoiselle should discover her having allowed me to go to Maud's bedroom with her.

She at once began railing at her, abusing her for her folly and carelessness. Maud was calmly arranging her hair at the glass.

Elise's eyes soon felt on the bed. She screamed as she noticed the deep carnation stains on the counterpane and flying at Maud, she shook her violently.

"Whatever have you done? Whatever have you done? You are ruined. You have ruined me. I shall lose my place; my character is gone," she shouted, beside herself with fright.

"Mademoiselle will kill you; she will flay him alive. Fool that I was! I might have known what you were up to. She will turn me out of the house the instant she discovers this."

And Elise flew to the bed, swept the quilt in a bundle on to the floor and kicked it underneath the valance.

"I know what you have been about. I might have guessed what would happen. You are ruined, Miss Maud; ruined! You have been prostituted by — by — that beast," she exclaimed in a tone of deep anger, red with fury, and pointing to me with scorn and indignation.

So I *was* right after all.

Maud gave a little cry. The language certainly profaned our loves.

"You must not use such words, Elise," she said. "Be sensible; he is my cousin. What is to be done?" and, looking at me, she added: "Never mind her, Julian."

"Never mind me! No, I dare say not; but you will mind Mademoiselle. Your cousin, indeed. Your husband, I think. It cannot be concealed. Impossible! You will have a baby. You will," she shrieked. "You will be disgraced. Where will it end? Mademoiselle to save herself will throw all the blame on me. However, I will have my revenge.

"Come along, Master Julian," rushing at me and seizing my wrists. "Come along to my room. I will hang you up and lash you till you are insensible."

"Oh, Maud!"

"Julian, Julian," said the dear girl throwing her arms about me; "no, no, she shan't take you; I will not have you cruelly used."

"Don't interfere, Miss Maud. He must come; he must not be found here. Put on that *peignoir*, and come along instantly."

I was paralysed with fright. I felt Maud was powerless.

At that moment the door opened and Mademoiselle appeared.

Elise stood speechless. Maud looked confused. I stood naked and did not know how to hide myself.

Mademoiselle had just returned from riding. She looked admirable in her riding costume which set off her superb figure to perfection. She stood holding up her habit with both hands, disclosing her dainty boots, and she looked round with an amused expression trying to take in the situation.

She gazed at Elise, at Maud, and then at me.

She was evidently in a good humour and in high spirits. She had been riding a young half-broken colt, and carried a heavy training whip — by no means the delicate little weapon she had made me acquainted with in her dressing room.

"Well, Elise," she said at length in her calm, clear voice, "what is Miss Julia doing here naked in Miss Maud's room? Come, I can see from your face there is something wrong; do not try to deceive me.

You will not succeed and it will only be the worse for you!"

"If you please, Mademoiselle," began Elise, trying woefully to look as collected and unconcerned as possible, "Miss Maud required a model for a statue and came and begged me to allow Miss Julia to go to her studio for an hour. As Miss Julia had been well disciplined I thought there could be no objection."

"Her studio indeed; this is her bedroom. How came you to bring him in here, Maud?"

"Oh, he only came in here to undress," replied Maud, with a readiness which astonished me, but which unfortunately did not impose on Mademoiselle.

"His undressing seems to have caused you a vast amount of confusion," she rejoined in a dry tone, flourishing her whip. "However, we won't waste time," she ominously continued, gathering her skirts into her left hand: "I will teach him that he cannot be found in a young lady's bedroom naked — absolutely naked — with impunity, and I will teach you next, Miss Maud, that you should have had more modesty. Come," disengaging her right hand and arm. "You are just in the condition for being flogged, and I am in the mood, too."

"Oh, Mademoiselle — indeed — oh, pray —" cried I, frantic at the sight of the whip.

Mademoiselle's eyes flashed. Walking firmly up to the bed she directed Elise to put me across it.

"Oh, Mademoiselle, please, please," cried Maud, throwing herself at the governess's feet and clasping and wringing her own hands, "please do not punish Julian; it was not his fault — I brought him here —"

"Hold your tongue, Miss. You won't escape, I can promise you; now, Elise!"

Elise dragged me, struggling, to the side of the bed at which Mademoiselle was standing and tried to push me over it, face downwards. I sobbed and resisted frantically. "Hallo!" said Mademoiselle, her attention directed to the couch. "Where is the coverlet — and the bed is disarranged, too! However, one thing at a time."

Elise, without answering, redoubled her efforts. To cover the condition of the bed, by making it worse, was, I believe, her real intention; but, ostensibly for the purpose of getting me into position, she scrambled on to the top of me and slipped off at the other side, leaning heavily over my shoulders and holding my arms with all her strength.

"Put his head between your knees, Elise," ordered Mademoiselle, striking me with the whip.

Elise tried to catch my head between them, outside her petticoats. "No," reiterated Mademoiselle, "underneath your skirts."

Elise dived with one hand for the ends of her garments, slipped my head under them, and soon had it fast between her warm legs higher up than her knees.

As I have before had occasion to remark, a woman's whole strength lies in her thighs. Elise needed all hers to hold me as probably Mademoiselle knew.

"Now for being found naked in a young lady's bedroom you shall receive twenty-five lashes, Miss Julia."

"Yah, yah, yell, yell!" I turned and twisted. I writhed and tried to bite Elise. Like red hot iron over my bottom, my legs, and my back, Mademoiselle rained the blows with slow even regularity and merciless force.

"Keep your seat, Elise," she cried, as mad with pain I almost struggled free, and Elise then sat close, holding on like grim death, my head well down under her bottom. My struggles must have given her extreme pleasure.

I heard Mademoiselle say to Elise towards the end, "Outside your petticoats, indeed — you idiot. You would not have had the enjoyment."

I became almost senseless from agony.

"Twenty-five," at last exclaimed Mademoiselle. "There he is well waled. Let him go. He won't sit comfortable for a week or more."

I rolled on the floor, sobbing and writhing with agony.

"Now, Maud," said Mademoiselle, "it will do Miss Julia good to see you whipped. I warrant she will forget her pangs and ridiculous contortions, which are quite indecent, in order to see you catch it. Take off your drawers, Miss. Where is the coverlet, Elise?" asked Mademoiselle, tapping the blanket with her whip; but noticing Maud standing still, she did not wait for the answer, Maud's obstinacy attracting her attention.

"Take off your drawers, I tell you," she repeated in a higher tone for the third time — on this occasion with a cut of the cruel whip across her shoulders, at which Maud screamed.

"Oh, I can't, I can't; oh, let me off this once!" said Maud in despair.

When Elise seconded this appeal, Mademoiselle began to smell a rat.

"Why can't you?" she asked suspiciously and sharply. Maud did not reply but trembling like an aspen leaf began to fumble about her dress. Mademoiselle watched her narrowly.

"Why, what have you got on your drawers and on your *chemise*, too? Tumble her over the bed." Maud, sobbing and terrified, was powerless. "Blood, I declare!" screamed Mademoiselle as Maud was thrown over and her petticoats turned up to her waist. "Where is the coverlet?" she demanded at the top of her voice.

Elise raked it out. Mademoiselle eagerly spread it open and examined it with a horror-struck look. Elise mournfully shook her head. "It is evident what has happened. He has seduced her. *Mon Dieu!* How long have they been alone? I have been in twenty minutes — these stains are not dry. Run, Elise, I will settle with you another time — run for a syringe."

Mademoiselle threw down her whip and tore Maud's clothes off. Elise rushed off and speedily returned. They held Maud down and squirted into her with warm water and alum violently for ten minutes. They turned her over and lashed her until she bled. More dead than alive, they strapped us back to back on the floor.

"What's done cannot be undone. You will remain so until I consider what is to be done with you. In the meantime, Elise, come with me," said Mademoiselle, leaving the room and banging the door behind her.

With this catastrophe, a turning point in my career, I will close my first volume.

END OF VOLUME I

VOLUME THE SECOND

CONTENTS OF VOLUME II

Chapter I

Retrospection

When Heracles in consequence of the murder of Iphitus was ill of a serious disease, and received the oracle that he could not be released unless he served some one for wages for the space of three years, Hermes accordingly sold Heracles to Omphale... [By *whom he became the father of several children!*]

Yes; this I very well recollect, for, no doubt, as the Reader has observed, the adventures, or perhaps this adventure, of Hercules made a solemn impression upon me; and excited exceeding interest in my breast. I always thought Hercules exceedingly fortunate in his punishment, and you may observe the corroboration of the justice of my view in the apologetical, parenthetical, and, as it were, quite irrelevant statement that by her he became the father of several children. Happy man! We all know the torso of Omphale; I have never met with a full length representation. What a coquettish little head and piquant nose — what a resolute and yet voluptuous chin — what large eyes, in which lays a glorious light; eyes which, if she was put out or vexed, or found Hercules hurt her, while she administered those stripes for his clumsiness in the workroom, would swim and look like blue water lilies in a clear transparent lake. How withering the first reproachful glances, how rapid the transition from the melting mood to the fiery gaze, portending vengeance. How promptly Hercules would find his corset inconveniently tightened by the united efforts of all the Lydian hand maidens and he himself transported by the same means to the Queen's dressing room, where, no doubt, fastened down upon his back (he would otherwise have been altogether unmanageable), he paid the penalty of his misdemeanours to that charming woman, completely by divine appointment as well as by her own charms, his sovereign mistress.

It is remarkable how this story has been tabooed by an apparently universal (male) consensus of opinion. There are few, if any, representations of this period of Hercules' life. Venuses beating Cupids abound; in the Salon a few years ago was a canvas depicting Psyche lashed by the fair goddess' orders; Circe, too, reposes in her chair naked, her foot upon the head of the armed and prostrate Ulysses. Where do you find Hercules beaten by Omphale, or even, excepting the statue in the Borghese Casino, in petticoats?

Omphale ruled like Mademoiselle by force and love, not like Beatrice by the last alone. I have come to the conclusion that women rule all men; why is the subject, the truth, ignored? It would be some help, some consolation to me, as I continue this narrative of my own subjugation to the petticoat, if it were not. I am conscious of the existence and encouraged by the knowledge of many fellow victims, but can obtain no openly expressed sympathy. A club of hen-pecked husbands, if started, would find but one member, myself, and I doubt whether even I would venture to send in an application to join unless — unless she compelled me to do so; and it is exceedingly likely she would.

"Several children." Happy man — yes, undoubtedly, Hercules must have been fastened down by force or held down by love and devotion, and Omphale, reversing what I suppose is the usual order of things, must have lain on the top of him, until he was exhausted. Exhausted as the individual mentioned by Brantome, who awoke his wife. The story is well known. She placed him underneath her upon the bed. She made him perform and discharge the primary obligation of matrimony once, twice, thrice, even a fourth time, and left him fainting there, *"Hein!* you will not wake me again, I dare say — I think I have given you a lesson!"

Mademoiselle Hortense de Chambonnard had now such a hold upon me that I dared not resist in the slightest anything whatsoever that she might take it into her pretty little head to do with me, and I feared greatly, and quaked and trembled exceedingly, as I wondered and marvelled what that would be. My fate, my destinies, my fortune, were now completely in her hands, and hopelessly at her mercy, as formerly my unfortunate body had been.

Formerly there was necessarily some limit, for she had no hold upon me. But now, by my own act, with Maud's assistance, I was at her mercy and my future, I felt, was in her hands.

Dire were the threats she used that evening when she had me brought down to her bedroom. I quailed before the storm and not understanding all that she threatened me with I took the earliest opportunity of consulting a dictionary.

I was to be taken up to London to be unsexed, to be circumcised, to be castrated. I did not wish to become a Jew or a gelding. When I read the meaning of the words I all but fainted. Mademoiselle depicted my act in the blackest colours. But when after rating and abusing me for a quarter of an hour, she began to say that I had done Maud an irreparable injury, I wept, for my heart pulsated, transiently, but really, for that dear girl. I was still under the influence of the ineffable delight which she had given me in her arms. I still felt as though her soft, warm, yielding form lay beneath mine. And while we had lain on the floor naked, strapped back to back, we had exchanged vows of perpetual devotion, an offensive and defensive alliance which was to terminate with but the life of one of us.

The upshot — the immediate result — of the matter was that Mademoiselle concluded that when she had had Maud well syringed she had done all she could do.

Things were to go on as before — if she had before beaten me with whips, she would now do so with scorpions.

It was arranged that in three days Mademoiselle and Elise would take me to London to be unsexed, circumcised, and castrated; that the meantime was to be spent by me in Mademoiselle's bedroom and the room opening off it where I was to sleep, so that I might be a close prisoner and never out of her sight; that I was to spend those three days naked, and upon bread and water, and was to be birched each morning — first by Maud, then by Beatrice, then by Agnes; then, on my return, I was to be handed over to Lady Alfred Ridlington, who was invited to pay Mademoiselle a long visit.

The idea of being unsexed filled me with nervous terrors as I stood quaking and naked before my furious governess who looked simply lovely in her anger. I consoled myself by the reflection that I had at least escaped the remainder of my term under Elise and her diabolical cruelties also. And I think my quiescence somewhat mollified Mademoiselle. I was devoutly glad the secret was to be kept from my parents.

Nothing befell Elise. Mademoiselle no doubt found it impossible; the deprivation of my three day's subjection to her was, I suppose, considered penance sufficient.

As for Maud, for some time I could not learn her fate. I know it now.

Beatrice was told nothing.

I gazed at Mademoiselle and hope sprang in my bosom; now, now that I knew all, now that the cat was out of the bag, might I indulge it?

She too gazed at me voluptuously. My appearance was not lost upon her, as her movements as she lectured me shew.

"Come here," she said, at its conclusion, putting her legs apart as I advanced.

And for my part, as I have hinted, Mademoiselle's appearance was not lost upon me; it was ravishing, and gradually as I stood meekly before her, it obliterated my tender recollections and thoughts of Maud and the sensation of the embrace which still lingered so vividly that I could have almost believed it still endured.

"Come here," said Mademoiselle, moving voluptuously, in her low musical voice, her liquid eyes resting upon me with a slight sparkle of amusement in them as she observed my confusion which was increasing minute by minute.

Mademoiselle's tone had however been so severe and her attitude so angry and indignant that I feared to give the slightest indication which might lead her to imagine I felt there was any relaxation of her strictness. She had spoken to me *de haut en bas*, sharply and uncompromisingly. Were I to ignore all this, pay no attention to it, brush it aside, go on as though nothing had happened, and as though I was conscious of no fault and she was scolding and purposed punishing me simply *pour les convenances* and not from sincere displeasure, I felt that I should do for myself.

I was reassured by her direction to approach her and by the movement which accompanied it. One which I intuitively knew presaged my having to make amends to a very sensitive part of her exquisite frame — a part which had evidently been tickled and much excited by the occurrence upstairs in Maud's bedroom.

Anything, any little thing of this kind I could do to please and propitiate Mademoiselle, I was only too eager to execute, congratulating myself that it was no worse. And fatigued as I was by the experiences of that day — sore from the frequent castigations of Elise, sore and my bottom and thighs waled by the merciless thrashing Mademoiselle had administered on the spot with her riding whip — still I felt my passions and emotions welling up within me as I watched my beautiful governess, and as a consciousness of my absolute nakedness before her and of the offence with which I was charged stole over me.

Elise had been sent for me to Maud's room. Poor Maud had been for some time suffering very much from the cramped position and the tightness with which we had been buckled together. What my physical sensations would have been had not the anguish I was suffering from the whip prevented my adverting to them I do not know. My wrists were strapped to Maud's wrists, my ankles to hers. We were back to back, and there was a heavy strap buckled tightly round our waists keeping us in close and exciting contact with each other.

We had been strapped together as Maud lay writhing on the floor, having just had her bottom waled, as I had had mine by Mademoiselle; and hers being more tender, no doubt the infliction had been proportionally more severe.

We made several attempts to rise, which were all unsuccessful, and resulted only in our rolling over each other.

Maud, I must say, was very generous. When her bitter tears ceased to flow and the acuteness of her pain passed away, she did not reproach me as I almost dreaded she would. I felt that it had been to some extent my fault. For although she had obliged me to place Mons. Priapus into her wet, warm, burning moustached mouth, yet when I encountered the obstacle, she had bidden me desist, although her eyes swam and were kindled by what I now knew to be desire and her cheeks burned with the rosiest, loveliest blushes. I had not desisted. I had not heeded her in the smallest degree. I had, on the contrary, thrown myself upon her with animal rage and fury, driving all before it, had torn open her delicate body and deluged her internally with the essence of myself. I felt aghast when I contemplated my deed. I felt it was kind and generous of her not to reproach me.

She was very anxious about the consequences.

"Beatrice had forbidden me to be a model for your Apollo," said I.

"What can Bee know?" answered Maud. "Even I do not know

why all this fuss is made. Of course I know it was very dreadful your putting that terrible thing of yours into — into me — where — where *you did*." I could feel her flush as she said this. "And then it went into such a fit, such throbs, like a steam engine. I could feel it to my finger tips — to the tips of my ears. Oh, Julian, it was nice! And really, I believe, because it was so naughty. And then it shot out some delicious wet that was like balm to a sore place. Oh, to think of it! Oh, how nice! Still, was it dirty? I suppose that is why Mademoiselle had me syringed so quickly before it could poison my blood or anything. But I do not see why they should make such a fuss about it. Mademoiselle does many worse things herself, as she must know I am aware. If you had not torn me open, you bad boy, they would never have found out. It was the blood that betrayed us. But I do not feel at all sore. In fact — in fact — oh, Julian, do you know, I should really like you to do it again. I feel I want it. I wonder whether there will ever be a chance?"

I was amazed at Maud's ignorance, and amused too; pluming myself on my superior knowledge. She spoke slowly, a sentence at a time, and I did not interrupt her, for I wished to ascertain exactly what she knew and I learnt she knew nothing! I was bursting with anxiety to impart my knowledge but I held my tongue until she had quite finished. Then I said, "Don't you know, Maud, I should have been a model for a living Apollo."

"Whatever do you mean, Julian?"

"Why, that is how babies are made!"

"How babies are made!" she cried. "Nonsense! How do you know?"

"Mademoiselle told me."

"Told you! Did — did you do it to her?" Maud's tone suddenly changed towards me as she asked this question. Had I answered in the affirmative I was convinced she would have been so jealous, that for a time, at any rate, she would have had nothing to do with me. Fortunately, I was able to answer: "No."

All the years that have elapsed since the period I am speaking of, have failed to teach me the reason of this desire in each individual woman to exclusively possess all the men whom she favours. My petticoats, my being so long treated as a female, my experiences with Lord Alfred Ridlington in the conservatory have given me a great insight into the mystery of female feelings, into the sensations of a woman when bestowing her choicest favours. And what I have yet to relate has deepened this insight. But although I can understand her coveting exclusive possession, I have never been able to regard it as reasonable.

"No," repeated Maud. "Then how can you know? Do you mean Mademoiselle told you in so many words? She can never have had the face to do that!"

I was on the point of saying like a fool that I had longed to do it to Mademoiselle and so found out, but I stopped in time.

"She gave me a psychological lesson and I discovered it incidentally," I said with as much nonchalance as possible.

"And what can Beatrice have meant about the Apollo? You and Bee were chums from the first. She must know."

I confess I felt very much puzzled myself as to what Beatrice knew and the real reason for the promise she had so pertinaciously extracted from me. I recollected also that I was bound on parole to Beatrice for five years and it struck me that if she discovered what had occurred between Maud and me it would be excessively awkward for me. She would, no doubt, regard it as a breach of allegiance to her for I knew that I had for a time given myself to Maud as completely as a man can give himself to anyone and yet I was not my own to give.

These reflections seriously increased my discomfort. It was bad enough to find myself absolutely in Mademoiselle's hands and I was far from pleased at the prospect of a score to settle with Beatrice as well. Strange to say I felt more disturbance on her account than on Mademoiselle's, and I explain the fact by Beatrice's possessing much more control over my spiritual being than Mademoiselle, the confines of whose sway were my animal existence.

A spark of the divine fire of love had fallen from Beatrice's eyes into my bosom and had there kindled a flame which permeated all the ramifications of my existence. One curious result was that I willingly submitted to corporal punishment from her as it appeared to bring my sensual organisation into subjection to my soul, which was hers, and consequently in some esoteric mode gave me the gratifying sense of being possessed by her, of being wrapt in her, of having the same springs of life, of drawing our existence from the same source; of having my mind, my feelings, and senses bounded by her own; of, in short, entire subordination to her.

Maud's limbs were beautiful, round, and plump, her skin was white and clear, and my happiness had been great. Why did I torment myself with the unseen and the mental, possessing so complete a sensual anodyne as I did. Maud was not complimented by my silence while my brain was occupied by these ideas, and giving me a jerk with her hand, repeated the question: what I thought Beatrice could know, as she had forbidden me to become a model?

"Oh, I suppose she did not wish you to see me naked! She did not wish you to study me anatomically."

"What nonsense! We have all seen your anatomy, your *bottom*, and — and — that thing you put into — me. Don't you remember how often we have birched your bottom, and besides yesterday, when Elise had drawn your skin back, and you had to ask us one by one to set you right — what more is there to conceal?"

"I had petticoats and things on then — being completely naked before you would give you a more exact idea of me which, I suppose, Beatrice wished to keep for herself."

"Greedy thing! Anyhow — oh, Julian, I have had such thorough possession of you — at that supreme moment not long ago, I seemed to be *you*; to know and control your vital centres, mental and physical. You had no secrets then from me; the revelation you made of yourself was complete."

"Yes, Maud, dear; and it ought to be incarnated and reproduced."

"Oh, Julian, do you think I shall have — have a — a *baby?*"

"That abominable syringe may prevent it."

"Oh, what a crime. And yet imagine me with a baby and unmarried. You would have to marry me, Julian!"

Now I must frankly confess that I could not marry them all.

I did not wish to marry Maud.

However, maiden like, she saved me from the embarrassment the necessity of a reply would have occasioned. When she uttered these words she pressed herself amorously against me; she did not stop there.

She was lying on her left side, I, of course, my back being against hers, was on my right. She moved her right arm, which was strapped to my left, backwards across me with pretty hesitation, and soon grasped her friend Mons. Priapus and played with him.

"If — if you — married — me —" she ejaculated, "how — how — I would make that fellow work."

And her body was suffused with a warm glow.

I slipped my left arm through, between her and the floor, and returned the compliment to her womanhood.

I do not believe that equality of the sexes will ever be established until the seat of a woman's womanhood is transferred from between her legs to her head. A man exists for something else than for procreation. But it is the beginning and the end of a woman.

"Love," says the poet, "is woman's whole existence." It is all that she seeks, whatever she may affect; and if you can tickle her clitoris, either with your fingers or by way of her imagination, she will obey you as exactly as a vessel with steerage obeys the helm.

It is all very fine, though, for me to boast, for I remember how I was made to obey, a few days later, when a female hand proved to be a very effectual rudder.

"Maud, dear, take care! If you excite me too much, whoever comes to fetch us will find out. I do not want any more whipping."

"No, poor boy; you have had your share. How Elise smacked you in the workroom! I told you," archly, "you would soon find out you were powerless in the presence of petticoats. A lady's whip and birch can bite, cannot they? Never mind, Julian, we shall have more fun yet. Oh — oh — oh. Naughty boy," she exclaimed, as I tickled her. "Oh — oh — oh — oh, do stop. I do not wish to be whipped again either, I can tell you."

"What a nuisance these straps are. They must be making you quite sore, Maud; they hurt me very much. I wonder whatever Mademoiselle will do."

"Oh," replied Maud, "she cannot do much; but she will, no doubt, make us both *feel*, and excruciatingly too."

"The mixture of pain and pleasure is odd. In fact, some pain is pleasure."

"Oh, Julian, I wish you would tell me how you felt when Mademoiselle first birched you. How dreadful it must have been for you, a big boy, to have had your trousers taken off before us girls and your bare bottom birched by your governess in her bedroom."

"The sting soon drove all ideas of the kind out of my mind. It is all pleasure and no pain," said I, anxious to turn the subject; for I knew that if Mademoiselle found I tattled, I should lose all chance of sugar-plums from her, "to be here fixed to a beautiful big girl" — putting my finger into her — "quite naked."

My old trick of analysing, into which I hereupon again fell, then kept me quiet.

It will be remembered, perhaps, with surprise, that I had not seen any female quite naked until Elise, having syringed Maud, very violently stripped her with Mademoiselle's superintending assistance, and laid her, as I had myself been laid across the bed, to be flogged. I had been in Mademoiselle's bed between her legs, I had also been between them underneath her petticoats. I had been made rudely acquainted with the maid's bottoms, but had only seen pieces of nakedness — breasts — legs — thighs — at one time. The statues in Mademoiselle's *boudoir* were my nearest approach to knowledge of the divine feminine form in a condition of absolute nudity. I now called to mind their exquisite shapes, their full bosoms, their admirably rounded backs, their thighs under which I longed to be crushed. When Maud had been stripped before me, my own sufferings from the cruel whip were much too severe to permit me to dwell upon the spectacle. But now I was back to back with her absolutely naked. It was the fact that she was a girl, that she was feminine and I male, which gave such piquancy. But she had possessed me while she had on her petticoats, and they certainly emphasized the difference of sex. I distinctly recollect that when she was undressed a vague sense of disappointment stole over me to find that after all she had a body and two legs like myself.

Wherein does the charm, the esoteric feminine magnetism, lie? In petticoats? Verily petticoats, drawers, corsets, long silk stockings, have a powerful and mysterious influence.

Maud, naked, did not possess the same power over me as Maud in her petticoats. When I lay extended in an absolutely nude state before Beatrice, it was the fact that she was clothed and I naked which I felt so keenly. Had she also been naked I should not have suffered so much shame. There is no severer ordeal for a young man than to be naked in the presence of clothed damsels. Whence the subtle influence of clothes? If women abandon their garments in favour of a "rational" costume, they will at the same time lose much of their empire over men.

Macaulay, in his history of England, reflects that: "The poison which they (certain writers) administered was so strong, that it was in no long time rejected with nausea. None of them understood the dangerous act of associating images of unlawful pleasure with all that is endearing and ennobling. None of them was aware that a certain decorum is essential even to voluptuousness, that drapery may be more alluring than exposure, and that the imagination may be more powerfully moved by delicate hints which impel it to exert itself, than by gross descriptions which it takes in passively." Certainly, if woman be an image of unlawful pleasure, she, I reflected, thoroughly does understand the whole art and craft of associating her lovely self with endearing and ennobling petticoats, frilled, and tucked, and laced, with a glimpse half revealing the exquisite beauties stimulated imagination then depicts as concealed.

Had I lived in the times when Courts of Love were held, I should have proposed the question:— Whether a lover was happier who saw his mistress naked than he who saw her *en grande tenue*, and I should have required at the hands of every member of the tribunal a written and closely reasoned judgment.

For another aspect now presents itself of the question. If I was in possession of my mistress naked, I should wish to be clothed! Here my soliloquy was interrupted by Elise opening the door.

Elise! I dreaded to see her again.

Maud also had her own cogitations, for the moment before Elise's arrival she had remarked to me: "I do not think Mademoiselle will dare to say much to me when she hears that I know she shewed you the way. She shewed him the way, she shewed him the way to woo," hummed Maud.

There was no time for reply. But it struck me that we might be a very happy family and the father and mother of a whole generation if things were only properly and sensibly managed. On the other hand even at that age I plainly, with a boy's acuteness, perceived that if Mademoiselle Hortense de Chambonnard found that she was becoming entangled and in danger of losing prestige, she would choose the most favourable opportunity for bursting the whole thing up. There was one thing I could plainly perceive my Haughty governess would never endure and that was restraint of any description. I believe my father himself was afraid of her.

Mademoiselle had all my letters and the only news she vouchsafed to me was that my parents were quite well and glad to hear that I had arrived safely and that they hoped I would be very good and obey Mademoiselle in all things.

Chapter II

Retribution — "Saeva Venus"

"Now, you beast, you horrid pig! I cannot bear to touch you! I wonder Mademoiselle has left you close to your cousin whom you have outraged — lent to her, taken to her studio — to abuse these favours — to outrage her — to put that beastly rank thing into her. Ah! Miss Maud, if I had my way, I would put something hot into his arse."

Elise unstrapped us.

"Why do I not send for a dog whip from the hall? Why do I not lash you both on the floor? *Hein!* I should enjoy it! What will become of me? What will Mademoiselle not charge me with? I trusted you. Miss Maud, you betrayed me. Mademoiselle has said nothing, not at all. Dat is worse," went on Elise, in her fright forgetting her English, which she usually spoke with great correctness. "Dat is ver bad. When Mademoiselle say notink, she mean a vast deal. She will turn me out — out into de guttah, and all becos dis beast, dis animal, dis lecherous goat here. And I had pinched him, and smacked him, and pulled him, till I thought he was emasculate. I did; and den he go and get you with tild. Beast! *Sacré —.*"

I arose; so did Maud. Elise grasped Maud's arm, led her to the bedstead, and passing her arms round one of its posts, strapped Maud's hands behind her, confining her to the bed.

Full of my reflections, I gazed into her eyes. Her form was displayed to me and there was no pain to distract my contemplation of it. She flushed a lovely pink as I gazed, and instantly recalling my own nakedness I averted my eyes.

This was due to the presence of a third person. Hereafter, when one mode of Beatrice's chastisement of my fault is narrated, this will be remembered.

Elise, who was exceedingly crestfallen, then took me by the ear with her left hand. She gave me several sounding spanks upon my sore bottom and finally slipped her hand through, from the back, to my testicles.

Of course he soon reared his head.

Elise turned me towards Maud: "Now, Miss Maud, if I had my way you should be made to suck that thing with your mouth — yes, with your mouth."

I hung my head in ignominious captivity, Elise nipping my ear. Maud said never a word. Ignoring Elise, she looked at me significantly, and perhaps a little sadly. What a lovely prisoner she made. Would that I had been in the room alone with her fixed in that manner, her breast, her body, her limbs exposed and helpless.

Elise led me out into the passage, along it, and down the stairs, perfectly naked.

"I won't go naked," I had exclaimed, and had received such a blow in reply that I went. The blow had been administered upwards from behind, just avoiding what it might have seriously injured; and then Elise again slipped her hand through, and holding my ear with the left hand and my virility with the right, marched me on.

"Where are you taking me to?"

"Where do you think? To Mademoiselle."

We met Agnes on the way.

"Oh, Elise," she exclaimed, gazing at me, "stop a moment." She blushed all over. Elise vigorously fingered me. "Oh, let me look at him! Oh! Oh! Oh!" and she was plainly overcome by her feelings.

Elise told Agnes to be ashamed of herself; and quickly pushing me along the corridor, ushered me into Mademoiselle's bedroom.

"Perhaps you would like Miss Agnes, you pig!"

"There, I told you that you would have cause to remember this room. Mary pointed it out to you the very first day of your arrival. Get in, you pig," giving my ear an extra pinch and jerk. "I hope she will leave you to me. If she does —"

The twilight of the May evening had already fallen when Elise opened Mademoiselle's door, and I found the curtains drawn and the lamps lighted.

Mademoiselle had taken off her riding attire and was clothed in the softest and most bewitching *deshabille*. Her tea wrapper of delicate pink *batiste* showed her bosom beneath it; her feet in morocco slippers and pink stockings, dangled over the side of the couch on which she luxuriously reclined. Beside her, on a delicate little table, was a Sevres tea service, and the room was redolent of orange Pekoe. Her dark eyes were full of light, not of anger, but of pleasure I think, as I was led naked into her presence and bidden stand before her. She raised herself and directed Elise to retire and wait downstairs until rung for.

"So, Master Julian," she quietly said, "so, Master Julian, or how am I to call you with that great thing wagging in front of you?" I covered my face with my hands. "Mock modesty, I declare, I declare," she cried. "You seem shame-faced before me, but yet you put that thing into your cousin between her soft legs," moving, "into her warm flesh — so, you beast, you animal, you were determined in spite of all my lessons, to pluck the forbidden fruit!"

"Oh, Mademoiselle!"

"Yes, and although you professed such love, and such admiration for me — what are all your professions worth? What shall I do to you, wretch? You have ruined Maud, I shall write to your father — yes — I shall disgrace you."

"Oh! Mademoiselle!"

"I shall disgrace you; unless body and soul you give yourself up to whatever fate I may determine for you. You will?"

"Yes."

"Kneel down. You shall be naked for three days in that room," pointing, "and here you shall have two hours' exercise naked, daily, and I will take care your cousins play with you. You shall be birched every morning first by Maud, next by Beatrice, and then by Agnes; then I shall take you to town and you shall be unsexed."

"Oh! Oh! Oh!"

"Circumcised."

"Oh! Oh! Oh!"

"Castrated — that thing cut off — so that you will be for ever unable to take any more maidenheads. You wretch, how could I otherwise keep you!"

I held my tongue. Why place obstacles in a torrent's way, to make it eddy, and whirl, and foam?

"Will you submit to all this, or shall I write by this post to your father?"

"Oh, Mademoiselle, I will," said I trembling, "submit to you." Strange infatuation, but any fate out of *her* hands, would, I felt, be certainly worse than any in them.

If I had taken her at her word and declined her terms I know she would have been in a fix.

"How dared you, you bold bad boy" (this was better) "put that dreadful engine into your cousin? I shew you what it would do. How had you the face to let it work inside a girl? Come here," she said, ravishingly moving her leg. "Come here, I will give you a dose really this time!"

She pulled a stool to the side of the couch and placed a cushion upon it. I approached her. She bid me lie flat down with the back of my head on the cushion. She lifted her garments and her left leg. She had pink silk drawers on and they whisked across my face. Her hairy mouth soon touched mine. "I shall punish you with that," she said. "You have been whipped enough."

The pressure was so great that I used my hands to lessen it.

"Get up," she cried; and tying my hands behind me with her dainty handkerchief, she soon had me underneath her again, but now altogether unable to help myself. I knew where my duty lay and I performed it. The event happened. I was still held.

"Have you swallowed it *all*?" she asked, lifting up her petticoats so as to uncover my head and give me a welcome sight of her shapely thighs and limbs encased in the wide pink satin drawers, the make of which left what I had been kissing and the insides of her legs naked.

I had a full view of the Mount of Venus and of the bushy wood in whose recesses dwelt the spring of her being. The thickness, strength, and luxuriance of her black hair both astonished and alarmed me. Then slowly carrying my glance upwards from her exquisite navel to her face and looking into her mischievous eyes, I answered with my mouth all sticky: "Yes, dear Mademoiselle, I have swallowed it."

"All?"

"Yes, all."

"Very well. Now I shall give you something to wash it down with."

She wriggled in the sofa as she said this, and slipping quite to its edge I again felt the weight of her divine form oppress my head. I dreaded what was coming; I shuddered but dared not move or protest. She carefully removed her drawers and chemise from about my face and head to prevent their being wetted. Then she rubbed herself about me until she had parted the hairs and placed the wet lips of the mouth with a moustache against mine, holding me fast with her thighs meanwhile.

She did not content herself with mere contact, but continued with firm determination to press me until my mouth was wide open and she felt her clitoris against my teeth and tongue. I at once tickled it with the tip of my tongue and she gave a gentle movement or two plainly denoting satisfaction.

But as the horrible idea struck me that possibly she intended not to restrain herself and meant to drench me in that position a feeling of deadly sickness spread over me. I broke out into a cold sweat, and made an involuntary attempt to escape. Down on my back under my governess, held by her strong thighs, my hands tied behind me, this attempt was abortive, and only increased the strictness of her grasp.

I felt the taste of her warm and liquid flesh in my mouth and its rawness. The rolls of flesh unfolded themselves more and more each time she rubbed me. I knew how she was exciting herself and the pleasure she enjoyed both by this expansion and by the quick breathing which accompanied it. Little love calls and exclamations of rapture, dulled by the clothing over me, also stole upon my ears.

Suddenly was a longer breath than usual; then another — in fact, a sigh. I had hardly begun to tickle her again with my tongue, when, while it was yet extended, the floodgates were opened.

I endeavoured not to swallow and my mouth consequently was soon filled and it overflowed into my nostrils, my eyes, and ears; choking, blinding, and drowning me. I was compelled to cough and splutter and swallow a quantity to save myself from suffocation. I struggled, but Mademoiselle held me deliberately and rigidly. She gathered up her skirts to prevent their being drenched, but kept me fast until she had quite finished.

Mad, exasperated, and sick, I gulped and gulped, and, willy-nilly, swallowed mouthful after mouthful. A large quantity ran on the rug, on to the floor, but quite a stream was forced down my throat.

"There," she said, triumphantly, "how do you like that? I do enjoy pissing upon you above all things; it is the only thing you really seem to mind. It does take it out of you and punish you."

I spat and spluttered, too disgusted, too horrified, and too angry to speak, too much tamed to show any anger.

"Now," continued Mademoiselle, looking complacently at me, "I shall try an experiment which has been recommended to me by a German friend as a capital means of curing bad boys' indulgence of uncontrolled passion."

Chapter III

A Hint from Caesar

I continued to cough and splutter and wished to spit, but I dared not. Mademoiselle, with refined severity quietly waited, for she had noticed my coughing up what I could, until I was obliged to again swallow what I had coughed up.

Then, with a wicked smile, she directed me to walk over to the wash-hand-stand. Upon it stood a jug whence she poured a quantity of musky-coloured water into a tumbler and placed it to my lips, bidding me drink it. I protested. I said I could not possibly hold any more, but Mademoiselle was inexorable, and holding my head by the hair, forced the rim of the tumbler between my lips (my hands were still tied), and its contents — warm mustard and water — down my throat. I was made to drain the glass. It was an emetic, intended to make me sick. To that in itself I did not object, but the idea of the passage of all that wine up again through my throat and mouth made me feel very bad indeed.

Then Mademoiselle made me kneel down. She placed a pot in front of me, and stood opposite. I noticed she had in her hand a long quill pen with feathers on both its sides. I was not long left to wonder what use she intended to put it to.

"Now, Master Julian," she said, standing over me with her left hand resting on my bare shoulder, "throw your head back as far as possible and open your mouth as wide as ever you can."

I already began to feel qualms and did not at once comply.

"If you do not immediately do as I tell you," observed Mademoiselle very sternly, "I will gag you as you have been and then try again."

I meekly threw my head back and opened my mouth.

"Now," said Mademoiselle, her left hand upon my forehead, and proceeding to tickle first the roof of my mouth, then the palate and sides, then the uvula and throat, making occasional dabs down it with the feather which soon made me retch, "now you must submit to being punished by me. It is doing you good already; that male factor between your legs," she cried, glancing at it, "is not half the size he was when I commenced."

"Ugh — ugh! I shall be sick."

"Hold your tongue and keep your mouth open."

141

I knew I must soon vomit. What a diabolical idea! What a horrid, disgusting mode of treatment!

"When Julius Caesar — no, you must not attempt to catch the feather with your teeth" — giving me a slap in the cheek — "visited Cicero, the latter was extremely flattered by Caesar's taking a vomitory before dinner. He regarded it" — I felt I should faint; a deadly paleness, a cold sweat, a fearful feeling of sickness possessed me; Mademoiselle's words seemed far off — "as an earnest good fellowship, as an assurance on Caesar's part that he intended in good faith to do full justice to his hospitality. Now you will please vomit. Yes, here, before me into that vessel as a punishment, in obedience to me, your mistress; and to show the good disposition you have to do honour to the bread and water which is all you will have for the next few days, unless, indeed, it should again enter my head to give you some other beverage, and" — looking fiercely at me — "perhaps some other food, too."

She could not mean — she would not dare! My condition, the constant retching, prevented my continuing unbroken any thread or sequence of ideas.

"Yes," she went on, confirming my worst apprehensions, "Elise has just reminded me that there is something behind as well as before by which you can be punished; and, as she said, you are such an utter reprobate I really think you deserve it."

My mouth filled. I spat it out. Mademoiselle pulled my head back and tickled my throat more vigorously and lower down. A cough, a choke, a perfect flood. A few minute's rest, a few groans, during which Mademoiselle let me rest against her. Again that irresistible overpowering sense of sickness.

"Shall I send for Maud, to console you?" asked Mademoiselle.

"No; only let me lie down." The mere idea of having anything to do with a woman was at that time abhorrent to my soul.

"Ah! I see," said Mademoiselle, "my friend was right. Her prescription was a good one. I have never seen this thing," she said, touching my shrivelled affair, "so small, so lifeless, before."

She made me rinse my mouth with Condy's fluid and water, and then put me to bed in the other room, leaving the door between it and her own room open. She covered me up and I soon fell asleep.

Chapter IV

Elise — The Last Time

When I awoke it was evidently late in the evening for Elise was undressing Mademoiselle and what had awakened me was the angry sound of Mademoiselle's voice.

"You must do as I order you, Elise, or leave the house tomorrow morning without a character. You allowed him to outrage Miss Maud, and if I am to retain you in my service, you must be punished by being yourself outraged in the same way. Go and fetch that great big canvas linen bag. You have finished my hair. You may take twenty minutes to make up your mind while I see how he is."

"If I do, Mademoiselle, I will give it to him, I will torture, I will tear him, I will —"

"You may punish him as you please," Mademoiselle answered in her calm unruffled tones.

Elise left the room and Mademoiselle came to me.

She was in a dressing gown and her lovely hair, falling over her shoulders, was tied in large knots at intervals for the night.

I lay on my back with my eyes open.

Mademoiselle asked me how I was, and brought me some chicken broth and delicious white Vienna bread, with a glassful of some clear sparkling frothy liquid.

I was startled, was it — just fresh?

Mademoiselle laughed. "No," she said. "No, Julian, it is not — not — not Elixir — it is Veuve Cliquot. I mean," quickly catching her words, "not widow's water, her wine — Champagne."

I was not quite satisfied even yet. It might, I thought, still be a joke at my expense. Mademoiselle's mischief knew no bounds. She, however, put the glass to my lips, and I could not refuse to take a sip. It was wine, and excellent.

There was a knock at the door, and Elise, bidden to enter, came through into the room in which we were. Elise, wearing such an angry, depressed, crestfallen countenance as I had never thought possible for her, held in her hands a great brown canvas bag — one of the bags in fact in which the household linen weekly went to the laundry in the outbuildings. "There," she said, throwing it on the floor with a gesture of disgust.

"Well, Elise, have you decided, have you made up your mind?

Will you submit or go?" Mademoiselle asked, amused at Elise's air.

"Mademoiselle," she answered, choking, "it is too bad, too wicked, too disgraceful, to treat a young woman so —"

"Now, Elise," interrupted Mademoiselle, "yes, or no?"

"I can't say no."

"Exactly! You are aware your breach of trust, your abominable dereliction of duty, deserve the severest punishment. Miss Maud no longer a virgin — through *your* fault; and this jackanapes here is in possession of the experience necessary to enable him to beguile every woman in the house into becoming a mother, all through your fault," said Mademoiselle, standing in the middle of the now brilliantly lighted room, her eyes flashing. "Undress yourself," she added, peremptorily.

"Not before him," retorted Elise, growing pale.

"Yes, before him. Stay! Get up, Julian — stand with your back to the bedpost." And drawing my arms round it behind my back, she tied my wrists together with her handkerchief, fixing me exactly as Elise had fixed Maud upstairs.

Mademoiselle then told Elise to undress.

Slowly she did so, until, at length, she too was stark naked.

Looking foolish, but still more angry, she went into Mademoiselle's room for a birch which she brought her mistress and handed to her upon her knees. Mademoiselle caressed the green slender well-budded twigs positively with affection and twisted the rod three or four times through the air with supreme satisfaction. Elise had then to lie over a *pouf*, placed exactly in front of me, and to spread her legs wide asunder. I saw and gazed at all she possessed — her muttering did not prevent my doing so although it undoubtedly sounded ominous — but as I had already made a full acquaintance with her thighs and bottom, I wondered why she troubled to conceal them with petticoats. I was struck by the very different impression given by a partial view of nakedness from that given by the complete revelation. Elise was a lovely girl, not so slender or delicate as Mademoiselle, but certainly lovely.

She placed herself in position and received thirty-six slow, deliberate stripes which Mademoiselle delivered with all her force.

Elise writhed and twisted, but took the punishment bravely, not crying out but sobbing quietly.

Presently, however, she shrieked. At the close of the punishment with the birch, Mademoiselle bade Elise remain as she was, and went into her room, when I heard her open a drawer. She returned holding a round stick about a foot long and as thick as the butt end of a billiard-cue, in her hand; from its end depended several knotted pieces of whipcord. The moment Elise, who was still lying on the *pouf*, caught a glimpse of this, she jumped up and danced about the room.

"No, no, no, Mademoiselle! Oh, no! Oh, I pray, I do beseech, I do implore" — she cried aghast with terror. Mademoiselle, for all reply, lifted her arm and gave her a swish about the buttocks. Elise screamed.

"Elise, lie down directly; or I shall give you a dozen instead of half a dozen. And do not scream any more unless you wish to be gagged," directed Mademoiselle, quietly, but severely. Elise seemed positively beside herself — positively distraught. I thought she was mad when she lay down on her back.

"Spread out your legs," said Mademoiselle.

Elise obeyed.

Mademoiselle lifted her arm and giving the cords full swing, brought them down with a vicious force, lengthwise, between her legs, full upon "Miss Elise," whom I had had to kiss more than once. I shuddered and trembled. The torture appeared severe beyond expression. Five times more Mademoiselle's arm rose and fell with the utmost precision and deliberation, and at each blow Elise yelled.

This is the mode in which in Spain, in Holland, in Paraguay, the Jesuits punished their naughty female penitents; and, strange to say, notwithstanding the pleasure subsequently felt, quite extinguished the pain, under which it is not unusual for the delinquent to faint.

Elise did not faint but lay gasping, totally oblivious of the exhibition she was making of herself to me, when Mademoiselle had given her the sixth lash.

I recollected reading in a note to Gibbon's *History*, of the Empress Theodora, Justinian's wife, having lain on her back in a theatre in public, her clothes turned over her breast, while geese pecked from her abdomen and navel and generative organs the gilded grains of corn which had been scattered over them in order that they might endure the blows of the bird's beaks.

There lay Elise, like the Empress Theodora, in a strange trance.

I dreaded to attract Mademoiselle's attention in her then mood — I did not know but that horrid little scourge might be turned upon me — but what with the warmth of the apartment, the state of nervous erethism in which I was from the terrible discipline of another kind I had gone through, and what with the spectacle I had witnessed, I found myself in a state of extreme erection.

Mademoiselle unloosed my hands. Her feelings appeared to be such that she could not speak. Leaving Elise, she took me violently into the next room, threw herself into a chair, reclining almost on her back, and, apparently dead to all idea of modesty, drew her skirts up to her waist, displaying her beautiful naked limbs to my admiring eyes.

She pointed between them. Three times again had I to indulge her passion with my mouth and tongue.

Elise was lying on the bed, her head on her arm, when Mademoiselle led me again into the room.

Mademoiselle led me up to the bed and again fastened my hands behind me.

"Lie on your back, Elise. Excite him with your hands, ask him to — to fuck you."

"Oh, Mademoiselle, before you! Oh!" fingering my testicles, her legs stretched out on each side of me as I knelt on the bed over her. "Master Julian —" moving to and fro.

"Oh, Mademoiselle, oh, I can't ask him! I will make him — it is too humiliating to ask. Beside I cannot say dat word."

"Obey, Elise, or you shall have another half dozen cuts."

Elise put her arms about me and drew me now to her face, at the same time placing one of her legs across my back.

"You shall be put to bed with her as a horse is put in a box with a mare, you animal," said Mademoiselle. "Come, Elise, put it in. Stop though, first say what I told you."

"Please, Master Julian, will you fuck me?" And then, having uttered the terrible word, she spasmodically caught me to her bosom.

One hand forced me into her wet warm body. Mademoiselle gently birched me. Then Mademoiselle, with her hand upon the piston, counted the throbs.

"Now, Master Julian, for fucking my maid in my presence, you will have a dozen lashes on the soles of your feet!"

Mademoiselle easily fixed them to the bedrail at the foot, and gave me half a dozen stripes on the sole of each foot with the birch rod. They hurt a good deal, and caused a curious tingling sensation in my feet and legs which lasted many hours.

I felt disgraced beyond measure at what I had been compelled to do in Mademoiselle's sight to Elise. Nakedness! Nakedness was nothing to it. There was now no secret function of my frame unknown to my governess.

As we still lay on the bed Mademoiselle picked up the canvas linen bag and bid Elise hold me. Elise again wound her arms about my shoulders and her legs about my own. Then Mademoiselle opened the mouth of the bag (which was closed by means of a running tape), as wide as it would go, and slipping its mouth under Elise's heels she gradually worked it up to her shoulders, enclosing Elise and myself inside the bag.

Horror of horrors — how long was I to be kept, my hands tied, in that close proximity to Mademoiselle's maid? She was much stronger than Maud; just now when she had "had" me, I felt as if she were drawing my life out of me, her power of suction was so enormous. No sooner had Mademoiselle got the bag above Elise's shoulders and up to the nape of my neck than Elise's hands had immediately sought out my male engine. "I will punish him, I will," she hissed from between her teeth.

I gave a slight scream. She was twisting my testicles round and round with her hand and then had caught hold of the foreskin and was forcing it back.

"One moment, Elise," said Mademoiselle, placing one of her hands on the mouth of the bag while with the other she drew the tapes tight so that the mouth closed round our necks. When she had closed it so that our heads were fastened closely together, she knotted the strings and put them where neither Elise nor I could get at them.

"There, now do what you like, Elise," her hand over my body, outside the bag. "Acquit yourself like a gallant youth, Julian!"

On to the top of us she then bundled a feather bed, and over that a large eiderdown, and so left us in the dark. Elise's breath and mine mingled. We soon began to perspire, to sweat, and to stew. Elise would not keep her hands quiet, and I could not protect myself, deprived as I was of the total use of mine.

"Now, you vagabond, you wretch who have made me be prostituted, you will just beg and pray and beseech me to pardon, and I will punish you as I did upstairs."

Whereupon she caught my unhappy implement, swollen as it

was by her exciting fingers, and notwithstanding my cries and supplications, forced back the foreskin, hurting me cruelly, rubbing my raw flesh against the bristling hairs of her navel — her leg across my back preventing me from moving my body even so slightly away as the width of the bag would have permitted.

The greatest, because the most perpetual and unavoidable cause of discomfort was undoubtedly the narrow tape running the wide hem at the mouth of the linen bag for the purpose of closing it. Had the tape been wider, had it been fastened about any other part of our bodies — the annoyance would have been less. There was my face fixed close to Elise's as she snarled at me. I could not avoid catching her breath or breathing into her face to her great vexation.

When she spoke, and, forgetting the string, attempted to move her head to the ordinary distance, she found herself brought up by a sharp jerk emphasised by the tape and finding my face still close to hers, notwithstanding her endeavour to remove from it, she was, of course, the more exasperated.

And, vice versa, if I moved, in blushful forgetfulness of the tie which bound us, I gave her a pull which she promptly resented.

She could not get out her hands to slap my face; she therefore slapped my body with all the force she could muster in the confines of the bag, pinched it, and gave me sudden blows with her knees.

She complained of the warmth of my breath, and of my weight; every movement was checked suddenly and unexpectedly by the tape — a perpetual source of irritation, a very ingenious contrivance on Mademoiselle's part.

For the prayers which now, at Elise's order, I entered upon for forgiveness, were seriously hampered, having to be uttered in her immediate neighbourhood. However, my only hope of pacifying her lay in their accomplishment.

I found it difficult to put much heart in them principally because, as Mademoiselle had said, I was gone on the subject of being incarnated. It may have been because Elise was a lower order of animal that I cared nothing about her receptivity, her passion, her being. Besides I was being forced into the most abject entreaties to be permitted to do that which I did not at all desire to perform.

Elise made me beg and implore her to permit me to do to her what Mademoiselle had made her ask me for.

She had a smooth skin, a beautiful body, which I felt close against mine; this was my only encouragement. A purely animal one. I had no psychical encouragement, but intense psychical aversion to overcome. This was, of course, the point of Mademoiselle's punishment; this was why she chose to confine me with a woman in a bag.

Elise's hand had not been quiet all this time. Tired of my weight upon her she had placed me at her side.

She had much interrupted my thoughts by the manner in which she twiddled my testicles, interlaced her legs with mine, rubbed my bottomland pressed her fingers forcibly against my rear. When she did that, Love used his wings and I felt myself become a beast. Her evolutions seemed to excite her more than myself.

Pressing her lips against mine, she inserted her tongue into my mouth, and at the same instant catching Mons. Priapus, moved her hand to and fro upon him drawing the foreskin to and fro with it, thus performing with her hand the office her hairy mouth should have performed. All ideas of decency, love, prostitution, copulation, stallions, mares, dogs, cats, Mademoiselle, Maud, Beatrice, quickly vanished from my mind under this treatment.

"Oh, Elise, let me put what you have in — your hand into — into you."

"Pig, you want to put your nasty rank smelling stick into my body — a fine, a modest idea! How dare you suggest such a thing to a lady! You would be at the tricks with me you practised with Miss Maud!"

She continued all the while exciting me to distraction.

"Oh, Elise! Elise! I know I have done very wrong; but forgive me, have some kindness for me!"

"Some kindness for you! What will that thing do when it is inside me?"

"Oh! You know."

"Yes, I do know. It will wet me, it will pollute me. Why should I have its nasty — injection — in my body?" kissing my lips and inserting her tongue.

"Then, why excite me so?"

"Excite you! Because I choose to. *Tiens!* I had to say the shameful word, so shall you."

"Now, Miss Elise. I do beg and pray of you."

As she moved her head she suddenly burst out: "Damn and blast this accursed tape —"

"Ah! Miss Elise, you are throttling me!"

Half reclining upon me she inserted one arm down my back between my arms which were bound together. The other hand she placed in front of me. I spasmodically contracted all my muscles in a supreme effort at fortitude.

Not one minute had passed, during which Elise's hands, which had suddenly seemed to become much stronger, were hard at work in back and front, before I cried: "Yes, yes, yes."

"Now ask," said Elise, abating the punishment.

"Please, Miss Elise, do let me —"

"Say the word."

"F—fu—fuck you. Please, Miss Elise, do let me fuck you."

She moved lasciviously.

"Do you want to, very much? Must you now — an hour hence, will that do?"

"Now, now," replied I, catching fire from her. "Now, let me, oh, pray let me fuck you."

She placed her lips to mine and rolled over on to the top of me. She clasped my shoulders with her arms, my body with her legs. One hand she put underneath me behind. She inserted him into her terrible engine. I feared he would be sucked off. He was inside her up to the hilt.

As she moved up and down, I felt myself becoming Elise. Her soft breasts, her body and legs, gave me much pleasure by their contact. The confinement of our heads was very irksome.

I forgot who she was individually. I recollected only that she was a woman.

The deed was done.

I lay happy and reconciled in her arms until the morning.

Chapter V

Maud

It was a long time after that I heard what had become of Maud.

In the first place for six weeks she was degraded to the rank of a scullery maid. All her own clothes were taken away and locked up. She was dressed in the short frocks and the coarse and common underclothing of a rude little village maiden. She was not permitted — great girl of twenty though she was — to wear drawers. In these short garments she was compelled to wash and scrub floors, dust the staircase, mount steps, and clean windows and pictures.

For the first ten days she was whipped, birched, three times each day. For rebellion or slovenliness she received smacks with the tawse, the fringed edge of which she hated and dreaded more than the birch.

She was sometimes dressed in a very short *chemise*; hung by the wrists to a bedpost, her feet only just touching the ground; or made to stand in the stocks in a stiff backboard, the collar of which was raised extravagantly high for long periods.

She was, at other times, fastened naked across the bed, well whipped, and left so for several hours. Every Tuesday and Friday she had to wear, during the morning, a nettle petticoat, and in the afternoon bunches of nettles were hung underneath her clothes.

Sometimes she was kept quite naked for several days so that she had the utmost humiliation to go through, and, in addition, she was repeatedly whipped in front.

It was many years later when I learned all this from Maud's own lips in Beatrice's presence; and her punishment proved to be a very efficient mortification of whatever pruriency she possessed.

This parenthetical notice of her fate seems to be needed here; her own description of her discipline must be referred to for an adequate idea of her punishment and of its subjective results.

Chapter VI

Short Frocks

I fell asleep under Elise. We managed somehow to sleep and to breathe.

Mademoiselle awoke me by unfastening the bag, shaking Elise, and bidding her get up.

What a relief to be freed from the oppression and load of the feather bed and eiderdown under which we had sweated and fumed all night!

How my arms ached!

Mademoiselle unfastened them, covered me up, and bade me sleep.

The thought crossed my mind, that possibly I might be admitted to her bed. A moment's reflection convinced me of the more than groundlessness of this aspiration. Such a fastidious creature as Mademoiselle would not allow me to touch her after the night I had passed.

A feeling of horror and despair came over me when I reflected she would henceforth hate me — be disgusted with me.

And I looked at the woman who stood naked for a moment at the bedside, with whom I had been in such close contact all night, who had been impregnated with my very essence.

Elise wrapped something about her and left the room.

Mademoiselle covered me up. Freed from the restraints I had suffered so long, I slept soundly and happily.

I hardly knew Maud when, three hours later, she was brought into the room. I had a bath and some breakfast and my hands having been again tied behind me, I was sent naked into Mademoiselle's room.

Maud looked as though she had been crying. Her hair, instead of being rolled coquettishly upon her head, was done into two long plaits at the back. She wore a common print cotton frock which came only to her knees. Her stockings were of white, coarse, unbleached thread; her shoes heavy and clumsy. She looked thoroughly humiliated and punished.

Mademoiselle spoke as rudely and roughly to her as to the lowest servant. Her sleeves were rolled up to her elbows and her hands were red. In the middle of the floor was my old acquaintance the oak bench.

"You are to birch this young gentleman soundly. He has been misbehaving himself."

She answered falteringly, "Yes'm."

She had evidently already had a schooling.

I thought as I was being strapped down of the haughty, faultless, proud Maud. Could this be she? I knew she would not spare me for having seen her humiliated in that manner. My surmise was right. A green birch, which had been soaked in Mademoiselle's urine, was put into her hand, and she gave me three dozen sound strokes.

She was then dismissed.

Mademoiselle seated herself and, opening a book, pretended to read.

Church time came. Maud had to wash up the breakfast things and peel the potatoes for the day's use. I was locked up in the bedroom, to learn the Epistle, Gospel, and Collect for the day, Mademoiselle informing me that I should have no dinner unless I could say them perfectly.

That night when I was put to bed, my hands were strapped to my sides and a bunch of thistles was placed before and behind me, kept into position by a lady's towel between my legs I could only lie upon one side or the other. Consequently, if I moved on to my face or on to my back I was unmercifully pinched.

The next morning Beatrice birched me with less severity than Maud had used.

Dear Beatrice, I fell in love with her again as soon as I saw her maidenly little figure. I hoped some day to belong to her.

On Tuesday I was flogged by Agnes. I think I felt my nakedness most before her. In fact I was quite ashamed. Beatrice looked at me with her calm gaze, unmoved, but glancing demurely as if she saw nothing extraordinary, nothing unusual in a naked body.

Agnes blushed, looked conscious, simpered, cast her eyes down, and was greatly confused. Her breath came and went so quickly that Mademoiselle told her she should herself be whipped there and then unless she behaved.

I should have liked to have seen those dainty legs uncovered, her skirts turned up, her drawers opened or taken off, and her prudish little bottom well cut.

I wished to possess Agnes. I wished to be possessed by Beatrice.

I need scarcely say that the whipping Agnes gave me did not

deserve the name.

Then I was dressed in trousers, waistcoat, and jacket — placed over a silk vest, a cambric *chemise*, long stockings, girl's boots with high heels, long cloth drawers, a corset, and a *camisole*.

The effect of the change of dress was startling. Amongst all the girls I felt much happier dressed as a boy, and had a greater capacity for enjoyment; and no sooner had they seen me so attired, than they one and all gave themselves their little feminine airs and graces which they had abandoned more or less with me whilst I was in girl's clothes. Mademoiselle, however, destroyed this bit of conceit, which she quickly perceived.

"He only appears a boy — really he is a girl," she observed, with superciliousness. At this remark we all blushed and Agnes giggled. It was quite plain that Agnes and I would have to settle accounts. I anticipated the reckoning with satisfaction. I determined to exact the ultimate, the very bottom farthing. Agnes was such a cleanly made girl!

My feelings of elation, however, soon yielded place to humiliation when I looked at the dainty feminine company and remembered but too vividly what they had seen and what they had done. Then I felt overwhelmed with confusion.

And indeed so much changed was I and so sensible of it, that as I stepped off the hall door steps into the Brougham, I wondered whether I was actually the same Julian Robinson, who, but on the previous Wednesday, had for the first time, alighted in that porch and passed through those massive oak doors.

Chapter VII

Sat Upon

Mademoiselle was accompanied by Elise. The carriage door was closed — the girls waved *adieux*, their graceful figures giving an unusual charm to the grey building. Beatrice looked into my eyes with a slight pout and we dashed down the long avenue to the road for Stowmarket, which was formerly the county-town, and whence Mademoiselle decided to travel to London. Instead of taking the more interesting route for Cambridge.

The horses sped along, and turning out of the gate, jolted me against Elise, who was seated opposite Mademoiselle. Mademoiselle had totally ignored my presence till then. The few remarks she made were addressed to Elise as though no one had been present. She was so angry with what she was pleased to describe as my "idiotic mooning," that for the rest of the way she made me kneel down on the floor of the Brougham, between her and Elise.

It did not, however, last long. The horses were quick trotters and Stowmarket but some five miles distant. In about twenty-five minutes we had reached the railway station.

"Julian," said Mademoiselle, "stay still — let Elise get out first."

I had attempted getting up before the porter, who opened the carriage door, and the stationmaster, who was standing at the entrance to the booking office, could see that I had been kneeling, an effort frustrated by Mademoiselle, to my bitter chagrin.

I hoped however, it might be thought that I was engaged in a search for something which had fallen down, and I endeavoured to retain my composure. If either the stationmaster or the porter observed me, they preserved the most praiseworthy unconsciousness and stolidity. They were absorbed in watching Mademoiselle as she gave her imperious orders and her appearance seemed fairly to bewitch them — they flew about, they changed colour, they trembled before the gaze and the words of this elegant haughty French damsel.

I trembled, glowed with colour one minute, and became ashy pale the next, in rapid succession. I had not a word to say myself — even walking into the station, whither Mademoiselle led me by the hand, was a severe trial to my terrible self-consciousness.

"Elise," said Mademoiselle, "we should have dressed him like a little boy, in knickerbockers; his frilled drawers would have showed then. Why did you not suggest it?"

I am sure some of the bystanders overheard, and I nearly sank down to the ground in shame.

Why did Mademoiselle lead me by the hand instead of allowing me to see to the baggage and get the tickets, as might naturally be expected of a tall youth of my age? She led me by the hand as though I was a helpless idiot anxious to run away. All my sprightliness, presence of mind, and assurance seemed to have vanished.

The idea of the vest and girl's *chemise*, the corset, drawers, and long stockings, of the flannel petticoat, which I had narrowly escaped having tucked into my trousers, haunted and reduced my mind to silliness and made me perfectly soft. But I felt a substratum of indignation. It was all very well in the precincts of Downlands Hall, in its gardens and in its terraces to be under Mademoiselle's thumb, but here, in public, at a railway station, with numbers of people to observe and to comment, it was quite another thing.

As we walked about the platform, I feared it would certainly be noticed that I had girl's boots on, and high heels, and that I was tightly laced up in a lady's corset, which could easily be noticed under my jacket.

As the light things had been removed from the carriage I had been curiously scanned, but Mademoiselle had given her orders where the luggage was to be labelled for and from that instant all interest in me appeared to have determined. I felt certain it would be noticed that the baggage was all feminine. I had not been permitted the honour of a *portmanteau*. A dress casket and an imperial; there was nothing else.

"Coachee," I heard one of the men say, "you have left the young gent's box behind."

At length with the bustle usual at places of absolutely no importance, the train ran alongside the platform. It drew up, and the stationmaster who gave me a very searching look, came to conduct Mademoiselle to the compartment he had reserved for her. What a relief to escape into the privacy of a railway carriage from the quizzical gazes and the prying eyes of these people. Mademoiselle had spoken to one or two acquaintances, and the amused stare they gave me, a kind of intelligent look, was positively insulting and maddening.

With great deference the stationmaster led Mademoiselle to the carriage, and I had yet bitter dregs to drain in the humiliating cup. She made me jump in first just like a child.

Mademoiselle pointed out the seat I was to occupy — the centre one with my back to the engine. She took the far seat opposite to me, next the window.

Elise sat at my left. The door was shut; the stationmaster nodded to the guard who was beside him, he blew his whistle, held out his arm, the engine gave an acquiescing scream, and we were off.

"What a noodle, what a nincompoop, what a fool you are, Julian. I longed to smack your face on the platform," and she gave me a sharp pat with the back of her gloved hand on my mouth. If anything was needed to complete my abnegation it was this.

Mademoiselle relapsed into a reverie, her shapely legs crossed, her chin resting on her hand, her ankles displayed.

We soon reached Ipswich, the run of twelve and a half miles from Stowmarket thither taking only seventeen minutes or so. The platform there was crowded and there was great commotion and many people, Suffolk farmers, talking and dreaming in beery fashion of oxen. It was market day of course. No one invaded our sanctuary although many looked in with more curiosity and openly displayed admiration than I considered polite, and at which Mademoiselle laughed heartily. Her high spirits were contagious, and when we were again under weigh, I felt myself emboldened to utter some joyous remark, and warranted in an effort to throw off my restraint.

Mademoiselle gazed at me for a moment during which I felt my courage ebbing away and I became terrified at my own audacity. Then she spoke as I shrank into my shoes. "This is not a pleasure trip for you, Master Julian. How dare you give yourself that insolent air and impudence, and attempt to treat it so frivolously; do you not know you are to be taken to London for serious punishment? Have you already forgotten the fault, the crime you have been guilty of?"

"Shall I punish him, Mademoiselle?" asked Elise, looking significantly at her mistress.

My blood ran cold. "Oh please, oh, please, Mademoiselle," I cried, clasping my hands, "I did not mean anything, I did not intend to be naughty." I dreaded being punished there in the train.

"Yes," replied Mademoiselle, moving. "Yes, Elise, punish him," she said, dwelling on the word, "and then sit upon him, until we reach Colchester."

"Oh! Oh! Oh!" I exclaimed, wriggling.

"Be quiet, you little ass," said Mademoiselle. Elise arose and took her bag down from the rack over her head, and opening it on her knees, having again reseated herself, drew out a handkerchief which she folded and placed between her teeth.

Mademoiselle looked on intently all the time. Elise then caught me by the wrist, drew me up, and made me stand before her. There was no occasion for her to slip her other hand, as she did, violently between my legs, hurting me a good deal, and exciting me more.

"Now, Elise," said Mademoiselle, threateningly, as she observed what Elise did.

Elise then turned me round and fastened my hands together tightly behind me. She next encircled me with her arms, unfastened all the buttons in front of my trousers, undid the braces, and there, in that public railway carriage, and before Mademoiselle, promptly took down my trousers.

"Now," she said, making a lag, "you, young rascal, lie down across my knee."

My cheeks flushed scarlet with shame. I dreaded being whipped. There was the exposure. The people in the neighbouring compartments would certainly hear, and I should be publicly disgraced.

"Oh, oh!" I besought. "Don't whip me. Don't. They will hear in the next carriage. Oh, don't!"

"It would serve you right if they did," rejoined Mademoiselle, shaking with laughter. And then she continued: "You are not to be whipped this time, Julian. I am going to see if I can really impress upon you, that you are a girl."

Elise nodded acquiescence as she said: "Come, no nonsense," and drew me down. Reassured, but wondering, with some consternation, whatever was about to be done to me, I lay down.

Elise put her right leg across mine, and her left elbow between my shoulder blades. She opened the drawers behind, and drew up my *chemise*. Then she took something out of her bag which was on the seat beside. Next I felt her hand on my bottom which she pressed and fingered, advancing gradually towards its centre. Horror! She had something cold and hard in her hand, which the motion of the carriage jerked about; but, terrified at her attempts, lying there on my stomach across her knee, I grew more scarlet, more ashamed, than ever.

"What a pretty bottom," observed Mademoiselle. "I really do not think I have noticed it before."

Still Elise pressed whatever it was she held against the passage or orifice of my bottom. Terrified, I gave a little scream, and tried to jump, tried to writhe off Elise's lap on to the floor, to slip from under her arm. Useless! The only result was a stinging smack. Then — horror of horrors — the train slackened speed, slowed, stopped!

We had reached Bentley, a junction six miles south of Ipswich.

"Keep him there," called out Mademoiselle, getting up and throwing a rug over me and over Elise's lap; only my feet sticking out, Elise holding me as in a steel vice. So during the whole stoppage while the porters and passengers rambled up and down the platform and looked into the carriage.

Suppose someone got in! Whatever would happen to me. However, no one did. In three minutes or less we were off.

"You must wait, Elise — keep him as he is. We shall be at Manningtree in a very few minutes. When we leave Manningtree you will have a quarter of an hour before we get to Colchester."

As soon as we had left Manningtree Mademoiselle walked along the carriage, and, standing at my head, held me by the shoulders.

"You must submit," she said. "You have put a certain wicked thing into a certain part of your cousin, you must now have something put into — a — certain — part of you."

Elise had got in her hand an ivory knob, about three inches long, shaped like a closed crocus flower, with a narrow flat band about a quarter of an inch wide, chased or cut round into it at its base. The base was fixed to a narrow, thin, and pliable silver crescent.

Elise immediately and more vigorously recommenced operations. She got the apex of the thing in my rear and forced it into me. I resisted with all my might, stoutly and vigorously. She pushed firmly. The resistance hurt me very much, and, besides, the attempt Elise was making excited me to so great a degree that I could scarcely contain myself. The combat lasted several minutes. Mons. Priapus grew larger and larger against Elise's knee.

Her continued efforts convulsed me.

"The beast," Elise exclaimed, looking at Mademoiselle. "The beast — he has gone off — spent."

At the same instant, however, owing, I suppose, to the

involuntary relaxation of the muscles upon the supervention of the venereal orgasm, she succeeded in getting the plug right in.

No sooner had she done so, than removing the arm which until then had been pressing my shoulders, she slipped it round my waist in front, and made me stand up.

Elise, as I stood shaking and trembling before her, quickly drew up my trousers and buttoned them. The knob inside did not exactly hurt, but was immensely inconvenient. The predominating sensation being that there was a bomb inside, which might explode at any moment, and which I could not get rid of.

Mademoiselle evidently hugely enjoyed my condition.

"How do you like that?" she enquired. "We have discovered a vulnerable point. Perhaps you will have more regard for young ladies in front now that you know they can avenge themselves on your rear. And indeed you suffer less for that thing will not do what yours did."

"But Mademoiselle," said Elise, "if you will permit me, I will make it work too."

"Oh, Mademoiselle, pray, don't; it is enough, too much to have it there," and I flushed scarlet again at the idea.

"Maud might have said the same to you and yet you pumped what you could into her."

Again the idea that Maud had asked me at the last moment to desist crossed my mind. There was now no time to dwell on the subject.

"How do you like that?" Mademoiselle triumphantly asked. "Now sit down."

Sit down! How could I sit down? Sit down on that thing! No, I was going to remain on my feet for the rest of the journey. I shuffled from one foot to the other.

"Sit down," she reiterated, "at once."

"Oh, Mademoiselle, I can't."

"Put him down, Elise."

Elise placed her hands on my shoulders and forced me down with a cruel bang into the seat which I had occupied before. I was made to sit well forward so that the cushion pressed the knob well up and for another purpose too.

"Now, Elise, sit upon him."

Elise stood before me, looked with a smile at my lugubrious countenance, and then, turning round her back to me, calmly sat down on my abdomen and legs. Her weight was considerable. What little resistance I had been able hitherto to make to the pressure of the cushion was now absolutely out of my power.

The thing was driven well up afresh, and Elise's weight was constant and drove me down upon it. Then she leant back upon me exactly as though I had been an armchair, pressing her strong shoulders into my chest, the nape of her neck and her back hair into my mouth, nostrils, and eyes; and there she continued to sit, treating me as an inanimate piece of furniture, moving, crushing, pounding me with her weight, as the whim took her, so that I panted for air. The inconvenience of the knob seriously increased and added to the excruciation of the circumstances.

Mademoiselle quietly read.

My groans, my inarticulate exclamations, my puffings and blowings amused Elise vastly. Occasionally she would give me a thump with her elbow, or a series with each one alternately in my ribs, bid me be quiet, bid me hold my noise, knocking all the breath out of my body and reducing me to the brink of tears.

I was glad when we reached Colchester shortly after two. But Elise showed no symptoms of stirring.

As the guard, with a serious face, came up to the window, followed by a girl, with very pale yellow hair, dressed in brown, Mademoiselle looked at Elise, and signalled to her with her hand. Whereupon Elise, to my inexpressible relief, dropped into the seat beside me. What a sigh of delight I gave as I sat up in the posture which enabled me to feel that implement inside me least! Mademoiselle noticed it with a frown, which made me regret my rashness.

Chapter VIII

Gertrude Stormont

The next moment the guard unlocked and opened the door, and taking his cap off, requested Mademoiselle to permit a young lady who was going to London to have a seat in her carriage as the train was too crowded.

I felt certain she knew that something had been going on.

However, she got in as soon as Mademoiselle had politely assented, and sat down at my right hand, and in a few minutes we were off again without the prospect of a stoppage until Liverpool Street was reached at half-past three. So miles passed in silence. The newcomer had got out a novel which it was plain to me she but pretended to read.

Mademoiselle condescended to make the same pretence. Elise kept looking at me menacingly and then at Mademoiselle.

Now, I really could not sit still with that thing inside me and kept snuffing my feet.

"Sit still Julian," said Mademoiselle.

The yellow-haired damsel looked up interested.

She had a beautiful neck and pretty little ears; her features were not particularly striking, but the form of her body, her arms, bust, and lap, were good.

"Why don't you sit still, Julian?" said Mademoiselle, and then after a pause, speaking slowly and deliberately:

"If you make me speak again," looking full at me, "I shall thrash you soundly."

The stranger moved in her seat, a slight flush ran over her countenance, and she put her hand up to the knot of her hair at the back of her head, displaying her well-shaped arm.

"Is this young gentleman under petticoat-government?" she asked in rather severe tones. "Now-a-days, when boys are so unruly, it really does one good to find one who is made to mind."

"I am very pleased," answered Mademoiselle, with that courteous smile which I hated, "to hear you express such an opinion. Yes, he is certainly under petticoat-government — under petticoat-punishment, in fact. My maid was punishing him just before you entered the carriage."

"He seems a big boy for it," said the new arrival, scanning me curiously. "He must be eighteen, I should think. And pray how was she punishing him? I wish I had been here to see. I thought he looked very conscious and shamefaced, when I came to the door; and then when I heard you speak sharply to him, I at once guessed that, notwithstanding his great size, he was kept in strict subjection."

"Yes, he is," responded Mademoiselle, "and he requires it. And as for his size and age, petticoat-discipline is more salutary at his time of life, than if he were still a hobbledehoy. A youth of just eighteen, which, as you observed, he really quite looks, is particularly susceptible to women's influence; in fact, I think it would be a capital thing for all youths, when they leave school, to be in a young lady's hands, as he has been, to be kept in subjection until at marriage the yoke is forced upon them once for all. There would be fewer young fools silly with conceit in the world if this plan were followed. There is nothing like subjugation to a girl for taking the conceit and nonsense out of a young man."

"I quite agree with you; but is he not going to college?"

"No; he has been entrusted to me instead; he so misbehaved himself at home that he is to be deprived of that privilege."

Now this was the first intimation I had received of this decision, and it came as a revelation and disappointment; for at times when my thraldom felt most bitter, I had found some consolation in the reflection that before long I must go to the university. Besides, it was my right — it would affect my whole position in life.

"Oh, Mademoiselle," I burst out, "of course I shall go to college, of course I shall go and take a degree. I must have one."

"I shall not permit you to go — my petticoats are your university; how dare you interrupt and speak to me in that tone?"

"Indeed, I should not allow it. I am quite shocked. He evidently needs a most severe *regime*," said, with pious horror, the pretty light-golden-haired damsel in closely fitting brown frock which set off her plump figure to perfection.

"And has he not been to school?"

"Oh, yes, but they could not keep him there."

"Oh, Mademoiselle, indeed this is not fair. It's not true," said I in desperation, "I was not strong enough for school. That was the reason I was sent home and you know it."

An exclamation of fresh horror on the part of the young lady, in which Elise seemed to join, greeted this audacious outburst of mine.

A very angry look appeared on Mademoiselle's face.

"I certainly should not permit such — such impudence to pass," said the stranger, drawing herself up, and sitting back on the seat. "I understand he was being punished when I got in. I see he richly deserved it. Pray, do not let my being here prevent his receiving the treatment he merits," and she covered me with a look of serious and solemn displeasure.

"Thank you," calmly said Mademoiselle. And then to me: "How dare you, Julian, contradict me? How dare you insinuate that my statement was untrue? Kneel down there this instant!"

The train was rushing on and the carriage oscillating very much; but, astounded at my own boldness, it never occurred to me to refuse. I sighed deeply because I knew what was coming, and knelt down. My hands remained all the time fixed together at my back.

As soon as I was in position, Mademoiselle gave me several stinging slaps on the cheeks with her gloved hands. At the pain and the humiliation I nearly burst into tears. "Beg my pardon," she ordered. I did so.

"If he were my pupil, I should wale his bottom for him with my lady's riding whip until it looked like a latticed window with the setting sun shining through."

"You hear, Julian," said Mademoiselle. "That shall be the penalty of your naughtiness. And now apologize to that young lady for behaving so before her."

Her little mouth looked very stern and there was a curious light in her eyes, as I addressed myself as gracefully as I could to this task. There was a delicious perfume and atmosphere about her and she told me she thought she too should inflict some chastisement on me.

"Pray, do," cried Mademoiselle, only too pleased. "I will do something to him," she said flushing a lovely colour, the more remarkable because of her clear fair complexion, "that my young brother, who has to wait and attend upon me, particularly hates. It has the advantage that it can be done anywhere, and it punishes severely." Proceeding to unglove her dainty hand: "Sit down!" I sat down.

"Why does he wriggle about on his seat like that? Is there anything wrong with him?"

"The fact is," answered Mademoiselle, "the young rascal has been making too free with a cousin and is being taken to town for the express purpose of being unsexed. I thought, when he tried to make light of the matter, it would be well to remind him he was no longer to be a boy, by directing my maid to insert an ivory instrument —"

"Into him? Capital!" cried the girl, clapping her hands. "Into him? Behind, you mean. Oh, do take down his trousers and show me. There is plenty of time; we are not near town yet."

"No, no, no," I cried, I prayed. What an exhibition they proposed making of me to that strange girl! It was bad enough with them alone.

But Elise, with a smile, had already placed her arm about me, again unfastened my trousers, and had thrown me over her lap and uncovered my bottom.

"What a nice one," said the girl, for whose benefit this had been done, giving it a few slaps with her hand, off which she had taken the glove, and stroking it as well.

"Put your legs apart. There, you can see the silver plate."

"Take it out and show it to her, Elise. He may as well have the employment of having it taken out and replaced."

"Oh, please, Mademoiselle! Oh, please, Elise! Oh, oh, don't! Oh, no, Miss — Miss —"

"Gertrude Stormont, if you mean me, you bad boy."

The thought flashed through my mind. I recollected that women named Gertrude, Aline, Laura, are always inexorable and fond of using the birch without that voluptuous mercifulness which characterizes the discipline of an Ellen, a Julia, or a Mary. Names are a certain index to disposition amongst ladies in society anyhow. A Violet is strict, but always by coldness, never by active infliction. It is true my governess was Hortense and her maid, Elise. Anyhow, the moment I heard the name Gertrude, I felt my fate was sealed.

"If you were in my hands," she went on, "I would take it in and out with you over my lap for perhaps an hour for my own private amusement."

Elise slipped her thumb and finger underneath the plate, and regardless of my exclamations and cries, pulled the thing out, holding me down as she handed it to Miss Stormont for her to examine.

"Capital," she said. "And I see there is a hole through it into which a tube can be screwed. I hope he will find you make use of it."

"Undoubtedly," observed Mademoiselle.

The implement was then handed to Elise who set about replacing it.

"Keep still — don't wriggle so, lie still, will you?" and she pushed, and puffed and poked me. Her efforts were useless until she slipped her left hand down my front. The counter irritation deprived my resistance of all force. The thing was reinstated.

"Now," said Miss Gertrude, "before his trousers are buttoned up again, please, let him come to me. I was about to punish him, you will remember, when I asked to be shown that thing; and I should still like to be allowed to do so, if I may. I will give him a peculiarly feminine infliction," she added, with a pretty menacing gesture.

"By all means," said Mademoiselle.

"I should have done it without taking his trousers down," she coolly continued as she drew me towards her with a firmness I could not withstand, especially on the part of a girl: "but, as they are down, so much the better. Come here, close to me. So. Now lie backwards. Yes, backwards, across my knee. Sit on my knee and lie back across the arm of the seat. Now, no nonsense," she went on, with charming peremptoriness putting her left arm across the front of my chest and firmly pushing me backwards into the position she had described. It gave me the oddest and most disagreeable sensations to find myself thus face upwards in the arms of a strange girl, my middle, with its disarranged clothing, all exposed to her, her plump round arm pressing me down. Bending across me, with a flushed face and flaming eyes, she made me stretch my legs well apart, pressing the knees alternately to separate them.

"It increases their punishment," she explained, glancing first at Mademoiselle and then, for a moment, looking into my own eyes (I noticed hers were swimming), "to let them see who is doing it."

Assuredly, if queer sensations can be considered punishment, I received it in full measure. The embarrassment of the position to a bashful and susceptible young man was extreme.

"Why, good gracious," she exclaimed after a slight further examination, "I declare he has got a corset, *chemise*, lady's drawers, and stockings on. His attire puzzled me a moment ago. What a splendid idea! Now, young gentleman!"

Tightening the pressure of her left arm, she slipped her ungloved hand down between my legs and slowly moved it upwards from my knees. Coming into contact with the sensitive nerves at the insides of my thighs gave me many a pungent twinge. It was the last place in which I should have desired a strange young lady's hand to be. I could not avoid moving about.

The little hand soon reached the angle and to my intense bewilderment was not withdrawn, as I should have expected, when it came into contact with what was there. On the contrary I was soon made very sensible of its cool, soft, deliberate pressure upon a very sensitive organ which it grasped, accompanied by a fresh liquid look into my eyes, without the slightest hesitation. I uttered an inarticulate murmur of pleasure. I could not resist or protect myself now that she had touched me — indeed, I did not desire too.

But the next instant when with her left hand she commenced to gather up the chemise and my legs being wide apart, to completely expose me, my feelings again altered, and I would have protested if I could. I wriggled about, notwithstanding that the plug from behind hurt me when I did so, but I could not help it, it was so embarrassing, so confusing to find a girl's hand, without leave asked, quietly playing one's secret anatomy.

In a moment I was quite exposed. She scanned me carefully and leisurely. The look was even worse than the touch. I asked her to cover me up and received a little mocking laugh in reply as she continued playing with me. I drew several deep breaths, sighs, almost groans, and as I gazed at her, at her pretty face, her bewildering hair, her bewitching little head and ears, the graceful form of her back and sides, and felt upon me the atmosphere and perfume of her beautiful body, and remembered she was a stranger, and realized what she was doing, what she could see, I became much excited, and Mons. Priapus grew and grew regardless of the presence he was in.

"I can plainly see the mischief my eyes are doing," she observed to Mademoiselle. "I must confess" (with a winning smile) "I have often wished when a gentleman gazed into them, I could just slip my hand in and gauge their effect exactly. Some naughty boys have a slit in their trouser's pocket for the purpose."

"Have they, indeed?" said Mademoiselle, moving.

"Yes," answered Miss Stormont, calmly fingering me all the time. "I found it out from one of my brothers, who is at Eton — not the one I have already mentioned to you. I discovered that all his trouser's pockets had each one side of the top unfastened, and I caught him one day with one of the housemaid's hands in his pocket. He tried to pretend she was merely seeing for herself whether the pocket was empty as he had declared to her it was. She was a very pretty girl. Then I called him to me, and slipping my hand through, shew him I knew the truth."

"How dreadful! Whatever did you do?"

"I sent him up to my bedroom, and the girl too. I deprived him of his trousers, made her hold him down, and whipped him soundly. Then I punished him before her as I am about to punish this youth. After that, he was made to wear a kilt without drawers for the rest of his holidays — about town as well as in the house."

Miss Stormont then directed her attention again to me. After my experience I had not much doubt how she intended to punish me; and I can safely affirm I squirmed considerably. She increased the pressure of her leg underneath me, and her arm above, adding to my troubles and excitement, by driving the plug yet further in. Then she caught hold of my lance which stood out in the air, her dainty little hand about it made it grow still more. She moved the foreskin up and down, causing the most poignant sensations a woman can give a man. I sighed and sighed. She would not desist. The more I wriggled the tighter she held me, the more she smiled. Then, at last, with a cruel jerk, which made me jump and exclaim, she forced the *prepuce* right back over the swollen animal, leaving his wet, raw, red head exposed and wagging in the air.

"There," she cried, with exultation, "now show yourself to Mademoiselle," and making me stand up and holding up the garments with both hands, which I could not do myself, as my hands were tied, she obliged me to turn round and, to my shame, display myself.

Mademoiselle looked, and so did Elise, with pretty shocked exclamations and heightened colour, whilst Miss Stormont complacently enjoyed her triumph, and the train rushed on. When they had gazed as long as they cared, Miss Stormont dropped the garments and began pulling up my trousers.

Mons. Priapus decreased in stature and girth, but the skin did not right itself.

"Suppose we leave him so for an hour or two," quietly observed my fair tormentor. "What he has behind is on your account. What he suffers in front will atone to me — he has to thank me for it, and it will teach him in future to restrain his impudence and to behave himself in the presence of strange young ladies."

She was so charming that really I did not very much regret having something to thank her for, but I felt woefully uncomfortable, notwithstanding.

"Yes, certainly," cried Mademoiselle, delighted. "Button him up, Elise!"

Elise caught me roughly, and without ceremony bundled me over to her, and drew up, adjusted, and fastened my clothes. Then I was again made to occupy the seat between Miss Stormont and herself, my hands still bound, wretched in front and behind.

"Just before you came in," observed Mademoiselle, "my maid was sitting on him. Shall she resume her place — or as you have taken possession of him in front, will —?"

"To be sure I will," exclaimed Miss Gertrude with alacrity before Mademoiselle had time to finish her sentence.

She jumped up and plumped flop down upon me without another word. I wriggled into as comfortable a posture as possible and panted for breath. The more I moved the more closely she pressed me with her thighs and her pretty back. It was a more agreeable experience than Elise's sitting on me and she did not treat me so roughly; although I was pressed well into the arms and cushions, and thoroughly well oppressed by her, she did not give me the severe and painful nudges Elise had given me, nor thump me with her elbows. And so the minutes and the miles passed, Mademoiselle and her new-found friend chattering and laughing, utterly ignoring me. They compared notes, chiefly on education; spoke of various instruments of punishment, told anecdotes, discussed the corset, strait-waistcoat, stocks, backboards, callisthenics, &c.

Mademoiselle amused her friend hugely by describing the perplexity of a lady, the mother of a boy and girl, who had been left a legacy on condition that she dressed them both alike until they attained twenty-one years of age. She did not know whether to dress both as boys or both as girls.

"I should have had no difficulty. I should have dressed both as girls," said Mademoiselle.

"Of course," exclaimed Miss Stormont with a determination and conviction which settled the question.

Chapter IX

Hotel, Piccadilly

By the time we had reached Liverpool Street, Miss Stormont and Mademoiselle had, to my great dismay, struck up a close friendship and agreed that they would take rooms at the same hotel. She had given my governess an account of the slavery in which she kept her young brother and of the floggings she gave him periodically, not always because he was naughty, but because she considered them good for him; and I was very much frightened.

At Liverpool Street I was waddled across to a hansom cab and obliged to get in first and sit in the middle.

By the time we reached the hotel in Piccadilly what little spirit remained in me had disappeared.

As the train had sped along, and I had become warm under Miss Stormont, and my pulse seemed to throb with hers, and our beings seemed to mingle, I had ventured upon a little affectionate pressure, at first with extreme hesitation. She took no notice of it for some time; I repeated it with more assurance.

Her hair, the back of her head, looked so beautiful, she was so coquettish! Would she betray me? I was not left in doubt long. The pressure was gently returned, and if she and Mademoiselle had struck up friendship by the time we reached the station, so had I struck up a warmer one, and as we got out of the carriage had had a little glance which told me I was understood. This made me very happy. But the drive to Piccadilly extinguished it; only for the time though. I could not help feeling indignant at the calm air of possession with which the majority of the women we met had plainly contemplated me, as if I were annexed, and definitely subject to the petticoat, and they knew it.

The smiling hostess of the quiet private hotel where Mademoiselle stayed increased my dismay by her curious and intelligent looks at me.

My bedroom as at home opened off Mademoiselle's, and the landlady pointed it out incidentally and quite as a matter of course, taking it for granted it was what Mademoiselle would wish.

I should have expected her to consider it strange that a youth of my size should sleep in a room to which there was no access but through a young lady's; and should have been much gratified to find my expectation realised. But the fact that Mademoiselle was my governess appeared quite sufficient explanation to her. And if I had been but five or six years old, I could not have been treated with more indifference by these women.

I found that Mademoiselle frequently used the hotel, and was well-known there.

Miss Stormont's room was on the opposite side of the sitting room.

Of course my hands had been unfastened just before we alighted from the train. The first thing Elise did when we got in, and I was waiting in the sitting room while the apartments were being decided upon, was to tie them up again.

Chapter X

Vivien

And then, with great scorn, they got Sir Dinadan into the forest there beside, and there they despoiled him unto his shirt, and put upon him a woman's garment, and so brought him into the field, and so they blew unto lodging. And every knight went and unarmed him. Then was Sir Dinadan brought in among them all. And when Queen Guinevere saw Sir Dinadan brought so among them all, then she laughed that she fell down. So did all that were there.

Mort d'Arthur

The chief effect of my treatment at the time was undoubtedly a delicious delirium of priapism which fitted me for the accomplishment of one of the reputed labours of the redoubtable knight, the Sieur Hercules, who, in the course of one night got fifty girls with child, if my memory does not deceive me.

There was a delicious contrast between Mademoiselle de Chambonnard and Gertrude Stormont.

Mademoiselle, dark and peremptory, and "capaciously serene," to use an expression of Wordsworth's, reminded me of Zenobia, Queen of the East, while Gertrude was the impersonation to me of Vivien, in the *Idyll of Merlin and Vivien*.

It is difficult to convey in words the multiplicity, the multifariousness of women upon me, to which, at that moment of fatigue after my journey, I felt exposed, and my effort to convey it may appear somewhat rhapsodical. With the influence of Mademoiselle and of Gertrude was joined that of my laughter-loving Venus, Beatrice, and of Maud. Agnes was an indistinct, undivided part of the potion which made me love sick.

My second feeling was an extraordinary and ecstatic exaltation of all my faculties, particularly of my memory.

I had an extraordinary envy of old Merlin always. No doubt he had Vivien towards the close of that dreadful storm before he told her the charm, and no doubt it was delicious to have a creature like she was.

I think it was Miss Stormont's light golden hair, which, as she sat on my lap, was very conspicuously placed before me, that first set my thoughts rambling on the "wily Vivien."

> A twist of gold was round her hair; a robe
> Of samite without price that more express
> Than hid her, clung about her lissom limbs,
> In colour, like the satin-shining palm,
> On sallows like windy gleams of March.

And then that glance I had just as we were getting out of the carriage, lit up by the fire of her hazel blue eyes after:

> She had made her little arm round my neck
> Tighten, and then drew back and let her eyes
> Speak for her, glowing on me like a bride's
> On her new lord, her own, the first man.

How well I could imagine Gertrude saying in her petulant way:

> They, ladies, never made unwilling war
> With those fine eyes: she had her pleasure in it,
> And made her good man jealous with good cause.
> And so I longed for this beautiful gilded summer fly.

Beatrice was far away. Mademoiselle would keep. Gertrude might vanish tomorrow. I longed to love them all in her, and herself above all. I longed to possess the paradise beneath her petticoats.

My heart panted as I hoped.

I felt nothing. I thought of her lovely figure in its beautiful setting of close-fitting ruddy brown, which, like Vivien's samite robe, "more express than hid her." I listened for her voice.

But Gertrude was even more delectable in my opinion than Vivien. She possessed the latter's wiliness, limberness, lissomness, clingingness; but Vivien was something of a witch, venomous, spiteful, and Gertrude was not. Gertrude was a much more comfortable, robust, voluptuous girl with no disquieting airiness, without the subtle penetrating brain, too acute to be sensual.

I knew Gertrude was sensual or she would not have taken such delight in torturing me as she did. I know she was so, for she looked for some response from me. Oh! When should I feel my face between those soft, satiny thighs which had so long oppressed me; when should I feel my lips in contact with the fountain of her being, and know that she was expiring from the delight that I gave her?

When should I die with delirious joy in her arms possessed by a fair prospect of being at last incarnated by some woman!

The door opened. A tall and beautiful parlour maid advanced to the table. Mademoiselle had given standing orders that no men were to come to her apartments. We had had a substantial luncheon before we started at noon. There was a large dish of sweet biscuits, three glasses, and two small bottles of Perrier-Jouet. The maid looked at me and departed, too well trained to give a sign of any sort.

Where was Mademoiselle? Where was Gertrude? How would she look without her hat?

Yes, Gertrude had Vivien's sweet eyes, but they were blue-hazel, and Vivien's must have been a shade of brown, she was so deceitful — a harlot.

Having concluded my reverie, I began to feel uncomfortable. I was grimy and dusty; and besides my condition in front (and I really feared the thing would strangulate), and the plug behind, there was something else.

We had lunched substantially at twelve, and had gone direct from the luncheon table to the carriage. Whether I had drunk more than usual, or whether the corset was tighter than usual, I do not know; but I longed to be alone, with my hands free, in a bedroom for a few moments. Had my hands been free, I think I should have risked all and ventured into the corridor, even asked that stately, distant, silent, observant parlour maid for a lavatory. I had not to wait much longer. Mademoiselle and Gertrude entered the room together. They looked fresh and bright.

"Julian," said Mademoiselle, "Miss Stormont will occupy that room, and you — you — are to sleep in the little one off it" — nodding to the apartment I had understood was to be hers — "and I shall place you free in Miss Stormont's hands. She has begged you from me till tomorrow morning. I congratulate you and hope you will prove yourself not altogether unworthy of the honour."

I flushed with delight, exclaimed eagerly: "Oh, Mademoiselle!" and looked with love, gratitude, and admiration at Gertrude.

"You see ladies can be kind sometimes," Gertrude remarked, looking at me with a look that spoke; "and as you are to be made a girl tomorrow, I have asked Mademoiselle to let me have what remains of the boy. But," putting up a finger, "you are not to consider yourself anything more than a boy, and" — giving her petticoats a whisk — "I shall treat you exactly like a child."

While she said this Mademoiselle undid my hands and gave me a playful pat on the cheek by way of emancipation.

"I am going out presently with Elise," said the Mademoiselle. "I have arrangements to make and people to see. We shall dine at eight here. Mind you are very obedient while I am away."

Gertrude looked at me.

"Yes," I said eagerly, willingly, "I will do all she tells me, all she wishes."

She smiled.

"Not too fast," she observed. "Remember that hollow tube; remember the faults you have to expiate; remember my little riding-whip, and your impudence to Mademoiselle in the carriage."

I own I felt a little terrified at this category. But to be for hours in Gertrude's possession, alone with her all night, what a prospect of intense happiness unalloyed. Suddenly a fear struck me.

"You are not going out, too?" I exclaimed.

"No," she answered, amused at my eagerness, "and I am going to stay here and look after you."

"Come, come, Julian," laughed Mademoiselle. "Come and make yourself useful. Do not stand there as if you were in an enchanted palace, some bewitched prince, and we two princesses who have captivated you. Open that wine."

"Ganymede!" uttered Gertrude.

Variable and changeable indeed, thought I, oh, Virgil, are women.

I opened the wine. We ate sweet biscuits and drank it. They petted and fed me. Gertrude made me sit by her, and call her "Mamma." That was the culmination of my bliss.

The disconsolate Elise appeared and gave me an angry look. She was laden with Mademoiselle's walking things. Mademoiselle had changed her travelling dress and looked more lovely than ever in her stylish hat and gown. She gave me her hand to kiss, nodded to Gertrude with a merry smile. I opened the door; they passed through it. When they had gone some little way along the corridor, I shut it. Turning round I saw Gertrude reclining in an easy chair, watching me, and I was alone — alone with her.

Chapter XI

Mamma

"Well, Julian?" she said softly.

"Oh, Miss Stormont, Miss Stormont!" I exclaimed, flushing all manners of colours.

"Miss Stormont!" she repeated. "What do you mean? What did I say you were to call me?"

"Mamma," I exclaimed, kneeling by her side, and, catching her hand, I pressed it to my lips, while she moved in her chair in a way I immediately recognised, intoxicated with the knowledge that I could give her pleasure.

"Yes, Mamma," she repeated, stroking my hair with her hand.

"And now, you bold boy, you seem to be very much in love. Pray with whom are you so taken?"

"Oh, Miss Stor — oh, Mamma! With you — whom else?"

"In love with your mamma!" she said with mock severity, but moving again. "Don't you know," flushing, "that is very improper, very wrong, very wicked. Pray, what do you want your mamma to do? I fear you would like to commit incest!"

She moved again. Her legs were uncrossed and wide apart. I could hardly believe my eyes. She was plainly love sick. I became vain and conceited on the instant.

"Yes," I said, flushing the colour of a crimson peony. "Yes, that is exactly —"

She put her "lady palm" across my mouth.

"Go into my bedroom, you bold boy, and I will come and talk to you there."

I went and leant against the pretty bed. The room was thickly carpeted, the window curtained. Gertrude came in and locked the door.

"I must see," she said, coming up to me, "how you are. I do not think it is good for you to remain any longer in the condition in which I put you in the train."

She seemed to have quite forgotten my declaration.

"Besides," she went on, "you were left in the sitting room, while Mademoiselle and I were changing our things. You must want to wash your hands and face — and — and — to do something else, too," with a delightfully quizzical look, which embarrassed me extremely. "And there is some hot water here; and this —" as she opened a drawer and shew me a long tube with a bulbous thing in its centre. I knew what it was and turned pale. "And yet you want to love your mamma, you indecent boy!" with a pat on my face. I caught her hand and kissed it.

"Well, you must first obey her," as she unbuttoned my trousers.

Her soft and nimble fingers quickly undid and drew them down. "Naughty boy! Its mamma must really take its little trousers off. Take off your jacket and waistcoat first, Julian. Now your shoes. Now slip off the trousers — yes, right off."

She next unfastened my corset and drawers, and I stood before her in *chemise* and stockings.

She turned me backwards over the bed, with my *chemise* over my breast; from the tops of my stockings to it, I was exposed to her searching gaze, and she gloated upon what she saw.

"Poor fellow!" she said, presently. "How swollen, how red, how inflamed he is! I must set him right."

Her soft hand was soon upon me, and a little very exciting determination effected her purpose. I gave a sigh of intense relief.

"Now you must turn over," she ordered, leaving me and going to the wash-hand-stand where she poured out some hot water into the basin and tempered it with cold. "Mademoiselle has told me how you behaved to your cousin Maud. I feel it my duty to make you feel something of what you did to her."

"Oh, please, Mamma! Oh, please, please, Miss Stormont!"

"Now," she said, lifting her finger, "you must obey. Remember, I have a little whip. I am not at all sure that I am not under an obligation — a promise — to wale your bottom for you, you great, big, naughty child! I advise you not to recall it to my recollection. I shall not hurt you, Julian," she added, as she observed my look of consternation.

As she uttered the word "bottom," she blushed divinely. I turned over. She put a chair by the bed beside me, and an end of the tube into the basin of water, which she set upon it.

"Oh, Mamma," I said, "please! I do not know how to tell you, but there is something I want to do, must do, first."

"You must tell me!"

"I can't! Oh! Ever since lunch — all the way in the train, I could not get out; and here I have had no opportunity."

It was such a terrible thing to have to tell a woman, and my thoughts reverted to Beatrice, and to that night in the bedroom. I was glad that now it was not quite as bad as then.

"I can guess," said Gertrude slyly and sweetly. "It wants to be held out, the big baby!" What a womanly girl she looked.

"Yes," I said blushing.

"Well! Say, please, Mamma, may I pee before you punish me?"

"Oh, Gertrude!"

"Gertrude! Sir, how dare you!"

"Oh, please, Mamma!"

"Well go on —"

"Oh! I was going to ask, don't make me say that —"

"I daresay — you must say it, if you want to, or you shall not do it. Now, choose!"

And before my beautiful Vivien, I had to say those words; hiding my face, doing all I could to conceal it. I seemed to give her wonderful pleasure, and I suppose I looked very artless and attractive, for she kissed me.

"Get the pot," she said, her eyes full of mischief. "Put it on the chair."

"Now, come," she said, taking hold of me and walking me over to the chair. She put her right arm round me from the back and held up my *chemise*.

"Now Baby, Baby, tiddley, tiddley — be quick!"

I laughed. "I can't," I exclaimed.

"Nonsense, Baby. Baby *must*."

"Oh, Mamma! You darling," I exclaimed.

"Baby be dear boy. Baby do what his mamma wants him to, and not keep her waiting."

This aspect of the affair settled the matter.

Baby did.

"Good boy!" said his mamma.

Then baby put the vessel under the valance and lay face downwards on the bed.

His mamma, charming girl that she was, stroked his bottom and explained his wickedness to him while she screwed in the tube. Then as baby groaned, she filled the bulb full, and with an arm and a hand on the small of baby's back, squeezed it, and I felt the warm water enter into my bowels.

"Baby not be naughty with his cousin any more," she said, her sweet womanliness overpowering me as releasing the pressure of her hand she let the tube fill again, "for his mamma does not like to have to punish him but when he is naughty she must," squeezing the now full bulb again.

"Oh! Oh! No more." I felt I should burst. "Oh, Mamma! Oh, Gertrude! Oh, my dear Mamma! Oh! Oh! Oh!"

"Yes. Baby must be thoroughly punished; his bottom must be made to suffer."

The idea of her being conscious of what I was undergoing; of her, Gertrude Stormont, the stranger who had entered the railway carriage at Colchester, the beautiful girl in the brown dress with the golden hair and her ladylike refinement, doing this to me, filled me with all manner of sensations, pleasant and unpleasant. I could not escape.

Again the bulb was pressed, and at last the gurgle in the basin told me the allotted portion was exhausted.

"There," she said, withdrawing the whole instrument, "I think I have punished you well."

"Take this dressing gown of mine; put it about you — there is a bathroom at the other side of the passage. Go and have a bath and then come back to me."

I went. I cannot describe the multitude of feelings with which I was overwhelmed.

I bathed, and did more; the bathroom possessed all the necessary accommodation of course — though really the sanitary arrangements of these private hotels are not all up to date, not all that could be desired.

Wrapping myself up, I returned up, I returned to Gertrude. Her hair was down; the snake of gold which had withheld the braid had been removed. She was combing its lovely, gorgeous, waving masses with a maidenly pride.

"Oh, my beautiful Mamma!" I exclaimed.

She had removed her dress also, and was in a pretty *peignoir*. My dressing gown was all I had on; the stockings and *chemise* I threw on the bed.

Without a word she got up and taking hold of the dressing gown, opened it, and threw it off my shoulders. She made me walk about the room and at length said: "Now, Julian! What have you to say to me?"

"Oh, Gertrude! I mean Mamma, I — I — love you!"

"You, very naughty boy!" she answered with mock

disapprobation but smiling and evidently well pleased as she moved towards a satin-covered couch on which there was a great square pillow and reclined upon it her golden hair like an aureole about her fair face. "Don't you know, don't you remember, I have already told you that it is very wicked to entertain such feelings for your mamma?"

There was a strange gleam in her eyes as she said this which immediately excited my wonder. I did not know what she was driving at and was considerably puzzled. As to my feelings, however, there was no opportunity for being puzzled. How attractive, how desirable she looked, as she lay there in a dishabille of the most alluring kind, one slender leg unveiled almost to the knee and the other far away from its sister at the other side of the sofa. When a young lady sits edgewise upon a table, she is said to be in want of a husband; when she lies on her back in the presence of a naked young man, careless about her clothing, her eyes aflame, and her legs well separated, it may safely be affirmed she wishes to welcome that young man to her arms. But then why baulk him with all this talk, this fiction of being his mamma? I suppose it excited her. No doubt the idea of being possessed by, of yielding to her son, gave a peculiar, a poignant zest to it, which the ordinary humdrum everyday copulation of a youth and maiden would have been without. And to this sense of double possession and power must, I think, be attributed the treatment most stepmothers accord their stepsons. It causes a peculiar especial flavour to the lust. A strong stimulant to the imagination, which no woman can say "No" to, and as they are too conventional, or want the courage to act as Parisina, they take it out on their stepsons with their riding whips, or slippers, or tawses under cover of salutary discipline.

My "Mamma" bid me kneel down by her side and tell her all about it.

I obeyed and clasped her lithe form with my arms, her clinging and thin garments permitting me to feel her soft plump form beneath them, and as I grasped her she thrilled.

"Julian," she said in low sweet tones looking at me with her swimming eyes, "in the train I felt you, yes, actually felt you making love to me and — and —"

I slipped my hand on to the lovely leg nearest to me and let it move upwards. I felt she had no drawers on, my hand was upon the smooth roundness of her thigh. I moved up her clothes and saw the delicate pink flesh which I kissed. Her own left hand upon my shoulders drew me from my kneeling position over her.

"How dare you?" she said.

"Oh, Mamma, Mamma, I do love you so!" And I gazed into her eyes and ventured to kiss her ruby lips.

She put her right hand round my back, and holding my mouth to hers gave me a long clinging kiss, inserting her tongue between my lips in quest of my own, moving up and down as she did so.

"You — you — must say what you want, you must ask me — to — let you —"

I guessed what was necessary. How strange it is that the more refined the girl the more she loves to be shocked.

"Oh, Gertrude!"

"Gertrude," she repeated scornfully.

"Oh Mamma dear, please let me — fuck you —" and I hid my face in her breast.

Her arms were about me instantly.

"Did Baby want to do anything so naughty to its own mamma?" she asked. "Well den it sail, kiss me den!"

With my lips upon her warm, wet, open mouth and my eyes fixed upon hers, half covered by their drooping lips, I removed her petticoats and ensconced myself between her limbs, naked from the tops of her stockings, rejoicing in the contact of her flesh with mine. Her legs enlaced themselves at my back and made me a happy prisoner. I opened her *peignoir* at the neck, and caressed the full round globes of her bosom, removing my mouth from hers to cover them and her neck with burning kisses. Her right hand had not been idle. It had been playing with that instrument which was to outrage her so sweetly and had excited it and enlarged it greatly.

"It must be put in *there*," she said, directing it. "It is nicer having itself uncovered by me there than by my hand, isn't it, Julian?"

"Yes," said I, beside myself.

"Oh! Oh! Oh! Naughty, naughty boy! Oh, Julian! Oh, Baby! Oh! Oh! Push him further in — there," as she embraced me with all her strength.

"Oh, Mamma! Dear Mamma!" I exclaimed as, after a moment's sweet tossing by her, which I felt to my fingers' tips, and a moment's determination to keep the position I had gained, from which, indeed, her strong legs at my back made any retreat impossible, I shuddered, and sank upon her luxurious form, as, with passionate force, the spasmodic injection of the essence of my being into hers was accomplished. Her bosom rising and falling rapidly, herself in a lovely, exquisite love sickness, she held me tightly, scarcely relaxing her grasp.

"Baby has — done — it — to please himself. Now he must do it to please his mamma."

Now what with the fatigues, excitement, and experiences I had gone through, added to which was the tremendous outburst of passion I had just given her, I was very much afraid I could not repeat the performance; but at any cost, I would not confess this impotence. She moved up and down, and moved her hands about me and I puffed and blew and endeavoured to realise where I was and with whom, with some success.

She grew a little impatient.

"Do you really deserve to have lady's drawers and petticoats on? Come, Julian, how did you feel in them? Very naughty, eh? Is it not much nicer to be — between a lady's legs — to be inside — actually inside her — than merely — to wear — her clothes? I shall whip — you — if you don't obey. I shall — replace that thing — *here*," she said, moving her fingers to the very spot, and finding how it excited me, kept them there, "if — if you are not quick — only think — your mamma — what a privilege! What a favour! Come, Julian, do as your mamma wishes, or — she will smack your — your *bottom*. She will whip it and cover it with wales if you don't."

How she harped upon being my mamma while I was in that position!

"Come, Julian — you must — must — fuck your mamma again, because she tells you to," blushing with exquisite confusion.

The chief delight to her lay not in the gratification of love, or lust, but in the simulation of incest. How curious, how odd, the fascination of vice! How depraved, what a thorough woman Gertrude was! And, strange to say, I liked her the better for it.

And I was between her legs, in the closest possible contact with her. And then the idea of the lady's drawers, and of the little whip wielded by her alabaster arms which made such delightful bracelets, so warm, so soft, so yielding, and yet so strong for me. My passion again culminated; again as she gasped with love, I gave her whole desire, in the strong convulsion of ecstasy.

"Oh, Gertrude Stormont! Oh, Mamma!"

She kissed me, called me "good boy," drew me to her side, and placed my head next hers on the pillow, covering me with her garments, and then we must have both fallen asleep, the last thing that I remember being her placing her right leg across me. Her arm lay across my neck and the gentle pressure of her form thus upon mine inspired me with delicious dreams.

I was awakened by her shaking my shoulder. Why does the woman always wake the first? Probably because she is insatiable.

"You lazy boy! You lazy Julian! Now — Baby — Baby — awake! It is" (kiss) "just" (kiss) "seven o'clock." And she locked me in her arms. "Jump up, and help your mamma to dress!"

"Oh, Mamma!" I exclaimed, rubbing my eyes, and smiling at her. "Oh, Mamma dear!"

That night I was attired as a young man for once again in my life — trousers, a stiff shirt, an open waistcoat, socks. It positively felt a strange garb and I felt at a loss and uncomfortable in it. I retreated into my room; I washed, dressed, and returned to Gertrude. I found the stockings she wished to wear, changed those she had on for them; and anyone who has done this office for a lady will understand how much the words mean — the tremulous blushes, the stolen looks and touches they include. I found her her silken *chemise* and drawers, her satin corset, which I laced, and her evening dress, which I fastened. I handed her her bracelets and jewels, and admired her shapely arms as she knotted up her hair and fixed it with a stab of an agate pin studded with diamonds.

Chapter XII

Bacchus Docens

When she was dressed Gertrude turned and gave me a glittering smile looking so fresh and beautiful in her exquisite *toilette* of faint pink, that, without delay, I fell in love with her over again. It was this lovely form, I reflected, that had sat so long upon my lap in the train, those hands that had invaded my privacy, and subjugated my rebellious male sex, those bright eyes that had seen all I had to show.

She smiled at me and daintily raising her voluminous and clinging drapery from her feet, showed me her low-cut shoes and slender ankles in the pink, open-work silk stockings I had had the privilege of putting on for her; so high did she raise them that I gained a glimpse of the trimming of her pink silk skirt-drawers.

"Oh, Mamma, Mamma!" I exclaimed, falling on my knees and clasping my hands before her divinely corseted and dressed form. I kissed the backs of her hands one after the other as they held up her skirts.

"Julian, how impressed you appear to be! Would you," with a lovely flush, "like to lose yourself, to be smothered in all this drapery — under — under my petticoats?" And she gazed at me inquiringly and archly half lifted them.

"Above all things!" I cried with enthusiasm.

So with a charmingly mischievous air she walked across to where I was kneeling and threw her skirts over my head and lifted her legs, one by one, across my shoulders.

"Oh! Oh! Oh! Julian!" she exclaimed, moving rapturously. "Oh, Baby! Whoever taught you to do it so well?" as I found, amid her glowing flesh, her well-developed clitoris and tickled it vigorously with my tongue.

"Oh!" she cried. "Stop! You must let me lean against the bed." There I continued my delightful task and tasted and swallowed the divine nectar of the woman I loved.

Mademoiselle very soon returned and we went to dinner. Mademoiselle was in very high spirits, declaring London of all places the most charming, saying she was positively obliged to me for having occasioned the visit.

"I have got a box for the Gaiety tomorrow night and you shall attend us in your smartest corset, Miss," she said to me. "Your smartest corset! Oh, I have seen such lovely ones! I wonder how you will like the regime of the stay-lace!"

Gertrude's pretty assumption of authority over me thrilled me as did also her constant glances. I looked at her silently in reply.

Towards the end of dinner Mademoiselle made an observation to me to which I replied rather petulantly.

"His trousers make him uncommonly pert," observed Mademoiselle.

"Yes," rejoined Gertrude, "he shall be punished after dinner by being deprived of them and of all his masculine garments; and as we have no others to give him just now he will have to remain without any at all."

Mademoiselle looked at me with a provoking little smile and a sparkle of satisfaction in her eyes as much as to say: "How will you like that, I wonder?" Aloud she said: "I am glad your mamma keeps you well under her thumb. She evidently knows how to deal with a precocious boy."

The prospect of being despoiled of all my male finery which gave me position and dignity and a sense of my importance by these two exquisite damsels upon whom I gazed noting their lips and features, their busts, their unveiled, swelling, and rounded bosoms, their shapely arms, their waists, and their petticoats, filled me with a delicious tremor and a sweet confusion. A sense of their feminine sex overwhelmed me, intoxicated me. My heart palpitated to such an extent as almost to suffocate me and effectually prevented my eating. I knew as sure as fate that as soon as the dessert had been cleared away I should have to undergo my doom.

Fresh glasses were put on the table, the dinner things had all gone. Mademoiselle had informed the maid that she would ring if anything was required. The coffee was filling the room with its fragrance when Mademoiselle flung herself upon the couch and placed a cigarette between her lips.

"Now, Julian," said Gertrude peremptorily, "I really am very sorry but I cannot overlook your disrespect to Mademoiselle. You must be taught to behave properly and with due deference to young ladies. Come here! I must deprive you of your trousers and of these other things," she continued, twitching my shirt, "which seem to inspire you with such boldness — you are evidently not fit to wear them. Your discipline does not even yet seem to have impressed you with sufficient awe of the petticoat. Perhaps when you have no clothes on your feelings will induce you to behave more decorously."

"Oh, Gertrude! Oh, Mamma! Someone may come in," cried I, standing up and trembling, while Mademoiselle smiled on the sofa sending little rings and wreaths of smoke up to the ceiling from her dainty mouth.

"I cannot help that," replied she, taking me by the shoulders. "If they do, you must regard it as a part of the penalty you have to pay!"

She slipped her hand down to my waist as she faced me and unfastened the buttons all the way down the front of my principal garment. Then she undid the braces and pulled them down. She next did the same with my drawers.

She made me seat myself and took my clothes including the shoes and socks off and deposited them on a chair some distance away. "There! I have taken charge of them. Now, come, your jacket, your waistcoat, no nonsense!"

And I stood there in my shirt, which barely came down to my braces. She undid my tie with scant ceremony and took off the collar, unfastening the three studs of my shirt. Notwithstanding my protests, she gathered up its skirts and lifted it off over my head. My vest scarcely concealed my nakedness and the next moment that too was unbuttoned and I was deprived of it.

"This I believe," she said pulling me in front, "this ugly thing is, I believe, the cause of all your naughtiness!"

"He will have it cut off tomorrow," calmly observed Mademoiselle.

"Oh! Oh!" I exclaimed shuddering. "Not really?"

"We shall see," she remarked.

"Now, Julian, tomorrow morning when you have to dress you will have to pay for these garments before I shall give them back to you," went on Gertrude menacingly.

"I think he should be well birched," remarked Mademoiselle, who had an inordinate affection for the birch. "The birch," she exclaimed, "warms a bold boy's bottom more to a lady's satisfaction than anything else. It is so delightful to feel that one has made a boy's bottom smart, and burn so much that he ardently wishes he had not one."

"I dare say you may find it very desirable to birch him,

Mademoiselle, but he will not get his clothes back without becoming acquainted with my little riding whip. I long to lay it across his bottom," said Gertrude, passing her hand over that part of me which they both took so much strange delight in repeatedly naming.

"For your vest and shirt you will receive three strokes each; for your drawers, as a more important and indispensable article, six; and for your trousers as the most important, and the most emblematic garment, a dozen."

Chapter XIII

Hortense

"Now go," continued Gertrude with her delightfully imperious and dictatorial manner, "now go and kneel before Mademoiselle and beg her pardon."

"Pray, Mademoiselle, forgive me," I said scarcely venturing to raise my eyes to her face. She took no notice of me for quite ten minutes. When she had finished her cigarette she sat up.

"Come closer to me," she ordered, "and keep your hands behind you."

Then, with her bare arms and dainty hands, she slapped my cheeks.

"Now I shall slap something else," she added. "Lie across my knee."

I lay somewhat bewildered with the shock of the pretty palms across her silken gown, and received a severe, nursery punishment from her dimpled hand.

"Thank me!" she ordered, when it was over. How her little hand could sting!

I obeyed.

"Gertrude," she said, "he has made me so naughty, you really must let me subject him to my petticoats."

By all means!

Mademoiselle moved to a low armchair, bade me seat myself in front of her, and while Gertrude cracked walnuts and drank, or rather sipped, Burgundy at the table, Mademoiselle held my head between her exquisite thighs and I was made to kiss and lick her mouth with a moustache, which I found in a very excited state indeed.

"I see where he learnt that before," observed Gertrude.

"Oh — so — you — oh — oh Julian! So you — made him — oh, oh, oh — do it to you?" observed Mademoiselle as she lay back in her chair in the most abandoned attitude, her arms dangling at each side of her, her beautiful chest expanded, her legs stretched straight out across my shoulders tightly grasping my head, almost fainting with the love sickness I was causing her.

I was soon deluged but was not allowed to rise. She retained me in that position while she and Gertrude chatted. She stretched out her hand for her glass. At intervals I kissed her. I determined now to excite her to please myself without waiting for her bidding. She kept me there and must take the consequences, so I determinedly inserted my tongue.

"Oh, you naughty boy! You naughty boy!" she cried moving violently and much more energetically. I could feel her flesh. I persisted tickling her clitoris with all my might; at last she was overcome and obliged to give me what she had before obliged me to receive.

"Oh, Julian! You have gained quite a little love victory of your own. Would you like now what you wanted so much that morning?"

"Oh, Mademoiselle!" I cried, at length released, my eyes sparkling. "Yes, yes, above all things!"

"Are you quite sure you want it still?" she asked, in her pretty teasing way. "Are you not" — delight in tantalising me — "too tired?"

"Oh, no, no, no! I do want it. Oh! Above all things."

"Very much — are you sure?"

"Oh, Mademoiselle!" I exclaimed, gazing at her, speechless from my delirium of delight. The idea of possessing or being possessed by that exquisite being who had inspired me with such feelings towards her almost took away my senses.

"Very well; you must ask your mamma's permission first though."

"Please, Mamma," said I instantly, addressing myself to Gertrude. "Please, Mamma. May I do what Mademoiselle wants?"

"Oh, you wretch!" exclaimed Mademoiselle, again reclining on the couch. "What you want to do with me, you mean."

"What I want to do to her," I repeated.

"Whatever can that be?" said Gertrude, pretending to be puzzled and looking up with a horrid little smile at the ceiling affecting an air of absolute innocence.

"Please, Mamma, may I —"

"Well what?"

"May — may — may I *fuck* Mademoiselle?" and I hung my head and again covered my face with my hands.

"You indecent young rascal. How dare you? Mademoiselle, do you wish this boy to — to *fuck* you?" (How Gertrude, like other refined young ladies I have known, loved to say naughty words!)

"Yes, yes!" exclaimed Mademoiselle. "He must."

"Must!" exclaimed Gertrude. "Dear me. Well, you may, but you must do it before me."

"Come," said Mademoiselle eagerly, her hand already lifting her skirts.

"Oh, I hope — I hope — we shall have a baby!"

"Oh, you Monster!" exclaimed both the girls.

Mademoiselle drew me to her breast between her legs, and at last I lay in that paradise I had so longed to enter.

She was nicer, softer, and warmer than Gertrude. I lay upon her as though I had found everlasting peace after a long quest.

Gertrude stood over us. I never until then felt what nakedness was. My intense appreciation of it transfigured me with passion.

"I must feel how he does it," she said, placing her hand upon me.

Mademoiselle strained me to her bosom.

Gertrude's hand urged me to the delicious task I had to perform.

A pause, another long sigh, Mademoiselle's eyes softly closing, her mouth apart, her lips deliciously moist, as I entered further and beyond the gate, as she came more and more under the divine influence.

My whole being seemed to be concentrating itself in the spasm that was about to overtake me — it came. My love, my soul, my existence were conveyed to my sweet cruel mistress amid her soft inarticulate murmurs more grateful to my ears than any other music could be.

"How the little heart does beat!" exclaimed Gertrude, who would not even then remove her hand which, upon my highly excited nerves and sensitive organ, stimulated them almost to frenzy. I begged her to remove it.

"No, I shall not!" she said, still holding me tightly.

I feared she would rupture me.

"Have you been sufficiently — fucked?" asked the naughty Gertrude.

"Oh, Gertrude! Oh, Julian, you dear boy!" cried Mademoiselle, kissing me.

"Now come with me to my bedroom," said Gertrude. "How dare you behave like that to a young lady, you naked animal? And before your mamma, too!"

Chapter XIV

That Night

"Now, into bed," she said, leading me to it, giving me a big bumper of red wine. "I shall come to you presently."

I lay dozing. Gertrude awoke me after some little time. She was as completely naked as myself.

"I will teach you that a young gentleman does not come to his mamma's bed to sleep!" she said, with a pleasantly menacing tone, slipping into the bed. I was on my back. She extended herself upon me, holding me close with one arm, while, with the other, she excited my virility in a way she knew to perfection, even more than Mademoiselle. This was the revenge of her jealousy!

Her being over me was a strange — a new experience to me. She pressed me down and I lay completely at her mercy. Her legs held me and I could not escape from the tight wedding ring she slipped off and on to Mons. Priapus, up and down, until he was beside himself, and kept him there.

"Now, Julian, not till I tell you, *mind!*"

She proceeded to work herself into an ecstasy of excitement, positively perspiring, glowing with her efforts, kissing me passionately. I restrained myself as well as I could.

"Oh! Ah! Oh, Gertrude! Oh, I must, I must!" The contact against mine of her breasts, of her hair, the extent to which she made me feel the fire of her eyes, excited me to distraction.

"Not yet," she answered. "You must not yet. You must restrain yourself. I will teach you to please a lady. You must not, without permission — you shall not!"

"Oh, oh, oh! What shall I do? Gertrude — my own!"

She increased my trial by playing with my testicles with her hand, covering my mouth with her dewy, little, unfolded rosebud of a mouth.

At last I felt her flush.

"Now," she said. "Good boy to have withstood so long — now — now" — in a soft low tone — "now — fuck your mamma."

A sigh — throb — throb — throb — throb — throb — throb — throb — throb.

"Oh, Julian, you angel!" as she at the same moment gave herself to the love fit.

"Well," thought I, "love makes life worth living. No wonder it is said to make the world go round!"

We fell asleep, and awoke not until the morning.

"Time to arise," then exclaimed Gertrude. "Go and get the chocolate. You will find it on the table outside the door — no, go as you are; yes, naked. I love to see you so. You look so interesting with that shame-faced look. Shame positively becomes you, you naughty, naughty boy, to have slept with your mamma!"

Before I went I kissed my mamma well on her face, eyes, mouth, inserted my tongue into her pink, seashell-like ears, descended to the red and white roses of her bosom, thence downwards along the Via Veneris.

I brought in the chocolate; we drank it very happily together.

"Julian, what are you dreading?" asked Gertrude, noticing a certain amount of gloom upon me, which was caused by my dread that that night would be the last of my joy, as Mademoiselle had expressed her determination to have me circumcised and castrated.

The Jews, I knew, were circumcised, and yet had plenty of children. It was the gelding, the castration, I feared.

I told Gertrude my dread.

"Mademoiselle will, I believe, have you circumcised, but I am equally certain you will have nothing more done to you. Mademoiselle is determined that you shall be punished for seducing Maud and that you shall bear the marks of her displeasure as long as you live. It won't do you any harm. Besides, she would be afraid to keep you with the girls unless you were so punished as to make her pretty sure you would not repeat the offence with Bee or Agnes."

"But does it hurt?"

"Yes, I think it does — like having your ears pierced; and you will be sore for quite eight days. Have you not read the Bible?"

"Oh, Gertrude! — Oh, Mamma! Could you not beg me off?"

"Certainly not! I think you deserve the punishment."

Chapter XV

Morning

There was a knock at the door.

Elise told Miss Stormont that Mademoiselle wanted me in her bedroom.

Gertrude lent me a dressing gown and Elise conducted me thither. A strange, tall girl was in the room. I trembled. Were they going to operate there?

"This is the young lady who has the superfluous hairs on her face," explained Mademoiselle.

"Will you not try electrolysis?" asked the stranger.

"No, shave him — her, I mean," directed Mademoiselle.

So I had to sit down and was lathered and held by the nose while the strange girl shaved me clean.

"There are very few hairs," she remarked. "She will not need shaving very often."

Then I was turned into the bathroom.

Immediately after I sought my clothes.

"Mademoiselle," I exclaimed, "what am I to dress in?"

"Oh! Miss Stormont has your clothes; go to her."

I immediately remembered the events of the preceding evening and shuddered at the prospect of that little riding whip. I trembled as I knocked at Gertrude's door.

"Please, Mamma, may I have my clothes?"

Gertrude was dressed in a charming spring *toilette*; her tightly laced waist struck me at once.

"Must you have them?" she asked.

"Oh, you know I must."

"And you know," with a whisk of her petticoats, "that you must" — imitating my emphasis — "pay for them!"

I changed colour. She went to a drawer and took out a dainty little feminine whip with a jewelled handle.

"Lie on that couch," she ordered. I did so with reluctance and she put two straps round me, one round my shoulders, the other round my legs at the back of the knees.

"Vest," she remarked. "One! Two! Three!"

The little whip bit and stung fearfully. I cried out and tried to escape, to turn.

193

"Shirt," she went on. "One! Two! Three!"

The strokes were deliberately and well laid on and bit horribly. She paused a few seconds between each.

"Drawers. One! Two! Three! Four! Five! Six!"

I yelled — I lost my breath! That was an awful dose. She smiled.

"Trousers —"

"Oh, Gertrude! Oh, Mamma! Oh, Mamma! Oh, stop! Yah! How it hurts!"

She did not stop for a moment and put her hand through from behind and played with my testicles.

"Oh! Oh!" I exclaimed. "Oh, for the sake of our — our love — of — our — night together!"

"Yes, if you will come about town with Mademoiselle and me without trousers" — momentarily suspending her strokes.

"Oh, Gertrude, how unkind!"

"Nonsense! You must suffer the petticoat. Now, Julian. Trousers! One! Two! Three!" With a will from the right side.

"One! Two! Three!" With a will from the left. "One! Two! Three!" With a will from my feet. "One! Two! Three!" With a will from my shoulders.

I fairly yelled and shrieked. She unfastened me. I rolled on the floor.

"There are your clothes," she laughed; "and if there was time I'd make you kiss what — made me enjoy whipping you. Your bottom is certainly beautiful waled. Don't you wish you had no bottom for a girl to punish?"

She left the room and me to dress before I could reply.

I was a considerable time for I could not recover from the pain and shock.

"I am glad your mamma has whipped you well!" exclaimed Mademoiselle, seeing how tenderly I seated myself, when, at last, I entered the breakfast room.

Chapter XVI

The Ladies' Shop

As soon as breakfast was over a hansom was called and I was again placed in the middle of the seat between my two dear tyrants. I had not on this occasion that thing behind to incommode me but the whipping had made me quite sore enough to counterbalance the pleasure arising from its absence. We drove to a ladies' shop, not ten minutes' distance from Leicester Square. The window was full of corsets, chemises, drawers, mysterious combinations, and triple garments! Inside, behind the counters, the assistants were all girls, and in front of them numerous customers, all ladies and their daughters.

"I have brought," said Mademoiselle in a loud voice, "this young gentleman to be fitted with a tight corset and lady's underclothing."

What she said was distinctly heard over the whole shop. Some of the daughters tittered, the mammas looked pleased, the shop assistants changed colour.

I felt overcome with confusion and I wished the ground would open and swallow me.

"Certainly, Madam," said the tall handsome shop walker. "Will you walk into a fitting room with me?"

"Miss —, attend to this lady." She singled out a girl whom I had noticed as soon as I had got into the establishment, one who had dark brown hair rolled up in masses over a ruddy face, a voluptuous mouth, black eyes with heavy lips, and a sensual chin.

She had observed me noticing her and had glanced at me.

"What corset would Mademoiselle desire?"

"Oh!" said Mademoiselle. "A severe one with very stiff busks, long waist, high under the arms, long in front, and twenty-three inches in girth."

"I quite understand; here is one, Paris made, which perhaps might do with a Venus shield; it would not wrinkle over the hips in the fitting of the dress or break; or," she went on, "here is a Newmarket Corset, very deep in front (she eyed me) or, here is a Rational-Corset, in fact we keep all kinds; or of course we can make anything you please. And do you wish for silk underclothing, or the ordinary linen?"

"Linen and silk too," replied Mademoiselle, "both."

At the prospect of a large order the manageress became yet more deferential in her manner and gave some hurried whispered directions to her underling.

"These things will be tried on?" she then asked, looking severely at me, and hesitatingly at my governess.

"Certainly," replied Mademoiselle. "In fact I wish him dressed in them now."

"We do not keep dresses; but we can send to — a few doors away for some likely to fit, if you choose?"

"Do so," said Mademoiselle.

The woman bowed. "Now, young gentleman," she said, addressing herself to me, "I must trouble you to take off these things," and she took hold of my jacket.

"Indeed I won't; here — before — you all," I almost whined.

"Julian," exclaimed Mademoiselle, plainly laughing at my piteous tone.

"How dare you?" ejaculated Gertrude. "Have you forgotten my whip?"

"So has he been whipped, and I am sure he deserved it thoroughly, I can see what a naughty boy he is. He is under petticoat government, I think," and she looked enquiringly at Mademoiselle.

"Yes," she answered, "he decidedly is."

"A very good thing too. We have had several gentlemen to dress as ladies and it does them great good."

"Then it is not unusual?" exclaimed Gertrude.

"Oh! Dear me, no; not in London at all events. Many gentlemen do it to please themselves, others, because they are made to. Come, Sir! You must take off these things and your trousers too. We do not allow trousers here unless they are linen and trimmed, or silk and open, you know — this is a ladies' shop."

Miss —, the underling, returned at this moment with an armful of silk drawers, *chemises*, petticoats, corsets, &c., and deposited them on the couch.

There was a large glass in front of me and two others on each side. Mademoiselle and Gertrude were seated on two chairs a little distance away.

"Thank you, Miss —, now please send a messenger to Messrs. — and ask them to send round a few ready-made dresses to fit a young lady; waist twenty-three inches, bust so and so and length,

Madam?"

"I think," said Mademoiselle, after a slight pause, "they had better send a few frocks suitable for a girl of twelve, or — say fourteen, as well as the long dresses."

"Certainly," said the lady pencilling down the directions with indecent glee on a pad which hung at her waist. And tearing off a slip she gave it to the girl, "And pray, Miss —, return as soon as you can; and bring a broad steel stay-busk or two with you."

"I think," she said, looking at me, "if he is troublesome, we shall find a means of compelling him — of making him only too glad to obey."

While I was wondering what she meant she succeeded in slipping off my jacket and waistcoat.

She had just begun fumbling about my trousers when Miss — returned. Needless to say that I could scarcely stand for shame.

"Miss —, please hold his hands and give me those busks," by which she designated two long pieces of steel, buttoned the one on to the other, sloped and curved, and very pliable.

"I thank you," and she put them down, within reach.

"Now I think, Madam, we shall be able in a moment to cure this young gentleman of his refractory disposition; if you will allow me?"

"Certainly," said Mademoiselle, "do what you please!"

"I have had some very refractory ones to deal with, but I think they have all had to submit at last," and she slipped her hand underneath me behind.

I vainly tried to jerk my hands from Miss —, who was standing in front of me, grasping my hands tightly about the wrists with hers, and smiling in my face.

"Oh! Oh!" I cried. "Don't — how dare you?" and I grew very pale.

"Indeed," she retorted, "how dare I? How dare you?" and she gave me a sound smack upwards upon the testicles from the back, at the pain of which I turned very faint.

I gave a little scream of pain.

"Hold your tongue, Sir, if you don't want another."

Miss — held my hands tightly, and almost laughed outright. The punishment deprived me of the power of resistance completely and of all my bounce too.

"I see you know how to manage him," remarked Mademoiselle.

"I wish I had him under me for a week. He would not hesitate obeying me whatever disgrace obedience might cost him," replied the manageress with conviction. She then unfastened and pushed down my trousers and drawers. Next she lifted my shirt off my bottom and took up the busks.

"You must always," she observed, "obey a lady. I can see your bottom has been well waled — look, Miss S—! I should have thought you would have learnt that already by this time — but as you have not, with Madam's permission," whack, whack, whack — "hold him tight, Miss —" — whack, whack — "take off your trousers, shirt and all?" — whack, whack, whack. Miss — held me as if in a vice, her dark eyes full of deep pleasure.

"Oh! Yah. Oh, you hurt! Oh, stop, oh, yes, I will, I will, oh, Mademoiselle! Oh, Gertrude, oh, Mamma!"

Mademoiselle and Gertrude shrieked with laughter at my utter discomfiture.

The manageress though was really quite angry, and gave me several more gratuitous stinging blows. Miss —, holding me, then looked very serious.

"Stay busks" — whack — "don't" — whack — "make such a litter as a birch — they are —" whack, whack — "quite as effectual though, don't they smart? — No nasty buds and bits about the floor, not such a noise as the swish of the rod, and besides they are an article of lady's attire you are punished with — what" (a sounding whack) "has compressed your governess's form. I trust" — whack, whack — "if ever you have a wife she will govern you severely — it is a capital thing for a man; and that she will make you dread her stay-busks. Now I think you will be more docile. Do you know, Madam," she said, recovering her breath, "many ladies bring their husbands or lovers here to submit to the *regime* of the stay-lace? Only the other day — yesterday in fact — was it not, Miss —? — a young lady brought her *fiancé*, and explained she had promised to marry him, but only on condition that he would wear one of our tightest corsets, and a pair of lady's drawers under his trousers to teach him he was no longer his own master but now under a mistress, and her property."

"And did he submit?" asked Gertrude, with undisguised curiosity.

"Yes! He had to; in her presence he was laced up and she chose the drawers and took away his own with her; he had half a dozen pairs, richly trimmed with lace; and then he begged as a sign of goodwill on his part, to be allowed to wear ladies' stockings too — she clapped her hands, and was delighted — she gave him a kiss as a reward, and made him show her what she should possess after they were married."

"And did he?"

"The poor gentleman looked very shamefaced, but I held his hands behind him and made him stand before her seated on that very couch and she had a good look; examined him carefully I promise you."

"Did she touch him?"

"No. Now, Miss —, now young gentleman, if you do not want more flogging, strip yourself, Miss — will help you; and as soon as you have taken your things off you shall have this nice *chemise* over your head."

Miss — did help me. In fact she stripped me and I stood naked before these four women.

"Whatever has he to be ashamed of? A back and thighs like a woman's, I declare; and such a smooth face. He will make a capital girl!"

A silk vest had been slipped on under the *chemise*, then long stockings, silk, next the corset.

Mademoiselle finally fixed on what was technically described as an Ideal Sylph-Corset with a very small long waist. It was very high under the arms and inconveniently long in front, and it was laced with great severity, Miss — holding me, while her fellow conspirator tugged at the laces and *made* it meet.

"Drawers," Mademoiselle explained. She would not have combinations.

"We always advise wide old-fashioned drawers for young gentlemen who are to be unsexed. They can be easily removed for purposes of punishment and combinations cannot be." At the sight of the flannel petticoat I rebelled again. I was not a girl, I would not wear the thing.

"Bring him here," cried Mademoiselle, exasperated. "Give me the busk. Across my knee this instant, Julian."

Miss — pushed me over. Whack, whack, whack.

"Oh, Mademoiselle! Oh, Mademoiselle! Oh, you hurt!"

Sobbing and trembling, the white flannel petticoat was then tied on.

"Now, Miss, your dress —"

When I was fully equipped, a cab was called and we were driven to a lady's *coiffeur*.

"No, I will not have my head shaved."

"You must," said Delilah with a stamp.

"It is not necessary, Mademoiselle," remarked the hairdresser.

"*Mais je le veux*," exclaimed Mademoiselle, with another stamp of her little foot.

So my head was shaved, and I was furnished with a woman's head of hair. Several wigs were chosen. Another cheque. Then to Rathbone Place, to a bootmaker's.

"This young lady requires boots and shoes very tight, very high heels. Two pairs to lace halfway up her legs, halfway to the knees," ordered Mademoiselle.

My feet were then forced into girl's tight boots, which were laced up, the five-and-a-half-inch heels feeling like mountains under me.

When we reached Oxford Circus, Mademoiselle would look in at a shop in Regent Street where she saw some marvelous corsets with horrid belts below the waist, more like instruments of torture, more like strait-waistcoats than any I had seen before. I was willy-nilly taken in; the assistants were very much more hoity-toity here than nearer Leicester Square. They could hardly find a corset large enough for me and plainly regarded me as a hoyden. Of course they found out that I was a boy. They entirely ignored the fact although their winks to each other seriously embarrassed and discomforted me.

But when the belt below came to be laced, there was something in the way. Their discovery of my sex had already cost me several sly pushes and touches, which, with feminine spitefulness, they gave me at every opportunity in the most promiscuous manner. One of them then whispered to Mademoiselle.

And as a result a principal was consulted.

"Yes," said the haughty and stately personage, "a young lady of abnormal development and construction, in fact a hermaphrodite. I quite understand. We have met with several cases of it. The abnormal organ had better be turned under the belt, Miss —"

This was ruthlessly done.

I recollected Lord Alfred Ridlington's observation in the conservatory, that he had met several young ladies with that thing in front. Oh! Would they — would they after all believe me to be really a girl? Walking was now more troublesome but Mademoiselle insisted on it and we went down Regent Street, along Conduit Street and Bond Street, and so back to the hotel.

Luncheon, alas! I could scarcely eat, so tightly cased up was I.

Gertrude had to leave that afternoon. I bade her *adieu* with tears. And then I was suddenly revived, for Mademoiselle reminded her of the theatre and induced her to stay until the next day, when Mademoiselle purposed returning to Suffolk.

Chapter XVII

A Lady Doctor

After luncheon Mademoiselle and I drove to a lady-doctor's.

Horror! I cannot dwell upon it.

First my ears were pierced, and I was forced to wear gold earrings. The doctor and her assistant held me during the operation — a painful one!

Then I was placed on a table, on which were several cushions, and fastened down on my back.

My petticoats were turned over my head, my legs well separated and fixed to the corners of the table. Some chloroform was given me to smell which threw me into a dreamy, relaxed condition.

My corset was unfastened, and Dr. Mrs. — stood at my side, an arm over me.

"What a fine one!" I heard her exclaim, in a far-off way, her hand aggressively upon my generative organs. "Now, young gentleman, you will be punished for seducing your cousin, punished by your governess' order, this lady here." And she caught my testicles and slipped her fingers on to the penis, which she, with firm pressure, pushed under the skin, then gathered the *prepuce* well forward, and pinched it between her finger and thumb.

I could have offered no resistance even if I had not been too drowsy. The lady-doctor held me very rigidly with her left hand, and with a sharp instrument in her right, snipped off the proper portion of the *prepuce*.

A styptic soon stopped the bleeding. The wound was bandaged scientifically. I was unfastened, told to rest on the sofa, and presently given a small glass of dry sherry.

"I have had occasion," I heard the doctor say to Mademoiselle, as she slipped the fee into her hand preparatory to departure, "lately to punish a surprising number of young gentlemen in this way. You will find it of great service, especially as you tell me he is being educated as a young lady with others; besides it will be of great benefit to him hereafter and improve the character of his offspring. He will be all right in a week and not so prone by a long way to transgress in the mode of which I hear he has been guilty."

I felt very sore, in some pain, and so queer from the chloroform, that I could not walk.

"Take him home in a cab, put him to bed for a few hours in a well-ventilated and airy room; let the window be open; it is a warm afternoon. Oh, yes! I should think he would be well able to go out with you tonight, but do not let him have any stimulants stronger than claret and not much of that; not eating, if you please. Thank you. Good afternoon."

And so we were bowed out and we drove home. Mademoiselle was extremely kind, really tender to me.

"Now, Julia," she said, tucking me in her own bed, "I trust in future you will be a very good girl," and she gave me a delicious kiss and bade me sleep.

Gertrude was out when we got back.

I awoke very much refreshed about seven o'clock.

Gertrude came in to see me and she and Mademoiselle helped to dress me.

My wardrobe had come from the shop and it included a low dress. I was dressed in all respects like a girl, with opera-cloak, flowers, and ornaments in my hair. My ears were too sore to be touched; the plain gold earrings, Mademoiselle declared, were the only false note about my otherwise *chic* and smart *toilette*. Both Mademoiselle and Gertrude with the kindest thoughtfulness and consideration avoided exciting the slightest sexual emotion in me.

A chicken was roasted especially for me and I was permitted a half bottle of claret.

After dinner, Mademoiselle in her lovely diaphanous robes, and Gertrude who looked radiant in a severer costume more suitable to her more Circe-like features, entered the Brougham, and we drove to the Gaiety.

How I enjoyed the performance! How happy I felt.

We returned and had a delicious little supper. I drank soda-water and milk.

Mademoiselle claimed me that night, and, to my intense joy, I spent it in her bed; but, alas, was obliged to do so, as if in very truth I had been a girl.

The principal incident of the next morning was the sale of all my masculine garments to someone who had been directed to call for them. When they were carried away I felt irrevocably a girl.

Then Gertrude bade us, "good-bye," promising to come to see us in a few months at Downlands.

And finally Mademoiselle, myself, and Elise, with augmented

impedimenta, drove off to Liverpool Street.

My travelling costume was a very fashionable and becoming one.

"Good-bye, Julia, you dear, dear girl! Don't forget your mamma," said Gertrude. "Be a good boy — girl I mean. Never attempt rebellion. Resign yourself to the petticoat and you will find it sweet."

As we started I felt that I had bidden *adieu* also to Julian Robinson; as though I could never remember having been a boy any more than last night's dream.

Chapter XVIII

Downlands Hall Again

We arrived. Beatrice and Agnes rushed into the hall, and Mary descended the steps to the carriage door. Maud, still unforgiven, did not yet appear.

We went into the drawing room; Elise helped Mademoiselle off with her travelling cloak and hat and gloves, and did the same kind office for me with less ceremony and more promptitude, and then Maud entered in her short frock with the tea-tray and cast a reproachful look at me. The proud beauty evidently felt very keenly the position to which she had been degraded, as, under Mary's superintendence and orders, she set out the tea things. Mademoiselle noticed both the look and Maud's manner and glanced at Mary who seemed to have been waiting for it.

"Yes, indeed, Miss," she instantly said, "we have had great trouble with her; she would not wash the vegetables or peel the potatoes and has been trying to get at her own dresses. She locked herself up in her own room yesterday afternoon and set me at defiance."

"It is a shame, a disgrace," burst out Maud, looking beautiful and flushing with rage, "to dress me like this, to treat me like a servant; I wonder what my uncle —"

Mademoiselle, seated in her chair quite at her ease, looked at her with that dangerous smile I had long ago learnt to dread.

"Take off your drawers," she ordered.

"No, I won't," said Maud, with a stamp, "here in the drawing room before him; or" — with hesitation, "anywhere else either."

"Him!" retorted Mademoiselle. "This is Julia, your cousin, a girl like yourself," and she got up there and then and gave Maud a ringing slap on each cheek.

"Take them off," Mademoiselle repeated.

Maud burst into tears and sobs.

The trimmed ends of her drawers were visible below her frock. At Mademoiselle's reiterated command she gathered it up about her waist, the sting of the slaps proving sufficient motive, and took off the clothing.

Maud was put across an ottoman, weeping. Her pretty bottom was exposed, her skirts turned over her head.

Mademoiselle then gave her two dozen lashes. The lovely pink and white skin quickly became scarlet, and in some places there were blue marks. She rolled and wriggled, displaying herself under the influence of the smart with absolute recklessness. Mademoiselle then gave her with deliberate severity which took my breath away, a third dozen. At its close Maud appeared to faint in an ecstasy of delight. Beatrice and Agnes could not sit still. Mademoiselle's eyes sparkled with a strange light.

"Will you obey — will you submit?" she asked, as the strokes fell between Maud's separated legs. "Are you sorry for your insubordination?"

"Yes, yes, yes," convulsively gasped the unfortunate girl, "I — I — I will — obey, I — will — will, oh, stop! Oh, I will — I will — obey."

Mademoiselle positively caressed the fragments of the rod as she finished the castigation and ordered Maud to lie as she was until she had permission to rise.

She kept her so during the whole time that we were at tea; and then Maud had to get up and take away the tea things, disturbed and trembling, covered with shame, flushed and disordered.

Maud was in penance until the end of the month.

The bedroom to which I was taken was that I originally occupied. It communicated with Mademoiselle's room by a door of the existence of which I had been unaware until this evening.

When the dressing bell rang, Elise shew me into it. She had unpacked my things and dressed me for dinner.

My dress was not that of a young lady, but of a mere chit of a girl, scarcely coming to my knees. It was of some white fluffy material and underneath it I was compelled to wear a stiffly starched petticoat which made it stick out and disclosed my limbs almost to my waist.

Mademoiselle without seeming to do so made me occupy positions which set off my costume to the fullest extent.

"Has it really been cut off?" whispered Beatrice to me in the course of the evening, all her inquisitive, prying looks failing to satisfy her. And Agnes, behind me at the door, slipped her hand under my skirts and felt my possessions.

"No," she said, "he is still a boy."

Agnes' own skirts did not reach her ankles and I longed for a revenge.

Beatrice in her quiet, matronly way rejoined: "You know, Julia, you are mine. I have a score to settle with you. You have broken your oath. Wait; an opportunity will soon come."

What infinite disdain she managed to throw into the tone in which she uttered the word "Julia!"

Three or four weeks passed in very monotonous routine by which time I had quite recovered from the operation I had undergone in London; and to my surprise I found myself more susceptible and longing in a more reckless way to put my instrument into the middle of my charming tyrants with whom I was so intimately and familiarly associated. I longed to see them blush and tremble under me as I probed with my most sensitive and shame-dealing organ the secret recesses of their beautiful bodies.

All this time Beatrice maintained, notwithstanding my numerous mute appeals, a distant and cold reserve towards me.

And one day, when Agnes, while we were out walking, complained of my impudence and disobedience because I would not climb a tree to please her by displaying my nakedness, it was Beatrice who suggested to Agnes to whip me with nettles.

The punishment was cruel. Agnes stung me more than she whipped me. While I lay on my face on the soft mossy bank, held down, my Beatrice slowly drew the bunch up and down between my legs and did not forget to include Mons. Priapus and his purse. For three days subsequently I suffered great pain.

It was upon one of our half-holiday afternoon rambles that Beatrice first attacked me.

We were in a lonely and out-of-the-way part of the wood, and Agnes in her romping with me had very much disordered my clothing. My drawers Beatrice had already removed and they were stowed away in her pocket.

"Now, you harlequin," began Beatrice, seating herself upon a mound of grass under the green spruce firs and looking very imperious in her luxurious girlish beauty, "just you come here and reply to my questions."

"Here is a sceptre," gaily cried Agnes, putting into Beatrice's hand a bundle of fir twigs; and, sitting down beside her with a smiling countenance, she regarded me with a comical expression of mixed solemnity and amusement.

"Kneel down there, Julia, in front of us."

"I'll tell you," cried Agnes. "We'll strip him, tie his hands, and make him sit or lie on the ground between us."

No sooner said than done. Agnes flew to me, and quickly rid me of all my clothing, notwithstanding my frantic opposition. My cries and protests were unheeded. Agnes grasped me violently while Beatrice quickly divested me of every single garment, and sat upon them.

Agnes then tied my hands behind me with a handkerchief and forced me back, downwards on to the narrow strip of green ground between her and Beatrice who towered over me, holding the rods in her hand.

"So Elise sold you to Maud and she took you to her studio. What did she do to you?"

"She — she —"

"Be quick, Julian!"

"She undressed me."

Agnes here squeezed me pitilessly in front.

"Oh! Oh! Oh, don't! Oh, don't, Agnes, you hurt!"

"Of course, I do — I intend to."

"She undressed you?"

"Yes, Mademoiselle came in suddenly and found me."

"Found you!"

"Ye — ye — yes; found me like this — naked in Maud's room."

"Oh!" said Agnes; and she leant over me, playing vigorously with me, and gazing into my face.

"Turn him over!" said Beatrice.

A slight struggle accomplished this.

"Now I shall whip your bottom before we go any further for being naked in my sister's room."

And Beatrice administered a sound flogging with her wretched twigs.

"Now, Master Julian!" said Beatrice, recovering her breath by deep inspirations: "Please account for the blood on Maud's *chemise* and on the coverlet of the bed. Oh, yes! I saw both before they went to the wash."

"No doubt the blood came from you," continued Beatrice derisively; "the effects of the flogging Maud gave you, no doubt; but I want to hear it from you yourself."

I was aghast.

"Concealment is of no use. Confess!"

"Well, Beatrice, Maud wanted me to stand as a model for a

statue; and you know you had made me promise I would not do that, and so I resisted and objected and made excuses.˶

"And so Maud whipped you; hence the blood, eh?"

"No, Maud began coaxing me and playing with me —"

"Like this?" suggested Agnes, suiting the action to the question.

"Oh, oh, oh, Agnes! Oh, yes!"

"And you slipped your hand underneath her clothes?"

"Yes — no — yes."

"And then she —"

"She lay on the bed."

"Yes, and you became a model for a living statue?"

"Yes!" I gasped.

If my hands had not been bound, I should have covered my face with them.

"And you were mine for five years, and gave yourself away?"

"Oh, Beatrice!"

"Now, just tell us how you did it?"

"She — she — lay down."

"On her back?"

"Yes, on — her — back; and I lay face downwards upon her, with what Agnes has got in her hand inside Maud."

"You wretch! You beast!" exclaimed Agnes.

"Inside her! Where?"

"Oh, inside —"

"What she pees with?" asked Beatrice sternly, and peremptorily.

"Y—e—s."

"You monster!" exclaimed Agnes.

"And what next? Did it shoot something into her?"

"I had — had to — she made me — I forced it in, and Maud bled and then —"

"You went into a convulsion?"

"Yes."

"Very well," said Beatrice. "And now, when last I saw this thing, it had not a red head like that, it was covered with skin. What did your governess do to you?"

"She took me to London and had the skin cut off."

"By whom?"

"By a lady-doctor."

Agnes was listening intensely.

"This is all a mystery to me," she observed.

"Let him lie in your lap a minute, Aggy, and I will show you."

"Oh, no, no, no, I *won't*. Whatever will Mademoiselle do?"

"Mademoiselle! You are mine, do you forget? Lie on your back, dear."

Agnes soon rolled over.

"Now, Julian!"

I reluctantly reclined upon her.

"Beg her permission to tickle her with your tongue."

"Put his head — *there!* — Between my legs? Oh, Beatrice!" cried Agnes, with a deep flush.

"Yes; he knows the way. Now, Julian!"

I tickled the soft virginal aperture and stiff little clitoris with my tongue until Agnes was almost fainting with pleasure. But before anything happened, Beatrice made me lie upon Agnes; her *chemise* was between her and myself.

"Now," said Beatrice, "Agnes, dear, imagine that that thing you have been amusing yourself with is inside you, inside where he has been kissing you."

"Oh, how — dreadful!"

"And hold him tightly." She did so, and Beatrice whipped me gently.

At last the spasm overtook me.

"Oh! Oh! Oh! Julian!" cried Agnes, biting my lips with her pretty mouth.

On examination the *chemise* was found to be well wetted on both sides.

"There, that is what he did to Maud, only actually inside her. Should he treat our sister as a harlot?"

"Oh, the wretch! He ought to be hung."

"As I find your word is not enough, Julian, and your bondage must be more severe, you shall be mine, not for five years or ten, but as long as you live. Mine, body and soul. What a slave I shall make of you! And as you did what you did to Maud in utter disregard to your promise to me I shall not consider you have expiated your offence until you have besought and implored me to let you do it to her again after our marriage, and have gained her assent, and then you shall do it in front of me. I shall tell Maud at the first opportunity and get her to meet us on our honeymoon. There!"

"Now kiss your mistress," she said, "and receive your fate; when you are married to me I promise you, you will spend more of your time between my legs than anywhere else!"

I yielded. I kissed my hairy mistress with a queer sensation that she was to be my wife and my tyrant for all my days.

"Now, Julian, I consider we are engaged!"

"Yes," I cried eagerly, "yes, Beatrice!"

"Well, as he is mine, I will give him a kiss," and the dear girl touched the top of Mons. Priapus with her ruby lips, tickled him with her little tongue, and bit him with her pearl like teeth.

"Does that give you pleasure?" she asked, gazing with liquid eyes into mine.

No need to chronicle the response.

"You are having all the fun, Bee; it is not fair, playing with and sucking that great big thing as if it was a sugar stick!"

"Indeed!" cried Beatrice, with a quick fierce glance at Agnes.

"Very well," with an air which I knew meant mischief, "you shall have your share!"

"Come," she said, gathering her skirts up a little, and spreading her pretty limbs apart, "come and sit down between my knees, your back to me — so" — as Agnes readily complied.

"Now lie back, your head down in my lap, and give me your hands."

I noticed that Beatrice crossed her legs across Agnes' middle.

"Well," Agnes exclaimed, "what next?"

"Now, Julian," continued Beatrice, "kneel across her and me; lie down upon me, your face close to mine."

"Oh, Bee!" cried Agnes, turning pale. "He has got that thing against my face. Do let go of my hands for one moment, or it will be in my mouth!"

"Yes, that is exactly what I intend," calmly remarked Beatrice, holding the struggling girl firmly, "you wanted your share of the sugar stick, you shall have it. I will take good care it is none of it wasted. Put it into her mouth, Julian, well in; imagine it is inside me, and make it do what it did inside Maud, and half an hour ago in her own lap."

"Oh, no, no, no," cried Agnes, "I — I won't —"

I stopped her utterance by promptly popping Mons. Priapus between her pretty lips, well into her little mouth. She was transfixed. I felt the back of her throat with his head.

In two minutes I shot my appreciation of Beatrice down Agnes' gullet.

It was intensely *bizarre* and exciting to give to Agnes the emotion that Beatrice had evoked.

"There," said Beatrice, "I hope you enjoy and appreciate your lollipop!"

"It is much nicer than I thought it would be," naively remarked Agnes, sputtering and wiping her mouth with her dainty handkerchief.

And then, looking at me, she gave me a sound smack on the cheek.

After a moment's silence she added: "You must lend him to me sometimes, Bee, and next time, he — must — put it — else — elsewhere," and a rosy blush mantled over neck and face.

Chapter XIX

Incidents of an Afternoon

Elise one afternoon told me I was to get ready for a drive with Mademoiselle and soon her prancing ponies and pretty carriage came round to the door.

It was the first time except when returning home that I had been outside the grounds dressed as a girl and the prospect gave me a fresh shock.

My hat and thickest veil emphasized my girl's costume as I reclined by Mademoiselle (who drove herself) in ladylike fashion holding up a little parasol.

I felt quite naughty when I saw her whip her ponies which she did with a will. She had two whips. One for occasional and special use was short and heavy. She positively employed it to castigate, with deliberate, conscious archness, the off pony's private parts. He frisked and pranced to the satisfaction of Mademoiselle and to the intense merriment of the miniature groom in the rumble, who would have a fine story for the servant's hall and the stable loft.

Fortunately for the near pony Mademoiselle could not get at him; but he received many a stinging cut horizontally across his buttocks delivered from over my head.

Mademoiselle noticed how her use of the whip asphyxiated me.

"Julia," she said, loud enough for the tiger to hear, "if you don't behave, if you ever show the mulish spirit of these ponies, I will flog you just in the same way. I'll tie you up naked to a trapeze by the wrists and — lash you!"

"Oh, Mademoiselle!"

She turned and the flame in her eyes set me on fire.

We returned after a drive of about two hours which had, owing to its incidents, served to reawaken all my old naughtiness. I longed for anything Mademoiselle would give me.

When we got home, Mademoiselle held a *séance* by way of afternoon lessons in the schoolroom.

My good fortune was nearer at hand than I had anticipated but at the cost of much more preliminary excitement.

Beatrice had not looked at her Dante and came to terrible grief over a difficult passage. To make matters worse she lost her temper and angrily told Mademoiselle, she herself knew the construction of the passage as little as she (Beatrice) did.

Mademoiselle rose in her majestic fashion without a word. We expected the heavens to fall, while poor Beatrice looked flushed and dumbfounded, as she stood before her. No doubt she knew her fate and it was one no girl could contemplate with equanimity.

Mademoiselle rang the bell.

Mary answered.

"You must be birched soundly on your bare bottom," remarked Mademoiselle to Beatrice, who drew her breath quickly and defiantly. "Julia" — I gasped — "Julia shall give you two dozen. Remove your drawers, Miss!"

I caught my breath, and felt as though I should faint. I whip Beatrice!

"I won't be whipped! It is a shame and disgrace! It is not fair! I know the meaning of the passage as well as any old commentator of the lot. I don't believe the author himself knew what he meant. I won't be exposed, I won't" — with a desperate stamp of her little foot — "to — to — to him. I won't let him whip me."

"A third dozen for impudence and insubordination. Now, Julia, lay them on well, mind! Mary!"

Mary promptly took Beatrice's hands — her perturbation and nervousness were so great, that she could not resist — and led her, sobbing, to the couch.

"Take off your drawers, Miss," reiterated Mademoiselle, who invariably insisted on this self-degradation.

I had never seen Beatrice naked — naked as she would be to be whipped. I had, of course, been placed by her herself under her petticoats, but there was not sufficient light to see by, and, besides, she was pressed closely to my face. I longed to see her bottom and legs and thighs. That prospect filled me with exultation and I therefore resolved, at all hazards, to seize the opportunity, and to give her a thorough, downright flogging.

She would respect me all the more for it.

When Beatrice saw that Mademoiselle was inexorable she sobbed, but she knew resistance would be worse than futile. Still sobbing, she gathered up her skirts with both arms, unfastened the string of her drawers, and stepped out of them.

Mary laid her across the cushion and held her arms. She gathered up her dress and petticoats in front and at the back, and Mademoiselle placed a nice, new, green elastic birch in my hands.

I contemplated with rapture the plump, white thighs, the private parts, the curving back of my future wife now exposed to me for punishment.

"Now, Julia!" cried Mademoiselle.

I recollected how Mademoiselle had birched me, and how I had often been birched since, and resolved to better the instruction.

Maud and Agnes looked on with blanched faces and heaving bosoms. Mademoiselle moved in her chair in a way I understood. Mary was scarlet. I felt a strange kind of fire, a lust for flesh, thrill and bound in my veins, and I thirsted for blood.

Slowly and deliberately as Mary counted, with all my force I flogged Beatrice's bottom soundly. She yelled and screamed, and writhed, and twisted, but Mary held her fast. Before long she was reduced to the most abject submission. No obstinacy can withstand the birch.

The last strokes were given lengthwise, and I made the buds hit, and the supple twigs embrace that protuberance I had had to kiss. Beatrice shrieked at first, but then sobbed quietly, and seemed to go into a delirium of delight as the last stroke fell. She was thoroughly whipped in every sense.

"Now, Julia, come with me," ordered Mademoiselle with astonishing energy.

She led me straight with swift silence to her *boudoir*, the happy scene of my first initiation, of my first experiences.

Once there, she, apparently beside herself, tore off my dress with a divine fury which alarmed me. She threw me down on my back with enrapturing violence upon the large yielding divan and its great soft cushions. For one instant she contemplated me there in my disorder before her. The next, with a deep and satisfied inspiration, she gathered up my garments with both her arms and tossed them over my breast. I made no resistance. I was conscious of my nakedness, but made no attempt to conceal it. Then she threw herself upon me and gathered me to her warm bosom, her breath fanning my face. She had lifted her own skirts and against my nakedness I felt her own.

I was at her disposal completely; her face above mine, her form close to my own. I felt every emotion that thrilled her as she toyed with my being as the wind toys with a feather. I was carried away by the vehemence of her passion. She placed herself upon me and I knew that our physical organisations were joined, were united, had become one.

With what force, with what rapture, with what transport she threw herself upon me, how hard and quick her breath came and went, how her eyes swam, how her lips clung to mine, with what vigour she moved to and fro, up and down, exciting me to an enormous size and pressing me vigorously and relentlessly home!

"Now, Julia — now — if — if — you don't — at once — I will whip you, I will whip your — bottom — until — until it bleeds — I will flog it."

I did not need this spur. I clasped her sweet crushing form. I twined my legs round it and I gladly and with profligate rapture exposed myself to the full fury of the storm.

Oh! Oh! Oh!

And the lovely girl sank yet more closely and more intimately into my embrace.

What a strange circumstance that the sight and infliction, even the thought, of whipping should produce and inspire such a tornado of passion.

I felt, no doubt, that it was seeing me whip Beatrice that had so inflamed Mademoiselle, but I recollected the flame in her eyes when during our drive she had told me how, if necessary, she would correct me. Beatrice's whipping had only brought about the climax.

This was my first experience of an embrace since my circumcision; and it was eminently satisfactory.

To my supreme surprise and delight I found the entrance into paradise much easier, the contact with my mistress much closer, I could preserve it longer, and my power was greater; whilst the annoyance and discomfort caused by the forcible retraction of the tight skin had altogether vanished.

Mademoiselle, in her entrancing disorder, looked into my eyes and kissed me again and again. Her thick hair had partly fallen. Her lovely limbs in their exquisite underclothing were visible to my enraptured eyes which dwelt on their shape; and I was happy to be oppressed by them.

"Did you enjoy whipping Beatrice, Julia?" she asked mischievously as she stood up, her hands behind her head, re-knotting her magnificent hair.

"Yes," I answered, with a smile.

"Naughty girl! Have I made you happy?"

"Oh, Mademoiselle! Oh, my darling!"

"No, I am your mistress, Julia!"

"My darling mistress, then."

"My yoke is heavy, is it not, Julia?"

"Love makes it light," I replied — a reply for which I got another kiss.

Mademoiselle's passion lasted long. Although she would not then permit me a second embrace, yet its fires were not all assuaged or extinguished.

Before dressing for dinner she bathed. That night I was ordered to spend in her bed.

There was no preparatory ordeal on this occasion, but I had to take up the same quarters as on the first, down under the bedclothes, under and amongst the skirts of her night robe, my head between her legs, at once my pillows and my gaolers. I kissed her frequently, but she did not let me again explore the grove, or the recesses of the humid temple of the Cyprian goddess, which existed hidden in its luxuriant growth, except with my tongue. To do that, however, was the task imposed upon me and exacted rigorously.

In the morning, when I awoke, Mademoiselle had already arisen.

Chapter XX

Not a Wedding Ring

It is an ill wind that blows nobody good! The advantage of the operation I had undergone did not only lie in the greater ease and comfort with which I employed the best agent and the cleverest advocate of my feelings, but also in the fact that I ran no risk of having him flayed out of mere wantonness — an act Elise had perpetrated on me on more than one occasion.

Neither my cousins nor Elise could now slip their hands up my petticoats, excite Mons. Priapus, and retract his covering, leaving him raw and bald until they were pleased to re-hood him, or to permit me to do so myself.

But his head now reminded me of a vulture clothed with plumage up to the neck and bare beyond. In fact Elise made some remark of the kind as she dressed me and suggested that she should make a nice, soft warm cap for the poor chap. I did not respond either "yes" or "no."

In all respects I was now treated as a girl. All day long my ideas, wishes, and desires about exercise, about reading, about work, about sport, were pruned down, and assumed, as a matter of course, to be those which should influence the actions and life of a young lady of my age. What yet remained of my masculine propensities suffered great repression from this process.

It was a masterly measure and decidedly checked flirtation. But Mons. Priapus — abnormal or not — was there and free. And four or five days after the first day when Mademoiselle had admitted that I was restored to health I must narrate that certain appearances had (under extenuating circumstances, undoubtedly — a peeping ankle will do so much mischief) made themselves remarkable in front, just underneath the end of my corset, lifting my petticoats and skirts in a peculiar manner, making quite a little mound in front, and raising the garments higher off the ground than usual, and also further away from me so that they stuck out.

This was first noticed as I was standing one afternoon in the schoolroom reading in choice Italian some of Boccaccio's tales to Mademoiselle and my three cousins who were working. I was carried away by what I read and not caring to recall my thoughts from contemplation of the delightful ideas suggested by the author at first did not notice that I had not the attention of my audience, that the girls were tittering, and that Mademoiselle was gazing at me with amused anger, biting her lips either with vexation, or to repress her laughter. There was nothing laughable in what I read. I thought it was some of their tomfoolery and read on. I felt naughty, but never dreamt they would be able to discern any indications of it. At the end of the paragraph I came to a full stop.

"You may well stop, Miss!" remarked Mademoiselle. "A pretty exhibition you are making of yourself," she continued, laying aside the embroidery, upon which she had been engaged.

"It is an unfortunate interruption," cried Agnes. "I was much interested in the adventures we were listening to. I wonder whatever the Signora did with her lover. Julia, I wish your abnormal development was — was —"

She dared not conclude her sentence before Mademoiselle, but her eyes told me what she meant.

"Was inside me," is what she would have said.

Through the perplexity and embarrassment I suffered I felt the germination of the same desire. I would have given her a reason for no longer laughing at me. But I dared not dwell on it or the phenomenon would have again become noticeable!

"Julia!" said Beatrice, "is not responsible. It is all Mr. Boccaccio's fault."

Beatrice had evidently not forgotten the whipping I had given her a few days before.

"I really cannot permit," broke in Mademoiselle, "such an indecent exhibition. I cannot pass over it — Julia, I am shocked and ashamed of you — a young lady should know how to restrain herself, and if she does not know she must be taught. Beatrice, take your cousin and put her down on that couch upon her back, and hold her arms over her head."

Sinking with shame, afraid to say a word in self-defence, I was led to the couch and laid across it. It was in a prominent part of the room.

"Maud, lift up her skirts — throw them over her head — take off her drawers — spread out her legs."

These directions were all speedily obeyed. I resigned myself with a choking in my throat.

"Now keep her so, until I return," ordered Mademoiselle.

"I shall have the birching of you, Julian, in a few minutes. I knew," said Beatrice, "I knew my revenge would come. Won't you catch it!"

"I declare," exclaimed Maud, "your remark has made the thing positively rear its head."

"Oh, Julia!" went on Maud, first clasping her hands before her and then kneeling between my knees, almost touching "him," for whatever my sex, *he* was certainly masculine.

"Oh, Julia! Do you remember?"

"Remember what?" angrily exclaimed Beatrice.

"Mind your own business, Bee. He is just as much mine as yours."

If Maud had said more mine than yours, she would have been more accurate, nearer the truth.

"Indeed," rejoined Beatrice scornfully, "he has sold himself to me long ago. I know what happened in your studio, Maud."

"You don't," screamed Maud, an angry flush rising and spreading itself all over her countenance.

"Yes, I do," quickly replied Beatrice, "and he is to marry me for it; and I shall compel you, Maud, when we are married, to ask for a repetition of it."

Maud's angry flush died away. She thought it wiser not to pursue the subject; instead she caught her skirts with both her hands, and slightly raising them asked, "Now?"

"I think your assumption and airs of proprietorship quite absurd," she continued. "He is not his own to give away or to sell, and as you say you know all about it, no doubt you are aware that Elise, in whose possession he was by Mademoiselle's own order, sold him to me."

"That's all very fine," quickly retorted Beatrice, with a readiness a lawyer might have envied, raising herself up, throwing her head back, and speaking the words with great defiance, "but he was to have been only for three days in Elise's possession even if you had not interfered; and you surely do not imagine that she could have sold him to you for a longer time than she was to have had him herself?"

"My interference indeed! How dare you? You would have done the same yourself, and as to Elise's selling him or his selling himself, he is Mademoiselle's slave."

Beatrice during this altercation held my hands very tightly by the wrists over my head. I wondered what my fate would be.

"Look here," cried Agnes as I contemplated the stylish forms before which I was so shamefully exposed, "if Mademoiselle catches us squabbling you know we shall be flogged all round; do shut up. You have got him now, Bee, at any rate, so what is the good of wrangling?"

"Oh! Maud is always setting everybody to rights."

"I don't appropriate other people's possessions anyhow.'

"Because you can't get them."

"I have had more than you."

"And yet you say you don't appropriate other people's possessions."

"No more I do. I bought them."

"Bought them. Prostitute!" hissed Beatrice.

"Beatrice, shut up! Goodness, she must have heard!"

Mademoiselle, at that instant, opened the door.

"Which of you young ladies used a word with which I will not sully my lips?"

They all hung their heads.

"Maud, was it you?"

"Beatrice and I were discussing what Julia had been reading to us. She declared that the lady was — was..."

It was very generous of Maud.

Agnes looked greatly relieved.

Beatrice threw a glance of grateful recognition at her sister for her presence of mind and generosity after which I certainly drew my breath more freely. Had Mademoiselle known the truth Beatrice would have been half annihilated especially after what had actually occurred between Maud and myself which, no doubt, Mademoiselle would have surmised Beatrice was maliciously throwing in Maud's teeth. Besides which Mademoiselle believed, or, as I really think, pretended to believe, that what had happened between Maud and myself was known only to Maud, myself, herself, and Elise. What she might feel bound to do if brought into contact with the fact that it was common knowledge, I dread to think. What an escape for Bee and for all of us!

"So, Beatrice, as usual, it is you who are in fault; it was you who used that word! Where are your modesty, your maidenly feelings? How could a young lady use such a word?"

Beatrice looked at Mademoiselle but said nothing. There seemed, however, to be something in her mouth.

"Well?" asked Mademoiselle.

"I really can't see any harm in the word: *pro*, 'before,' and *statue*, 'I place.' If I had said, *proseda*, or *procax*, or *togata*, or *meretrix*, or *cunnus*, or *pellex*, or *lupa*, or *scortum* —"

"Very well, Beatrice. Stop your obscene storm of words! Your vocabulary — *sacré bleu!* — you have a fine one. It does credit to your classical attainments. However, I have something else to attend to now. You shall be punished, after dinner, in a way which will test your candour. If what you have said to me is true you will not feel the penalty: but I doubt it very much. Prostitute indeed — a pretty word! As it is of so little significance please to write it in Roman capitals on a large card and hang it round your neck when you come down to dinner!"

"Oh, Mademoiselle!"

Mademoiselle had a flat steel ring or disc in her hand, the inside edges of which were serrated or indented like a saw. By means of a watch spring attached to it, it was fixed on to Mons. Priapus, and it was evident to me that if he enlarged himself in the least, the teeth would be into him and the more he grew the further they would penetrate.

"There," said Mademoiselle, having daintily fixed the instrument, "I think this will cure you; but in the drawing room I must direct Elise to replace that bandage you wore when Lord Alfred Ridlington dined with us. And now, Miss Julia, of course you know you must be birched. Beatrice, flog your cousin's bottom for her?"

Beatrice brightened up at the notion of whipping me. Mons. Priapus grew. I got fearfully pricked.

"Oh, Beatrice, let me go!" I shouted. "Oh, Mademoiselle, it is eating into me! Take it off," I cried desperately struggling, "take it off!"

Beatrice held me tight.

Mademoiselle was pleased to see her horribly ingenious little instrument work so effectually.

"Oh! Do not have me whipped with it on! Oh, Mademoiselle, please!"

"You may appeal to Beatrice."

"Certainly you shall keep it on; it is a capital thing for you. Come, turn over. Who shall hold him, Mademoiselle? and how many is he to have?" responded that damsel.

"You must put the straps across his shoulders, Beatrice. And Maud and Agnes — one at each side — can hold up his skirts. I should order him five dozen, but as he has that little bulldog on in front, we will say three. He'll bite, I expect."

I was strapped down, my petticoats held up, my buttocks exposed.

Beatrice turned back her sleeve displaying and freeing her supple wrist.

He did bite already, of course.

She walked over to me with determination and glee. I knew I should catch it and I did.

To begin with her strokes were delivered very slowly and with great force; and then, instead of spreading them about she continued to administer them as much as possible in the same spot aiming each stroke carefully.

I panted and called out — ended, in fact, by bursting into a paroxysm of sobbing. Of course my contortions and cries were no more heeded by Beatrice and Mademoiselle than if Beatrice had been lashing a feather bolster; neither did Maud nor Agnes seem to pity me.

I had whipped Beatrice, it was her turn now. My goodness! If she whipped me like this when I was married to her!

"There, Miss Julia," said Beatrice, with satisfaction as she concluded and drew the birch through her left hand quite affectionately and gratefully.

The bulldog did bite again, as I writhed on the couch, and it entirely deprived me of the power or wish to express the sensations provoked by my nakedness and castigation before the girls.

"Well, Julia," asked Beatrice afterwards when she met me in the gallery, "did I warm your bottom for you? Does it still smart?"

"Oh, Beatrice!" and I grew red as I looked at her.

"Thank me for the punishment. You deserved it."

"Yes. Thank you for flogging me."

"And you deserve another for daring to flog me?"

"Oh, no! I was obliged to."

"I have nothing to do with that. Do you deserve another for daring to whip *me*, or do you not?" — stamping her foot.

I grew pale. She had given me a birching I should not forget for a week or ten days and was intending to give me another. I looked at her splendid form.

"Yah!"

"What on earth possesses you, Julia?"

"That damned thing!"

Beatrice shouted with laughter.

"Oh," I soberly remarked, "it is all very well to laugh! It hurts confoundedly, I can tell you."

"So it ought! Will you please answer my question, Julia?"

"Yes, Beatrice, I do; but don't give it me yet."

"Good boy! As a reward you shall have it in a very pleasant way. Your head between my legs, your face upwards, while I hold your legs across my shoulders. You know — you remember — don't you?"

"Yes, under your petticoats?" asked I, slyly, for which I was given a slap.

"Oh! Oh! I can say no more," I was obliged to yell out; for the next moment this cursed contrivance bit me again. "I may have no feelings at all," cried I, clasping my hands to the middle of my lap. "I would sooner wear that diabolical bandage. Who is to whip me, Bee?"

"Oh, Agnes shall do that!" said Beatrice, scarcely concealing her merriment.

"Be it so. I hope you'll take this ring off."

Agnes' whippings were not very dreadful.

"We shall see," replied Bee, going away.

The ring I have since discovered is an American invention intended for the prevention of involuntary excitement during sleep. The teeth instantly wake the sleeper and — well, they at least deprive the act of its involuntary character.

A pleasant state of things! Was I to be permitted no sensations whatever? Again a fresh invention for teaching me a habit of restraint, of continence, by a method which itself violently excited just the contrary.

What my feelings were in the drawing room that night when Beatrice received her remedy for the use of that ill-favoured word and for her unwise defence of it I must leave to be told in another chapter.

Chapter XXI

Lord and/or Lady Alfred Ridlington

That same afternoon in her *boudoir* when my transports had become more vehement than Mademoiselle liked she had first threatened and then expressed her intention of handing me over to Lady Alfred Ridlington to tame, and Mademoiselle's laws were like those of the Medes and Persians which alter not.

There had been no question that afternoon of my sex, no allegation then of my hermaphroditism. I was then acknowledged to be a boy and in fact the whole point of placing me in Lady Alfred Ridlington's hand was that I was such. Since then however, my sex appeared to have been evaporated under the potent spell of Mademoiselle's subtle magic, of her rigorous treatment, and of the lady's garments in which I was constantly kept. Certainly the petticoats and the drawers had had a very powerful effect upon my constitution. I really hoped Lady Alfred Ridlington would prove to be that Alfred who had taken me in to dinner and afterwards to the conservatory where he had behaved so gallantly and had so delightfully shocked me — a modest damsel — with his fierce masculine nature.

Besides, of what use could I, a girl, be to his wife; or indeed, she to me?

The long summer days went by, and went by happily. We rode, and sometimes Mademoiselle took me for drives, lashing her ponies and making me pay the penalty in that famous *dormeuse* of hers, with which I became very well acquainted. Indeed, it was the means of imparting to me a wonderful understanding of Mademoiselle's nature, disposition, and temperament.

Maud had resumed her artistic pursuits in her studio, whither, however, I was now never permitted to penetrate alone, and she had to content herself with modelling my bust and arms while eagerly desiring to mould my legs in clay. I was flattered by this appreciation of my form and by the compliment to it.

Beatrice had found an opportunity of inflicting the whipping she had made me acknowledge I deserved.

It was on an evening of unusual beauty whilst Mademoiselle and Maud were rambling in the grounds after dinner in the summer twilight that she had taken me to her apartment and accomplished her purpose.

She was dressed in underclothing of unusual richness which I regarded, rightly or wrongly, as a special mark of favour to myself.

The dainty things were thrown across my head which was clasped by her ravishing thighs and pressed down by her no less ravishing body. I felt upon me that which was to be my wife and the consciousness thrilled me as I explored its recesses with my tongue while Agnes, excited and amused, whipped me with enjoyment as Beatrice held my limbs across her shoulders. The punishment was sweet, but severe, the more so because she would not remove the ring.

Agnes' pretty girlish form was stamped upon my mind; I can see her now, as in her low white dress and bare arms with a smile upon her lips and tightly compressed little mouth and a laugh in her eyes, she obeyed her sister's behest and birched my naked body exposed in so humiliating and defenceless a posture. For its tenderest parts were laid bare to her rod by the position.

The ring had not been removed. For three days I was compelled to wear it; and afterwards a bandage was put upon me when there was any danger of a manifestation to strangers of what I had shown in the schoolroom. But there, and while with the girls and Mademoiselle, I was usually without it, so that I might learn to restrain my feelings, or at least that expression of them.

The result of the discipline and of the effort, I am convinced was to lessen the force and power of Mons. Priapus, who in connection with all those girls, and above all Mademoiselle, was so dear to me. I therefore upon this account much regretted it.

I felt that time was indeed flying, and being lost, since that May morning in Mademoiselle's bed had passed — the impression upon me that it would never come again was strong. I could now never beget that child which had been summoned and (alas!) dismissed. But these girls, and she too, seemed ignorant of this.

One afternoon we were in the drawing room after lunch in the warmth of the glorious summer's day, too lazy to carry out any of the plans and projects about which we gossiped. The roses were in full bloom, the breeze made soft music with the heavily leaved beeches and sycamores and elms, played with the frantic aspen trees which tremble at the slightest motion of the air and lose their heads in even a zephyr, and seemed to annoy the stately Wellingtonias and Deiodaras that gave grace and beauty to the pleasure grounds. We heard a carriage dash up to the door. And a few minutes after, as Mademoiselle quizzingly glanced at me, Lord Alfred Ridlington was ushered in.

He could not have appeared at a more opportune or propitious moment as, indeed, he very soon gave many indications that he had quickly perceived. He greeted Mademoiselle with a frank and debonnaire gallantry that was particularly charming. How bright and engaging his manner was, how merry his tone, and how unembarrassed the freedom of his laughing eyes. He had driven himself over and he assured Mademoiselle he had at last come to fulfil his promise of paying her a long visit.

"Ah, Miss Robinson," he cried, grasping my hand, as I blushed, "deeply in love again, I suppose. I am so delighted that the moment of my happiness has arrived at last. Mademoiselle promised my wife some time ago a wild boy to tame; but I have persuaded her to reconsider that matter and to favour me by allowing me to place myself at your disposal; that will be much more agreeable," he calmly asserted, casting a lingering and amorous look at me which caused me an overpowering consciousness of my petticoats.

He had bowed to my cousins and had shaken hands with Maud who appeared perplexed. Beatrice looked as angry and as threatening as the sky before a storm and Agnes seemed provokingly intelligent. It was evident that only Maud and myself were in the dark. They all three soon took themselves off but Beatrice managed to leave a very uncomfortable impression upon me and it was clear that I was in her black books again.

"Ah, Lord Alfred, you naughty man!" exclaimed Mademoiselle, cheerily. "I fear you will find Julia as difficult to deal with as Lady Alfred would have found Julian. I recollect very well that evening when you dined with us and your elopement from the saloon afterwards. Remember it, if you do not."

Lord Alfred glanced at Mademoiselle very meaningly and possessed by an apparently irresistible spirit of mischief, passed his hands down the backs of his thighs in so comical a manner, that I fairly laughed outright, and Mademoiselle smiled, and bit her lip.

She was vexed, I suppose, because she thought he was revealing too much to me; but what Elise had said to Beatrice in my hearing on the same evening, had already informed me of the truth and made guessing, which would have been easy, if necessary, altogether superfluous.

"Oh! We shall get on capitally together, sha'n't we, Julia? Mademoiselle, you know, is a very old friend of mine; and although she looks so stern, she loves a joke."

And he calmly put his arm round my slender waist, and kissed my lips.

"Oh, Lord Alfred!" I cried, flustered and blushing. "How dare you."

While he and Mademoiselle rattled on, I wondered, whether this could possibly be Lady Alfred Ridlington, and then scouted the question as impossible and ridiculous. It must be *Lord* Alfred. He looked it. His cheeks, lips, and chin, bore signs of the razor. Lady Ridlington would certainly not have shaved, but then his form was wonderfully round, his limbs astonishingly plump for a man's and his breasts too did not look under his swelling waistcoat like the mock mamillae which men possess. On the other hand his closely cropped hair, his gestures, his manners, were, I was secretly delighted to notice, decidedly and emphatically masculine.

"*Julia*," presently said Mademoiselle to my relief, for I began to feel *de trop*, when her visitor had taken a chair and seated himself near her and had commenced a low conversation with her alone, "you had better go to my *boudoir*, amuse yourself there with that passage in the *Medea* you could not construe this morning or with Aeschylus or Sophocles —"

"Or Sappho," he broke in; "or, better still, Ovid's *Art of Love*. Mademoiselle has a *rariorum edition deluxe*, illustrated, and altogether sumptuous, if you can only find it."

"Lord Alfred!" said Mademoiselle, menacingly.

"Mademoiselle!" I heard him retort in a mock-pleading tone, his head a little on one side, as he looked at her. And I left the room.

END OF VOLUME II

VOLUME THE THIRD

CONTENTS OF VOLUME III

Chapter I

Summum Bonum

Why had I not been allowed to go out with my cousins as usual? Why was I sent to Mademoiselle's *boudoir!* These were the questions which first suggested themselves to me; and then in a flutter partly agreeable and partly the contrary, I looked at the statues and at the pictures in a vague search of some assistance to determine Lord Alfred Ridlington's sex and my own!

At last my attention was caught and engrossed by a truly sumptuous edition of Theophile Gautier's *Mademoiselle de Maupin*, a work I then saw for the first time — one which has ever since fascinated me and which to my mind possesses a greater charm than the writings even of Rousseau himself.

The steel engravings were all that the most exacting imagination could desire, executed with consummate art, and possessing a still atmosphere of perfect luxury and voluptuousness which imparted itself as an additional delight to the letterpress.

Mademoiselle had with difficulty obtained the copy in Bond Street on our last visit to London and had paid £15 for it. She had it bound, at an additional charge of three guineas, in a rich chaste cover.

I threw myself down on the great divan with the volume in my hands, opening it at random. I arranged my skirts and myself comfortably, exactly with the feelings of any other girl, leaving my pretty ankles and shoes sufficiently visible for my own delectation, if for no one else's.

I opened my new acquaintance with avidity, intent upon the entertainment promised by the engravings. My thoughts, without any direction on my part, however, momentarily returned to Lord Alfred Ridlington. But only for a moment.

The fact is the puzzle had by this time become a bore.

It worried me; it excited positive neurosis, it set up neuralgia. Impatiently and petulantly, therefore, I dismissed the subject to stew in its own juice and to evolve itself as fate might ordain. As to a welcome refuge I turned to the volume between which and myself these intruders had ventured to insinuate themselves.

Then, with the scent of the glorious roses smiling in great bowls wherever within the little sanctuary, my eyes chanced to light, filling the atmosphere and my nostrils, I read.

The balmy air — soft, cool, and in gentle motion — gratefully fanned my cheeks and neck. A sense of deep rest, of intense peace, as distinctive of this apartment as of its mistress, settled itself upon me, leaving me free to concentrate my undisturbed attention upon a narrative which speedily absorbed it.

From the lawns and terraces of the gardens beneath the large window, shaded by an ample awning outside, came the sounds made by Juno's proud birds, wheeling themselves out with pride, expanding their blue, green, and gold tails to their utmost dimensions, stretching downwards their wings so that their rustle along the ground, as they strutted to and fro, rivalled the noise made by a modern belle and her garments. Then, with the burst peculiar to them, they allowed their pent-up magnificence to escape, only to recommence the performance, their discordant cries startling me from time to time with their dissonant harshness.

The hum and buzz of the myriad of summer insects were unceasing. More than one industrious and adventurous bee sailed about the window, and having reconnoitred the lady's apartment and the lady within, withdrew with polite reserve.

Amid these ideas and surroundings and under the potent spell exercised by them, one to which by temperament I was more than ordinarily susceptible, to which indeed my peculiar circumstances, my vesture, and what I had undergone, exposed me in a special manner, I opened the book of all others fitted for that place and time.

> This the golden book of spirit and sense,
> The holy writ of beauty.

The engravings did not retain me long. I desired to become acquainted with Mademoiselle de Maupin herself.

I felt satisfied as my eyes fell on the clear text and I read with slow rapture, in order to prolong the delicious impression made by my imaginative expectations and their gradual and entire realisation. Here is what I read.

> "You know the eagerness with which I have sought for physical beauty, the importance I attach to outward form and how the world I am in love with is the world that the eyes can see; or, to put the matter in more conventional language, I am so corrupt and *blasé*, that my faith in moral beauty is gone, and my power of striving after it also... I find that the earth is all as fair as heaven, and virtue for me is nothing but the perfection of form.
>
> "Many a time and long have I paused in some cathedral under the shadow of the marble foliage, when the lights were quivering in through the stained windows, when the organ unbidden made a low murmuring of itself, and the wind was breathing amongst the pipes; and I have plunged my gaze far into the pale blue depths of the almond-shaped eyes of the Madonna. I have followed with a tender reverence the curves of that wasted figure of hers, and the arch of her eyebrows just visible, and no more than that.
>
> "I have admired her smooth and lustrous brow, her temples with her transparent chastity, and her cheeks shaped with a sober virginal colour, more tender than the colour of a peach-flower. I have counted one by one the fair and golden lashes that threw their tremulous shade upon it.
>
> "I have traced out with care in the subdued tone that surrounds her, the evanescent lines of her throat so fragile and inclined so modestly. I have even lifted with an adventuring hand, the folds of her tunic, and have seen unveiled that bosom, maiden and full of milk, that has never been pressed by any except divine lips.
>
> "I have traced out the rare clear veins of it even to their faintest branchings. I have laid my finger on it, to draw the white drops forth of the draught of heaven. I have so much as touched with my lips the very bud of the *rosa mystica*."

"Oh, Mademoiselle! Oh, Gertrude Stormont!" I exclaimed, and sighed involuntarily, and as I lingered in my contemplation of Mademoiselle's bosom, which the above lines exactly described, I sank into a soft transport, half closing my eyes and dwelling upon my recollection of the contact of my mystical rose, recalling the lilies and the roses of the exquisite mounds, out of which it grew and the azure veins which I too had traced with my eyes.

I had then no further opportunity of pursuing this train of thought, or of reading any more of the words of one who so fully understood and expressed my ideas.

I heard the *portiere* removed and someone took hold of the door handle. I hastily glanced at myself to ascertain whether my pose was satisfactory and my drapery as it should be. No doubt it was Mademoiselle, and yet perhaps — I kept my eyes down upon the book, I dared not raise them yet — perhaps it might be Lord Alfred Ridlington!

What if he should find me here alone in that turmoil of mind, in that little sanctuary at my devotions to Venus, carried away by her sacred inspirations?

The door opened and closed again. Someone came across the thick soft carpet towards the couch. With a blush, which must have been perceptible, I looked up. It was he, it was Lord Alfred Ridlington — and alone.

"Julia!" he said, gazing at me.

I returned the look in silence, not knowing what to say.

"At last," he murmured, a suppressed eagerness in his tone, and an earnestness too which startled me. I blushed afresh.

I was satisfied with my posture and my appearance and saw that it had produced all the effect that I could wish. A certain light came into his eyes as I unconsciously made room for him to sit himself beside me. His eyes, I noticed, rested on my ankles and seemed to travel up my legs. I knew intuitively he longed to see more than was exposed.

Approval of what he did see, however, was plainly expressed in his looks. He seated himself beside me and was very careful, I observed with secret amusement, not to terrify my obvious timidity. He instilled a wonderful gentleness and softness into his manner as for a few moments he silently sat at my side.

If I had done what I wanted, what I should have liked to do, I should have thrown myself upon him. I, however, let my eyes serve as the mirrors of a human form — his. But one man then existed for me in the universe. Many girls, I doubt not, have to make this confession.

Yes, I honestly avow and confess, that if I had done what I longed to do, what all the fierce passion surging in my breast prompted, I should have thrown myself upon him, gathered him in my arms, and scattered our clothing to the winds.

But something — my maiden coyness, my virginal modesty (your virginal modesty! Oh, Julia!) — withheld me. He was still silent but not from want of feeling. I was sensible of the passion radiating from him like the heat from a furnace. How could I encourage him?

He must make the first advance. Suppose (terrible idea!) he did not do so! What would become of me in that case? Suppose he had merely intended to propose a saunter or a ramble in the grounds?

He took my hand, jewelled with lady's rings.

I involuntarily glanced at the door.

"Oh!" he cried, in a reassuring way. "Mademoiselle has gone out — gone out in her phaeton, I think. She told me she was going to sketch some ruin or other, miles away. No one will disturb us."

I looked relieved.

He took my hand, and approached me more closely. His hot breath, which began to come with more rapidity, played about my cheeks.

I did not draw myself away. Why should I not take what the Gods provided? Why should I deprive myself of what I desired above all things? I did not draw myself away, nor did I repel him.

Now this is strange; for what I myself like in a woman is boldness, and an entire, imperious disregard of all *les convenances*; and how I enjoyed that embrace of Mademoiselle's after whipping Beatrice, because she had given the violence of her passion full scope, and had thrown herself upon me in headlong fury.

And I know, too, there are some women who love to be outraged, who care only for "the ponderous weight of the steer, rushing to enjoyment." However, with Lord Alfred Ridlington, I felt it would be the greatest blunder I could commit and so I made no advances.

He held my hand imprisoned in both his. What soft, plump hands they were, for a man's! He looked at me.

"Julia," he said, tenderly, "you remember that happy evening in the conservatory?"

"Yes," I answered, affecting to wonder what was coming next.

I suppose there was a tell-tale tone about the monosyllable, for he bent over and warmly kissed my lips — a very different kind of kiss from that which he had in sport given me in the drawing room.

"Oh!" cried I. "Lord Alfred, you really must not."

And I grew hot all over, and red in the face.

"I love to make the roses bloom," said he. And he gave me a second kiss.

How warm, how soft, how clinging his lips were! Their contact was like nectar to a thirsty soul! They thrilled me through and through. I felt a disturbance about the centre of my lap. Good gracious, if he should observe anything there!

"Julia," he pleaded, "kiss me back!"

I looked at him coyly and archly.

"Will you not love me one little bit?" he added. "I love you so much!"

His eyes rested on mine and shone with the strong but soft and subdued light of one in love; they were moist, and their lids drooped over them.

"Do you?" I said, innocently. "Well, then, if I must."

And I put my mouth up.

"You dear girl!" he cried, in a transport, throwing his arms about me and raining a perfect shower of kisses upon my lips, my eyes, my brow, my cheeks, and my lips again.

I yielded to the embrace. I was glad I had made no blunder.

I kissed his lips in return; and I must acknowledge that, catching fire from him, I inserted my dainty little tongue into his mouth in search of —

"Oh! Oh! Oh!" he cried, in ecstasy.

"Does that give you pleasure?" I asked, coquettishly, my maidenly reserve fast thawing and vanishing like a patch of snow that has lingered too long on some Alp below the snow line when the surprised sun espies it.

His hand slipped down to my feet.

A terrible dread came over me. Suppose, after all, Mademoiselle was wrong; suppose I was not an hermaphrodite; suppose I was altgether a boy!

I should be cheated of the happiness which seemed within my grasp; the cup of which I had already tasted the sweetness by anticipation would be dashed from my lips. I should be as disappointed — and more so, than that unfortunate child whom I could never forget, when Mademoiselle had so heartlessly refused to incarnate.

And yet — to become a mother!

Should I become a mother? I recollected I had wondered what I should do. I had wondered — when I had believed myself altogether a boy — what I should do with Lord Alfred Ridlington if he made hot love to me as there seemed every probability that he would.

Beatrice was to be my wife. Yet, how could I be another man's wife if I was to be somebody's husband? Beatrice must be in the dark. The reflection was a slight cloud upon my happiness.

He slipped his hand underneath my petticoats and I lay back across his other arm. He travelled upwards, and caressed my limbs. For a moment he played with Mons. Priapus, then his hand slipped to my back.

"Oh, Alfred, Alfred!" I cried. "Don't, don't!"

"Does it hurt?" he asked.

"Yes! Oh, yes! No, it — doesn't hurt — but don't put your hand there — it makes me so ashamed," and I hid my face in his bosom.

"You," he continued, "are like a girl there because that thing in front you know is abnormally large," and he continued to play with my buttocks and endeavoured to insert his finger.

"You have to wear petticoats because you are really a girl, Julia. Do not be deceived about it, and," he provokingly added, "Mademoiselle has told me you are such a naughty one, and I know how dear a one! Now, Julia, I cannot take off all your clothes, my dear, here; neither can I disrobe myself — you must wait until tonight for that happiness — but we can have something now. Lie on your face, my darling."

And he turned me over on the soft cushions. I knew he was undoing his own trousers and a moment later he turned up all my petticoats and uncovered my bottom.

"Oh! Oh!" I cried, and endeavoured to turn over but he prevented this. "If I am really a girl I do not mind; on the contrary I am so glad — but I hope I am."

He did not reply. He lay down upon me and I felt his weight with rapture. He pressed his hands round my waist, got them beneath my clothes, and played with what I understood was an unnaturally overgrown clitoris.

He removed one hand to insert something behind. It felt like the tube Mademoiselle had pushed in there. It burnt me, but delightfully. In a few minutes it throbbed with violence and I felt deluged with warm moisture. My clitoris also responded.

He sank upon me without reply, for his passion was too intense, pressing me closely to him.

"Oh, Alfred! Alfred! Oh, my dear Alfred!" I gasped.

In a few minutes he said: "Again, Julia."

"If — if you like."

He made the attempt, he replaced the weapon, but he was unsuccessful in the accomplishment to the end. It did not throb. He excited me however into a second paroxysm which he appeared to delight in.

He withdrew himself, let me turn round and repose in his arms.

Presently I kissed him.

"Do you think, Alfred, do you think I shall have a — a baby?"

He smiled curiously and enquired whether I should like one.

"Above all things," I promptly answered.

He laughed. "Oh, Julia! What a confession."

"And do you know, Alfred," I continued, "I — I — really thought once — just for a short time, that you might be *Lady* Alfred Ridlington dressed in your husband's clothes! Wasn't that absurd?"

"Yes; what on earth put such an idea into your silly little head?" he asked, with a look of deep affection.

"Oh! I don't know except that you have such a beautiful well-formed figure which would be a credit to any girl or woman, and because Mademoiselle —"

"Well?"

"Mademoiselle said she would, when I thought I was a boy, get Lady Alfred Ridlington to discipline me because I wanted to make too much love to her. And —"

"And what more?"

"Oh! Because she said that Lady Alfred Ridlington thrashed her husband and — wore his breeches. There!" Looking curiously at him with depreciation of my own credulity.

"Indeed, I am extremely obliged to Mademoiselle," he replied. "Lady Alfred does not thrash me and does not wear my breeches. And I think I have proved to you —"

"Yes, indeed you have, that you are a dear, delicious, naughty man! Would you like to do that again?"

"Not now, dear, thank you — it would be too exhausting for you."

To my surprise before many minutes were over, I felt very "unwell." I at once knew why Mademoiselle had endeavoured to show and to teach me how to contain myself. I felt I was going to be "unwell."

Mademoiselle had injected much more into my womb than Lord Alfred had and I had had to wait twenty minutes, so that I might easily wait a little longer now. But I could not — I had no towel on — the quantity of the injection did not affect the matter. I looked terrified. He saw something was up. What could I say or do?

"Hallo, Ju!" he cried, springing up. "I declare I hear the girls' voices on the lawn, let's have some tennis — you will come and join us presently, won't you?"

"Yes," I said, looking fondly at him as he stood before me; and as, giving and receiving a kiss, he disappeared, I rushed to my room. What a narrow, what a fortunate escape!

I leisurely put my things on before the glass, a hat, a pair of tennis shoes, and changed my skirt for a tennis one. I looked at myself, and thought: "Now, Julia, thank goodness! You know you are a girl, and are, perhaps, going to have a baby."

I recollected my rude, hobbledehoy, hoydenish days, when I believed I was a boy and wondered at the change so surprising, so far reaching, so complete, that had overtaken me.

My former rudeness and roughness and violence positively shocked and astounded me. I felt ashamed of them and blushed deeply. They were so disgraceful in one who all the time should have been in petticoats.

So thorough was this system of discipline that to this day when I know all about it and understand how I was mystified, the impression is still strong upon me and exercises a most wonderfully taming and domesticating effect.

On the way down I met Mademoiselle.

"May I congratulate you, Julia dear?"

"Oh, Mademoiselle!" I cried.

"Am I cut out?" she asked, with that playfulness which she never lost.

"Oh, Mademoiselle, no!" I answered, a little indignantly.

"But how about Alfred? I suppose he is now —?"

I blushed deeply. My wits came to my rescue.

"You know," I said, in very low, hushed tones, "you said I was an hermaphrodite. I belong to you just as much as to him."

"You are a dear boy — girl, I mean, Julia." And she kissed me.

"Never mind the tennis. Come with me to my *boudoir* and tell me all about it. We'll have some tea or chocolate or what you like."

And how delighted I was to obey.

Chapter II

That Night in the Drawing Room

As I returned to my room for the purpose of substituting for my short, tight skirt (fitted for tennis but not for the dalliance of Mademoiselle's *boudoir*) a loose tea gown and high-heeled shoes, a rush of memories flooded my mind in an unaccountable fashion — memories of that evening, now some days past, when I saw the rich, full bosom of Beatrice, in her low-cut evening dress, hidden by an ugly oblong card suspended by a scarlet ribbon from her radiant neck on which was inscribed, in letters an inch long, the word —

PROSTITUTE

What thoughts, what notions and ideas, what immorality and profligacy, this single symbol — this single expression — on the swelling bosom of my future wife evoked!

"Oh, Beatrice!" Agnes had cried, clapping her hands, as Beatrice entered the brilliantly lighted drawing room before dinner. "What a — a — charming one — you are! If only I were a man!" Beatrice's anger, rising at the first half of the sentence, was momentarily diverted by its close. She looked at me full and distinctly betrayed the fact her chief concern was as to how I should take her disgrace. Without being aware of it, I felt flattered.

And I suppose it was the sense conveyed by this assurance of her concern about me, lingering upon my mind, that caused me now to stand and think and wonder instead of hastening to Mademoiselle as I should have done.

Agnes, however, did not escape, for Beatrice, averting her eyes from me, and returning to her first impulse, walked up to her, her teeth clenched and her eyes flashing and hissing the words "You wretch!" gave her two sound boxes, one upon each ear, before Agnes could recover from her surprise at the storm she had raised.

I abandoned myself somewhat inopportunely and somewhat to my own surprise, to a *resume* in my thoughts of that delicious, eventful evening — delicious, principally, I verily believe, because Beatrice had to undergo then what she was so fond of inflicting. I delighted in the discomfiture and humiliation the proud beauty had suffered.

Agnes looked pretty and girlish in her elegant frock. At the blows she changed colour but appeared more disturbed at the threat with which Beatrice followed them up.

"There, you impudent baggage! Just you wait awhile and I will make you wear a card like this behind and before!"

Agnes dared not reply, but I could see her pretty bosom heave and grow crimson whilst a defiant glance shot from her eyes.

Maud was in the room and watched what went on with quiet amusement; but, as usual, was too careless, too serenely indifferent, to take any active part. She had looked up at Beatrice's entrance and at Agnes' remark, but then, with an impatient kick of her dress, and a disdainful pout, she continued her perusal of the novel she was reading while we waited for Mademoiselle and the gong.

The whole scene returned with surprising vividness to my mind though I was much puzzled why it should do so at that particular moment.

The current was, however, too powerful to resist, and as I stood before my glass, fondling my arms, admiring my breasts, noting my drooping eyelids and their long lashes (I had thrown off my gown) I was forced to abandon myself to it and I may as well relate my reminiscences in the order in which they most impressed me, which was at the time when I most cogitated upon them, although not the time of the actual occurrence of the events.

What then, to be honest, was the significance of that magnificent *diamante* bracelet, the gift of Lord Alfred Ridlington to me, worth several hundred pounds at least, which now adorned my dressing table and which I had more than once fully appreciated and admired when clasped upon my arm, and had made up my mind to wear that very evening although I felt very uncertain whether or not to tell Mademoiselle beforehand of the gift? One of the articles of her favourite code of love enjoined strict secrecy in love matters. Had it — disquieting hateful thought — been given to me as wages?

How I loathed the notion; and under its influence the red-gold and sparkling stones for a few seconds appeared to be a badge of servitude. Was I a prostitute?

After all, the gift was made to me in accordance with custom, for I was a girl and should have all the trouble of the baby.

How should I, and I looked at myself in the glass when asking the question, feel with a great card on these swelling breasts of mine with the word "prostitute" inscribed in enormous letters upon it?

Poor Beatrice! She had accused Maud of prostitution because she had bought me from Elise and had herself to suffer as though she were the criminal. How delicious to consider Beatrice in that light!

What a strange qualm, strange thrill, shot through me, as I recollected the exquisite happiness she would sell. Those soft, warm, yielding thighs opened wide to the shower of gold as were Danae's to her god! My imagination faithfully depicted the well-stockinged calves, the daintily perfumed underclothing, the glimpses of pink flesh, the alluring posture, as she reclined with outspread arms and inviting looks, the drooping lids, the languishing air. Verily, as Agnes said, she would have made a splendid one, hence no doubt the sting of the observation. What a scrutinizing piercing glance she had thrown at me, as Agnes had added, "how I wish I were a man." Did Beatrice after all know the secret and the truth? Was I a man and did she long for me?

I wondered what Mademoiselle would do, for what use could a prostitute be amongst women?

I had helped to dress Mademoiselle that evening and she had never looked more stately nor more queenly than when in the drawing room upon that occasion.

She, of course, noticed Beatrice directly, and looked at her with well-feigned surprise as she observed Beatrice's carnation hue and shamefaced appearance.

"Well, Miss," she exclaimed, "what is there about the word that so disturbs you? *Pro*, before and *statuo*, I place," mimicking Beatrice's tone; "if it were *cunnus* or *pellex*, or *scortum*, or — or *meretrix*, did you not say?"

"Oh, Mademoiselle!"

"Perhaps you have been round to the OEdiles and announced your intention of joining the ranks of the *pro-fessce*, and this card announces — until a tailor has provided you with a toga."

"Oh, Mademoiselle! You know no free woman —"

"No free woman could become a harlot. True — but as you have carefully explained, it is not harlot or — or — or a worse name that you bear; it is only *prostitute*."

"It is too bad, it is too shameful," cried Beatrice, beside herself with anger, "to label me prostitute!" and she tore at the card. But before she could rid herself of it Mademoiselle stopped her. "I forbid you to take it off. I cannot suppose," with delicate scorn, "your excuses for the use of the word were insincere — so you will please keep it on. And who knows, after dinner we may find some one anxious to fill your lap with gold. Julia, for instance," added Mademoiselle. Then slyly to me, "Julia, what pocket money have you left?"

"Julia is a girl," retorted Beatrice scornfully; in her turn scanning Mademoiselle very closely.

"Julia is an hermaphrodite," replied Mademoiselle, calmly.

"We shall see."

"Never!" shouted Beatrice, reddening to her forehead.

"Or if you do not think her sufficiently powerful, I dare say we can find someone else. There's the gong. Julia, take in Madam Beatrice. Maud, give me your arm — run along, Agnes." During this passage of arms, we had stood open-eyed and open-mouthed, wondering what the end of it would be. Even the sedate Maud had relinquished her book and I would have given a great deal to learn what was passing in her little head.

"Oh! Oh! Oh!" I cried, for my excitement had occasioned a growth, and I got myself unmercifully bitten. I blushed painfully; in fact the pain was so severe that I thought I should faint.

Mademoiselle stopped, really astonished.

"It is that wedding ring of his, hers I mean," said Maud.

"Oh! I had forgotten. There, Beatrice, already," observed Mademoiselle. "I fear his remaining guineas are in serious jeopardy."

"Julia," said Beatrice, in desperate tones, as she took my arm, "if you don't take care, if you don't look out, I — I — I will tear the thing off you."

"I really could not help it, Beatrice," I expostulated.

"You *must* help it," she replied, giving my arm a vicious pinch.

So we marched off to the dining room.

The maids who waited at table looked at Beatrice and looked very significantly at each other. They were too well trained to give any other sign but I am sure I heard tittering behind the screen, and the one who handed me my soup gave me an intelligent although almost imperceptible nudge.

There was Beatrice next to me, that great card in her way, unable to lift her spoon to her mouth without sprinkling it, to such an extent did she tremble, to such unusual nervousness was she reduced; and all because there was that word upon it.

During the meal Beatrice was unusually silent, almost sullen.

What she was thinking of I puzzled myself very much to imagine. I was too much occupied with my own thoughts to take much part in the conversation always dominated by Beatrice's flaring announcement; for whatever subject was broached it seemed to be very quickly exhausted and attention returned to the placard.

I noticed that Beatrice drank much more than she ate. Glass after glass of red wine disappeared, until, at length, I observed Mademoiselle noticing the frequency with which it was emptied and refilled.

In these matters we were always left to our own devices. Mademoiselle never condescended to interfere in them, although she was ready enough to amuse herself with the consequences of any indiscretion.

It soon became plain to me that a spirit of perversity had seized Beatrice and that she was resolved to do justice to the character which had been ascribed to her. She had been made to declare herself a prostitute; she intended, evidently, to fill the part.

I knew the quantity of wine she was imbibing would make her utterly reckless. She drank and drank and her air and demeanour soon gave her the appearance of being so.

Before dinner was over she sat bolt upright resting against the back of the chair, her cheeks flushed, her eyes wild, her hair slightly disarranged. The naughtiness of the word seemed to have entered into her; and her legs were well apart, her eyelids drooped, and her gestures were very free.

The two other girls looked very much astonished, Mademoiselle looked amused, and I was frightened. I did not want Beatrice to make an exhibition of herself and she was evidently on the high-road to it.

In my solicitude, without exactly intending it, I involuntarily took an opportunity of pushing her glass from her, when I thought no one but herself would observe me, by way of giving her a gentle hint.

"You little ass!" she at once exclaimed, looking angrily at me, and quite loud. "Are you going to spill it over me again? Do you want me to slap your face for you as I did the other day? Leave my glass alone!"

I gave up in despair. I felt quite sad at the failure of my well-meant interference, and rather small at the notion of having my face slapped by one who was herself evidently more in need of control than able to exercise it.

"Julia," said Mademoiselle, "take care! Beatrice, I expect, will slap you somewhere else next time."

"That I shall! I shall put him across my lap, and warm his other end!"

And she pushed her chair back and appeared ready there and then to execute her threat.

The result was that I had recourse to the anodyne myself; for Mademoiselle, noticing Beatrice's condition, merely smiled and bit her lip — that dangerous smile which I knew betokened mischief.

In the drawing room Beatrice sank into a low, easy chair with a review on her lap, which, for some ten minutes or so, she attempted to read. Maud and Agnes went to the piano and Mademoiselle made me sit on a stool at her knee and talk to her. Beatrice soon began to nod and Mademoiselle to tire of inaction.

"Julia, why, with that alluring, appetizing spectacle before you," asked Mademoiselle, slyly, and in a voice audible to me alone, "do you not forget your petticoats? Look at your cousin," she continued, half turning and motioning with her hand towards her; "what an attractive attitude! What do not those pretty ankles promise! Observe her air of perfect *abandon*, her lap gaping, her arms outstretched. Why do you not fly to her?"

Beatrice's pose was indeed all that Mademoiselle described it. Her shapely legs were stretched out and well apart, her skirts had travelled half way up to her knees, disclosing her close-fitting, open-work stockings and slender ankles. Her knees had fallen wide apart, her arms rested, one upon each of the arms of the wide *dormeuse*; her breasts, rich, full, and snowy white, rose and fell evenly, and with them the card bearing that dreadful name; her eyes were closed; her lips slightly open; a soft smile was upon her face and her cheeks were touched with a soft glow apparently borrowed from the scarlet ribbon round her neck.

She did indeed, as Mademoiselle said, look most attractive, most alluring, most appetizing. Her figure was most voluptuous and full of promise.

"How can I forget my petticoats?" at length I asked my governess, discontinuing my contemplation of Beatrice, and refusing to enter upon the dreams her beauty inspired.

"How can you?" rejoined Mademoiselle ironically. "Did you not forget them with me, with your mamma, with Maud?" and

Mademoiselle looked down into my face, with a soft smile.

I at once felt my suspicions aroused and myself set upon the alert. This was some deep ruse of Mademoiselle's to entangle me and to discover the true state of things between Beatrice and myself. I had learnt enough of feminine nature to be well aware that, where such preference existed, it was impossible to withhold it from the apprehension of any feminine being. They inhale its existence with the air they breathe. It is an epidemic, and I thought the smile signified a *soupcon* of jealousy on Mademoiselle's part.

I have never understood, this being the fact and no hallucination of mine, the necessity of a lover's formal declaration of his passion unless it be that he must lay himself open to a breach of promise.

No woman could find that on intuitive perception. I felt that my situation was an extremely ticklish one. The real object Mademoiselle had in view was to discover who really was the possessor of my heart. She herself merely owned my body.

How I congratulated myself upon the avoidance of the snare. I rested my head against Mademoiselle's knee, and, with a wisdom in advance of my years, murmured as I did so, Hamlet's words to Ophelia: "Here is metal more attractive."

"That is all very fine, Julia, but what good are your petticoats to me?"

Mademoiselle positively blushed as she asked this. "You made me wear them."

"Don't you want to eat between meals, Julia?"

"It's not fair to turn the tables upon me like this, Mademoiselle. I thought I was only — a — a — youth then."

"And now you find you are both that and a girl too — as Lord Alfred Ridlington will show you."

"Lord Alfred Ridlington! I thought you said Lady —"

"Oh, yes! That was before your adventure with Maud — you have been unsexed since, and I have invoked his aid instead of hers."

"Oh, Mademoiselle!" And I hid my face in my charming governess' draperie.

"Why, Julia, what has become of your aplomb? It is so long since you have been birched — by me at any rate — that I really think I must have recourse to those dainty twigs to enliven your wits. There is a lady asleep. That ring, I suppose, forbids your enjoying the privilege claimed by those who possess but one half of your dual nature. Come, I will remove it. Is a young lady to announce herself 'prostitute' in your presence for nothing?"

Mademoiselle made me stand up, and slipping her hand underneath my skirts, she removed the horrid implement.

She did not stop at that. She caught hold of Mons. Priapus and his purse and by her dexterous manipulation of both very soon evoked various inarticulate exclamations from my lips and an irresistible impulse to move myself to and fro in her hand.

"Now go to Beatrice," she ordered presently, "and do what you like, what you wish, or as much as you can — and if you want encouragement, let me tell you that if you don't forget your petticoats you will have good reason to remember a certain oak bench and my birch!"

For a minute I felt quite at a loss what to do. How much did Mademoiselle know? How was I to undertake such a task as she suggested with the girl I was engaged to? Should I blurt out the truth at once and say it was impossible with my future wife. And then there were Maud and Agnes. They might fly at me, Maud especially. And Agnes. I recollected that day in the wood, as no doubt did she. "Should he deal with our sister as with an harlot?" Beatrice had asked her and had made me teach her the exact meaning of the query.

"Go!" said Mademoiselle, and she stood up, pointing to Beatrice, and gave me a slap on the back below the waist just as though I were an infant in frocks.

I considered the subject no further. I felt compelled to obey, trusting to my usual good fortune for extrication from the mess. And notwithstanding Beatrice's threats, which I knew were perfectly sincere, notwithstanding all my apprehensions of the bondage I was perfectly certain was in store for me as her husband (apprehensions, I may observe, since fully realized), I was possessed by some strange infatuation for Beatrice which made me anxious above all things not to offend her.

What could give her greater offence than to violate her under cover of the card Mademoiselle forced her to wear?

Of course I felt naughty, but my passion was dominated by this reasoning.

"Oh, Mademoiselle!" I exclaimed. "You are punishing me, not Beatrice."

"Nonsense!" she answered. "I have not birched Beatrice. I shall birch you if you are such a recreant knight."

"It is immoral."

"Oh, no, Miss Julia! Love is not immoral. Perhaps, however, you do not care for your cousin."

"I — I — I think I care for her too much."

"And pray," instantly retorted Mademoiselle, "what then about your professions to myself?"

I was dumbfounded. I felt as though I had been struck.

In a dazed state I went without another word up to where Beatrice reclined and knelt down between her feet. I placed my arms round her and kissed her lips.

She murmured. I repeated the kisses. She opened her eyes in a dreamy way and looked at me.

"Oh, it is you, Julian!" she uttered, putting her arms about me, not sufficiently awake to know where she was. "I was dreaming. Dear boy, you may kiss me again! I suppose they have gone to bed. Where am I? What's this thing on my breast? Don't press it against me."

I kissed her again and she kissed me. I slipped my hand down underneath her dress, on to her knees, and let it glide higher up.

"Oh! Oh! Oh! You must — you must kiss me there!"

"Beatrice!" exclaimed Mademoiselle.

At the sound of her voice Beatrice started up and rubbed her eyes, leaving me still kneeling.

"Oh, I must have been dreaming!" she declared, flushing up to her eyes. "Julia, you wretch, how dared you take advantage of me?"

"Nice dreams for a young lady! Kiss me there!" went on Mademoiselle. "Where pray?"

"Oh, Mademoiselle!"

"And what about that card? Sit down again, Miss. Lift up your skirts to your waist — all of them. *Statuo*, 'I place,' Julia, *pro*, 'before.'"

"Why shouldn't I?" rejoined Beatrice. Desperately and with ravishing carelessness she obeyed Mademoiselle's injunction.

"There," exclaimed Mademoiselle. "Maud, Agnes, look at your sister. See how she absolutely gives herself up to the embraces of the first person who invites her. Wicked, abandoned girl. Go to my room instantly. And you, Julia, come with me. The heroine of the novel, a prostitute indeed! I suspected there was more than you wished me to suppose, Maud."

"Indeed, Mademoiselle," began Maud.

"Go to bed," interrupted Mademoiselle, "and you, Agnes, go too."

Beatrice, accustomed to the *role* of *bete noire*, went off without saying anything more. Maud and Agnes bade Mademoiselle good night and left me with her.

As soon as they had gone Mademoiselle turned to me with a certain amount of anger in her gesture.

"Have you ever kissed Beatrice like that before," she asked, scrutinizing me closely.

I at once remembered the night of the dance. I recollected the whipping I had from Agnes by Beatrice's orders for whipping Beatrice herself, my head under Beatrice's petticoats, I —

"No need to reply, I can see it in your face. And Agnes —"

"Yes," I replied, hanging my head.

"Maud of course, and myself, and Elise, and your mamma — every woman you meet in fact."

Now this seemed unfairly hard upon me. It was their doing more than mine.

"Go along," continued Mademoiselle, "to my room with me."

When we arrived Beatrice was standing by the fireplace. Mademoiselle entered the room with an imperious sweep of her garments.

"Undress yourself at once and completely," she directed Beatrice.

Beatrice immediately commenced sobbing.

Mademoiselle opened a drawer and took out her jewelled whip.

At the sight of it, the culprit, without delay but not without protests, unloosened her bodice, her gown, her underclothing, petticoat after petticoat, her drawers, until at last she stood in her *chemise*.

"Take that off," ordered Mademoiselle.

With a deep blush of shame but no hesitation, Beatrice obeyed, thus saving her skin.

Mademoiselle laid down the whip.

I gazed at Beatrice. She was surpassingly lovely. Her confusion heightened her charms in a most remarkable degree. But pretty bashfulness and alarm like that of a graceful fawn were not her only characteristics as she stood there in her stockings and shoes but otherwise completely naked, a condition which the contrast of the stockings rendered more emphatic.

"Now, Julia," exclaimed Mademoiselle, "do not stand there as if you were moonstruck, gazing and gazing in that idiotic manner. Upon my word you will wear out my patience. Take off your cousin's stockings and then undress yourself."

The contact of my hands with Beatrice's soft warm full limbs which resembled the delicious plumpness of a scarcely ripe peach, communicated a strong fire to my veins and caused my brain to whirl. I was in a state of violent commotion and the tender glances which fell upon me from Beatrice's half-closed eyes, greatly increased my enthusiasm, making me fully aware of her own state. It was very evident that my execution of Mademoiselle's direction was very agreeable to Beatrice. She pressed her legs against me more than there was any occasion for; and it is these voluntary and gratuitous caresses which I have always found the most irresistible and intoxicating.

When her stockings were off, Mademoiselle made Beatrice stand upon a low cane stool, which served as an admirable pedestal.

"Now, Julia," said Mademoiselle, from the chair where she reclined in easy comfort, "follow suit. You will then have an opportunity of comparing yourselves and of observing your points of difference. What a pity Maud is not here to model you both. By-the-bye, first hang that card again round Beatrice's neck!"

With a deep sigh and flush I slowly divested myself of my clothing and in a few moments stood before Beatrice and Mademoiselle absolutely naked, and feeling so guilty and ashamed that I covered my face with my hands. Beatrice's nakedness and Mademoiselle's full *toilette*, her low dress, accentuated my sense of my own state, and my consciousness of it, to a bewildering degree.

I am quite sure as I recall the scene that the whole spice of it lay in the difference of sex.

It was the sense of that difference which overwhelmed us both and so delighted Mademoiselle. With my feminine garments I felt I had put off all the nonsense about hermaphroditism — for nonsense I at that time felt it to be — though, now today, after my experience with Lord Alfred Ridlington, I stoutly denied to myself that it was nonsense; and as I now gazed at myself in the glass, and passed my hands over my body as I stood ready, in petticoat and body *camisole*, to do my tea gown, and proceed to Mademoiselle's *boudoir*, an indignant assertion of my hermaphroditic nature if not of absolute feminacy rose to my lips.

But to return to that evening.

When Mademoiselle had regarded us thoughtfully and amusedly with a somewhat triumphant air for several minutes, she bade me walk up to Beatrice and let her examine me.

Beatrice descended from her pedestal for the purpose and passed her hands over my plump body. I could not keep my hands off hers and we found ourselves locked in each other's arms.

Mademoiselle at length told Beatrice to lead me into the inner room where I had spent the three nights after my escapade with Maud.

There was a crimson silk coverlet over the bed and on it she made Beatrice recline. How lovely, how desirable, she looked!

"Now, Julia, kneel down. Beg for her embrace, ask her price. What do you value a night by her side at?"

"Beatrice," I said, in a trembling whisper, "may — may I spend the night with you here, in your arms, in bed with you?"

The last part of the suggestion appeared to me insulting.

Beatrice moved ravishingly. She had not the ordinary means of defence which women possess when clothed; and I could see how my question and the ardent longing expressed more by my eyes and looks than my words, agitated her form; and, to my great relief, under the influence of the rosy little god Bacchus or for some other reason, she entered into the joke.

"First," she said, "I must make the illusion complete."

And she threw away the card.

I am convinced of the rapacity of all women.

Beatrice did not scout the notion; on the contrary she took it most kindly.

"And what," she said, "are you willing to give me if I do?"

"Oh Beatrice!" I cried, hiding my face close to her lovely form, "all I have — love."

"Love!" she retorted, scornfully. "I can have love for the asking. I shall not give it for nothing."

"Quite right, Beatrice; make him pay," said Mademoiselle.

"Yes," Beatrice rejoined, "what will you pay?"

Mademoiselle laughed outright.

"Five — five — guineas," I stammered.

Beatrice's eyes brightened as an idea seemed to strike her.

"Very well," she answered, "give them to me and I will give you what you want all night long. And I shall take what I desire. Give them to me now."

I looked at Mademoiselle. "Tomorrow?"

"Tomorrow, nonsense!" exclaimed Beatrice. "You won't buy repentance at any price then. Now, before you feel you have any need of repentance —"

"Beatrice," I exclaimed, reproachfully.

"Oh, that's all very well. Five guineas, what are five guineas, five hundred thousand guineas?" and Beatrice looked significantly at me.

I understood. This damsel would want a fine settlement.

Mademoiselle laughed delightedly again.

"Your money is in a drawer of my *escritoire*, in the next room; the right-hand top one. Go and get your guineas."

I returned in a moment with them, and shamefacedly handed them to Beatrice.

She counted them singly and put them under her pillow, and then, throwing herself back, she opened her arms and said with a winning smile: "Come."

I sprang on to the bed and locked her in my embrace.

If the contact of her flesh which before I had touched only with my hands had set me on fire, I was now, as my body pressed against hers, ablaze with pleasure. I kissed her and she kissed me back. At last I made certain advances. What did I care for Mademoiselle's presence then!

To my astonishment Beatrice said: "No! I promised you what you desired, and I shall take what I want. Do you think that for five guineas you are to have what you seem on the point of taking?"

I knelt up, puzzled and disappointed.

Beatrice put her hands on my shoulders and pushed my head down to her middle, making me turn round as she did so. She caught my head with her thighs.

"There," she exclaimed, "that is what you want," as she rubbed herself against me, "and here," taking hold of Mons. Priapus who was now near her face, "is my toy. You shall sleep like that."

"It is not what I meant at all," I gasped.

"It is what I meant though," replied Beatrice, "and you shall stay so all night because I want this thing and will not be done out of him."

"Capital," exclaimed Mademoiselle. "Good night. Mind you keep to your bargain, Beatrice."

"I certainly shall," exclaimed Beatrice.

"There, Julia, you beast," she added as soon as Mademoiselle had gone, giving me a sound smack, and then another, and another, "there, I have outwitted her hand on you, and I have got you to myself anyhow. How could you consent to play such a part and with me too? You shall pay for it hereafter. Now kiss me at once! You know how. It is not the first time and I shall perhaps, just once, act Agnes' part with this thing."

She did so as I kissed her.

When we had rested she made me get underneath the bed clothes and dived into them herself, placing me in the same position again. What a night it was! I, as the hours — Hark! I hear Mademoiselle's voice; she is wondering what I am dawdling over. I must be off, and with a sigh I broke off my broodings about that night, put on my most elegant tea gown in frantic haste and rushed off to her *boudoir*.

Chapter III

Mademoiselle's Tea Table, and Other Things

"Julia," exclaimed Mademoiselle, as at last I entered her room in some hurry and confusion, "what on earth have you been doing all this time? Surely it cannot have taken so long to change your frock! There was no one with you, was there — Beatrice, or Maud, or Agnes?" she enquired with an uncertain and menacing air and a look which scanned me searchingly. "No?" she went on, relieved, and unbending her brows as she heard my denial. "Then what on earth can you have been doing? You knew I was waiting for you: the tea is cold long ago. I have a good mind to make you drink it as it is for a penance; but, I suppose, today you must be indulged; and so," going to the kettle, "I will make you some fresh tea. You must attribute this complaisance to the sympathy between our feminine natures. As a girl myself I can understand what you have been through."

I gave Mademoiselle a grateful look in recognition of her taking, in this good-natured way, my having kept her waiting so long, while the suggestion of a similarity between her eminently feminine nature and my own, caused a wave of feeling to pass over me not at all unpleasant in its effects, occasioning me a sweet sense of confusion and shame at the suggested positive allegation of my womanhood and the attendant irresistible conviction that beneath my lady's attire existed a veritable girl.

I felt ashamed of Mons. Priapus of whose existence I had become bewilderingly aware from the force of her words which excited very curious sensations, and I proceeded, impelled more by civility than by any other pronounced motive to make the best excuses I could.

"While I was changing my frock, Mademoiselle," I said, slowly watching her as I spoke, "various recollections rushed upon my mind which so absorbed me that I fear I dwelt longer upon them than I ought to have done; and, indeed, I was not aware how quickly the time was passing."

"Ah!" exclaimed Mademoiselle, with a little gesture of delight and a very intelligent glance. "I can easily understand and excuse you. No doubt you were dreaming of your first lover. Come, sit down here beside me"; and with a tone expressing much interest and sympathy, "tell me all about it, my dear."

Mademoiselle's manner was tender and delicately affectionate. It conveyed to me that she would consider my maiden bashfulness, if I could any longer consider myself a maid, or that, at least, she would not shock me by too rude an assertion of the change.

She treated me, indeed, as though I were a girl who had undergone some radical physical alteration, tacitly assuring me that she would make due allowances for its effects on my being.

Now this was very embarrassing to me. I had not become aware of any alteration in my anatomy, or, indeed, of any revolution in my ideas. What Lord Alfred Ridlington had done, had, in fact, been disappointing, or I was disappointed that he had not done more.

In what had taken place I had had no active part. I had been passive only, I had not received or actively acknowledged the receipt of anything. In fact I had felt acutely the want of the anatomical apparatus necessary to conceive. He had given me various sensations, resulting, as I knew, in nothing; for when he had so opportunely left me what he had given me was disposed of by me.

And he had done no more to me than what Mademoiselle had done on the first of June, than what Elise had done on the first dry day that I was under her; than what my mamma had done in her bedroom at the hotel when she had screwed that flexible tube into the ivory bulb which had been inserted into me during our journey up to town; but, of course, having all this done by a man to me in the character of a girl, had a queer, perplexing, and very exciting effect on my temperament. He had wooed me in the most approved fashion and had sought and obtained all that as a girl I had to give.

"I see," said Mademoiselle, "you should have had a honeymoon with your lover. You desire seclusion and quiet — an opportunity to compose yourself, to recover from the first shock of intimate acquaintance *with a man!*" (I shuddered and blushed.) "But come, Julia, there are no secrets between you and myself. Will you not confide in me? Has *he* —"

Naiveté, a delicious simplicity, and artlessness always characterized me. I therefore answered candidly.

"Oh, Mademoiselle! I was not dreaming of Lord Alfred Ridlington, I was thinking of Beatrice."

"Of Beatrice!" ejaculated Mademoiselle. "Of Beatrice!" and I know her thoughts ran upon all sorts of things in connection with that damsel.

"Mon Dieu! What are you dreaming of Beatrice for? Look at those cushions, look at that ottoman. They tell a tale, I want to hear about that!"

I blushed again and looked at her. There was nothing for it but to give her a full narration and I summoned up my energies for the purpose.

I sat down beside my governess under the absolute conviction that I was a girl like herself and I abandoned myself to the feeling while I hugged my petticoats about me as friendly things, the exponents of the truth regarding my sex. I felt very naughty and very happy. The happiness was due to the charming influence of my governess upon me and to the close proximity into which I felt drawn to her.

"Sometime ago," I said, looking into Mademoiselle's eyes, "I always wanted to be a boy for you, and now it seems so delightful to be the same as you are — a girl like yourself!"

"Well," said Mademoiselle, after a few seconds' pause during which we both followed out our thoughts, "Well?" and she moved her legs underneath her voluminous skirts in a peculiar manner. "Has that thing been cut off then?"

"No; only you assure me that I am a girl."

"Yes; certainly I do. *It* is punished by your being made to feel so." And she turned and looked into my eyes with an expression which searched the depths of my being and covered me with shame.

Mons. Priapus at once grew and all other feelings gave place to an ardent longing to be embraced and lost in that ample bosom, engulfed and annihilated by those firm round strong thighs.

"Oh, Mademoiselle!" I cried, my cheeks flushing.

Mademoiselle laughed.

"So you think, after all, you will want a girl to console you sometimes, Julian?"

"Julian!" I exclaimed.

"You see," she exclaimed, "you have the advantage or disadvantage of being both masculine and feminine, both Julian and Julia. You have a dual part to perform in life. You have to satisfy men and women. I wonder which you will consider the pleasanter task?"

And she again moved, tightening her skirts across her shapely limbs. "Sometimes you will want a lover, sometimes a mistress.

That is why you were dreaming about Beatrice," with a slight pout. "But I," she continued, "am determined by developing your feminine proclivities, to tame and counteract your formerly too aggressive masculine characteristics. You will," and she spoke more sternly and looked severely upon me, "always be under the petticoat. Now do you like what the petticoat exposes you to as a consequence of wearing it?"

I sat silent for some minutes, gazing at Mademoiselle, wondering, thinking, perplexed; very conscious of my pre-eminently feminine tea gown, headdress and general bedizening of the slender ankles belonging to long legs encased in stockings undoubtedly a woman's, and of the little feet shod in shoes also indubitably made for the gentler sex. And yet under all Mademoiselle's remarks lay a quiet tacit assumption that I was masculine. Her assertion of my double sex was made with an air that convinced me of its insincerity.

A feeling of indignation and of intense repugnance to my situation and garb began to reassert itself and when I thought of Lord Alfred Ridlington I grew hot and trembled. I think I almost loathed myself and certainly endeavoured to recall a chapter in Genesis, purposing to examine it.

"What was the sin of Sodom and Gomorrah? Was I in any way related to it or connected with its doings? Had it anything to do with a man being dressed in a woman's clothes, with hermaphroditism?" I must confess I felt very uncomfortable and began to kick my petticoats impatiently.

Mademoiselle ate her *bonbons*, and sipped her tea, and looked from time to time curiously at me.

How did I like what wearing the petticoat exposed me to?

If I was really a girl, or partly a girl, or a girl behind, and a boy in front, I suppose it was all very well that I should wear a petticoat and be treated as a female.

"I do declare, Julia," said Mademoiselle, disturbing my reverie, her patience at length worn out, "I do declare that I do not know what has come over you. Instead of the excited condition, the rapture, the enthusiasm, the *abandon* of the bride, the recklessness of one whose dearest wishes have been crowned with complete satisfaction, I find you morose, listless, dreamy, pale one minute, rosy the next, silent, not a word will you speak, there you sit munching your toast, and now looking at me, now at your clothes, now at those statues, then at those cushions — what is the matter? Why are you so *distrait*? What do you want? Whom are you dreaming of? Perhaps," she continued maliciously, and again moving in a manner which plainly shew her to be under the influence of very pleasant feelings, "perhaps you will reply that as a woman I should know, that your attention, your thoughts, are all of them concentrated inwardly upon the material *he* has supplied you with to enable you to make and reproduce an exact image of himself. Is it so? I can excuse you, if my conjecture is correct, and, indeed, shall feel bound to apologise for attempting to disturb your cogitations. A maiden suddenly converted into a woman, suddenly confronted with the necessity of answering the requirements of love by producing a child, may well desire to be left alone in order to collect and direct her whole energies to the work."

This would have been all very well if what Lord Alfred had given me had not travelled the same road as what Elise and Mamma and Mademoiselle had given me. There was nothing to work upon. If there had been I should have received it before, not behind. I was quite sure no one could make a child behind; not even the Venus Callipyge herself.

But how in a single-minded manner to discuss my difficulties with Mademoiselle, who stated one thing and implied another, who was evidently insincere and probably laughing at me, was quite another question.

It was no use hoping to discuss it with Beatrice, for she was blind to all possibility of my being at all feminine. Of course Lord Alfred Ridlington would only think me insane if I hinted my doubts to him. And besides I was aghast with terror at the notion of suggesting to him the possibility of my imagining he had behaved to a male as he had behaved to me.

So that there was nothing for it but to apply to Mademoiselle, and, indeed, this was probably the reason she had me there with her. She wanted to possess both my confidence and myself; so that, in spite of myself, I might be her absolute slave, body and soul.

Another question was latent in my mind, and that was the extent to which Lord Alfred Ridlington was Mademoiselle's fellow-conspirator or tool. However, it was necessary to rouse myself, for Mademoiselle's patience was evidently wearing threadbare.

As I considered my own frame of mind and really morose disposition, I wondered at myself. The influences and experiences I was under, and had undergone, were indeed calculated to produce a condition very different from this taciturn, cross-grained mood.

Mademoiselle was as alluring, as delicious, as ever. My chagrin may have been caused by erotic exhaustion. I was sensible of a nervous or cerebral fatigue and needed repose.

"Come, come, Julia!" cried Mademoiselle, impatiently. "You have sulked long enough. Answer the question I asked you long ago. You are in petticoats. How do you like what they expose you to?"

"You mean being made love to and treated like a girl?"

"Yes," rejoined Mademoiselle with a too frank smile. It was a smile — I saw it plainly — of laughter, of amusement, of ridicule, not of sympathy or of tenderness. "Yes; of having your secret charms invaded by the rude hand and weapon of a man; of his making himself acquainted with your nakedness and acquainting you with his own emotions at the same time that he learns your own most secret feelings. Do you like being a girl?"

"No, I do not."

"And pray, why?"

"Because I feel I can be more."

"More?"

"Yes. I was the wrong side up. Lord Alfred Ridlington may have enjoyed possession of me but I never seemed to possess him; and I do not think I shall have a baby. I had to run away almost directly. My womb retained nothing; there is nothing to germinate. I did not possess him as I possessed you and Mamma. I do not believe," with a burst of ingenuous candour, "that I am a girl or even half a girl."

"What nonsense!" exclaimed Mademoiselle, a little testily.

"What did he do?"

"Well, I was amusing myself with that superb copy of *Mademoiselle de Maupin*, when he came in and began to make love to me."

I blushed. Mademoiselle watched me closely.

"He took me in his arms, put me underneath him, removing my skirts, and pushed himself into my womb; and in a paroxysm of passion it happened, and it happened to me in front. I do not love him. Whatever my feelings at the moment I have ever since felt vexed, irritable, annoyed, and I do not want to see him again."

"You are a strangely inconsistent young woman — but I shall insist on your taking all the consequences of your garments. You will have to be Lord Alfred's mistress while he is here, so you had better not be refractory, or I shall make your beautiful back again acquainted with the birch — and in the meantime now to convince you of your sex I shall put something up behind."

"Oh, Mademoiselle!" I exclaimed. "Oh, pray, do not!" I stood up and clasped my hands, as I thought of the terrible suggestion. "Oh, pray, pray, do not! I will not be refractory, I will be as good a girl as possible."

"I cannot allow any nonsense of this sort," exclaimed Mademoiselle severely. "A little conviction will be good for your mind and will induce you to take more kindly to your lover and his embraces. I see you are not sufficiently broken in. I am glad I chose Lord Alfred Ridlington to discipline you instead of his wife whom I first promised you. You must have your feminine character indelibly impressed upon your mind — and upon your body. Come here."

"Oh! Whatever are you going to do to me, Mademoiselle? Oh, don't hurt me! I love my petticoats — I love being a girl — I will be as kind to Lord Alfred as ever he can desire."

"Come here, Miss, and let me tie your hands," said my inexorable governess, taking a long ribbon from a basket and placing it round my wrists, which she tied in front. Then, going to a candlestick on the mantelpiece, she took the candle thence. It had not been lighted.

"Now," she directed, "lie across that ottoman on your face and let me see this beautiful bottom of yours again."

She pressed her arm upon my back and as I reluctantly yielded to the position she indicated, I half turned round and with bated breath enquired what she was going to do with the candle.

"You are not going to burn, to singe me?"

"Oh, no!" with a smile. "I am going to convince you of the passage by putting this candle into it."

"I shan't allow you. I won't. You shan't," I shouted struggling vainly to free my hands, and half in tears.

Mademoiselle laughed. "I shall punish you all the longer for your obstinacy," she rejoined, forcing me down on my face.

I felt much surprised at the strength she possessed and exercised.

She held me down across the ottoman, one hand pressed on my shoulder while she ruthlessly turned up my tea gown and petticoats with the other. I kicked and struggled and consequently received a stinging slap as soon the skirts were sufficiently removed to expose me to it.

"There," she cried, as I tingled, "lie still or I will beat you until you do. I shall not permit this absurd nonsense, these crotchets. You shall just do as I bid you and be at the mercy of whomsoever I choose to subject you to without any questioning or reasoning on your part. I will have implicit obedience."

She opened my drawers at the back. The exposed behind completely upset my equanimity. She not only carefully exposed my bottom but the colder air upon my nakedness made me thrillingly sensible. Placing her elbow on the small of my back to keep me down, she separated my cheeks until she found what Lord Alfred had sought and pierced.

To my inexpressible consternation, I felt something, against the opening — a very persistent, very insinuating force, the thin edge of which all the voluntary and involuntary contraction of my muscles was unable to withstand. I sighed and groaned, but could not escape.

The instrument entered. Another push and I became conscious of an expansion. I was helpless to prevent the entrance into me of a larger mass which was pushed until I thought I was impaled on a stake and which seemed to penetrate my very nature.

"Now deny that you are a girl!" exclaimed my governess drawing the thing almost out again causing me excruciating sensations; and then, when it was almost entirely withdrawn, reinserting it.

"Oh, oh, oh, Mademoiselle!"

"You naughty girl!" moving the candle to-and-fro.

"Oh, I will never be so silly again!" I cried, abandoning myself, perforce, to the like to-and-fro movement. "Oh, oh!"

Mademoiselle continued.

I gasped.

"Oh, Mademoiselle! Will not that do? I am convinced I am a girl."

And I tore at the ribbon which bound my hands.

"No, I shall push the argument home. Was Lord Alfred like this?"

"Yes, but — not so big, not — so — strong!"

"Indeed!" exclaimed Mademoiselle, never relaxing her infliction.

And then she slid her hand round my waist, and over my clothes and caught me in front.

"A boy, too!" she declared.

"Oh, oh!" I ejaculated, at the fresh influx of feelings she now excited.

"Prove that to me!" she ordered.

I held my breath and my tongue, to overcome, to do otherwise.

The proof was soon given her and I felt absolutely exhausted.

But she continued to hold me.

"I shall behave better than he did. I shall not withdraw yet as you have given me so much trouble. Just a little more."

"Oh, Mademoiselle!" I cried, almost in tears, and clenching my teeth.

For quite five minutes she continued. Before she had finished I felt a very strange internal commotion. I buried my face in the cushion and submitted helplessly, hopelessly, quite reckless as to the consequences. It seemed an age, but at length it was over.

"A girl warranted not to have a baby!" remarked Mademoiselle as she at length moved away and allowed me to get up.

"It gives me diarrhœa," I foolishly observed as I got up in a very sheepish fashion.

"No, nonsense, Julia!"

"Oh, I must leave the room, Mademoiselle!" I asserted.

"Well, it is high time to dress and you may go, but mind you behave yourself tonight. I think I have smoothed things for you."

I returned to my dressing room to get ready for dinner and to prepare to meet my lover again; not without certain qualms, which Mademoiselle had taken effectual means to quell.

I felt that, willy-nilly, I must give myself up to him; and the consequence of her lesson was that I would not scruple further about the matter. Anything was preferable to being punished by her with that candle.

Chapter IV

"What Business Have You to Wear Trousers?"

We assembled in the drawing room. I in a very low dress, which Elise had helped me to do. I had on one of my strictest corsets, laced "severely," and I was chiefly occupied with the hope that I should survive.

My shoes were cut low, my legs were encased in openwork stockings, and the heels of the shoes I wore were fearfully high.

I had roses in my hair, and a cluster of them at my breast. I was perfumed with *eau de Cologne*, my face was delicately rouged, and I endeavoured to comport myself like a young married woman and to meet my lover or husband for the *noce* with *aplomb*.

He looked very well indeed, and I believe the girls envied me. Beatrice's face was a study; but just as I could not rid myself of the notion that I myself was acting, so an unholy and tantalising fancy kept bothering me that Lord Alfred Ridlington was doing the same.

Many symptoms appeared to me to confirm my suspicions. Notwithstanding all Mademoiselle's assertions and doings, I believed myself fundamentally masculine, and I began to think Lord Alfred Ridlington feminine.

However, the evening passed pretty much like that famous one which I spent for the first time in girl's dress when he had taken me to the conservatory, and my sensations were the same.

Lord Alfred took me into dinner and sat next to me. During it, and afterwards, he devoted himself to me, full of those little attentions so delightful to a girl. And upon this occasion we were quite en famille, there were no other men or guests.

At length, after a merry and exciting evening, I determined to exercise my prerogative and retire.

I kissed Mademoiselle as usual; and then, with a blush, I bade my lover good night. Prompted by some mischievous spirit, I said, as I did so: "You will not stay long in the smoking room, Alfred — you will come soon, won't you?" And I looked affectionately into his eyes. He gazed at me in return, first at my face and then at my gown and pretty ankles, which were disclosed by the way in which I had been schooled to hold up my dress when moving.

"Yes, dear," he replied, "at once if you like."

"Oh, no!" I answered, as a hot blush rose to my cheeks.

"Give me time to get into bed." And I smiled at him.

As I left the room Beatrice also got up and wishing Mademoiselle good night, followed me.

She overtook me on the staircase.

"Julian, you wretch!" she exclaimed, with great disdain.

"How can you behave like this? Don't you know you are engaged to me? Don't you know you are a boy, not a girl, and Lord Alfred — *Lord* Alfred indeed! Don't you know what he is!"

I very nearly dropped my candle.

"Don't you know?" continued Beatrice, with infinite scorn.

"You are no more a girl than I am a boy, and he is no more a man than you are a girl!"

"No!" I at length answered, summoning up all the courage I possessed; and turning round, I looked her full and defiantly in the face. "I do not."

Beatrice flushed angrily.

"Go along to your room — do not let us have a scene here. Go to your room, and I will follow you."

Mercy upon us! I wished to be alone. Lord Alfred Ridlington, then Mademoiselle and her candle, now Beatrice and after her goodness alone knows what. However, I too felt we could not have a row there and therefore slowly ascended the stairs to my room.

"You think, I suppose," continued Beatrice, "that because you wear all this borrowed plumage you are a girl."

And she set about enumerating it.

"Because you have girl's shoes on, and a lady's stockings right up your legs, and drawers, and a *chemise*, and corset, and petticoats, you imagine that makes you a girl."

Beatrice's flush had left her by the time we reached the bedroom and she had grown stern and pale while with her flaming eyes she glared upon me.

She so frightened me that I could only ejaculate: "Oh, Beatrice!"

"Oh, Julian!" she retorted, setting down her candle. Then she placed her arms and hands on my shoulders and forced me down on to the sofa.

There was no room for doubting *her* sex. A girl, a very lovely girl, and now a very angry girl. I trembled.

She looked at me and then without another word slapped my face.

"Don't you know the difference between a boy and a girl yet?

Have you not been often enough underneath *my* petticoats, and my hand often enough under yours? How can you be a girl with this thing?" And so saying she slipped her hand up my legs which fell apart instantly.

I gasped and shuddered under the violence of the assault.

"It is not my doing; how can I help myself?" I enquired coldly.

"Easily; you positively take a delight in belting your sex which is no longer yours to give away. Do you think I have not noticed all your tomfoolery with 'Lord' Alfred? I won't let you sleep with her."

"With her?"

"Yes, her."

"My goodness!" I observed. If *he* was *she*, the idea of sleeping with her was not, I must confess, altogether objectionable.

Beatrice saw she had made a blunder and I suppose this prompted the series of severe pinches she then gave me, the effect of which was to cause me to fall helplessly back upon the couch and to scatter all my ideas to the winds. She soon worked me into a condition of extreme excitement.

"There," she said, "how can you imagine yourself a girl now? Do you not long for me?"

"Yes," I replied, and in truth I did.

"Then lie flat down — on your back."

She whisked her skirts across my face and mine up to my middle. I very soon felt my mistress upon me.

"Now prove to me that you are a boy and I will satisfy you as to what I am."

Of course it had to be as she wished and it was so.

"Now get up," removing her exquisite leg from across me, "now get up, and undress and get into bed and imagine yourself a girl again if you dare. And try to be honest tomorrow!"

She took up her candle to go and I offered to kiss her, receiving another sounding and stinging slap upon my cheek in return.

"Very well!" I exclaimed, testily.

"Very well!" retorted Beatrice, at once stopping. "What do you mean? How dare you address me in such a tone?"

I looked at her but said nothing; I felt too indignant.

"Very well; just you wait one minute." Then she returned after a moment's absence with Mademoiselle's riding-whip. "Lie across the bed — on your face."

And notwithstanding my struggles, she forced me down, turned up my petticoats, held me with one arm, and inflicted some half dozen vicious stripes across my legs, over my drawers — a very poor protection, for the whip bit through them, and besides, their construction left an ample portion of my frame bare.

"Now," she said, recovering her breath, "it is very well!"

Before I had done writhing, she had left the room. As soon as I recovered I proceeded slowly to undress. I felt it could not be long now before Lord Alfred would join me and I wished to be in bed when he did come. As the shock and the pain gradually wore off I noticed my charms as they were one by one uncovered, and at last, diving into the heavily laced and frilled girl's nightdress which was placed for me, I jumped into bed. How delicious, how comfortable it was!

Silently, but angrily, resolving upon revenge on Beatrice, I ensconced myself at its further side. Its width and two large pillows pleasantly suggested what was to come. The long nightdress down to my feet, the lace ruffles at my wrists, the richly ornamented and bedizened *fichu* down my bosom, the cut of the garment fitting closely to my figure, impressed me with a deep sense of my girlishness.

I did not lie very comfortably upon my back because Beatrice's flogging had waled my thighs and had made them sore; but I lost the sense of discomfort in the sweet dreams promised by the night in store for me. The first I should have ever spent alone in bed with a man! The dim light, the warmth and luxury of my *entourage*, filled me with voluptuous enthusiasm and my mind with erotic notions and figures. I let my legs fall widely asunder. I little by little drew up the garment in front, the touch of my own fingers upon my legs strangely thrilling me.

I pictured to myself that it would be there Lord Alfred would lie; that his cold soft hand would make itself at home in that shrine, and prove but the precursor of the whole man himself, whom I should envelop with my being — then suddenly the thought struck me that I should have to lie not so — on my back — but on my face, and this disappointed me extremely.

I was still under the influence of the discontent this reflection had set up in my mind when Lord Alfred entered in his rich dressing robe.

"Julia," he presently said softly, his eyes sparkling and his voice resonant with a tone of deep complacency, "you shall not escape so easily now. Look here!" said the wicked man with deliciously cynical shamelessness and a recklessness which I enjoyed because it took my breath away. I looked and saw at the top of his legs — which, by-the-bye, I observed were plumper, rounder, and whiter than my own — and at the bottom of his exquisitely undulating abdomen an engine, fierce and formidable, exactly shaped as what I had in front of me but much larger. He wagged it with glee, menacing me with it so that I tingled from head to foot and hid my face in the bedclothes.

"Oh, no! No!" I cried.

"Yes," he rejoined with electrifying determination, "this is the great High Priest of Love who will take no refusal but insist upon entrance. He will unite you and myself."

"Oh, Alfred!" I cried.

"Come, my darling. You have instinctively assumed quite the proper attitude."

To my astonishment I was lying upon my face.

"Come, surrender to the tyrant!"

"Get into bed, Alfred!"

"No, Julia, you must submit naked this time."

Must submit naked! I did not feel at all inclined to abandon the pleasant warmth of my couch. I should have very much preferred his getting into it.

"Why, Alfred!" I said. "It has got no hair about it like mine, and — and — why have you those ribbons about your waist?"

"Oh! You see, Julia, Lady Alfred makes me work so hard, as you know from Mademoiselle, who has told you what she is, that the poor fellow has to be supported. These are patent American suspensory bandages. I am obliged to wear them; and the reason that he has no hair about him is that it has been all shaved off."

"Shaved off?"

"Yes," he rejoined quite coolly, repeating reflectively and sadly a minute or so later the same words, "shaved off."

"Why — how — because — because — you like shaving?" I enquired, perforce smiling at his lugubrious air.

"Oh, no!" he returned, with a laugh. "But just before I came here, Lady Alfred had reason to be displeased with me — I was really very tired at the time — and she shaved it all off." I felt completely puzzled.

"May I feel him?" I asked, moving across the bed and putting on my hand.

He let me do so. My manipulation of the engine did not seem to affect him or it in the least. I looked up into his face. He then began to affect throbs of passion. My observation was quite acute enough to convey to my mind that it was acting or affectation on his part.

"I really don't know what it is," I observed, discomfited and dissatisfied.

He did not appear to me altogether comfortable.

"Lie across the bed and I will show you," he reiterated.

The situation had made me feel naughty, and I was disposed to acquiesce; but I remembered, when he turned up my night robe, he would be sure to see the wales of Beatrice's whip. How could I account for them? They might suggest certain things to him and he might, besides, mention them to Mademoiselle and then there would be a row and more wales, undoubtedly.

However, I knew he would have his own way in the end, and that, then seeking a reason for my obduracy, he would be led to attach undue weight at the marks which he would be sure to regard as the motive. Delay, it appeared, would be a mistake, so I exclaimed.

"Oh, Alfred!" and hid my face.

"What a coy girl it is!" he cried, amused and delighted.

Pushing away the bedclothes, he uncovered me, and drew my right leg across the mattress away from its sister leg. Then he got between them both and embraced me. Removing a hand and arm, he inserted the implement and I noticed he kept his hand upon it.

My throes were very violent as he fell upon me, and before I went off in front, where his other hand had got to, he made the thing inject a quantity of warm fluid.

Then I got up. "Get into bed, Alfred," I directed, my suspicions fully aroused. "I shall tear that thing off when I return."

I hurried on a dressing gown and departed, knowing from experience the inconvenience I should suffer.

On my return I got into bed.

"Now," I said, "I shall play the part of a masterful wife! You shall be underneath, my boy!"

In the struggle the thing slipped; there was between it and him a total disconnection.

"Alfred," I exclaimed, "you are an impostor! I shall make you feel and receive the expression of what I feel."

I found an opening in front like Mademoiselle's; I pushed what I possessed into it. It was hairy like Mademoiselle's, but the hairs were so fair, so like the colour of the skin, that I could scarcely have detected them even if they had not been covered as they must have been.

I was extremely excited. Beatrice's reproaches rushed upon my mind. The unusual circumstances of being master also stimulated me. Notwithstanding protestations and observations, I pinned her down. I was really the stronger.

"Now I shall fuck *you!*" I cried.

She was silent, evidently meditating vengeance.

I did fuck her very violently.

"Lord Alfred," I then said, "you are a woman." I tore open her nightshirt and played with her breasts — of course they were a woman's.

I saw it all now.

"What business have *you* to wear trousers?" I asked.

"How dare you wear petticoats?" she retorted with a bitter smile.

This dumbfounded me.

Lady Alfred jumped up at the first chance. She was wild. "I shall call Mademoiselle," she said, and not heeding me, "he" hastily threw on a dressing gown and left the room.

Presently the door opened, and she re-entered; and immediately behind her came the stately form of my governess, carrying in her hand, to my great dismay, a long, lithe birch.

"So," said Mademoiselle, "you have turned a man into a woman, Julia, and insulted your lover."

"And he," I cried, defiantly, "has proved to me that I am a man after all."

I trembled and had grown very pale.

"I will argue with this," answered Mademoiselle, shaking her weapon.

Lady Alfred drew me, now incapable of resistance, from the bed, and put me on the couch. Then she dragged me across the end of it and held me down. Between them they got my nightdress up to my shoulders, and Mademoiselle then birched me until I was beside myself.

"There," she exclaimed at last, "now, Lord Alfred, I shall leave her to you. She has had a lesson she will remember."

I was too much overcome to object to the misuse of the pronoun.

I spent that night with Lady Alfred Ridlington, and she made me work very hard. She played the part of a husband, and I was made to lie on my back while she worked her wicked will.

Exhausted, towards daybreak we both fell asleep, and I dreamt that Lady Alfred Ridlington had metamorphosed me into a girl and had made my male attributes her own. I awoke to find her leg across me.

A long time seemed to pass before the matutinal refreshment came, as it did come at last, in the shape of chocolate.

"You are to be a girl and I a man still," she said, "because you must wear petticoats. I shall tame you. I know how you behaved to your governess just as she knows how you behaved to the nursery maid. You shall not pry underneath women's garments for nothing. You shall not make the indecent advances and the insulting propositions you made to your governess without punishment and therefore you will please understand you are a girl. Now turn over!"

The order was accompanied by the exercise of some physical persuasion, which, weakened as I was I did not know how to counteract or resist. The persuasion was indeed force; and from white feminine arms I could not withstand it.

It was terrible, though, to be outraged thus by a woman.

"You shall be made to be a girl to punish your naughtiness. I quite agree with Mademoiselle. It is the most effective punishment."

And so, before I got down to the breakfast room, I had to endure again, what I considered the last degree of degradation, three or four times.

My discovery certainly alleviated its severity, and the strangeness of the sensations gave me a certain animal gratification; but I knew that Lady Alfred Ridlington had no right to know me anywhere but in front.

Chapter V

He was his own Wife

If she would only wear petticoats, I thought, if she would be my mistress instead of my master, how much more I should enjoy it, or rather how much less difficult the yoke of iron would be to bear. My peculiar and constitutional susceptibility made it easy, perhaps pleasant, to me to endure all things from a woman.

This charm, this romance was dissipated to the winds, because Lady Alfred Ridlington would wear trousers, while I, the male, was made to wear women's clothing.

I was so fond of women that I did not always object to being in their garments, but I hated the domination of the masculine emblems, although covering a divine female form by whom the sway was exercised. Had Lady Alfred taken my trousers away and worn them herself while she compelled me to wear her drawers, the matter would have been different. And it would have been so, too, if she had really been Lord Alfred.

All the glamour of my being actually a girl had vanished at a blow. I almost wept as I thought I could no longer dream I was one — and one with a lover. Lord Alfred Ridlington no longer interested me for he was a fraud. He was his own wife. What a rude shattering shock to all my delicious dreams in the conservatory, to my anxiety to get a baby between us.

I felt overwhelmed with chagrin and despite, when I dwelt upon all the feminine airs and graces into enduing myself with which I had been cajoled by this imposture. And yet, after all, my tyrant was a woman. What a complexion, what a skin, what limbs she possessed! What knowledge of physical sensations, what physical ecstasy she could cause! How entrancing she would look in petticoats.

I wondered she had the hardihood, now that I knew the secret, to appear that morning without them. Mademoiselle knew it. Perhaps Lady Alfred was not aware that Beatrice was in it too. Without nicely weighing the consequences it struck me how gloriously I could revenge myself by letting the secret out at breakfast before the girls if an opportunity should occur. She would be overwhelmed with shame and confusion. Unless she was a brazen harridan, she must have sufficient womanliness and modesty left to be abashed and horrified when she was discovered to be a lady so wanting in proper feeling as to dress herself in men's clothes.

I did not in my indignation consider, as it would have been much better for me if I had, that I was in her power and in Mademoiselle's, and that they could turn the tables on me cruelly, and that they certainly would, if I so exposed my tormentor.

The three girls looked fresh and brisk in the bright morning light in their dainty maidenly frocks. They did not compliment me upon my appearance, Agnes remarking that I looked "quite haggard, and had black circles about my eyes," and proceeding in her kittenish way to tease me.

Beatrice remarked that "most brides looked so after the first night," an observation which made my hands itch to smack her face. Maud gave me an intelligent glance in which there was some desire and some sympathy. She whisked her skirts about her lower half, and so managed them as to make the form of her exquisite limbs very apparent beneath them, but faithful to the haughty indifference that characterized her, she said nothing.

Mademoiselle was more languishing than usual and her air conveyed that she possessed some secret source of amusement.

Lady Alfred Ridlington entered the room last and astonished me with her perfect self-possession. I regarded her with contempt as a fraud just as I suppose Beatrice regarded me.

I now carefully observed Lady Ridlington's round thighs, breasts, and form, and wondered however I or anyone else could ever have been duped into the belief that she was what her clothes denoted. But suggestion of a fact often goes so far as to make one discredit the evidence of one's own senses in respect of it.

She spoke quite gaily, quite *en preux cavalier*, to Mademoiselle, who responded in a similar tone of gallantry.

I was much entertained at Lady Alfred's perfect acting, and *debonnaire*, careless manner. Even before my eyes, which she soon perceived fixed upon her, she did not quail in the least, but in her own glance there was a latent threat and a cold stare as much as to say, "I have not done with you yet."

I did not concern myself much at the time with this, for my attention was occupied afresh with the idea how delicious she would be in her own raiment.

I was brooding thus when she asked whether Mademoiselle did not ever find the need of a tutor with such very masterful young ladies.

Beatrice shrugged her shoulders impatiently at this while a curve of intense contempt settled upon her beautifully moulded lips. Maud and Agnes looked up astonished. Maud, with slight disgust and impatience, Agnes, with open-eyed and innocent wonder.

Mademoiselle's eyes sparkled and glittered with the various frolics and high jinks the proposal suggested and I saw the colour come to her face as she bit her lip to repress the spirit of mischief which seemed to well up. The same idea, however, must have struck her as well as myself.

Lady Alfred looked young enough to be Agnes' little brother. Whether she was in reality older than Mademoiselle, who was not yet twenty-four, had been puzzling me all breakfast time.

Dressed as she was, she looked a baby boy — a chubby, smiling, careless, good-natured, overgrown baby. She was perpetually laughing and smiling.

When a woman's age perplexes me, I invariably endeavour to make her laugh heartily. The colour of the gums about the teeth, the teeth themselves, and, above all, the manner in which the skin wrinkles, at once enable me to make a shrewd guess at her age. An old woman who looks young when her face is in repose, will, when she laughs, immediately disclose lines, whilst her skin will have a more or less parchmenty appearance, however scientifically she has used her cosmetics.

Now Lady Alfred Ridlington was perpetually laughing, and her skin was as fresh as a child's — yet about the eyes there was a look of old worldliness which betokened a knowledge of life; and noticing closely Mademoiselle's demeanour towards her I came to the conclusion that she had lived a fast life but was some eight or nine months younger than my governess.

At times her eyes shone with a fierce white flame such as I had noticed in Mademoiselle's eyes when her erotism was violently excited, such as all women possess in some degree under like circumstances — Mademoiselle in a greater degree than most, and Lady Alfred in excess even of her.

At such times all laughter and smiles would leave her countenance, her face would lose its roundness, the cheeks become drawn, the mouth firmly shut, the whole soul concentrated in the baleful fires of her eyes.

Mademoiselle moved her legs under the table, and I knew, at

once, she had excited other emotions in her.

"Sometimes, I confess, I should like to have the assistance of a master, but he would need years to give weight to his authority," she presently said —

"And I," rejoined Lady Alfred with mock disappointment, "cannot pretend to them."

Now was my opportunity. I felt the danger of my folly but impelled by a boldness I cannot account for. I slowly lifted my eyes to Lady Alfred, and said very quietly: "Nor to the sex either, Lady Alfred."

Maud jumped almost off her chair. Agnes changed colour, and awaited events with quiet astonishment, incredulous at what I think she dreamt was a new form of joke.

Beatrice gave me an applauding look for my courage. And Mademoiselle plainly did not know whether to be vexed or amused.

Lady Alfred was furious. She jumped up. "How dare you, Sir! Miss, I mean!" she shouted in a transport.

"At any rate, *you* will feel my sex. Mademoiselle," she added, "you must let me break *him* in."

"You shall hear them their lessons, and whip them all round if you like, Alfred. But you, Julia, go to your room — or stay, go to mine at once."

"I think it disgraceful," remarked Beatrice, with real anger. "Suppose Uncle —"

At this Mademoiselle lost her temper — she glared at Beatrice and rang the bell. "Send Elise!" she ordered.

"Elise, take Miss Beatrice, strip her, and dress her in a shirt, boys' drawers, and trousers, and bring her to the schoolroom at half past ten. In the meantime, Alfred, you come with me. You other two," she added, looking at Maud and Agnes, "go to the schoolroom and set yourselves to work."

As I walked up in high dudgeon, I noticed the questioning and rather frightened look Lady Alfred gave Mademoiselle and her own quiet complacent air which indicated nothing to the unskilled, but which, I very well knew, meant danger all round.

I left Beatrice and Elise struggling and protesting together and before I had gained the door heard a succession of sharp sounds, followed by a sob or two, which told me Beatrice was having her face smacked, probably by Mademoiselle, while Elise held her hands. Foolish girl to resist.

My breath came and went more quickly than I cared to acknowledge to myself, but I was wise in my generation, and bent before the storm I had raised, and went at once to Mademoiselle's room.

The rustle of her garments was audible in the corridor before I expected it, and I shuddered at the sound. There was that horrid black oak bench before my eyes. How I hated it!

Mademoiselle came into the room with Lady Alfred Ridlington and took no notice of me, so fully occupied was she. She led her in reluctantly, white and flushed by turns, and protesting energetically, "No, no!" to something Mademoiselle was plainly bent upon.

I was very glad, as may be supposed, to take a back seat, and to fall into the background; and such was Mademoiselle's preoccupation that I doubted whether she was aware of my presence.

"You are a very naughty little boy, Alfred!" she was saying.

I opened my eyes at her tones of uncompromising severity and determination. I could scarcely contain myself. My head whirled. I thought I should burst my corset. I held my breath, transfixed with a strange ecstasy at Mademoiselle's fury.

"You are a very naughty little boy!" she reiterated, in tones which defied all contradiction of anything they might articulate. "A very naughty boy, Alfred! Tutor indeed! No doubt you would like to hear my pupils' lessons; no doubt you would like to have the punishing of young ladies; to turn them down on their faces, you young scoundrel, turn up their petticoats, see their pretty legs and drawers, uncover their soft warm bottoms, and flog them till they screamed and yelled for mercy. You would examine them; you would make them display their hidden charms, you indecent young rascal" (she jerked and shook her); "you would gloat over what you saw. Very well —"

"Oh, Mademoiselle! Indeed — indeed I —" And she seemed terrified.

Mademoiselle appeared, to my astonishment, thoroughly in earnest, and Lady Alfred thoroughly and really afraid.

"Very well," went on Mademoiselle, ignoring the interruption and not permitting her to say what she wanted, "you may thank your stars you have a governess who can manage you, and stamp out such improper ideas. You shall be deprived of your trousers —

here — now — exposed before me and this young lady" (turning to me) "and have your own impudent bottom well and soundly birched, and I trust it will do you good."

Mademoiselle went to a chest of drawers, opened the second drawer, and took out a fresh green, well-budded birch, which she swished in the air under Lady Alfred's nose.

"You shall be birched astride of that bench," said she, pointing to it; "and if you have any hope of concealing anything, say good-bye to that hope at once."

"Oh, Mademoiselle, it is not fair! I won't be whipped, and before Julia —"

"Would you prefer it in the schoolroom, before them all?"

"Oh — I — no, certainly not! Oh, Mademoiselle, forgive me! It was a wicked idea —"

I could hardly believe my ears. Was this Lady Ridlington, after all? My perplexity almost demented me.

"Take down your trousers, Alfred, at once — take them off — strip to your shirt. Fair or unfair, you are to be birched."

She flew to Mademoiselle and kissed her hands. For a moment she permitted the kisses; and then, giving her a pat with the back of one of her hands upon her mouth, withdrew them both.

"Undress!" she ordered. "Julia, put the bench in the middle of the room and the bolster upon it."

I did what I was told to but trembled so much and gasped to such an extent that I had hardly strength to move it.

"Now, Julia!" as I fumbled.

Mademoiselle fixed her eyes on me and perceived my condition in consequence of which she gave me a stinging cut with the birch across my shoulders which bit fearfully, although over my dress. I gave a little shriek, but I had no longer any difficulty in executing her orders. I placed the bench in position, and the bolster upon it.

Lady Alfred was still fumbling with her buttons, furtively glancing at Mademoiselle every now and then, to see whether there was the slightest appearance or sign of a disposition to relent. I had been in the same predicament myself and was devoutly thankful I was not so now.

"Come, come!" cried Mademoiselle, tapping the ground impatiently with her foot. "I cannot stay here all day to punish your bottom, Alfred. Be quick, off with your coat and waistcoat! Now the trousers and drawers, too — yes, everything, to your shirt, you bold, good-for-nothing boy! You'd much sooner see a girl in your plight and have a prospect of examining her bottom, and of whipping it, than of having to expose your own and to be whipped. Be quick, or I shall make you kiss Julia's bottom!"

"Mademoiselle!" she exclaimed, standing erect and aghast.

"Yes, I will. Be quick!"

The trousers and drawers were soon pulled down.

I saw a pair of plump, round, white legs and pretty round ankles, and white exquisitely shaped feet.

"Now stand across the bench. Julia, strap his ankles together."

I obeyed.

"Julia, hand me some pins."

I did so.

Mademoiselle put down the birch. Taking the tail of the shirt, she pinned it up to Lady Alfred's shoulders, and then did the same in front.

I looked eagerly at the young, but fully developed, fresh girlish form before me with the soft silky down in front at the navel. I noticed and gloated over the large well-formed hips, and the soft, white, shrinking little bottom. How could Mademoiselle find it in her heart to punish such a tender beautiful little back?

There was no implement in front now. Lady Alfred was a girl, and a beautiful one. The reason she was so anxious I should be absent was because she knew I was a boy. This was all plain to me now. My contemplations and cogitations were brusquely cut short by Mademoiselle's ordering me to put a strap round her waist and the bench, and to fix her together underneath it.

Then she stroked her bottom and talked to her; passing her hand through between her legs, she tickled what she knew how to find, agitating Lady Alfred's frame convulsively.

How dare she pretend to be a boy? How dare she wear trousers? She (Mademoiselle) would whip her follies out of her, cure her of immodesty and indecency.

And Mademoiselle immediately suited the action to the word in her finished style: scientific, methodical, deliberate, and cruel.

She punished Lady Alfred's bottom most soundly until it bled. I was made to stand at the foot and could see all.

Lady Alfred took the castigation with surprising courage until Mademoiselle came to the last dozen, which as usual she inflicted lengthwise. The ends of the fresh birch curled about the insides of

Lady Alfred's legs like vicious live things and all her fortitude vanished as if by magic.

She abandoned herself perforce to the agony; rolled and twisted, wrenched her wrists in the straps, and stiffened and relaxed her pretty, beautifully shaped legs.

Presently, unable to contain herself, she screamed again and again.

Mademoiselle appeared to be beside herself, her eyes positively flamed. Her transport terrified me. She seemed sensible of nothing but the writhing form beneath her. The last three cuts were delivered on the very centre of the very organ.

At the first she yielded, at the third and last she appeared to faint. Mademoiselle threw down the birch and sank into an armchair.

"Julia," she cried, "come here"; and she pointed between her widely and indecently outstretched legs. I flew to her and my head was soon lost in her drapery, and, clasped tightly by her limbs, was pressed against her navel.

The mouth was moist and the moustache was wet. I found the excited and enlarged organ with my tongue and tickled it. Soon the welcome spasm overtook her and with a sigh the humid expression of her feelings was shot into my mouth. She seemed greatly solaced, but kept me there, and a second time I repeated the task.

After a few minutes she arose. She was greatly relieved, but my paroxysm of passion was rendered more acute. And it was not by any means diminished by the sight before me.

There lay Lady Alfred Ridlington in a posture of the most abject humiliation, quietly sobbing now that she had come to herself, but her hands bound together underneath the bench, unable to use them to wipe her eyes, her legs separated by the rude bench which passed through the hallowed sanctuary they supported.

And there were her bottom and her rich thighs all well-waled, cut, and discoloured by the birch. In places the wales were latticed and they tended to the insides of her legs in an ominous fashion. On her bottom were spots of now congealed blood.

Lady Alfred turned her head from side to side upon the sofa. She had given her legs several jerks and had similarly signified her wish for the release of her hands. Her arms were concealed by the shirt sleeves as was also her back by that incongruous garment; but I saw enough of its graceful shape, white, elegant, and delicately curved, to make me long to see all. I thought of the picture in Maud's bedroom. I love the *vue de dos* of a woman.

What a strange whim on her part to wear trousers! to pretend to be a man! to have the pretence carried to the length of being punished like a boy! It was quite plain that it was this that gave the whole business its peculiar zest. What a mania!

Blasé, all legitimate ordinary sensations used up, she was obliged, in quest of novel sensations, to have recourse to this distortion and perversion of ideas and of all the functions of her body. What sort of beings would she give birth to? In what way would this love madness affect her offspring? A study of the hereditary instincts imparted to it and of their ramifications and results, would be worthy of Ibsen.

"Well, Alfred," at length asked Mademoiselle, arranging her hair, which her exertions had slightly disarranged, "I think you have been properly punished this time. Will you acknowledge your fault?"

I knew that my petticoats in front were quite wet, and I dreaded lest Mademoiselle should notice the little mound something made there.

I think if the strap round her waist had not been so tight as to make it impossible, Lady Alfred would have moved up and down. I could perceive from her drooping eyelids and general appearance that she was in an extremely erotic condition.

"Shall I let Julia unfasten you?"

"Yes, please."

"No, not just yet. You had better lie there a little longer."

And Mademoiselle looked at her, then walked over to her and gave her bottom a few well-applied smacks with her firm, cold hand.

"Oh, oh, Mademoiselle!" cried Lady Alfred, violently jerking herself all over. "Oh, don't! I can't bear more punishment."

Mademoiselle immediately after the slaps let her hand slip through.

"How wet it is!" she observed, as she tickled it.

"Oh, oh!" exclaimed Lady Alfred in very different tones.

What a longing, what an intense yearning, the interjection conveyed!

Then Mademoiselle reseated herself in her chair.

"Now, Julia," she said; her severe tone made me turn white

directly, and feel on the point of fainting. "Now, Julia, what am I to do to you for your impudence to Lady Alfred; how dare you make the remark you did? What induced you, was it Beatrice?"

"No, Mademoiselle! It was not — it was my — my petticoats."

"Your petticoats?"

"Yes, I am not a girl, and being treated just as if I was one, disgusted me, and made me so indignant, that I determined at the first opportunity to show up the hollow mockery."

"You had better let him come to Ridlington Court with me. I will teach him. Hollow mockery indeed! He is not half broken in."

"Julia, come here. Stand with your back in front of me — closer."

Mademoiselle put her left arm round my waist, and her right arm and hand underneath my skirts, between my legs through to the front. She caught the privy purse with her fingers and played with my testicles.

Of course in a few seconds I could scarcely contain myself.

"Will you acknowledge the power of the petticoat now?"

"Yes, yes — oh, yes! Oh, I did not mean — not seriously — any resistance! Oh, Mademoiselle, I will do anything you wish!"

She gave me a final and cruel squeeze of the globes, hurting me fearfully.

"Remember!" she said, sternly. "Now go," she bade me, trembling all over and half doubled up, "and unstrap Lady Alfred. It is your turn now, Miss."

"You won't flog me again?"

"Wait and see!" cried Mademoiselle, enjoying my discomfiture, and delighting in tantalising me.

I unstrapped Lady Alfred.

No sooner had she arisen than she tottered over to a chair.

"Take her some wine, Julia."

I obeyed.

"Make him strip, Mademoiselle, to his *chemise*," said Lady Alfred.

Again I felt all the colour fly from my face.

But Mademoiselle nodded, and with a sigh I undressed. The *chemise* covered me.

"I must have him, Mademoiselle."

"Very well."

Lady Alfred led me to the bench and fixed me down on my back. She drew down my arms and strapped my wrists together behind me and underneath it. Then she fixed my ankles in the same mode and drew up my *chemise* to my throat; displaying my nakedness in a shocking manner.

"What a splendid one it is!" she remarked to Mademoiselle.

"What full testicles! We really must find a tight glove for it!" And she lifted her leg across me and inserted me into her hot, fiery organ. "There, now I have the devil in hell!" And she lay down upon me, her burning breath playing about my lips which were parched by her scorching mouth.

The strap round my waist, although not tight, prevented my moving and so also did my posture; but Lady Alfred was not hampered in this manner and she pounded me vigorously, sucking the life out of my affair which was closely bitten and held by her vulva over which she appeared to possess as much control as over her lips.

Her arms enveloped me, her tongue was in my mouth, her weight oppressed me, my implement was lost to sight, up to the hilt, in her plump body. She gazed amorously into my eyes.

"Now, Julian," she said, "as soon as you like!"

Mademoiselle could not refrain from twisting and moving in her chair, crossing and uncrossing her legs. Her presence filled me with shame.

In the glass behind I could see my own legs twisted down and fastened below the bench and Lady Alfred's bottom oppressing me.

Various reminiscences flashed through my mind. I recollected the boudoir — the flogging I had just witnessed.

I felt the seminal receptacles fill, and a preliminary thrill shot all over me; and then with a gasp came the convulsion.

I sank back; and Lady Alfred, delighted, sank upon me.

I recovered.

"Now, Julia, again!"

"Oh, I can't!"

"You must! Remember the petticoat! You must be tamed!"

The reference to the petticoat stimulated me.

I clenched my teeth. Lady Alfred aided me vigorously.

In a few moments, the prolongation of which appeared to give her intense satisfaction, a second spasm was produced.

Still Lady Alfred did not rise.

"Won't that do, Alice?" asked Mademoiselle, who I suppose found the temptation too much.

Alice! How I thrilled at the feminine name! "No, it won't!" she returned. "He must do it again or be birched until he does. If he comes to Ridlington Court with me I will keep him always naked and he shall live between my legs. Besides, I determined to exhaust his impudence. I have the origin of it in my possession now and I will teach him to taunt me with my sex! I will teach him who really rules. I will make him understand, and admit, and feel that man is but woman's slave, soul, passions, and all that he possesses."

"I really can't — I should like to — but I feel already exhausted — empty!"

"Have you another birch there, Mademoiselle?"

My being underneath her made it much harder work for me, but the reference to the birch made me show I would really try though it should be my death.

Alice, seeing this, put her hand underneath Mons. Priapus, underneath his bag, upon the thick muscle that runs between the legs. She squeezed and rubbed it vigorously.

"I shall put a stiff hairbrush under you, if you give me any trouble," she informed me rising on her elbow but still holding my diminished organ inside her.

"A very good idea," cried Mademoiselle. "Here is one!"

Those moist, curved, cherry-coloured lips, the little head, with its closely cropped hair, the laughing, sparkling eyes, the tones, and the touch, and the embrace, all affected me very deliciously.

Alice must have been an expert in metaphysics. The suggestion of the brush thrilled me through and through and caused a growth which quickly delighted her. But she knew that the imagination would affect me more than the reality, which, by setting up a counter irritation, might possibly have altogether defeated her wishes.

She declined the brush, as she looked steadily at me; and I was glad, for her clemency had its due effect.

She replaced her arms about me, and renewed the pressure of her dear form, though really the muscles of my generative organs ached.

Then she talked of the birch, and Mademoiselle wriggled in her chair whilst she flashed glances at me.

The whole time Alice continued a process of very forcible suction; and the impression I was under was that she was drawing my life into her own body and desired the last spark of it.

Finding her efforts not sufficiently stimulating to please her and the response to them too slow — for I must have shown distress in various ways — she smiled and stood up over me, not moving her legs or the lower part of her body, with which she still retained me.

"Now, Julian, I will be good to you," she said, tenderly.

And she proceeded to remove that horrid shirt and vest and stood over me in all the glorious nakedness of her radiant beauty — a perfect woman.

"I will give you fresh inspiration. Look!"

I did look at her swelling breasts, like snow; at their scarlet nipples, like two strawberries in its midst; at her arms, so exquisitely shaped; and whilst I gazed, she moved up and down upon me and smiled.

"You know all my beauty, Julian, and" — again throwing herself upon me — "you possess it."

She pushed away the *chemise* and her velvety breasts, soft like cushions filled with down, rested on my own breast, her legs, against mine, our moist flesh was mixed. I felt that, exhausted or not, I must perform the function and give her myself.

With many efforts, many contortions, many throes, I accomplished her desire, which had become mine, too; and then lay absolutely limp, lank, and done for, beneath her.

For some minutes we rested, I cannot say in each other's arms, for mine were fixed behind me, but in the closest possible proximity.

"Good boy," she said, as she kissed me. "It shall not be whipped this time."

"He has achieved an Herculean feat, I shall unstrap him myself," cried Mademoiselle. "And tied down as he was, it must have been specially difficult. Drink this bumper, Julian, to your mistress' health. I must take care of your health, too. You had better sleep for a couple of hours.

"Here is my own nightdress," said Mademoiselle, taking it out of its scented case. "Put it on" (she threw it over my head). "Jump into my bed. You won't try to persuade me to follow you into it just now, I am sure."

I was glad to get into bed. Both Alice and Mademoiselle kissed me, and before I could recollect anything more, I had fallen asleep.

Chapter VI

My Lord's Afternoon

It was almost luncheon time when I awoke in the darkened room and I had not been awake many minutes before Mademoiselle and Alice came in. Alice was dressed in a suit of pyjamas, and Mademoiselle looked rosy and flushed, love sick like a bride, but without the calm satisfied look in her eyes which your properly used bride may be always supposed to possess. Indeed, her eyes were restless and wandered, but she bore other indescribable symptoms of having lately experienced the greatest possible physical and sensual enjoyment without, however, any psychological gratification. Of course, I could not tell how they had spent the morning. I guessed they had not been to the schoolroom, and indeed afterwards discovered that to be the fact. They had been in Mademoiselle's *boudoir*, and Alice, with her masculine artificial implement, had been playing the lover to Mademoiselle's heart's content.

"Now, Alfred," said Mademoiselle to Alice, "just dress yourself in trousers again. Julia is in the secret, and I have a shrewd suspicion that Beatrice is too. But even if they all were you should be compelled to wear trousers to punish your pruriency; just as Julia must wear petticoats."

Alice put on the underskirt and linen one, and was fumbling with the drawers, when Mademoiselle declared she must indulge in another look at her pretty bottom.

"Come," she said, seating herself in her great armchair and gathering up her skirts, making a lap between her shapely legs, "lie down here a moment in my lap." Alice, becoming red, walked over to Mademoiselle, and she proceeded to play with her as a cat does with a mouse. She turned up her skirt, examined and stroked her, and then, as if some sudden impulse carried her away, gave her with her arm tight about her waist a sound spanking.

"You have had your punishment for wearing trousers this morning and I have just reminded you of the birching I felt it my duty to give you. This afternoon you shall have your fun."

"You have amusement all day long, Mademoiselle. Have you ever been birched?" she asked, looking into her face with a delightfully saucy air. "If not, I propose that Julia and I give you a licking just to show you what it is like."

Mademoiselle certainly changed colour.

The idea of birching her asphyxiated me.

"Ah, ha!" shouted Alice. "I believe you would like it. I believe you would agree with me that after all, the birch is the next best thing to the masculine rod itself!"

"Alfred," answered Mademoiselle, now really rosy, "behave yourself."

I could see she had touched her; but if she was annoyed, amusement at Alice's triumphant air and tones afforded her a ready cover for its concealment.

Mademoiselle got up in a moment or two.

"I will not be tantalised for nothing," she said. "Lie on your back on the bench, as Julia did. I shall make you kiss my bottom, for your impudence."

Alice demurred, but quite uselessly. Mademoiselle was aroused and inexorable. She had to put herself in position, and I envied the squeezing she got, evidently only from her back.

Her countenance had changed when she got up.

"I do not like kissing you behind."

"Then hold your impudent tongue, or, next time this occurs you will not be allowed to get up until you have inserted it where it will indeed be punished!"

I was glad to see Alice taken down a peg or two, and to find Mademoiselle able to hold her own, as indeed, at all times and in all places she always did with a wit and self-possession peculiarly French.

In the afternoon, Maud, Beatrice, and Agnes were in the schoolroom where I went from luncheon which Mademoiselle had had served to herself, Alice, and me in a private room. Agnes instantly hailed questions upon me.

"What did she do to you, Julia? We thought we should never see you again. Where were you whipped? Let me look. What were you made to undergo and is Lord Alfred *really* a man? We waited and waited and waited and when Mademoiselle did not appear and twelve o'clock came, Elise took Bee away, and locked her up in some black hole. She is blinking like an owl at the light — that's why; but how tired you look, Julia? And I am sure Beatrice has had no lunch."

"Indeed I had, Agnes!"

"Oh, only the potato parings, and what was left on the servants' plates!"

Beatrice flew at Agnes, who, with a burst of laughter, made off.

"I wish you two would not play the fool," said Maud deprecatingly. "You will only let us all in for it if you do."

Beatrice did look queer in her youth's clothes — an Eton jacket and trousers. What a bottom she had!

She carefully averted her eyes from mine which she was determined not to meet. Her hair had been rolled up and she looked shamefaced to the last degree.

"Isn't she a great, big, rollicking tomboy?" enquired Agnes with intense glee and stealing up behind her.

Agnes, in the excess of her spirits, brought her hand smack down upon the redundant hemisphere which protruded at the base of Beatrice's jacket.

Beatrice turned round furious and Agnes would have received condign punishment from her had she not seen Mademoiselle standing stern and silent at the door. They were nicely caught in the very act.

"Upon my word," remarked Mademoiselle. "Lord Alfred, the very moment we open the schoolroom door the need of a tutor becomes apparent. I will leave you to deal with this."

"Certainly, Mademoiselle; only too happy."

Agnes had seated herself at the table and looked very crestfallen.

There was a rocking horse in the room — a great big one.

"Master Beatrice," ordered Alice, "mount that horse. We will deal with you presently, Agnes."

"Oh, I can't — I won't!"

"Have you a cane, Mademoiselle?"

"To be sure."

"Now, Master Beatrice, consider this little fellow. He will sting more" — swishing it through the air — "than your sister's hand."

The saddle was an old one, with a big knob in front and it was high at the place Beatrice would be wedged in between, and I knew where she would feel the pressure, especially if anyone was so ill-natured as to rock the animal.

Mademoiselle had seated herself comfortably in her armchair, and calmly awaited the progress of events.

The sight and swish of the cane appeared quite sufficient motive to Beatrice.

She mounted reluctantly and immediately put one hand on the saddle to relieve the pressure on the sensitive regions of her body.

"Julia," said Alice, "take her handkerchief and tie her hands behind her."

"Oh, no!" exclaimed Beatrice piteously, becoming white, red, blue, and green all at once. "Oh! The saddle hurts me."

"You do not suppose I desired you to get up there for your own amusement, do you? Do as I tell you, Julia."

So I was compelled to tie her hands as directed. She was almost in tears. When I had tied her hands Alice put her foot on the rocker and set the animal in violent motion.

Beatrice exclaimed loudly, turned very red, expostulated, threatened, and implored by turns. She was compelled to make the most ridiculous efforts to avoid falling off. That necessity made her squeeze the beast with her legs.

The rough usage they met with and which the nerves and regions between encountered made her positively glow with shame.

The combat in her countenance between shame, vexation, and sensuality was ludicrous to behold.

Mademoiselle laughed till the tears ran down her face and until her sides must have ached.

Alice bade me keep the horse going. I had had my turn of punishment in the morning and could now thoroughly enjoy the events of the afternoon free from all apprehension on my own score.

I rocked the horse with my foot as if it were on the pedal of a wheel, holding my handkerchief in one hand and my gown up daintily with the other.

Beatrice's oh's and ah's continued at each fresh jolt, and I could not avoid smiling and occasionally causing her a slight jerk by pressing the rocker down before the swing one way had been accomplished, upon which occasions I saw an angry red spot steal into her cheeks.

Indeed, before very long, I heard her suggesting:

"Gently, Julia! You may stop. No one will notice." And again: "Won't you catch it for —?"

With a smile I cut *that* short. It only required a little harder pressure of my foot than usual and the breath was jolted out of Beatrice's body and she found frantic efforts necessary to retain her equilibrium.

Alice then sat down and ordered Agnes to stand before her. She did so not very readily, obeying evidently only because she could not help herself.

"Do you know, Miss, the punishment a young lady deserves, who behaves herself during lesson time in so disorderly a fashion?"

"What is that to you?" said Agnes, pertly. "You are not my governess."

"Insubordination, in addition. Very well, Miss, you will have your bottom soundly birched."

Agnes flushed. "I won't!" she said.

"I think," said Maud, "it is a shame a man should use my sister so! I wonder, Mademoiselle —"

"Hold your tongue, codger."

I was afraid Beatrice would contribute her pipe next and so pressed my foot down strongly and suddenly. My pulses leapt and bounded; and, amid all my delight that these girls were going to catch it, I did not forget to rock Beatrice's horse with sufficient speed to keep her fully occupied with her own affairs.

How angrily Maud flushed at the word "codger"! That was what she had been named when made to work as a scullery maid. It shut her up effectually.

I was overjoyed at the thrilling prospect before me. These girls would catch it and the best of it was they would have to suffer the shamefulness of being punished by one whom they plainly considered a man while he was not really so. How deliciously they would be done!

They would have the salacious delight of displaying all their hidden charms to one they regarded as a man and then be bereft of their obscene enjoyment by being afterwards informed that the supposed man was, after all, but a woman like themselves.

What a disappointment it would be to them! For I know well that young ladies like being put to shame, having their nakedness exposed, and intensely enjoy anything that causes them an acute sense of immorality.

"What!" exclaimed Alice. "Here is flat mutiny. Maud, what business is it of yours to interfere with discipline? Get up, and stand beside your sister, Miss."

Maud looked very angry and threw down her pencil in a pet, but she went and stood by Agnes all the same.

"Now," remarked Lady Alfred, "I do not know which of you two young ladies is the worse, so I shall punish both your bottoms; and as the crime is really so serious, you must each have a dozen in front in addition. You must strip to your *chemises*. Maud, help Agnes, and you, Agnes, help Maud."

Long habits of obedience, the presence of Mademoiselle, the hopelessness of more resistance, I suppose, led them to acquiesce and obey. Rebellion would have been quelled at once by the assistance which Elise and the servants would have readily rendered, if summoned. And summoned we all knew they would be, upon the slightest provocation. They loved to see their young mistresses whipped and it would intensify their pleasure to see them flogged by a man.

Maud's and Agnes' frocks were soon off, their petticoats and corsets followed. They sat down and took off their stockings and shoes and drawers.

They were a beautiful pair of girls. Agnes' innocent blushes and cast-down looks were bewitching and almost compensated for the want of ripeness in her form as compared with Maud's.

"Before being punished you must lie on that couch and be examined."

"Oh, Mademoiselle!" exclaimed both the girls together, flushing scarlet, appealing to their governess against this fresh ignominy.

"You must obey, or you will find my whip about you, you refractory hussies!" was the only satisfaction they obtained from her.

"Oh!" they exclaimed. *"By a man!"*

Mademoiselle bit her lip.

"You will like it all the better for that."

Beatrice was going to say something, but an extra jerk shut her up. I could scarcely forbear from laughter at the control I possessed over her owing to my office of rocker. I knew I should have to pay for it hereafter.

"Agnes, come here! Lie down flat on your back, your head towards me," ordered her tutor.

Lady Alfred pulled her down and her *chemise* up, examined and passed her hand over her thighs, abdomen, and navel, and tickled, notwithstanding her choking exclamations, her clitoris. Then she rolled her over, and separated her legs as she looked at her pretty white bottom, and, placing her finger on the button between its cheeks, told Agnes she would *insert it* the next time she made punishment necessary.

"Monster!" said Maud. "Beast!"

Lady Alfred looked up, but said nothing.

Maud's turn followed. She was exposed and examined in the same way. When she had been rolled over, Lady Alfred enquired whether she had not called her a monster when she informed Agnes how she would be punished next time.

"Yes," said Maud defiantly.

"That candle, please, Mademoiselle — thank you."

"Very well, I shall insert this. That will teach you to control your tongue, I hope."

Maud threw herself about, screamed, kicked, cried, protested. Lady Alfred was much the stronger and got the candle well in; Maud yelled — she pushed it up and down.

It was quite plain she felt the punishment physically, as acutely as the degradation hurt her pride and self-respect. When it was over, she appeared to loathe herself, and to be unable to hold up her head. It was indeed a terribly humiliating ordeal for the proud immaculate Maud to have to undergo at the hands of one she deemed a man.

She cried quietly, altogether cowed as though indelibly stigmatised with disgrace. This is not the least of the effects of this horrid punishment.

In the schoolroom there was a long, narrow, but firm and heavy, four-legged table. It stood across the window.

Lady Alfred took two big sofa cushions and placed one at each end. Then, catching Agnes by the ear, she marched her to one end of the table, doubled her down across the cushions, folded her arms underneath her breast, and put a broad strap round her shoulders and the table, so as to prevent her getting up.

She next drew up her *chemise* at the back and afterwards in front, and wrinkled it up above her bosom round her neck. She then separated her legs by attaching one to each of the legs of the table which were quite three feet and a half asunder. A pretty picture Agnes looked. I became almost too much interested to continue my rocking.

Lady Alfred proceeded to fasten Maud in precisely the same way at the opposite end of the same table. Of course her head and Agnes' were thus close together.

It was plain though, she could not whip them both at once.

Stay, she was evidently going to try. She asked Mademoiselle for two birches, and holding one in each hand, standing at the middle of the table with her back to the window, she attempted to give alternate strokes with each hand to the culprits. She soon discovered she could not thus give them with enough force, and also that her position prevented her watching the effects of the punishment. So she made Agnes howl first. She did yell, and well she might; her bottom was soon crimson. She howled in Maud's ear to that damsel's disgust, but she, knowing that it would be her turn in a moment, endeavoured to put up with it without making any perceptible protest. I do not think Agnes had ever had such a flogging before. I thought it would cure her for a long time of her kittenish tricks. When Lady Alfred whipped in she seemed to become delirious.

Having punished Agnes, who was weeping bitterly, she next turned her attention to Maud and flogged her in the same thorough manner. She too yelled while Agnes was crying quietly; and with good reason she yelled. Her beautiful bottom was soon cut.

I wonder whether it was any consolation to her and Agnes to yell in such close proximity to each other.

The next step was to fasten the damsels face upwards. Lady Alfred did not spare their thighs in front, when she had done so, nor their pussies; as I contemplated Maud's affair, I recollected and thought of that memorable afternoon in her studio. Maud felt this mode of punishment most. Her contortions were terrible to witness.

Afterwards, they had to thank Lady Alfred for having taken the trouble of punishing them.

The bell was rung, Mademoiselle sent for the two housemaids with a clothes basket, and ordered them to take away all the clothes which Maud and Agnes had taken off, while these two young ladies were then made to stand in front of two large mirrors with their chemises pinned up about their throats.

"Now, Master Beatrice, it is your turn. As an Eton boy you must be so well accustomed to the birch that a cane will be a nice change for you; and as you are horsed already, we need not disturb you. Lean forward over your steed and put your arms round his neck. Julia, undo his hands. Now I am sorry, but I must take down your trousers."

Saying which, Lady Alfred encircled Beatrice's waist and took them down.

The horse was so high that a fall would have seriously hurt

Beatrice. She was, however, only fixed by her hands being tied together under the horse's head, her arms being round its neck.

Her boy's drawers followed her trousers, the tail of her shirt was tucked up, and her pretty bottom exposed fully to view.

Swish, swish, swish! And the cane whistled through the air biting her bottom, and leaving angry red wales.

Beatrice writhed and choked. Her posture protected her feminine apparatus, luckily for her. The punishment was painful and ignominious, but nothing so severe as what Maud and Agnes had to undergo.

Beatrice cried and looked remarkably beautiful and alluring in her sorrow. Her distress made her so unusually attractive, that, in spite of her boy's clothes, I really trusted I might find an opportunity for consoling her.

So ended Lady Alfred Ridlington's afternoon amusement — one she had really earned by her sufferings of that morning. Mademoiselle's strong arm had made her undergo, I am sure, quite as much pain as she had inflicted.

The two girls were forced to do their lessons in their *chemises*, and had afterwards to walk in them along the passages to their rooms.

Beatrice, after her caning, got down from her horse in order that she might be compelled to show her really pretty legs to advantage. She was deprived of her trousers; and her shirt, shorter of course than a *chemise*, only served to make the display more remarkable, especially as it was open at the sides.

So the three girls spent the afternoon in undress.

Chapter VII

Ridlington Court

It was resolved, in the course of that evening, partly to my consternation, partly to my delight, that I was next day to accompany Lady Alfred Ridlington home to Ridlington Court, in order to be thoroughly subjected to a woman who was utterly unscrupulous, and to undergo that discipline which Lady Alfred Ridlington convinced Mademoiselle was impossible at Downlands Hall amidst my cousins.

I knew that she was a volcano of sexual passion, and I well remembered her assertion that, if she became possessed of me, I should spend the greater part of my time between her legs. To this, notwithstanding what I had experienced in the morning, I did not object. It was the other features of the programme that troubled me.

It appeared that the real Lord Alfred was an old fogey twice his wife's age, who, for reasons best known to himself, had married a frisky girl; and she, of course, was overjoyed at the proposal of having a youth at her beck and call for some ten days or a fortnight.

She explained that her husband's niece, whom she called Ellen, acted as her principal maid, and she told Mademoiselle I should have to act as her assistant. She said that Ellen was a sprightly, vivacious, charming girl, and would take charge of me when she herself was otherwise engaged, and that there was not the slightest danger of discovery.

Mademoiselle consented, after some hesitation, to a ten days' visit. Elise was directed to put away for me such apparel as would suit the *role* I was to play.

We dined together as we had lunched. Fortunately the three girls were in disgrace and consequently easily disposed of.

The question then arose as to where I was to sleep that night. I had a secret wish that I might spend it with Mademoiselle and I flatter myself there was a corresponding desire on Mademoiselle's part; but hospitality towards her guest induced her to give me up to Alice, whose airs of proprietorship were at once exasperating and delicious.

I hoped, fatigued as I was, she would let me sleep that night. Otherwise I felt certain I should cut a poor figure upon the morrow.

All she did that night was to introduce me to my mistress of the next ten days, as agreed. Her mode of doing so may be guessed. It was merely to make me kiss her where I believe ladies always prefer to be kissed if they could only be induced to own it.

Mademoiselle had said something about a nettle petticoat on the morrow or a thistle or two hung round my waist; but Alice had declared that it would spoil our drive and the first day.

We breakfasted early. Mademoiselle kissed me and bade me be a good child and hoped she would have a good account of me, saying, that, when I returned, I should in all probability find my mamma there, meaning Gertrude Stormont; and finally, gave me a slight slap on my cheek to remember her by. I did not see any of my cousins.

I was dressed in a plain black gown, fitting closely to my figure, and Lady Alfred Ridlington was in a tailor-made costume, which did not in my opinion become her *mignon* style; though she could not be described as short, she was not tall, and the severity of the gown, &c., did not suit her voluptuous character.

Of course she drove herself. All the luggage had been sent on in a couple of carts. And about eleven, on a beautiful, bright, exhilarating morning, we started, Alice managing her prancing bays with great address, I seated beside her.

Ridlington Court was between sixteen and twenty miles distant. A groom had been sent for in the morning and the individual's presence at the back embarrassed me.

To Alice's surprise, my high spirits seemed to be blown away by the morning breeze. I confess that my remarks were monosyllabic, that I was awkward and preoccupied. I understood that I was to be in a sort of menial position as her maid, and already felt the bonds rivetted upon me.

I admit that I did not like the idea, but there were many counterpoising considerations. In what intimacy with this charming woman I should spend the time! Had she not declared it would be passed principally between her own legs? What, after all, did the rest matter?

And Ellen — I wondered what she would be like; whether she would be a termagant. Her husband's niece! How could a Duke's granddaughter be lady's maid to her uncle's wife? But then, I recollected, she might be the niece of a sister-in-law in uncertain circumstances.

Here, however, was Ridlington Court at last, a very substantial reality, and I was glad to sweep up its spacious avenue under the old elms, the sycamores, and limes, in the carriage of its mistress.

She was not sufficiently romantic to suit the scene, but possibly her very want of sentimentality and her breezy, matter-of-fact air, and the absence of womanliness she affected, formed an inspiriting contest.

The undulating glades of the park dotted with clumps of oak, and here and there with single great trees in the shade of which the fallow deer browsed and lay, presented a charming picture of rural peace and plenty.

At some distance I saw the sea spread out like a cool sheet of silver in the sunshine, its surface occasionally ruffled by the movement and scream of the water hens and other waterfowl.

The house itself was large, low, and appeared to cover an immense expanse of ground, but it had no architectural pretensions of any sort. It looked comfortable but ugly, in fact like a great overgrown farmhouse with too many windows. In the pleasure grounds some fountains and statues alone redeemed its character. I noticed with a qualm the presence of a few silver birches, peculiarly a lady's tree — but a rare one in these parts.

When we arrived we went straight up to Lady Alfred Ridlington's apartments and into her bedroom.

As she took off her things, I was introduced to Ellen.

The manservants in the hall, the silvery haired butler, the three or four stately footmen, and my Lord's man in plain clothes, who gave Alice a message from her husband as she passed up the stairs with me, gave me a totally different impression from that which I had received upon my entry to Downlands, where, in the house, there were no menservants at all.

The men looked at me and I felt uncomfortable, but soon found myself lifted out of the life of the house, and entirely confined to milady's portion of it. In fact, my very existence there might have been, and except for my passage through the hall probably was, unknown to everyone in the establishment except to its mistress and to Ellen.

Ellen was a gipsy like girl with very dark eyes and smooth blue-black hair, thin, and of dark complexion, observant but reticent, with hot temper and very little good humour. Her laugh was cold and not hearty, and I dreaded her.

She possessed an utterly unsympathetic nature, and while no one could be more punctilious or attentive in her duties, she remained always closely wrapt in herself. There was an inner Ellen, to which no one penetrated or seemed to care to penetrate. I concluded she had been crossed or disappointed in love. Her nature had evidently been originally a warm-hearted and affectionate one, which some hard black frost had congealed into thick-set ice that nothing could break up.

Now, although I wore a very plain black dress, my underclothing was of the richest descriptions.

When I had been introduced to Ellen, Alice made me lift up my skirts, to shew her my heavily laced drawers; there were triple rows of lace round the knees, and a long frill of it up the back of the legs.

Ellen had glanced at me in a very equivocal fashion when she first saw me. When I coyly displayed my garments to her, and attitudinised with first one shapely leg and then the other, her eyes became thoughtful and flashed.

"You must let me see better for myself," she said, leading me to a sofa upon which she threw me backwards. Her hand very soon set her doubts at rest. "So he is a boy," she exclaimed to Lady Alice who was nonchalantly arranging her hair at the glass.

The manner in which she had felt me was so cold and passionless that it had not aroused the least excitement.

"Yes," answered Alice, "he *is* a boy to be broken in to petticoats. He is to attend to me, to be my maid during his visit, and under you — under your orders."

"I understand," answered Ellen grimly, giving me a stern look which made me feel very uncomfortable.

Alice presently went down to lunch and left me with Ellen. I helped her to unpack Lady Alfred's things and she gave me various dresses to brush and boots and shoes to clean. She showed me our workroom, where, she told me, we should also have our meals — a very plainly furnished apartment, but with a pleasant view across the park.

Our bedroom was a good-sized one, with two small beds in it. She had, besides, a small sitting room of her own, in which were some books, and flowers, and canaries, who plainly, from the glance she gave them, were the pets that possessed all the softness which yet lingered about her.

I did not at all like being ordered about as I was, but very quickly discovered that Ellen would stand no nonsense.

The thought of the two beds in the same room also filled me with consternation.

"I cannot allow you to wear such drawers. Come with me into my bedroom. I shall take them off; they are a great deal too fine for a maid. In fact, at present, I shall not permit you to wear any drawers at all; and I do not approve of this dress, it makes you look too dignified and stately for your place. You must wear a frock, with a low neck and no sleeves; and I think, too, that as you appear anything but respectful and submissive, it will be just as well at once to correct and improve your disposition. My lady had not told you that I am Scots in great measure, and a firm believer, consequently, in corporal punishment. I can see plainly that severe chastisement periodically administered will greatly benefit you."

"Oh, Ellen!" I exclaimed, turning all manner of colours.

She walked to her room bidding me follow her; and when I had entered, she shut the door behind me.

"Take off your drawers and hand them to me, if you please," she ordered, dryly and peremptorily.

I looked at her, I looked up, and I looked down, and she steadily looked at me, not repeating her command, but waiting for its execution and evidently wondering how long I was going to keep her waiting.

Some magnetic force impelled me. To my astonishment I found my arms under my skirts, loosening the bands of my beautiful baby drawers of which I was proud and very reluctant to part with.

"Bring them here," said Ellen.

And I obeyed.

"Thank you. Now take off your dress, your petticoat bodice, and your petticoats, and be quicker about it."

I again looked at her involuntarily; I suppose with the view of ascertaining what possibility there existed of successfully rebelling. Ellen very calmly and determinedly returned the gaze. Neither of us spoke.

I proceeded to divest myself of my dress, &c., as directed, and stood in my corset, *chemise*, and stockings before my mistress.

"You will not require those things again; fold them and put them away in this drawer." She went to a walnut chest of drawers and opening one, left it open, and said: "Put your clothes in there."

Under the power of her eye, I, with reluctance, in spite of myself, put my dress and petticoats in.

"Now shut the drawer."

I pushed it with my knees.

"Now you will inform me how you have been accustomed to be punished. Have you had a governess or a tutor?"

"A governess," I stammered out, hanging my head.

I am sure it was not my imagination that Ellen's form dilated at this reply. A keener light came into her eyes and a more set look into her countenance.

"I am glad to hear it. And pray, has she punished you?"

"Yes."

"Often?"

"Yes."

"How?"

"In various ways."

"Has she whipped your bottom?" asked Ellen, looking full at me.

"Yes, she has."

"With a birch, I suppose?"

"Yes."

"Across her knee?"

"No, on a bench, or across an ottoman."

"A fine thing for a big boy like you to be *whipped* by a girl," exclaimed Ellen scornfully, "and your bottom too!"

I blushed.

She walked to a drawer in an old-fashioned *escritoire*, opened it, and took out a black leather strap, four or five inches broad and about thirty inches long; its end was sliced into a number of thin strips about six inches long.

"Have you ever seen anything like this before?"

"Yes, I have," I answered, very pale.

"What is it?"

"It is a tawse."

"Yes, it is, and there is nothing I enjoy so much as using it. Every morning and every evening as long as you are here, I shall beat you severely with this," she said resolutely.

"Oh, Ellen, not today!"

"Yes, we may as well begin directly — at once."

"You will not be severe — oh, please!"

"I shall beat you until I am absolutely satisfied, until you are reduced to the most abject, the most grovelling subjection, until you beg and implore, and pray for pardon."

Ellen then walked up to me. Why it was that I could not resist her, I do not know, but I could not. She put me face downwards on a low, broad ottoman, evidently the top of a box for dresses; lifting the skirt of her dress, she held my head between her thighs outside her petticoats, but under her gown, and fastened my hands behind me. Then she lifted my *chemise* as much as the corset permitted and I could feel her contemplating my legs. I was already sobbing; her grip was ruthless, escape from it was hopeless. She then lifted her arm, continued to lash my bottom and thighs with blows, and commenced to lash me with her heavy leather tawse.

The pain was frightful. I writhed and struggled. She let go my head, pushing me down with her blows well-delivered from the shoulder.

She appeared to be possessed by some demon, to be in a frenzy. Mute with agony I rolled on to the floor, where, spurning me with her pointed shoes, she continued to rain blows upon me.

At last I shrieked and prayed and begged for pardon and mercy, as if my very life depended on it. My supplications appeared to give her intense gratification.

"Will you acknowledge me as your mistress? Will you acknowledge that you are the absolute slave of the petticoat? Will you worship the ground on which I tread? Will you — will you — will you?" she demanded, in a fury.

"Yes, oh, yes! Oh, Ellen! I beg, I implore! Oh, oh, stop! Oh, I will! Oh, I acknowledge I am absolutely subdued, absolutely conquered, absolutely your slave!"

"Then kiss my feet; take off my shoes and kiss them." I obeyed and she placed them roughly on my mouth as I lay on the floor beside myself with pain.

"You must come with me to my lady's *boudoir* now."

"Like this?" I exclaimed.

"Yes," she answered.

Lady Alfred was dozing in a light summer *toilette* over a novel. A short frock disclosed her pretty ankles in pink silk stockings, so short indeed, that I could see up to her knees.

She looked pleased and amused at my appearance.

"I have been obliged to deprive him of his dress, drawers, and petticoats already and have just beaten him, milady, soundly."

"Very good, Ellen, let me see. Lie across my lap, Sir. You can leave him with me till tea time."

"He has had no lunch."

"Then he can go without. Lie across my lap. Upon my word, she has beaten you! What a pretty bottom! How red, black, and blue! Is it very tender?" asked Lady Alfred touching it and exciting herself voluptuously. "Ah, here is something to tell me all about it!" she exclaimed, grasping me in front.

And then rising, she seated herself in a broad, low armchair, the back of which made a very obtuse angle with the seat.

"Lie between my legs. Put it in. Now, Julian, how do you like having your bottom flogged by a girl — by my maid?"

The suggested idea, the position, soon enabled me to express to Alice several times how I appreciated my bondage and its cruel discipline.

As she said, I was the greater part of the ten days between her legs. Naturally, I became tired, fatigued, perhaps I should say, exhausted; but upon those occasions Ellen was requisitioned to lash me with her tawse until I fully satisfied her mistress; and I had some periods of rest when her social duties took Lady Alfred away.

One evening she went to a ball, or, to speak more correctly, to a dinner party, a dance.

I had to sit up to undress her; and when she came in about two o'clock in the morning in all the pride and splendour of her beauty and dress, it appeared that nothing would satisfy her. The champagne at supper was the wrong brand; the chicken was overdone, the salad was not fresh, and whoever heard of a salad at two in the morning. She abused the butler who came up with the tray and the man who carried it; she berated Ellen and she smacked my face.

Ellen took things very quietly while Lady Alfred was fretting and fuming and not knowing what she wanted.

Ellen asked whether she should punish me as I had been very lazy and indolent all the evening.

"Certainly," cried Lady Alfred, "the very thing."

So Ellen took me across her lap.

Lady Alfred then discovered a remedy for her perturbation of feeling. The spanking was no good. She made Ellen go for a birch and stripped me naked and then flogged me mercilessly. It restored her to a good humour. When I was in ribbons held by Ellen, and Lady Alfred had gloated over me to her heart's content, she put me underneath her on the sofa.

I tickled her a few moments with my tongue, exciting her to the highest pitch.

In a transport she removed her leg from across me. "He must come to my bed; and Ellen, you must come too."

She took hold of me, not by the ear, but by my instrument, which she seized very tightly with her right hand, making me jump with the vigour of the grasp.

"Come with me!" she ordered. "Ellen, put out the lights and follow."

Absolutely naked, with a flat silver candlestick in her hand, she marched me off to her bedroom, in all the glory of her evening dress, her face flushed, her eyes wild, her hair loosened, and tugging every now and then like a Maenad at my testicles.

When we reached the bedroom Alice threw me on the bed and bade me wait. She tore off her clothes and flew to me.

Turning down the bedclothes she forced my head between her legs, and, putting my feet on the pillow, drew my virile organ to her mouth with her hands upon it. She bit and pulled it as though bent upon making a meal of it.

I returned the compliment, catching her own fury. It was soon as impossible for me to restrain myself as it was for her. I returned her what she gave me, but I was exhausted before she was.

She made Ellen get into the same bed. When she had satisfied herself somewhat, and in the full glare of the lights, she made Ellen have me, while she kept her own hand upon my engine, seeming to derive intense satisfaction from the emotions, the throbs, the convulsions, she occasioned and felt.

At last, exhausted and drowsy, she told Ellen to get out of bed and turn down the lamps and made me sleep between her and her maid.

It must have been nearly eleven when we awoke. I woke first, but, not daring to move, I could only contemplate my two fair tormentors, naked on each side of me, in all the *abandon* of slumber.

Then Ellen awoke, and pinched and pulled and slapped me. She got up, threw on a dressing gown, and left the room.

"Where is Ellen?" asked Alice, presently awaking, and fondling me.

"She got up about half an hour ago."

"Ring," said Alice; "or stay, Julian, just once before you ring," and she played with me, looked at me in the most ravishing manner, and asked: "Can you once, Julian, can you? You must put this fellow into me — into this wet, burning, insatiable flesh of mine. I must have your flesh."

I had been dosed with champagne the evening before and I was anxious to get up for a certain purpose.

As Alice clung to me I craved a moment's excuse.

"No, I shall not let you," she retorted with charming presumptuousness.

"You must put him in there, whatever happens, *at once.*"

A few moments later there was a knock at the door and Ellen entered with the chocolate.

The windows were opened; we took loose garments and breakfasted.

Afterwards, Alice amused herself by making me try on all sorts of stockings and petticoats, drawers and *chemises*, and finally deciding on a *bizarre*, fantastic, but pre-eminently feminine costume, made me dress her as I wore it. First, I had to bathe her, and then to rub her delicate flesh, as she lay on an eiderdown of crimson silk, all with my hands.

When Lady Alfred was dressed and had gone, the inexorable Ellen came to give me the matutinal beating which I bore as best I could. Afterwards, dressed in plain clothes and in coarser linen than I liked, there were Alice's shoes to clean, her dress to brush, her things to put away, and the thousand-and-one little duties of a maid to perform.

So the ten days passed. And she returned me to Downlands Hall considerably tamed and very much effeminatised.

Chapter VIII

Mamma

I was driven back in a high dog cart to Downlands Hall, on a fine breezy morning, and there in the approach to the house stood Gertrude Stormont, my mamma, my Vivien, her hair as golden as ever, her form as lithe and supple.

I stopped the cart, jumped out, told the man to drive on to the house, and ran up to my mamma, both hands outstretched. She came to meet me, and clasped them both.

"Julian!" she said, in her low tones, velvety and sweet.

"Oh, Mamma, Mamma," I cried, "at last! Oh, I am so glad! How long have you been here?"

"Only since the day before yesterday. And are you still a boy and as naughty as ever? Come, let us stroll through the woods. We shall get back for lunch at half-past two."

We made our way through the park, till we came to a mossy bank in a sequestered glade. Gertrude threw her parasol down and seated herself.

"Sit beside me and tell me all."

I readily obeyed and caught her in my arms. The violence of my kisses brought a crimson glow to her face; and before I knew what I was about I had slipped my hands up underneath her petticoats.

"Julian, how dare you?" she exclaimed, with entrancing anger, and yet I knew she liked it. "No, no, no; not here."

"Yes, here, now, in the open air. I will commit incest. I will have my mamma, without another word. I will violate and outrage her. I will tell her all in that way."

"Julian," she said, with charming mock severity, "I fear the nettle petticoat, the thistles, the birching, the ride, have all been forgotten. Well, if it must, it shall!" as I continued to tickle her. "How he has grown!" she exclaimed, feeling him. "But I think it is very wrong, and what will Mademoiselle say at your outraging her guest in the green fields in this manner?"

But I only replied by pushing her down, kissing her lips so vehemently as to choke her protests, and removing her garments. I advanced into the interior of the paradise before me.

As soon as she felt the cold air upon her uncovered limbs, the whole situation struck her so forcibly that she was carried away by an excess of voluptuousness, and becoming utterly reckless, twined her limbs about my body.

"Oh, oh, Julian! You bold boy! But I will punish you afterwards. Now, Sir!" — moving up and down — "Oh, oh! Now — tell me *all*," and she fell still further back. "Oh, you dear boy! Oh! Oh! Oh!"

"Again!" I cried, a few moments later.

"Lady Alfred's discipline does not seem to have done *you* much good. I expected home such a demure, such a subdued, such a prudish Julia, and — oh, oh!"

"Oh, Gertrude, my own!"

"You darling boy! You are wicked, though."

And she smiled at me with her love-laden eyes.

We talked freely, unconstrainedly, and at ease, and in peace, which is more than most youths and maidens, when alone in each other's company, can say, and we did so as we had had the philosophy and the courage to satisfy nature first.

How she laughed at my experiences! How she rejoiced in my discovery of Lady Alfred's sex! How she gloated over the description detailed minutely, which she obliged me to give her, of the attempt made to make me believe myself a girl! What sly references she made about that ivory plug!

"And you are still in petticoats. Oh, Julian!"

"Mamma, I came into the world under them. And it is my belief I shall have to wear them until I leave it. How any man can escape them is to me a mystery."

"Indeed," she said, "but Mademoiselle has news for you. Shall I tell you? You are not Julian Robinson any longer. You — you petticoated thing! — are now Lord Viscount Ladywood. Your father has at length accepted an earldom. The general election was too much for him. He would not, he said, associate in the House of Commons with men he could not admit to his own servants' hall."

"Mamma!" I exclaimed, overcome by my new dignity.

"And Mademoiselle is determined to keep you in petticoats just the same. She declares you will feel them all the more. And what is more I believe the first thing Mademoiselle will do will be to make you take off your drawers to be birched by her, to prevent your head being turned."

"Oh, Gertrude!"

"And speaking of drawers," continued she, turning me over, "I shall take possession of them now."

Half serious and half in fun, she dipped her hands underneath my skirts, and despite my half-hearted resistance, took them off. She passed her hands over my sore legs and bottom, for Ellen had not omitted the tawse even on that morning, being determined to give me something which would make me remember her for a few days.

I cringed and shuddered.

"It is so sore still?" asked Gertrude, with a winning wile. "Women do nothing but beat you, and you do nothing but beat them with this rod of yours. But we must be going. I wonder if there are any nettles about here?"

"Mamma!"

"Oh, yes! That is all very fine. You expect to escape, but I know that unless I carry out my sentence myself, it will be unexecuted." And she looked about. "There are some, I declare."

Drawing her gloves on, she got up and went and picked two bunches of strong, rank, stinging nettles.

I also got up and made off as best I could.

She followed me. The chase was not long for she knew how to run in petticoats; hers indeed were shorter than mine, and my black dress had a train and her frock had not.

I tripped and fell and she was upon me in a moment. She drew a tape from her pocket.

At once the fact that she had a design in meeting me flashed upon my mind.

Oh, Woman! Woman! What a crafty, dissimulating creature you are.

I remembered hearing of a young lady who had gone down to Richmond with a man to tea. She carried a bag and when they found they could not return to town in due time and must needs sleep at the hotel the bag was found to contain a nightdress! How lucky!

I could not resist Mamma. She possessed too much influence over my being. She tied the nettles with her tape, which she fixed under my clothes round my waist, one bunch behind, the other in front, and then she made me rise and walk. I walked after a fashion — a most ridiculous one — which made Gertrude scream with delighted laughter. The expression of my face she declared was beyond anything — at every step I was mercilessly stung.

"Now, Julian, now, Lord Ladywood, pray, walk decently," and

she would give me a push with her parasol. "Come along, we shall be late! Come — your Lordship has had too much champagne — you seem intoxicated! Come, do walk properly! Give me your arm."

"How extraordinarily you walk, Julian," exclaimed Mademoiselle in her serio-comic way as, a few minutes after, we met her in the hall, looking in a puzzled manner first at me and then at Gertrude. "What piece of folly have you been perpetrating now? Whatever can Lady Alfred have done to you?" she remarked very gravely. "She surely has not — no, it is impossible — why cannot you walk? You are not ruptured, are you?"

Gertrude screamed with laughter and clapped her hands.

"Oh, Mademoiselle, I met this young lady, and we found some nettles, and she defied me. I felt bound in honour not to let her defy me, and — look!"

She lifted my skirts and shew my stung legs and the nettles.

"I deprived him of his drawers. If young men will openly defy a girl and then wander alone where nettles grow — they may find their defiance cost them dearly."

"Upon my word, Gertrude, you are too bad — you will have to extinguish the fire you have lighted. The irritation will make him wild for you."

"I think I should be so without it," I exclaimed, throwing an anxious look at Gertrude.

"Well," said Mademoiselle, "the luncheon bell has rung. Are you going upstairs first?"

"Yes," I exclaimed.

"Are you?" said Gertrude, coyly. "Not without my leave."

"Then take him," rejoined Mademoiselle, "and remember, no more fooling. I shall expect you both down in five minutes or you will have an account to settle with me."

How happily and merrily the days passed.

Gertrude used to insist, cruel girl, on birching me, and then taking me to ride with her.

I must not omit to state that Mademoiselle read me my father's letter with great solemnity and formality, and folding it up, added: "But you will remember that I intend to keep you in petticoats all the same, Lord Ladywood, so now kiss my hand; and recollect that nothing will emancipate you."

Chapter IX

A Maying

As I grew older, and as the year waxed and waned, as Lammas came, and we went to the Norfolk Broads for change, when we returned and the year died in winter, I loved Mademoiselle more and more.

It had taken a long time to awaken to more than a transient vibration any responsive chord on her part, but now at last a secret sympathy was established between us.

I loved her in her autumn boating costume made of flannel, which by its simple form set off and displayed her well-knit, robust figure to great advantage.

I loved her in her winter costumes, when she drove with fleet horses through the snow, galloping along the frost-bound roads in her sleigh. And how well she looked in her skating dresses, the contours of her graceful form outlined by the resistance of the air, by her passage through it, her skates increasing her height, her short skirts displaying her ankles, and the exercise itself compelling her to use her legs as if they were legs — a thing women are remarkably slow to do, considering the killing effect these limbs of theirs have.

And then the spring came — the spring, when one feels a new life welling up.

The fact of my being Lord Ladywood made her more *exigeante*, and anything like insubordination or impudence she put down at once, usually by a good sound birching, and by compelling me afterwards to apologise for my disobedience by putting me under, and making me kiss the lower parts of her beautiful body. Sometimes, in the passages, I would catch Agnes or Maud, and take liberties with them; and of course they birched and whipped me in the schoolroom just as often as I did them.

I loved to feel their pretty legs. Pretty frightened fawns! How they shuddered and reddened at a rude, invading hand upon their soft, naked flesh, and yet how they liked it! Maud especially. Agnes was not old enough to take more pleasure in this sort of frolic than any child ordinarily does in being tickled.

Of course I was kept in petticoats the whole time. The influence did not diminish by use. It was strange that it did not lose its force, and grow stale by custom.

One May afternoon, we read the "Golden Legend." When I reached these lines:

> I have heard it said, that at Eastertide,
> When buds are swelling on every side,
> And the sap begins to move in the vine,
> Then, in all cellars far and wide,
> The oldest as well as the newest wine
> Begins to stir itself, and ferment
> With a kind of revolt and discontent
> At being so long in darkness pent,
> And fain would burst from its sombre tun
> To bask on the hill-side in the sun.

a panorama of my year of gynecocracy passed before my vision, and I recalled with soft, voluptuous delight my "psychological lesson" — my night with Mademoiselle.

I was sensible of my blood beginning to stir itself and ferment with a kind of revolt at not having yet been infused into my sweet governess' organisation.

I looked up as I read the lines, and I knew there was a tell-tale tremor in my voice. Mademoiselle glanced up too, and our eyes met.

After dinner, Agnes, Beatrice, and myself squabbled in the twilight, in the drawing room; and I believe Mademoiselle, who had been on the lookout all the evening for something to seize on as an excuse, was glad of it. With unusual promptitude she was down upon me at once.

I had so far forgotten myself as to slap Agnes' face. Agnes, and her kittenish, apish ways, were especially tantalising.

"Bring me the punishment book at once, Julia," as soon as she heard and saw the sharp little blow on Agnes' peachlike cheek. She spoke sternly. "I cannot permit this insubordination. You are well aware how I insist upon constant respect and abject submission to the petticoat, even if you are wronged by it."

I looked ashamed, but said nothing.

I knew when she sent me for the book, that I should lose my evening, and was much chagrined in consequence.

"As you have slapped Agnes' face, she shall birch your bottom at ten o'clock in the schoolroom. You will then be sent to my room, where I shall take certain measures with you, which will, perhaps, make you regret your want of respect. In the meantime," she said, tearing out a slip from the punishment book and folding it, "you are to take this to Elise."

I trembled as I took the paper, and walked out of the room.

I went to my room and rang the bell twice, which would give Elise to understand both that the signal was for her, and that she was required to inflict chastisement.

I was aware that the servants would be going to supper about this time, and that Elise would be very angry at being called away. I debated with myself whether it would be safe to wait even ten minutes. I, however, only succeeded in satisfying myself that Mademoiselle's sharp ears would be waiting to hear the bell for Elise, and that any delay would involve me into fresh trouble.

So I rang and Elise came.

"Well, Miss Julia, what is it now?" she asked in a fury. "And I was just going to my supper. What have you been doing now?"

I grew white and held out my paper for an answer. Elise opened and read it.

"And so," said the lynx-eyed Elise, gazing gravely at me, "you are to be birched by Miss Agnes and then to spend the night with Mademoiselle as you did last year just at this time. What have you done?"

"Oh! They were squabbling, and I smacked that pert Agnes' face."

"And so she is to birch your bottom." Elise looked at me and smacked my face. "That's for bringing me away from my supper."

The smart made me lose my temper with the pretty maid.

"How dare you?" I cried. "That's not in the bill!"

"What do I care for that?" she retorted, and grasping me violently, she pulled me down across her lap, turned up my petticoats, and as she expressed it, warmed my bottom for me.

"That's not in the bill either," remarked Elise, as, satisfied at last, she allowed me to get up, half sobbing and wholly burning; "but it's a nice *hors d'oeuvre* to what Miss Agnes will do to you this evening."

Elise then took me to the schoolroom where she placed me in the stocks — two pieces of wood, heel to heel, and in a straight line at right angles to my person, and a lid with two apertures for the ankles was slid over my feet and locked. Then a cruel backboard was strapped on over an inordinately tightly laced corset, my hands or wrists were fixed behind to its tail, and its collar set so high that my head was thrown right back.

"There! That is how Mademoiselle wished you to be, but I remember last year," and Elise produced a red petticoat of my governess, which, having fastened at the waist band, she threw over my head. "There! So you shall remain until it is time to birch you."

I cannot express my sensations. Mons. Priapus was terribly distended by them; and my terror at being found in this state by my governess and cousins amounted almost to utter self-annihilation. But what could I do?

They arrived. Elise unfastened me. I was stiff. I had thought the time would never pass.

I was led to the scaffold, held down, and had my bottom vigorously birched by Agnes.

Afterwards, without much time for recovery, I was led to Mademoiselle's bedroom, and by her direction made just as on the former occasion, but without the preliminary ordeal, to get into her bed.

She soon came and enveloped me with her warm thighs, giving me such a squeezing that I can remember it until now, and making me kiss her behind as well as in front. At length we both fell asleep; I, of course, still between her lovely legs, in close contact with her person. What a curious sphinxlike affair women possess at the front lower end of their dear little bodies. What folds of flesh there are. How deliciously they unfold. What sweet moisture they exude. How they expand!

The morning had broken long before Elise came. Although still confined a very close prisoner between my governess' naked limbs in close proximity to the wet fountain of her being, the disordered bedclothes enabled me to see the daylight in the closely curtained, dimly lighted room. I could imagine the fresh morning air outside, I saw pencils of sunlight, and I heard the song of the thrushes and the blackbirds, and the soft sounds of the breeze amid the trees.

How delicious and voluptuous these morning hours are!

Elise presently entered with chocolate and cakes, drew the curtains, let in the May morning and its fragrance, and again my dear governess made me breakfast naked with her.

Elise had been dismissed. There were no hours to dread today under her. She could not come betwixt the cup and the lip, and tear me from Mademoiselle, upon whose form in its gossamer night robe I gloated.

She played with me, and love sick, I responded.

"Oh, Mademoiselle!" I exclaimed, as her taper fingers excited me beyond myself. "Listen to my madness now. Incarnate, conceive; we these days *must* end. Let us have a little one of our own. It can never be what it would have been last year. My virgin freshness has gone, and sorrow has replaced it. But let me, at any rate, unite myself, before I am older, with this dear ruler of mine. Let us have a little one of our very own to remember these days by — to personify all my devotion, all my love of you!"

"Lord Ladywood!" she exclaimed, as I made good use of my fingers. "How dare you?"

"Love is bold by right of love," I replied.

"And how do you know I love you?"

"Oh, Mademoiselle! How can I know otherwise?"

"This is a very impudent fellow," she answered evasively, playing with him.

"Conquer his impudence," I rejoined.

She lay back and drew me on to her.

"My love, my love!" I exclaimed.

She resigned herself to my fury, and I possessed her — not *Bacchus docens*, but this time of her own goodness.

I felt myself Mademoiselle and Mademoiselle me.

She loved me; her arms twined about my shoulders. Her passion startled me. Her legs wound round my body. She pressed me further into her.

"With all my heart!" she declared. "You have won! I will yield all my heart! I will embrace, will conceive, will reproduce you — if I can!"

I lay on her bosom. I felt myself inside her and felt the workings of her mind and body upon mine.

I was entirely engulfed, in her beautiful body. She felt the throbbing of my member, and its agitations were all understood and appreciated by the corresponding organ of her own feminine constitution.

I proceeded to beget a child, worthy, I hoped, of her and of myself. There would be some immortality in the result. These days at Downlands and Mademoiselle's sweet influence on me would not be lost. They would live in a child. The spirit now summoned would find a home.

Throb! Throb! Throb!

"Oh, Julia! Oh, Lord Ladywood! Oh, my love, my love, my own love!"

And Mademoiselle yielded herself up to the soft ecstasy.

Oh, that May morning! What ecstasy was mine! What rapture! What satisfaction!

Chapter X

My Wedding

My majority was approaching, and I was already the father of a beautiful girl, able in its infantine prattle to say, "Mam, mam, mam," to its own dear mamma, my Hortense. I confided to her the secret between Beatrice and myself. She had wished to be the mother of a child of love, not of marriage; and she promised to announce my engagement to my parents. They could not be astonished at it; and Mademoiselle told me I had made the wisest choice, notwithstanding that she felt sure Beatrice would always insist on having the upper hand.

My parents were pleased. I do not know whether I myself was or not. But I had quite satisfied myself that love did not necessarily mean marriage, indeed that marriage was a social necessity, probably excluding love.

And Beatrice's ample thighs filled me with passion. I might do much worse than be her husband.

One result of the engagement was a termination of my residence at Downlands Hall. It was not considered proper for me to reside before marriage in the same house with my bride select. Until engagement was known it did not matter. When once it was I suppose it was imagined I should seize the earliest opportunity of lying with her, and of plucking my rose too soon.

When our engagement was formally acknowledged, what importance it gave Beatrice! What airs of superiority she assumed!

I took rooms in town and then went on to my father's where Beatrice and Maud were invited.

Agnes and Mademoiselle came for the festivities to my coming of age, and then the engagement was announced to the world. The marriage was celebrated at St. George's, Hanover Square.

How queer I felt in trousers again and with what envy Beatrice eyed them.

My happiness with Mademoiselle made me impervious to all this, however.

I, of course, recollect my nervousness at the breakfast. I felt like a slave and Beatrice evidently felt like my owner.

She, indeed, slapped my face in the carriage; and, sliding her hand down in front of me, told me that that thing was hers now forever, to use as she chose.

I did not object to being possessed by the magnificent girl into which she had now grown.

But what had I promised? Or, rather, what had I not promised and sworn in the most solemn mode! We had no sooner got well away from Victoria on the road to Dover than she made me kneel down in the carriage and kiss and do homage to Viscountess Ladywood.

What a deluge she gave me! She had her maid in another carriage, and she informed me that in her overall were several birches.

"And you have no corset on, Julian. This freedom I shall not permit. I believe in commencing at once. I shall birch you at night at the 'Lord Warden,' after supper; and tomorrow, underneath your coat and trousers, you shall wear a *chemise*, corset, drawers, and stockings of mine."

"Oh, Beatrice!" I exclaimed, clasping and kissing.

"Don't you miss your petticoats?" she enquired.

"Yes," I replied.

"Well, then, get under mine."

She held me there as we rushed through Kent, whilst she pretended to amuse herself with a novel.

Her maid was a French girl, named Sophie — an intolerable termagant.

Of course my sense of possession of a woman gave me a certain importance. Beatrice was mine, to the exclusion of everyone else; and as I kissed her well-developed vulva, and tickled her large clitoris, I was proud of my possession. But this was quickly knocked out of me.

I did not exactly care about being treated as an absolute baby, and as such Beatrice and Sophie between them treated me.

Will it be believed, that, on our very wedding night, Beatrice locked me up in my dressing room, while she was being put to bed?

When once there, Sophie led me into my wife's room like a lamb to the slaughter.

As Beatrice lay in all her finery, Sophie undressed me before her, and put me to bed naked, not without a very careful examination and display of me. Then she undressed and got into the same bed herself.

I loudly protested, whereupon Beatrice held me, while Sophie smacked me.

"If you think Mademoiselle's lessons are thrown away upon me you are greatly mistaken," said Beatrice.

"I wish to have you all to myself. You are mine," I asserted.

"You are greatly in error," rejoined Beatrice, "you are *mine*. Lie down. Now I can have this fellow," she asserted, grasping him, "and Sophie will see that I do have him. Put him in! I don't want any nonsense. Sophie will see that you do it properly."

"Certainly, Milady," answered Sophie. "Now, Milord!"

Without any compunction this French damsel got her hand under me and inserted me into Beatrice, to whom, impelled by Sophie's hand, I gave too soon an evidence of passion if not of affection.

"It is all your own fault," I said, beyond myself.

"Fetch a birch, Sophie," directed my wife, holding me tightly with her arms and legs.

Sophie, with very great alacrity, skipped off for a birch.

As soon as Beatrice saw her maid re-enter the room, she stretched out her alabaster thighs and placed me between them, grasping me vigorously with her hands, in a manner which obliged me to catch my breath and to cry out. Being hauled about in this violent and masterful mode convulsed my being to its foundations, and caused me to tremble with delight.

Without explanation, request, or hesitation, she placed me against her, and clasping me with her powerful limbs, she said peremptorily: "Now, Julian, get in — right in."

She wriggled and pressed against me — pushed and pushed — so did I. She was very tight, and the accomplishment of her desire occupied some time, and necessitated considerable effort. She flushed violently and her pulse very much quickened. She began to look love sick, her eyes drooped and her lips grew moist, and opening slightly, shew her perfect teeth.

"Come — come, Julian!"

The effect of all this upon me may be imagined. It very nearly brought about the crisis before its time as on the first occasion. I pushed and pushed. Beatrice seconded my efforts.

"There," said my wife, at length, "there, now I have him right up to the hilt. Oh, how delightful! Now, do not slip! Now, Julian, now let me know how you love me — now," biting my lips and casting down her eyes, "now... *fuck* me!"

The word made me jump. Beatrice was so tight and grasped me so closely, so like a close, tight kid glove, that I felt as if I were in a vice — and although she kept up sufficient mechanical excitement to prevent my instrument decreasing, yet the physical destroyed the intellectual emotion, and I knew well as I drew a deep sigh, that there was no hope of an orgasm being accomplished like this, and very great danger before long of my shrinking out of her.

"Oh, oh!" exclaimed Beatrice, as Sophie stood beside us, an idle spectator, with a birch in her hand, and with a very amused and yearning expression upon her features, and as she and I gave ourselves up to the throes of the love struggle: "Oh, I declare, I can feel him at the mouth of my womb! Oh, Julian! Oh, Julian!" and she bit and pressed my lips, and breathed stentoriously. "Oh, Julian! Now!"

I contemplated her face. I drank in the love which flamed from her eyes. I gazed at her neck.

My wife looked at me with astonishment and contempt.

"Indeed, you deserved the petticoats," she exclaimed.

"Sophie, uncover him, whip him, birch his bottom severely, until he satisfies my desire, dastard bridegroom that he is! You shall catch it for this, Julian!"

Sophie pulled the bedclothes right down, discovering me naked between my wife's legs.

"Yes, Milady, I will birch him," said the pretty girl. "To be a log between his bride's legs, *Mon Dieu!* I will make him feel."

Beatrice contracted her legs and arms, holding me more tightly. Sophie raised her rod, made it whistle through the air, and it fell with a terribly stinging blow upon my defenceless buttocks. I felt it lessened my chance of success. But Beatrice announced her determination of having the punishment continued until I complied with her requirements. The birch had been well pickled and it hurt confoundedly; I could not, however, get away from those strong legs. Swish, swish, swish.

Sophie calmly scanned me all the time in my nakedness. She slipped her hand behind and played with my testicles. Swish, swish, swish, she then recommenced; I bounded up and down; so did Beatrice. "Oh!" I exclaimed at length, and Beatrice's eyes flashed.

"Harder, Sophie!"

Sophie, with a calm smile, continued her study of my anatomy, and the regular administration, slow and methodical, of her stripes, which, delivered as they were by a well-balanced and elastic birch, were very hard to bear.

Beatrice shut her mouth, and a curious smile overspread her face. I am sure she wondered how long I should hold out. In her glance there was a glimpse of unexpressed admiration.

Then she said, "Harder," and, needless to narrate, Sophie gladly obeyed.

"Whip well in," directed my wife.

Sophie, changing her position, delivered the strokes more between my legs.

I began to feel an unusual glow of warmth about my buttocks and thighs. In front, too, there was a sensation of strength caused by the increased flow of blood, attracted by the operation of the birch, more than by erotic images which should have caused the blood to flow in those regions in fuller streams.

Women are, indeed, very scientific in the matter. The birch is an admirable substitute for passion; and I suppose it is this connection with love functions that prevents a woman from ever referring to or hearing a reference to the birch without blushing.

"Beatrice!" I murmured.

"You good-for-nothing block! What is the matter with you?"

I clasped her soft, fleshy form — warm and flowing with life — more closely to me. I fell upon it in the enervation of love.

Beatrice made a signal to Sophie and the rod was suspended in the air. I wished more ardently than I can express that I had been covered and had not had to discharge this office naked under Sophie's keen and curious eyes; but I was not covered, I was fully displayed before her, and I knew she watched with eager attention my quickly accumulating passion.

Beatrice gave little calls and cries of love.

"You good boy, Julian, after all! I can feel you increasing, swelling inside me, filling me, gratifying all my longings. You good boy! Oh, oh, oh!"

Then the sense of being possessed by a female came to me. It struck me where I was, and, convulsed with passion, I injected into Beatrice, under all the auspices of marriage, that warm infusion, that germinating fluid, that essence of myself, which she claimed and demanded as my wife.

Before the spasm had completed itself, Sophie put her cool little hand on the cord of the instrument between my legs The shock of the touch fanned the dying embers again into a flame.

Beatrice was thoroughly satisfied.

"I felt you regularly inside me — in my womb, Julian. Nothing can please a woman more."

Then she kissed me and permitted me to lie beside her. Sophie put out the lights and jumped into bed; and indeed I was asleep almost as soon as I was conscious that she had done so, for I was quite exhausted.

We spent that day at Dover and the night at the same hotel, Beatrice enjoying the freedom with me alone so much that she was quite content that we should stay where we were; but on the following day we went on to Paris on our way to Switzerland.

Beatrice appeared to be absolutely insatiable. Her passions, her love, her lust, her appetites — what shall I name the fury that possessed her? — distanced even Lady Alfred Ridlington's.

I had wondered, too, in the old days, whether, when we were married, she would birch me as she did in them.

My speculations were very soon set at rest. Wherever we might happen to be, in public or in private, if I transgressed, Beatrice would inform me: "I shall birch you tonight, when we get in, Julian!"

How foolish it made me feel and look! I am sure the threat was understood more than once. I saw women glancing intelligently and sympathetically at the magnificent girl-woman, who was at once my wife and my governess.

Chapter XI

Swiss Honey

We had been a week or ten days in Paris when Maud arrived.

The sisters met with great glee and affection. Marriage evidently appeared to them to be emancipation, to open the door to fun and frolics without end, to justify all manner of escapades.

"How well, how beautiful you look, Beatrice!" exclaimed Maud, with genuine admiration. "What health you are in! Married life evidently agrees with you. And Julian," her eyes fell softly upon me, "he, too, is well; but I can see he is in pretty strict subjection."

"Yes," rejoined Beatrice, "I keep him well under, and it does him good. He knows what it is to have a wife who can use the birch. I keep him in much better order than Mademoiselle did."

"Is he very often punished?" asked Maud changing colour.

"Oh, yes! Are you not, Julian? I keep you in a very tender state. He particularly dislikes long drives because he has to sit so much."

"Is he so naughty?" asked Maud, seriously.

"A little difficult to manage, sometimes; and, by-the-bye, Maud, you and I have a score to settle."

"Oh, not now, Bee!"

"Oh, yes! I have not forgotten the Apollo and his disobedience. Go to my bedroom, Julian, and stay there until I come. We have nothing to do this afternoon, and we shall have time, before the *table-d'hote*, to amuse ourselves, and to take a walk too. You, Maud, will want to change your dress and it will be a capital opportunity for punishing you both, especially while the novelty of your arrival is upon you both."

I knew very well by this time what being sent to Beatrice's bedroom meant.

In these matters she always took the initiative.

If after a walk in the morning she had made a particularly good lunch and had found some wine to her taste, I was sure afterwards to be told to go to her bedroom.

The first time or so I was bewildered. I had done nothing to displease her and did not know why I should be sent into retirement in disgrace. I feared it was to be whipped. That, however, was not her object.

I heard her short skirts and her quick step rustling along the passage; she opened the door, shut, and locked it.

I was standing foolishly by the window, rather frightened and pale.

"Now, Julian," she said, in a strange excitement, her eyes flashing, her hair loose, her movements quick, as though she were under the influence of intense passion, "now, Julian, strip naked, you are to amuse me — to please — and to fuck me, twice, thrice, as often as I please. Be quick — off with all your clothes, Sir, every stitch of them, and come here!"

She seated herself in an armchair — her skirts above her knees, which had fallen widely apart.

"Get down there instantly, and kiss me, bite me, tickle me with your tongue, until I am contented."

I was soon enveloped, naked, in her garments, and when I had excited her to the highest pitch she sprang up, placed me down upon the sofa roughly, and threw herself upon me.

Putting a cushion under me, she soon forced me far into her burning flesh, and produced, by her delicious violence, the spasm of love.

I never knew at what moment I might be sent to her room. After breakfast, after dinner, after a drive or walk, if she chanced to see a scene, a picture, a book that excited her, off I was packed; but it was always at *her whim* and pleasure. There was, unfortunately, no reciprocity in the matter; the converse did not hold true, as I discovered to my cost.

One evening when we came in and Beatrice was changing her gown, I was under the influence of the glow of our walk and of her pretty figure, which I had especially noticed; and I felt particularly attracted towards her.

I had taken off her gown and boots — an office she always made me perform and as I gazed at her bare arms and neck in her petticoat bodice, still kneeling at her feet, I placed my hand on her leg under her garments, and, softly pressing it, looked up into her eyes.

"Beatrice," I said tenderly, "please, will you permit me now? Please, will you have me? Oh, I want you so much!"

"The idea!" she cried; and an angry flush at once mounted to her forehead. "The idea! What impudence! What next?" And without another word she smacked my face until my head sang, and then pulled my ears.

"How dare you suggest such a thing to a lady? Don't you know you must wait until you are asked? If you don't know, you shall learn."

She got up and rang for Sophie.

When that damsel entered the room, Beatrice told her that I had attempted to assault her indecently and had adventured to make improper overtures to her.

Sophie looked very serious indeed and said I must be severely punished for my uncontrollable passion.

"What shall we do?" asked my lady. "If Milady pleases, I have a *godemiche*."

"A what?" asked Beatrice.

"A little instrument to put here behind," explained the *soubrette*, touching me as she held me.

"Capital! That will teach him! Do it now, Sophie, before me."

"I will go and get it," she answered.

"How do you like what is in store for you?" asked Beatrice, stately, handsome, and smiling at my predicament.

"Oh, how hard you are to me, Beatrice! How you will disgrace me before you, and by this maid, too!"

"Before you want to put things into me you should consider whether it would be agreeable."

"I did ask."

"Yes, it is not for you to ask. It is for me. *A quoi bon etre femme?* You are my toy; not I yours."

Sophie returned with a box, which she shew to Beatrice, who, taking it, lifted out a great phallus.

"It is charged," observed Sophie.

I danced about the room.

Sophie came after me. "Come, Sir; come, Milord, I must take down your trousers, you must be complaisant, you must be good — you must suffer! Such impudence to Milady! Oh! You will find how a lady punishes; how she can make you feel here — behind. You like to have this in your *jesse* — in your what you call bottom. No? Oh, yes, you will! It will do you good ever so. Anyhow, you must!"

Sophie took me by the shoulders to the bed and fastened the affair outside her dress round her waist below her corset, and her gravity and the instrument made between them cut such a ludicrous figure that Beatrice laughed until the tears coursed down her cheeks.

Sophie, with a grim smile, unfastened and took down my trousers and drawers and pushing me down on my face very roughly, inserted her *godemiche*, whilst Beatrice walked over to the other side of the bed and held me down by the shoulders.

Sophie then commenced a series of strong thrusts at me which hurt badly and which overwhelmed me with shame and confusion. I groaned and resisted but the lively French girl was too much for me; slipping her hand round me to the front she grasped what she declared to my lady was the source of all my trouble. I, at once, spasmodically moved up and down and her persistent steady pressure quickly accomplished her purpose.

She moved the mock penis to-and-fro as Mademoiselle had done the candle. At length, at a nod from Beatrice, she gave it a squeeze and I felt myself deluged internally with a warm flood shot into me in jets.

"There!" said Sophie. "There, Milord!"

I groaned, lay still, and hid my face.

"He is too ashamed," said Sophie. "He hides his face — he must face his shame! Hold up your head, Milord!!"

Beatrice put her hand under my chin.

"Shall I do it again, while he lies in your lap?" asked Sophie.

Beatrice had been so much excited and was now in such a state of erotism that she at once jumped at the idea.

I protested vigorously and uselessly. My protests merely emphasized my degradation.

Beatrice returned to her armchair. I was placed between her legs. Mons. Priapus was inserted into my wife and Sophie's phallus into my rear. Beatrice was more tremendously excited than she had ever been before.

I never again ventured to make overtures of this sort to my wife.

But I was very frequently sent to her room. Other lady visitors or fellow travellers, with that rapid feminine perception which amounts to intuition, promptly understood my case, and congratulated Beatrice upon my strict subjection to the petticoat. But to return to Maud and myself.

There was nothing for it but to obey Bee's order and we all three went to the bedroom, Maud covered with blushes.

Beatrice made me undress. I made some kind of protest — uselessly, of course.

"You have done it before to Maud, why this ridiculous

affectation?"

Maud blushed.

"May I help him, Bee?"

"To be sure; and he shall help you."

"How queer it is," said Maud, "to take off a man's trousers! You know he had a petticoat at Downlands that day."

"What difference can that make?" said Beatrice.

"Oh, it does!" said Maud, red and hot all over, as she took off my clothes, slipping off my shirt and vest.

"Do you want him? I intend to make you ask for him, Maud."

"Oh, Bee!" she said.

"Yes, you know I do. Now, you'll please undress. Help her, Julian."

Of course I readily did so. She would keep me in countenance; and besides, had she not stripped me?

She made some resistance and seemed more than once upon the point of tears. When her petticoats had been removed and I was unlacing her corset and about to take off her shoes and stockings, she said to Beatrice: "I suppose you think it does not matter my being made to have him, because —"

"Rubbish!" returned Beatrice quickly. "You know you have had him already. I have heard the history of that stained bed quilt."

"Beatrice, it is too bad, your stripping me like this," said Maud, trembling, as the corset was unfastened and the other articles quickly followed.

Beatrice only smiled.

Maud's last garment — her *chemise* — was very soon slipped off over her head, and there we both stood naked before Beatrice, who, being herself dressed, made us the more sensible of our nakedness.

"You need not die, need not languish, Julian," remarked Beatrice. "You have had her once and shall again. When I took you it was understood that you were to be transferable."

"Oh, Beatrice — your husband!" exclaimed Maud.

"What of that? Now, Maud, do you not want him?"

She looked at me before she answered.

"Won't you ask him?" suggested Maud.

"Ask *him!*" replied Beatrice, with great disdain. "Certainly not. Why on earth ask *him?* He is not his own, he is mine."

"Oh, indeed!" said Maud. "Yes, of course he is."

"Now, Maud, you knew what there was between Julian and me

at Downlands —"

"Why, he had only been four or five days in the place! You don't mean to tell me you were engaged then!" cried Maud, forgetting in the heat of the discussion both her own and my nakedness.

"You knew," went on Beatrice, "what there was between Julian and me. You knew there was love; and you took him, and," looking at Maud's middle, "had him; and now you'll just ask for him!"

"Oh, Bee! But I don't care if I do! I am glad to have him on any terms."

Maud made no more ado about it. With entrancing ravishing coyness, very love sick and glancing at me, she requested Beatrice to permit her husband to fuck her.

Beatrice insisted both upon this naughty word and upon my being described as her husband. The feelings evoked in me may be surmised. I became wild.

Maud, on Beatrice's assenting, took me by the wrist and led me to the bed. She lay down, and drew me upon her white breasts and ravishing form. We clasped each other with our arms. I kissed her with enthusiasm. I complied with her desire.

Beatrice witnessed it.

"How dare you commit adultery under your wife's own eyes?" she asked me angrily when she had given our passion a few moments in which to subside.

I was stupefied. Had she not ordered me to do so?

She, however, fastened my feet to the iron foot of the bedstead, soles uppermost, and whipped them cruelly for my committing adultery.

"Oh, Beatrice! Oh, how severe you are! Has he not had enough?" said Maud.

"No!" shouted Beatrice. "He can't drive much because of the condition of his bottom; and he won't be able to walk much now because of the state of his feet. Before my own eyes to — to — fuck you, my sister!"

Lash, lash! Lash!

Beatrice worked herself into a perfect fury. When she had finished beating me she tore her clothes off. I must acknowledge I was weeping bitterly.

Maud looked at me with great concern, she saw what Beatrice wanted — what I had just done to her. No doubt she wondered whether I could satisfy my wife.

Beatrice lay down upon me in a perfect hurricane of passion, but I was equal to the occasion, and to her delight fucked her violently.

She then put me on the bed face up and stood across me, while, stooping over me and bending down, she inserted my member into her pretty mouth.

"You have excited me to such an extent, that I must taste him — I must eat him."

She tickled me violently with her tongue, while, with both her hands on my testicles, she manipulated them.

I glued my mouth to her sweet clitoris and our inflammation produced a spontaneous return to the natural posture, save that Beatrice was uppermost.

Chapter XII

Conjugal Rights

The honeymoon was quite too delightful while it lasted and it extended over a considerably longer period than a moon.

We returned to England in the autumn and went to a house which had been purchased for us on the southern slope of Compden Hill — a good-sized building, standing in about eleven acres of ground. Beatrice had had a voice in its choice.

I had not known that these three girls were heiresses, but so they were, and they had a couple of a hundred thousand pounds a piece, so that Beatrice, in determining that I should marry her, had not done me any wrong pecuniarily. We were not embarrassed, like some unfortunates, in our domestic arrangements, and we had a properly mounted establishment.

I am not going to enter into my political and social life. Later on I stood at a by-election, and have been ever since in the House, where I have ascertained that I am by no means remarkable for being under my wife's thumb. Most of the legislators who are married, that is, most of those whom I know anything of, are the same, and possess what may be conventionally described as a "mortal dread" of their better halves. I am not going to enter into all this. My history is a secret one, and is concerned with our *vie intime*.

Maud remained with Beatrice for more reasons than one — the two girls were fond of me, and Beatrice, I suppose, would have been lonely alone, and Maud had to look out for her Duke or Marquis, or her country gentleman with his thousands of acres, or her brewer, or whatever eligible person she could find. It was well understood, to my horror, that her marriage was not necessarily to be sanctified by love; it was to receive only the blessing of Mammon.

The answer to my expostulations was one to which I had no rejoinder.

"Oh, what does it matter, Julian? I shall always have you to console me."

It was a matter of surprise to me that the consolations I had administered to Maud, and the duties I had discharged towards Beatrice, had not altered the figure of either of those ladies in the very least. I pondered upon this. And after our return, when the honeymoon and its fooleries ceased to a large extent by Beatrice's commands, I found I was still expected to go to her room, whenever *she* pleased, and to Maud's whenever *she* liked.

I thought I would employ my heavy House of Commons manner in trying to make Beatrice understand the necessity of our having an heir, and the danger Maud ran in these days of fierce competition in the matrimonial and other markets, if it should chance to be discovered, as it certainly would be, that a little stranger arrived *via* Maud instead of *via* Beatrice, or that Maud had such wonderful subtle sympathy for the sister that she, without any ostensible wherefore in the shape of a man of her own, should produce a little stranger, too.

"You are an owl!" said Beatrice. "Go to my *boudoir*."

I went to her *boudoir*, although, upon my word, I wanted to go to my club.

In our travels we had passed twice through Paris, going and returning. In Paris, Beatrice bought a thickish quarto album, with a limp cover, and she made me collect all the photographs, prints, sketches and drawings that were obtainable, in which were depicted, with a rudeness and nudity which would have extended the reputation of Pietro Aretino himself, the subjugation of the creature man to his sovereign mistress; and she arranged and stuck them all in her album.

It was a collection rich and rare. One coloured drawing represented a youth, in girl's clothes, tied to a whipping post, and being flogged by his pretty mistress, whilst her maid held up his garments. Mons. Priapus appeared as large as life, with a very red head. It would be endless to describe them all; this favourite one is typical of the rest.

I was always compelled to wear underneath my clothes Beatrice's underclothing, long stockings and drawers, and a tight corset. I was not permitted a valet. Beatrice's maid, Sophie, attended to my toilette. This attire and this maid had a very subjugating effect, but the effeminacy they invested me with, made me a complete dandy, and I was the envy of many men whose wives were always twitting them at being outshone by me.

The division-lists in the papers were a perpetual nuisance to me. Beatrice always knew how I voted, and I had to vote as her ladyship pleased.

Once I failed to do so — only once, and she discovered it at breakfast. That morning I had a particular engagement with my broker, but I was not allowed to keep it. I may mention I am never permitted to leave the house without her leave, but on that morning she was deaf to all explanations, entreaties, or expostulations, and she certainly looked most uncommonly beautiful.

"You disobeyed!" she exclaimed, with a look of thunder, and in corresponding tones. "You disobeyed me! I do not care for Government whips, or for any other whips; and I wonder that you should. I should have expected you would care only for my birch. Go to my bedroom at once and wait till I come."

Maud looked triumphant.

"I have promised to go to Old Bread Street, where I have a most particular appointment with Messrs. —, and I am to see the Manager of the Bank —."

"Go to my bedroom, do you hear?" she repeated, stamping her pretty foot, the personification of pretty anger and of righteous indignation, in her elegant morning gown, with roses at her throat. "You may well look sheepish! I will make your bottom smart for you! Go!"

I went. I have described so many whippings, that I will not narrate what occurred when she came.

Beatrice, I may mention, had a regular supply of birch obtained by her through someone who once upon a time advertised in the *Saint James's Gazette*. I think they came from Aberystwyth. More cruel, more cutting, more stinging birches I never felt. They made me howl, and she always pickled them first in her own urine.

Maud and my lady then went out to shop in their Victoria.

When they returned, she lashed me with her riding whip, making me dance and scream with anguish.

"Oh, Beatrice!" exclaimed Maud, unable to sit still.

"Do what you like, Maud."

Maud took hold of me, sobbing and protesting as I was, put me on the sofa underneath her, and administered some certainly very sweet consolation.

Beatrice frequently handed over my punishment to Maud; and Maud, on the other hand, never scrupled to have me whipped by making a request to Beatrice, whenever she had a complaint to make, or for any occult reason of her own she wished to have me birched. Women are very inventive.

One last instance of my subjection. I was ordered to go to

Beatrice's *boudoir*. I went.

When she came I was deprived of my trousers, waistcoat, and coat. My petticoat-bodice even was removed, and my shirt, too.

She pointed to the ground in front of a low chair and I sat down on the floor. Taking up the album of which I have given a description, she whisked her skirts over my head, and sat down.

I — found she had removed her drawers; and while she amused herself, I had to kiss her. For quite two hours she insisted upon being pleased and amused thus. This is her construction of conjugal rights, and the bondage is the most severe imaginable: there is no escape.

I saw Mademoiselle and Julia, my daughter, shortly after our return. I am very proud of Julia, and so is her mother. She is a beautiful and as fine a child as children of love usually are, and I have settled ten thousand pounds upon her, which I did with huge satisfaction, feeling that I thereby gave society and its hypocrisies a nice slap in the face.

Mademoiselle did not condole with me though. She said she considered my discipline very wholesome, and when I expressed a hope that I should be some day emancipated and freed from the petticoat, with Beatrice's assent she put me in the corner for three hours with my hands tied behind me, my trousers down, and her red flannel petticoat over my head. At the end of the three hours Beatrice smacked me like a baby across her knee before Mademoiselle.

By this time I am resigned.

END OF VOLUME III

EPILOGUE

Ma femme est un animal
Original,
Qui tous les jours, bien ou mal
S'habille,
Babille,
Et se déshabille.

PANARD, *LE MARI MECONTENT*

The petticoat, as administered by Mademoiselle and then by Beatrice, after all is said and done, I consider extremely beneficial.

A woman can make a man. In the first place she has the monopoly of the making, for she alone can conceive and give birth to him, and in the next place she can make him by discipline, by instilling her common sense into him, and by keeping him rigidly under her thumb. I do not believe that I should be what I am but for this education.

I confess — whether I shall be pitied for it or not — that I love my bondage and I love my tyrant. She has developed me intellectually and physically.

The physical compensations are so many and so great. There is a wonderful luxuriousness and sensuality in being made to bow down before a woman, and to perform her behests, which is not experienced when one takes the initiative one's self.

My lady's stockings and drawers upon me give me, whenever I am reminded that I wear them, an electrifying thrill through and through. And as for the management of affairs, well, they are much better managed by my wife than they could be by me.

Still there is something in me which assures me that man was made for more than the petticoat. This world is woman's earth, and it is petticoated all over. Theirs is the dominion, turn and twist the matter as you will. Therefore, I conclude there must be some other world where men will have a ruling part to play.

Still, I trust even there, it will not be without woman, her influence, and the great mystery of sex.

Is this the reason why it is written that into a certain kingdom the effeminate will not be admitted?

I wish the word defined. What is effeminate? Effeminacy cannot be the product of wholesome discipline.

"Julian, writing still!" It is Beatrice's voice. "Go to my bedroom at once, Sir!" I tremble and go. I *must*.

Julian Robinson, Viscount Ladywood

THE END

BIRCHGROVE PRESS
Flagellant & Libertine Erotica

———————

Birchgrove Press specializes in producing new print and e-book editions of pre-1950s writings on sexual flagellation in English. Original editions of many of the books that we offer are difficult to obtain and are highly sought after. We are especially proud to offer new editions of rare Victorian flagellant texts such as *The Mysteries of Verbena House*, *Experimental Lecture by Colonel Spanker*, and *The Quintessence of Birch Discipline*. Birchgrove Press also produces new editions of libertine literature. We have published *Venus in the Cloister*, *The School of Venus*, *The Dialogues of Luisa Sigea*, and Isidore Liseux's translation of the Marquis de Sade's *Justine* (1791), *Opus Sadicum*, for example. For a full list of titles and formats, please visit our website:

www.birchgrovepress.com.

www.ingramcontent.com/pod-product-compliance
Lightning Source LLC
Chambersburg PA
CBHW051233260626
47162CB00002B/415